A CHANCE CREEK CHRISTMAS

By Cora Seton

Author's Note

A Chance Creek Christmas is book 1 of the Holidays of Chance Creek series. To read more about Ryan, Kerri, the firefighters and the Mountain Men, look for upcoming Holidays of Chance Creek Novels in 2023.

Meanwhile, head back to Chance Creek where it all began with The Cowboys of Chance Creek series!

Visit Cora's website at www.coraseton.com

Find Cora on Facebook at facebook.com/CoraSeton

Sign up for my newsletter HERE.

www.coraseton.com/sign-up-for-my-newsletter

CHAPTER 1

H E WAS NEVER going to get married at this rate.

Ryan Miller stood in the snow and surveyed the orderly rows of trees around him, phone pressed to his ear. Two years ago, he'd made a plan. It had been a damn good plan, too. Transition out of active duty with the Marines and head back home to Chance Creek. Take a job at the local fire station and join the reserves. Help his grandfather run the family Christmas tree farm when he could. Build a house of his own on their large acreage.

Find a woman to spend his life with.

It should have been simple.

But nothing was simple in this world.

"Sorry to have to break it to you right before the holidays," Ed Brookings said through the phone. "I would have told you earlier if I could, but I just heard back from the town council. There's no more room in the budget. I can't expand the fire department to offer you a paid position."

King's Mountain was quiet in the late November

afternoon as the daylight faded to a cold dusk. Ryan had drawn off one glove to answer the call, and his fingers were going numb.

"Thanks for going to bat for me," he managed to say. Ed was the chief of the Chance Creek fire department and would have been his boss if things had gone the way he'd hoped.

"I wish things had turned out differently."

"I wish everything had turned out differently." Ryan stopped before he said too much. Ed would understand what he meant, anyway. He'd been a constant presence throughout this hard year.

"If an opening comes up, you know you'll be the first person I call, just like last time."

"I appreciate that." But Ryan heard what Ed didn't say. Jobs hardly ever came available in the Chance Creek fire department. Ryan had known Ed all his life and had spent plenty of time hanging around the station when he was a teenager, making it clear to everyone who worked there he meant to join them as soon as he was old enough. He'd always been interested in the military, too. Ed, who'd served when he was a younger man, had been the one to tell him he could combine those interests as an Expeditionary Firefighting and Rescue Specialist in the Marines, and with Ryan's grandfather's approval, had introduced him to a local recruiter. They'd kept in touch after he'd joined up, Ryan updating him on his progress and the latest training he was receiving, Ed keeping him abreast of the goings on at the Chance Creek fire department.

When Ryan decided it was time to come home, he let Ed know right away. It had been pure luck that Lucas Freeman, who'd been with the department for thirty-five years, decided to retire around the same time. Ed immediately offered Ryan the job, and Ryan had arrived home in February expecting to start right away—

But that was before his grandfather was diagnosed with an aggressive form of cancer.

He swallowed against a surge of sorrow as he walked back to the clearing where his grandfather had sold his Christmas trees. It was empty except for a cluster of wooden supports ready to prop up the dozens of trees he planned to display this upcoming weekend. Before his stint in the Marine corps, he'd spent his childhood helping run the tree farm. He knew every corner of the operation, including sales and deliveries. A good thing, too, since this year he'd be on his own.

A chill wind brushed his cheek as he surveyed the sales area. His grandfather, John Miller, had run Miller's Tree Farm for over fifty years.

Now he was gone.

A thin, high-pitched whistle made him glance up at a nearby balsam fir. When he spotted the white-throated sparrow perched there, he nodded at it and automatically moved to grab a bag of birdfeed from the nearby shed. The bird had showed up daily this month, chirping at him until Ryan realized he'd forgotten to fill the feeders he'd constructed as a kid, a task his grandfather had taken over during Ryan's years away. Grandpa John was the one who'd taught Ryan the names of all the living creatures—animals, birds, fish, plants—that shared these Montana woods.

The bird whistled again as if to tell him to hurry up.

"Hold your horses." Holding the phone to his ear with his shoulder, he poured a mixture of seeds into the feeder and moved on to the next one. The little bird darted over, grabbed a kernel of millet, and flew off.

Ed broke off from his apologies and chuckled. "Maple getting restless?" he asked, referring to Ryan's Burmese mountain dog.

"One of the local birds getting a little uppity," Ryan explained.

"You going to be okay out there on your own during the holidays?"

Ryan knew what he meant. It was no secret it had been hard to give up the firefighting job before he'd even started it, but the next seven months had turned out to be far more difficult. Grandpa John passed away at the beginning of September. At first Ryan's grief had stopped him from doing much more than seeing to Maple's survival—and his own. He'd done his chores in a daze, once finding himself in the middle of an aisle at the grocery store, a basket in one hand and a jar of pickled onions in the other, no idea how he'd gotten there or why he was holding them.

After a few weeks of similar incidents, he'd begun to wonder if he, too, had been struck by some kind of disease, one that made his chest burn and his brain unable to function. His doctor had assured him grief took many forms and that time would soften its edges.

Ryan thought maybe it was the doctor who needed a checkup. He went to bed every night thinking about all the years he wouldn't get with his grandfather. Woke up only to be hit once more by the realization Grandpa John wouldn't be in the kitchen making his first cup of coffee for the day. Each time, the unfairness of it all pressed him into the mattress, making him wonder why he ought to get up at all.

One morning several weeks later, however, he woke thinking of the Christmas trees in the fields a stone's throw from the cabin and realized they needed to be tended. He was up on his feet before the grief hit him, and although it hurt as much as always, he found that having a job to do gave him something else to focus on.

Ever since, Ryan had been racing to prepare for the holiday season, determined not to let his grandfather's customers down. He was surviving on his savings for now, such as they were. When the holidays were over, he'd need to find another job, fast. The trees were a side gig; they couldn't finance his bottom line.

"I'll be fine." At least for now. When it became clear last February that Ryan would need to focus on caring for his grandfather, Ed had hired someone else to fill his position. No new ones had opened since then. Ryan had signed on as a volunteer with the department a couple of weeks ago, wanting to keep his skills current, and he was due to begin reserve duty in January, which would provide him with a little extra cash.

Even so, his life plan was in tatters. Instead of a

permanent position with the fire department, he had a part-time job selling Christmas trees. Instead of building a brand-new house, he was living in his grandfather's old cabin. He was about as settled as a teenager, with few prospects for the future. What woman would want to make a life with him now?

"Maybe something else will turn up," Ed said.

"Maybe," Ryan said, but he knew he couldn't count on it.

"I'd be glad to be a reference if you're applying for work at other places."

"Thanks."

He planned to apply for any job he could—once the holidays were over. Ryan was determined to stay now that he was home. He'd left Chance Creek craving adventure, and he'd had plenty of that. Now he was back, slipping into his role as a member of his community. Or rather, slipping into his grandfather's role.

"You'll be in tomorrow for our dinner?" Ed asked.

"You know it."

Tomorrow was Thanksgiving, and he would be celebrating it at the station. The day after, he'd make his first deliveries to the customers who'd ordered their trees ahead of time. On Saturday he'd open the tree farm to the folks who liked to come and cut their own. It might not cover all his expenses, but at least the Christmas tree sales would keep him from going broke for a little while.

"Okay. I'll see you then. Hang in there." Ed seemed reluctant to hang up. The chief was worried about him.

"I will," Ryan assured him. "See you then." He ended the call, wishing he could tell Ed there was nothing to worry about. He wasn't the kind of man who panicked when times got tough. He knew enough not to wallow in self-pity or take up drinking or any of the other dysfunctional ways people dealt with grief. He was fully aware of the facts of his situation and the difficulties that lay ahead of him. He'd find a way forward. He'd create the family he always wanted.

He just wasn't sure how yet.

Ryan stowed the bird feed away in the shed and whistled loudly.

The sparrow flew off in a whirr of wings. Maple, who'd gone exploring, came bounding out of the woods. Ryan stooped down to scratch behind her ears as she panted happily, her fur cold to the touch from the frosty air.

She'd shown up at the cabin barely three days after Grandpa John's passing. He'd woken that morning to a whining sound outside and opened the door to see her sitting patiently on the front steps. She'd trotted right inside, like she'd lived there for years. In his first stages of grief, trying to put his grandfather's affairs in order, Ryan had simply accepted her existence in his life, feeding her and allowing her to stay. Once he was over his initial shock, he'd made the effort to put up posters around town to find her owners, but no one had come for her, much to his relief. She'd been with him only a couple of months, but it felt like forever. She seemed to understand his moods and was even-tempered enough to go along with most of his commands.

He envied the dog sometimes. She was so content. She loved to run through the woods when they were at the tree farm, loved the rides in his truck in and out of town. Loved the attention she got when they were among other people and stretching near the woodstove at home when it was just the two of them. She didn't worry about the future the way he seemed to do all the time now.

Maple barked, bringing him back to himself, her wagging tail making a fan shape in the snow.

"You're right," he told her. "Let's go eat." He started down the path that cut through the woods to his cabin, Maple following behind. Both the cabin's driveway and the tree farm's parking lot connected to the paved road that wound around the mountain, but the path was a more direct route between the two than taking the road.

Maple bounded ahead of him as the cabin came into view and sat by the front door, waiting. He kicked the snow off the bottom of his boots against the cement stoop and opened the door, Maple pushing past him as he entered.

The old woodstove gave off a welcome heat, but the cabin's rustic furnishings offered little comfort to his soul. The place was too empty without Grandpa John around. It was his grandfather who'd filled it with a steady peace and companionship he'd always appreciated. Every stick of furniture was exactly where it had always been, which meant the place was full of memories. Ryan kept expecting his grandfather to come out of his bedroom, or in from outside, letting in a gust of cold air.

He never did.

Could he bring a future wife here?

Ryan wasn't sure.

Years ago he'd sketched out the house he wanted, a two-story, six-bedroom home big enough to hold the boisterous family he'd always craved. He'd never expected to inherit this small cabin so soon.

Heading to the kitchen area, Ryan poured himself a glass of water and heaved a sigh at the cramped dimensions of the space. Nestled in one corner, there was only a couple of feet of counter space. He'd planned to make chicken pot pie tonight, his signature dish, but he didn't have the patience for it anymore.

Ryan whistled for Maple, who came running. He crossed to the door, grabbed his coat and went outside, dog by his side. Forget the pot pie. He'd get something at Orchards.

He needed a hot meal and a cold drink. He needed people.

Women.

He'd been alone long enough.

"THERE YOU GO. All set," Kerri Olsen told Autumn Cruz, handing her a receipt for the transaction she'd just rung up.

"Thanks." Autumn picked up the wooden umbrella stand she'd purchased. It had stood in the corner of

Kerri's secondhand shop since she'd found it at an auction in Wyoming last fall. She'd brought it back to Chance Creek, sanded it down, painted it and distressed it until she knew someone would have to have it in their country-themed home.

"Thank *you*. Let me know if it works in your foyer."

"It'll be perfect for our bed-and-breakfast. Our guests always leave their umbrellas on the floor when the weather is rainy. This will keep our entryway tidy." The brunette left the store with a cheerful wave. Kerri came out from behind the counter to shift a few objects around to fill in the gap Autumn's purchase had made in her store displays. Ten minutes later she admitted she was delaying the inevitable. It was past five o'clock. Time to close up shop and go home to her huge, empty house.

Empty of people, she corrected herself. It contained enough possessions to fill her shop five times over.

She put up the closed sign, turned out all the lights and locked up behind her, taking a path through the snowy yard that led to the big yellow house her grandmother had left her along with the store.

She'd just made it up the seven steps to its wide front porch when her phone chimed. Relieved to be talking to someone, Kerri pulled it out as she took the mail from the mailbox and opened the front door, but when she glanced at the screen, she saw it was her mother on the video call.

Kerri hesitated. Should she take it? Her mom would only nag her about the lack of progress she'd made with her grandmother's affairs. On the other hand, if she didn't answer, her mother would simply keep calling back.

She accepted the call.

"Hi, Mom. Are you ready for Thanksgiving tomorrow?" She made herself smile, aiming for cheerful and knowing she was failing miserably.

"I'm not calling to talk about Thanksgiving. I'm calling to see if you got the envelope I sent you." Sylvie's face filled the screen, her chin angling this way and that until Kerri realized she was trying to see past her into the house.

Kerri dropped her purse on the hall console table, shut the door behind her and leaned resolutely against it as she sorted through the stack of mail. At the bottom was the envelope her mother had mentioned. A large, legal-size one. She tossed the rest on the console table and tore it open, all the while making sure the door behind her was the only thing her mother could see.

"What's this all about?"

"How many rooms have you emptied?" Her mother was still craning her neck, pinching her lips together in frustration.

"Plenty of them."

Her mother scoffed. "If that was true, you'd show me something other than the front door."

Kerri shrugged. "It's true," she lied.

"Prove it."

"What do you mean, prove it?" She couldn't believe they were having this conversation. She wasn't a child—

and even if she was, her mother had lost the right to police her actions a long time ago.

"Turn the phone around and show me one empty room in that godforsaken house you're living in."

"No way."

"Kerri—show me."

"No!" She was not going to give her mother a video tour of the house she'd inherited nine months ago. Grandma Bess's penchant for collecting things had gotten away from her a long time ago, and her mother's disapproval of it had eventually led to the two of them becoming estranged. It was Kerri who'd stayed with Bess when her mother left town. Kerri who'd taken over the secondhand shop when Bess couldn't run it anymore. Kerri who'd picked up the chores one by one that Bess stopped being able to do. Kerri who'd nursed Bess during her final days.

And it was Kerri who'd inherited Bess's house and store when she was gone.

Sylvie sighed. "We made a deal. I told you if you didn't clean it out, I'd demand you pay me the money you owe me immediately." Bess hadn't forgotten Kerri's mother in her will. She'd known Sylvie wouldn't be interested in her home or business, so she'd instructed Kerri to take a loan out against the property and pay her mother half its value.

"I told you last week I got the loan. You'll get your money in a few days." What on earth had her mother sent her? Kerri withdrew a fat stack of papers from the envelope.

"You told me you got a loan for *part* of the money—not the whole amount."

"I'm short only thirty-thousand dollars, and I sent you a payment plan for that. It's going to take me a few years, since I have to pay back the home finance loan, too, but the store has been doing really well." She wished the bank understood that, but the loan officer had explained that since the store had remained in her grandmother's name until she died, Kerri didn't have a proven track record as its owner, despite the fact Bess had renamed it Kerri's Collectibles years ago.

Her mother's brows drew together in a familiar way. "That store is the problem. You're going to turn out just like Bess, half your inventory ending up in the house instead of going home with your customers."

"I've brought only a few things home from the store since Bess died," Kerri argued. She was nothing like her grandmother in that regard.

"A few things? I knew it! I knew you'd turn out just like her."

"Mom," Kerri interrupted before her mother started in on one of her lectures. "I brought home a pair of hand-knitted gloves when one of my old pairs got a hole in it and a beautiful wool dress coat that would have cost several hundred dollars new. I threw away the old gloves and gave away my old jacket. That's a fair trade."

"That's the kind of thing your grandmother always said. Look where it got her."

Kerri sighed. They were going around in circles. "I swear to God, I'm not a hoarder and neither was Bess.

Not really."

"Just because she kept her house clean doesn't mean she didn't have a problem. There are six bedrooms in that house. Six. And she couldn't empty out a single one for you or me when we needed them."

Another old argument. Bess and her mother had fought about it at least a hundred times.

"Grandma Bess welcomed us with open arms," Kerri said quietly. "She loved us. You know she did."

"She loved that junk she filled her house with more," her mother countered. "Seems like you love it, too. I bet everything is the same as it ever was."

"I'm on it, Mom." Guilt spiked through Kerri because her mother was right. She hadn't touched a thing since Bess had died. She kept meaning to, but somehow she couldn't. Cleaning out the house felt like purging it of Bess's memory, and she missed her grandmother too much to be ready for that. "Right after the holidays I'll move all her collections to the store and sell them."

"*After* the holidays?" Her mother's face was pale with anger, and Kerri's heart sank. She'd seen her look like this only once before—the day Sylvie left Chance Creek thirteen years ago. "In other words, I'm right, aren't I? You haven't touched a thing. You haven't gotten rid of a single collection, and you never will. You'll keep adding to them instead. You'll be buried alive in that house, just like Mom was. I tried to be patient, Kerri. I really did. But I lost my mother to those collections, and I'm not going to lose you, too."

"You won't lose me." Kerri knew she'd hurt her

mother badly when she'd refused to move to Sacramento when she was fourteen. Bess had needed her, though. Besides, she loved it here. Loved every room of this big old house, despite the clutter that filled it. Loved this little town and all the people in it. Loved her friends and her school. Chance Creek was her home.

"I already lost you."

Kerri winced at the anguish in her mother's voice. She wished she knew how to convince Sylvie that wasn't true. She'd tried so many times.

And failed.

"I'll clean out the house *before* Christmas, then," she hastened to say. "I promise. Come for the holidays and see for yourself."

"I can't come for Christmas. I just leased a new retail space—in San Francisco." Her mother lifted her chin as if daring Kerri to find fault with that.

"A new space? Can you afford that?" Kerri's fingers tightened around the stack of papers. Her mother had already expanded her chain of boutiques to three storefronts, and she always seemed to be working when Kerri called.

"I can, as long as I get my share of the inheritance." Her mother paused. "*All* of it."

Kerri went cold. "Mom." She didn't like where this was going.

"I waited, like you asked," her mother said in a rush. "I waited for you to get rid of all that junk Bess accumulated so you could finally live like a normal person. I waited for you to get a loan so you could pay me my share—my full share. I'm building this business for you—can't you see that? It's your way out of that mausoleum your grandmother gave you. I refuse to let her win."

"This isn't about winning or losing. Besides, you're the one who wanted to leave, and you already went. Why isn't that good enough?" Why couldn't her mother leave her alone to grieve Grandma Bess her own way? She'd be ready to give up Bess's collections—someday. Just not now. And she'd tried to get a loan for the full amount. She simply hadn't been able to.

"How can I be happy if you're not free, too?" Her mother swallowed, her face tight with the emotions she was suppressing. "It's not healthy to live like you're doing. It gets under your skin, and you can't break free from it."

"I can break free. I will."

Her mother shook her head. "You have no idea how strong the compulsion gets once you let it in. Your grandmother never thought she'd end up the way she did. She wasn't always like that."

"I know. Mom, I swear. I'll get started going through it right now—tonight." She could spend an hour or two moving things to the store. She'd make more appointments with more banks next week. Maybe there was a different kind of loan she could get. One that would cover that final thirty-thousand dollars.

"You're going to have to. Like I said, I leased a new retail space, which means I need my share of the inheritance—now. Which means you need to sell up.

We'll take the proceeds from the house and store, split them fifty-fifty, and there'll be no need for any loans at all."

Kerri couldn't breathe. Sell the house—and her store?

"You can come out here and make a fresh start in Sacramento. You can manage my current stores while I open the new one. We're finally going to be the team we always should have been. You'll finally be free."

She didn't want to be free. She didn't want to leave Chance Creek. She'd always envisioned getting married here. Starting a family here. Filling this house with children of her own.

"Mom," Kerri started.

"No." Her mother cut her off. "I've filed a claim against you. The paperwork I sent lays it all out. If you don't pay what you owe me—all of it—by Christmas, I will force you to sell."

"You can't do that!"

"Yes, I can. I've got a lawyer, and I've got a court date right after Christmas." Tears were brimming in her mother's eyes. "I will save you from yourself, if it's the last thing I do!" She ended the call.

Kerri pocketed her phone in a daze and tried to read the very official-looking letter that topped the stack of papers in her hands. It was from a lawyer her mother had retained. Kerri went through the pages one by one. From what she could tell, the case would be tried right here in town if she didn't come up with the cash.

Some Christmas this was going to be.

She pushed off from the door she'd been leaning against and tried to see the front hall she stood in with clear eyes. Bess had done her best to keep this space clean and inviting. Almost every inch of the walls in the foyer and up the stairwell was covered with the photographs of Chance Creek she'd collected over the years, but the floor was free from clutter, the coat closet door could shut and the console table always sat empty, waiting to prop up a purse or a set of keys.

It was only when you turned to the left toward the kitchen or to the right toward the living room that you got a feel for the way Bess had lost control.

No, Kerri told herself. Bess had never lost control. She'd just...

Kerri steeled herself, walked into the eat-in kitchen and surveyed the vintage implements that covered the walls, the tea sets, boxes of fine china and serving trays of every variety stacked on the countertops, with more piled on the floor. The baskets of linens that filled the space where a table and chairs should have gone. The high bookshelf that contained only a portion of the cookbooks piled this way and that around the room. She didn't have to open the cupboards to imagine their contents. There were a few that still held pantry items. The rest were filled to the brim with glassware, cutlery, pots and pans of every description, silverware sets and more.

Kerri put the kettle on and fished a teabag from its box, maneuvering through the few square feet of space left open in the room. As hard as she tried, she couldn't stop her mind from tracing its way through the rest of the house. The living room was chockablock with vintage outdoor gear. Upstairs, each bedroom had a different theme. As a child she'd loved to explore them—to the extent she could. The sewing room with its stacks of fabric and sewing notions; the jewelry room with its boxes, cases and stands full of jewelry, some pieces beautiful, some whimsical, some downright ridiculous; the music room, which she'd never traversed without knocking over an instrument or pile of records; the library, with its musty towers of unread books. She'd loved the train room, with its dozens of tracks, hundreds of cars and mishmash of miniature scenery bits, and best of all, the cat room, full of every conceivable representation of the animal Bess had loved so much but couldn't own because of her allergies.

Her mother was right. Bess had become so enamored of her collections that by the time Sylvie had been forced to come home, baby in tow, there was no room for the two of them. Of course, by that time there was no room for Bess either. She slept in the music room. Long ago the instruments, sheet music, records, cassettes and other paraphernalia had forced her to get rid of the bedroom furniture she'd shared with her husband earlier in life and install a single bed in its place.

When she'd been forced to retreat home, Sylvie had reclaimed her childhood bedroom, forging a path through the towers of books that had swallowed it up, bought a single bed of her own and created a den for her and her baby among them. When Kerri had gotten too old to share, she'd been given a cot and put in with the cats, where she still slept—although she'd taken her mother's old single bed for her own after Sylvie left.

Kerri poured her cup of tea and sighed.

She knew it wasn't healthy to live like this, even if she scrupulously cleaned the house and its collections the way Bess always had. Sometimes she woke up in that sea of cats in fear they might come to life and smother her.

Her store couldn't possibly hold everything that was currently in the house, though. As she went through each room, she'd have to sort through what might sell and what she'd have to give away.

She'd start right now. Surely if she cleaned the place and showed her mother she'd done so, Sylvie would drop her claim and accept the payment plan Kerri had devised. If she didn't—

Kerri couldn't even think about that. She had no idea how to raise thirty-thousand dollars in less than a month. Her store didn't produce that kind of income. She could sell every piece of Bess's collections and barely make a dent in that amount. Her grandmother had collected things that held sentimental value—each one reminding her of a loved one she'd lost. They weren't valuable beyond that.

Kerri looked around the kitchen again. She'd salvaged a modicum of clean counterspace for food preparation. Underfoot, there were pathways to the stove and refrigerator.

If she started by sorting the china piled on the rest

of this counter…

She wedged her cup between the faucet and backsplash, reached for a china platter off the closest stack and ran a hand over it.

It had a peony pattern on a dark red background. No chips, but the colors were dull, as if it had sat in the sun for a long time. Could she sell it?

Maybe. If she priced it low enough.

She put it on the tiny amount of available counter and pushed it back until it bumped against the wall. That was the *maybe* pile, she told herself.

Kerri took the next platter off the stack. This one was a definite no. It had a chip missing and a crack that ran the length of it. She looked around for a place to put it, but there wasn't enough counter space to start a separate pile.

She scanned the kitchen helplessly. There wasn't enough space anywhere to put it.

Now what?

There was plenty of room in the hall, of course, but the rule was nothing went in the hall that didn't belong there.

Bess wasn't here to enforce that rule, she reminded herself. It wouldn't hurt if she made a couple of piles and left them there a day or two before moving them to the store or taking them to the dump.

But Kerri knew a pile was a dangerous thing. A person always started one meaning to clean it up, yet somehow piles never got cleaned up once they were there. She'd seen Bess slip up that way too many times.

Her mother had seen it, too, before she left.

Kerri set the platter back on its original stack with a shaking hand. Was Sylvie right? Was she like Bess? Was she about to lose control?

Swallowing hard, Kerri decided she couldn't tackle the kitchen like this. She needed a plan, and right now she was tired—and hungry.

Tomorrow was Thanksgiving. Her store would be closed all day, and she could focus on the house. Right now she craved food. People. Noise. Laughter.

Relief washed over her the moment she stepped from the crowded kitchen into the empty hall, picked up her purse and fetched her coat. With the kitchen and living room lights off, she could pretend the whole house was this organized. She let her imagination take flight as she had so many times before and pictured a fire blazing in the living room fireplace. Kids grouped around a table in the kitchen. Herself pulling a Sunday roast out of the oven.

A husband helping her get the meal on the table. Joking with the children. Giving her a kiss as they passed each other.

She'd been so sure her future was right here in this wonderful home.

She couldn't bear to think she was wrong.

CHAPTER 2

"**A**NY LUCK WITH the job hunt?" Jameson Ross asked when Ryan sat down at the corner table next to him at Orchards. He was a burly man with a full beard who lived alone high up King's Mountain. Ryan had a feeling he'd moved to the remote area to be alone with his thoughts. He wasn't sure what had happened to the man before he came to Chance Creek County, but he'd met others like him in the Marines. Men who'd seen too much. Who'd been shaken from the foundations of their world and were having to knit together a new way of being. He didn't ask Jameson a lot of questions. He figured if he was ever ready to talk about it, he would, and besides, Ryan didn't want to scare him away. He knew Nolan Mitchell harried Jameson just about every week so he'd show up at these gatherings. If he didn't, Jameson might never leave the mountain at all.

"Not yet." Ryan set the cup of coffee and bowl of chili he'd purchased at the counter down on the table. Nolan was already sitting next to Jameson. He was the one who'd started the Mountain Man Meetup, as Sunshine Patterson, the co-owner of the bakery and restaurant, had christened these informal Wednesday afternoon get-togethers. Nicholas King, Dane Moore and Adam Judge were there, too. Nolan had stopped by the tree lot one blustery March day soon after Ryan got home and invited him to join them. At the time Ryan hadn't felt much like hanging out with other people, but during the months Grandpa John had fought—and lost—his battle with cancer, he'd appreciated the easy camaraderie of these meetings.

He liked the guys he worked with at the station, too, but he found it hard to feel as at home there as the full-timers did. He was more relaxed here at Orchards with Jameson, Nolan and the others. They were bound by geography rather than jobs, living on or near King's Mountain. Men who'd chosen a rural way of life rather than to settle in town. They'd all served in the military and were in the reserves, too.

"There might be a position coming up at the bank," Nicholas said. He had dark hair and blue eyes, was quick to laugh and liked to drag everyone else on adventures. According to Nolan, he was the first to organize a night at the Dancing Boot or an excursion to the county fair. That didn't mean he was an easy man to know. Jameson might harbor secrets simply by not talking much, but Nicholas kept you so off-balance with his activities and antics, you never got around to asking him anything personal. "I was in there the other day and heard a couple of the tellers talking."

Ryan took his seat. "Not sure I'm cut out for banking." Just the thought of it made him restless.

"You're a steady thinker," Nicholas said. "Maybe you could move up after a while. Get into loans or something. You'd find out everyone's business." He said it like that was a good thing.

Ryan pictured sitting across a desk from a neighbor, turning them down for a second mortgage that could save their ranch. "No, thank you."

"Have you checked at the airport?" Dane asked. His sandy brown hair had a way of falling into his eyes, but he wasn't a slacker. His property was near the base of the mountain, and he was one of the few men in the group who made his living ranching. Where Nicholas practically crackled with energy, Dane moved slowly and thought about his words carefully before he spoke them. Dane's people had made Chance Creek their home nearly a century ago. Like Ryan, he was rooted here. "Could be work there."

"Too bad you're not mechanical like your grandfather," Nolan said. Wiry and intense, he'd turned his chair around and was straddling it. He never seemed comfortable being still for too long. "This town could use another auto shop."

"That's not my line." Grandpa John had owned an auto repair shop until he retired at sixty-two. It was his career, whereas the Christmas trees were a sideline. Ryan used to feign an interest for his grandfather's sake, but he never could get into motors. "I'll find something." He knew his friends' intentions were good, but it was hard not to feel the pressure of their suggestions.

"All set for Thanksgiving dinner at the station?" Dane asked.

Ryan was grateful to him for turning the subject. He nodded. "I'm not one of the cooks, so I just have to show up. What are you doing for the holiday?"

"Bachelor dinner, same as every year." Dane nodded at the other men, who nodded back. "You know you're invited."

Ryan did know that, just as his friends knew he'd eat at the station.

"None of you are going home to family?" he asked.

There was a general shaking of heads around the table.

"A bunch of people will join us," Dane said. "It ends up being a pretty big group."

"We meet at Jameson's place," Nolan said. "He's the Thanksgiving guy."

Ryan was surprised. "You are?" he asked the taciturn man.

Jameson nodded.

"I've got Fourth of July," Dane pronounced.

"He's got the best barbecue setup around," Nolan told Ryan.

"I've got Halloween," Nicholas said.

That fit, Ryan thought. He bet Nicholas loved Halloween.

"What have you got?" Ryan asked Nolan. "Valentine's Day?"

Nolan shook his head.

"I've got Valentine's," Adam Judge said. Until this point he'd been nursing a cup of coffee, content to let the others speak. He was in his thirties, hints of gray in his otherwise dark hair. He'd always looked to Ryan like the cross between a quarterback and a professor, muscular but serious. He knew Adam sometimes took off hiking for months at a time. He'd done the Appalachian trail one summer, the Pacific Crest trail another.

"I've got New Year's," Nolan said.

Ryan nodded. "Looking forward to seeing how you set up for that, if I'm invited."

"Of course you're invited. You're a Mountain Man, aren't you?" Nolan shook his head, as if the answer was self-explanatory.

Ryan supposed it was.

"Speaking of Valentine's. There's someone you should invite to your party," Nicholas said to Adam.

Everyone turned toward the door. Kerri Olsen had just walked in. Her cheeks were pink from the cold wind blowing outside. Her dark hair was a mass of curls. She unwound a forest-green scarf from her neck and approached the bakery counter with a smile. Ryan sat up a little straighter. He'd noticed Kerri a couple of times since he'd been home. In school she'd been a quiet little thing, but these days she was… kind of beautiful, he admitted to himself. Chance Creek wasn't a big town, and since he'd been home, he'd gotten a sense of which women here were single. He hadn't made a list of them or anything. At least, he hadn't written it down.

If he had, Kerri's name would be on it.

"Hi, Emma," she called to the woman behind the counter. Emma Larson was petite, blonde and curvy. An obvious beauty, where Kerri's good looks kind of snuck up on a person, or maybe that was because Ryan had always considered her just one of the people he'd gone to school with.

"Hi, Kerri," Emma called back. Soon the two women were deep in conversation.

"You've got a thing for Kerri Olsen?" Adam asked Nicholas. "Since when?"

Nicholas shrugged. "Bet she's married within the year. She's got that look."

"What look?" Adam demanded.

"That 'I'm ready for the next stage of life' look. She's got herself together, and now she's looking for a guy who's ready to settle down."

"And that's you?" Nolan's disbelief was palpable.

"I'm not saying it's me. I'm saying Adam's Valentine's party last year sucked because there were two dozen single men and about five women."

"There were not two dozen single men," Adam protested.

"But you agree there weren't many women," Nicholas said.

"There were women."

"Your grandmother doesn't count."

Ryan laughed with the rest of them. "Your grandmother was there?"

"Great aunt," Adam corrected. "She was driving through on the way from Boise to Minneapolis to see my cousin. She wouldn't take no for an answer. Nicholas is just mad because she beat him in ping-pong."

"I let her win!"

The argument faded into the background as Ryan watched Kerri chat with Emma, while Emma got her order together. Nolan was right; there was something different about her these days. In high school she had been one of the artsy kids. Not his crowd at all.

She'd inherited a property from her grandmother, and now she ran Kerri's Collectibles, a secondhand store that sat on one corner of it. She lived in Bess's old house on the opposite side. Bess had died early in the year, about the time he'd come home and discovered his grandfather was ill. He'd missed Bess's funeral and found himself wishing he'd connected with Kerri to make his condolences sooner.

Maybe he should do so now.

Another burst of laughter from the men at the table made him decide against it. If he got up and went to speak with her, they'd pair his name with hers and turn it into a running joke. He didn't like the idea of that. The joking, not the pairing.

Ryan sat back in his seat and toyed with his food, casting a glance her way now and then.

Kerri Olsen.

There was a woman who could keep you warm through a cold winter's night.

He scrubbed a hand over his face, trying to hide the smile that tugged at his mouth. What would a younger version of himself think about the way Kerri was affecting him today? She hadn't really been on his radar back then. He'd been a typical teenager, he supposed. Attracted to the flashier girls. Now he was old enough to know he was looking for something different.

A woman who was ready to settle down.

His younger self might have a thing or two to say about that, but Ryan had no problem owning what he wanted.

A wife.

A family.

A home.

When you served in the military, you got a good sense of how fragile life was. He was motivated to get to the part where he had a little kingdom of his own.

Kerri turned and caught him looking.

Ryan stilled. Could she read his thoughts from across the room?

He couldn't tell from her expression. She had big, dark eyes, framed by even darker eyebrows, a straight nose and full lips. Ryan bet they'd be soft if he kissed her. Just the thought of it had his body revving to life like a rusty motor left too long out in the rain, stuttering for a moment before roaring full throttle.

He turned away, pretending he'd been listening to the conversation among his tablemates, and when he next looked at the counter, she was gone. He located her at another table. Sunshine Patterson, who ran the restaurant side of Orchards, was joining her.

"Ryan?" Nolan asked. "Ryan!"

"What?"

"Dude, you awake?"

"Do my eyes look closed to you?" He had no idea what the other men had been talking about.

"No one's got Christmas yet."

Ryan waited, not understanding Nolan's meaning.

"We take turns throwing parties on the holidays, but you haven't been assigned one yet," Adam put in. "Seems pretty obvious Christmas should be yours. You've got the Christmas tree farm."

"You want me to host Christmas?" He was alarmed.

"Not the day itself. Have a party a couple of days before Christmas."

"Doesn't have to be fancy," Nolan said. Ryan had the uncomfortable feeling this was a conspiracy against him. They were trying to get him more involved. To get him living again.

"It can be whatever you want," Adam drawled. "Every holiday we do something different."

"Okay," Ryan said slowly, feeling their trap closing around him. He supposed he could throw a party. "My place isn't that big, though."

"You'll figure it out."

"ONE CUP OF sweet potato soup and a slice of cornbread," Emma said, handing the order over the counter to Kerri.

A chorus of male laughter sounded from the front corner window. Kerri glanced over to see Ryan Miller with several of his friends gathered around a table, cups of coffee and half-eaten dishes from their meal in front of them. As handsome as ever, Ryan rested muscled arms on the table, leaning forward to contribute to the conversation. She'd known him growing up, but after a stint with the Marines he'd come home a stranger, hardened, powerful and a little watchful.

"It's the Mountain Man Meetup," Emma quipped.

"Is that a real thing?" It sounded intriguing. She gave the men another look. They were all in their twenties and thirties. Unmarried, if she wasn't mistaken, although she figured they were all dating. Men who looked like Ryan wouldn't be alone.

"No." Emma laughed. "Sunshine gave them that name. They live on or near King's Mountain. Bunch of military guys. I guess they're reservists now, technically."

"They serve together?"

"All different branches, I think. Must have enough in common to make them friends, though. Whoever happens to be in town after work on Wednesday afternoon finds their way here for a quick bite and a cup of coffee. There's always at least two or three of them, but sometimes they all show up. This seems to be one of those days. Let me ring you in."

Kerri nodded, envying them. She'd bet none of those men had a mother trying to force them to move to Sacramento. Glancing over her shoulder one more time, she expected the men to be caught up in their conversation, so when she met Ryan Miller's gaze, she sucked in a breath of surprise.

His blue eyes assessed her for a long moment before he turned back to his friends, and she found herself holding her breath. Was it her imagination, or was there interest in his gaze?

Ryan Miller, interested in her?

"Kerri?"

"What?" She turned back to Emma. "Oh, hold on." She hoped her confusion wasn't evident as she fished in her purse for her debit card.

"Something wrong?" Emma asked.

"No. You caught me daydreaming, that's all."

Emma lifted her gaze to the corner table. Her lips quirked. "I see."

Done with the transaction, Kerri slipped her wallet into her purse, picked up her soup and hurried off to look for somewhere to sit. The last thing she needed was Emma teasing her about Ryan Miller. She was far too busy worrying about her mother's threats.

She chose a small table by the side window. Sunshine, emerging from the kitchen, plopped down in the chair across from her before she could even take a spoonful of soup.

"Did you hear about George Metcalf's basement?" she asked as she helped herself to a forkful of Kerri's cornbread. Orchards was a combination bakery and restaurant that catered both to hearty appetites and those on restricted diets. The food was vegetarian, with plenty of vegan, gluten-free and other options. Kerri was always surprised to find Chance Creek's ranchers among their customers, but Sunshine excelled in creating stick-to-your-ribs cuisine, and no one could resist Emma's baked goods.

"Hey!" Kerri blocked her fork when Sunshine reached for another bite. "That's a good racket. First you sell me food and then you eat it for me."

"Emma sold it to you, and I just took one bite. I'm hungry." Sunshine rested a hand on her belly. Kerri was glad to see her friend resting for a minute. Sunshine was pregnant with her second child, and she was always so busy with the restaurant.

"What's up with George Metcalf's basement?"

"Hot water heater burst. Flooded the place. He slipped on the stairs going down to see what was happening and ended up in the hospital with a concussion. You know he's got that whole train setup down there. I heard it's ruined, and it's such a shame. Sienna is going to be upset when she hears about it."

Sienna was Sunshine's seven-year-old daughter. Kerri could sympathise; she'd loved that train setup when she was a kid, too. George had hosted open house days for train enthusiasts for decades, and everyone who grew up in Chance Creek had gone to at least one of them on a school fieldtrip.

"Poor George." He was an elderly man who'd been widowed for some time. She suspected his trains were what got him up in the morning.

"I know, right? How do you replace a collection you've amassed over a lifetime?" Sunshine reached out with her fork.

"Get your own cornbread." Kerri warded off the attack. "If you eat any more of mine, I'll have to order another slice."

"Perfect. My evil plan is working." Sunshine smiled. "I want to do something for George. Maybe I'll make up a gift basket for him."

"That sounds like a good idea." Kerri decided she'd get him a card at the very least.

"You'd better start figuring out what women to invite to your party," she heard Nolan Mitchell say loudly. Kerri glanced their way. All the men at the corner table were focused on Ryan.

"Yeah, yeah," he said, lifted his gaze and met hers again. This time he nodded an acknowledgement. She nodded back, embarrassed to be caught, but it was hard to look away. Ryan Miller filled out his long-sleeved black T-shirt in a manner few men could. He'd been cute when they were kids, even handsome by the time he was a senior in high school. Now he was something else. Something that made her aware of him at a much deeper level. She wondered what kind of party he was throwing.

"Yeah, Miller, invite lots of women. I'm looking for a wife," Nicholas King pronounced. Kerri knew him when they were kids, too. The Kings had been in these parts forever.

The men's laughter rang out until people at other tables turned to see what was going on.

"You think someone wants to marry you?" Nolan asked him.

"Hell, yeah. I'm Chance Creek's most eligible bachelor."

Sunshine raised her eyebrows and leaned in closer to

Kerri. "Looking for a husband?"

"Not Nicholas King." He was a good enough guy. Handsome in his own way.

He wasn't Ryan Miller, though.

"*I'm* Chance Creek's most eligible bachelor," Nolan said. Kerri didn't know him well.

"Get over yourself. I am," Adam Judge said. He was older than Kerri. Had graduated from high school long before she'd entered it.

"You're all looking for wives, too?" Dane asked.

"If one comes knocking," Nicholas said.

"Don't look at me," Jameson growled. "I'm not looking for anything."

"Well, I'm looking for one," Ryan said. The rest of the men turned to him in surprise. Sunshine kicked Kerri under the table.

"Did you hear that? Ryan Miller is looking for a wife," she murmured.

"So?" Kerri refused to look his way, even though she had the oddest feeling if she did, she'd find him looking back at her again.

"He's pretty hot."

"And I'm not interested."

"That's a shame."

Kerri thought she might continue to press the matter, but Sunshine wisely chose to revert to their earlier topic instead.

"I bet George stores his Christmas decorations in his basement," she mused. "Did you ever go there as a kid at Christmastime? I've taken Sienna each year since she was four. He makes the whole train scene look like a winter wonderland."

Kerri nodded absently, trying to listen to what the men were saying.

"Maybe I should make a few casseroles to bring over to his house," Sunshine said.

"Who's house?"

"George's." Sunshine cocked her head. "Hello. You in there, Kerri?"

Kerri snapped her attention back to her friend. "Sorry. Just… thinking." Sunshine was right, she realized. George had always made a big deal about Christmas, setting up several artificial trees in his basement along with lights and garlands. An idea occurred to her. "What if we bought him a Christmas tree—a real one? That could tide him over this year until he replaces the old ones."

"A tree? From Ryan Miller's tree lot?" Sunshine asked innocently. "That's one way to attract his attention."

"From wherever." Kerri hoped she wasn't blushing. Thinking about Ryan Miller probably had prompted her suggestion, but she hadn't made the connection consciously. If she had, she wouldn't have said it out loud, given Sunshine's current penchant for matchmaking. She'd been a terror since she'd gotten pregnant again, as if she needed all her friends to be on the same wavelength.

"Even if George had a tree, what would he decorate it with?" Sunshine turned practical. "Like I said, I bet he had all that stuff stored in his basement with his trains."

Trains.

Kerri sat up. Why hadn't she thought of it before? "I have trains."

Sunshine raised an eyebrow. "I don't remember seeing any at your house."

"You haven't seen my whole house." When people came over, which was seldom, she was careful to shut all the bedroom doors, even though she never let anyone upstairs. Bad enough to let them see what the living room and kitchen looked like.

"What kind of trains do you have?"

Enough to rival George's collection, although they weren't set up nearly as well. There were big trains and small trains. Buildings, trees, bridges and other landscape features. Kerri knew from photographs that at one time, the train room contained a display worthy of George himself, but Bess kept accumulating more and more stuff until it was full to overflowing. George's basement was three to four times as big as that bedroom, though. Definitely large enough to hold Bess's collection.

"Different kinds," Kerri hedged. If she passed them all on to George, she could clean out a room and show it to her mother. Hopefully buy herself more time to scare up that thirty grand. They could take some of the smaller train cars and make ornaments out of them. She felt her spirits lift at the thought of the project.

"Okay," Sunshine said. "If you want to get George a tree, let's get George a tree. Hey, Ryan!" she called before Kerri could tell her not to. "Stop talking about matrimony and get over here! We need you."

"Maybe Sunshine found you a bride, Miller," Nicholas said. "While you're at it, find one for me, too, would you, Sunshine?" he called.

"I've got better things to do than to rope blameless women into matches with lazy men," Sunshine called back. "Find your own bride."

As the men grumbled, Ryan stood up and made his way to their table. Up close, he was even better-looking. Humor lurked in his blue gaze. A heavy shadow darkened his jaw, making him look just the slightest bit dangerous.

"Kerri needs a tree," Sunshine told him. "Can you deliver one to her?"

His gaze sharpened on her. The little flutter of awareness that had filled Kerri when he approached blossomed into something else entirely.

"I'd be glad to," he said slowly. "What size?"

"Um…" Kerri found her throat was dry. "About six feet." Ryan had delivered trees to Bess's house with his grandfather plenty of times when he was a kid. Why did the thought of him doing so now set her heart thumping? She imagined opening her door to find him on her porch. Maybe she could invite him in—

Kerri made herself focus. The remaining Mountain Men were watching this exchange with undisguised interest. So was Sunshine.

And she didn't invite in anyone if she could help it.

"Six feet tall?" Sunshine echoed. "I thought you said

a little one."

Kerri waved her away. She'd buy a twelve-foot tree if it would make Ryan keep looking at her like that. Besides, the bigger the tree, the more train cars she could fit on it as ornaments.

"White pine?" he asked.

That was the type her grandmother had always ordered. Had Ryan remembered that from when he was a teenager? Or was he making a good guess?

She wished she could ask him. Wished it was only the two of them here.

They had an audience, though.

"Perfect, but it's not for me. It's for someone else. Can you bring me a stand, too?"

That made him pause. "Sure. Do you want me to deliver yours while I'm at it?"

"Not yet. I'll want it in a week or so." She wasn't ready for her tree yet, although she wouldn't have been able to explain why. Christmas without Bess seemed... impossible.

"One white pine coming up, then. I'll deliver it to you tomorrow morning around ten."

"Thanks."

He nodded. Kerri watched him head back to his table, pick up his coat and say goodbye to his friends, then turned to find Sunshine surveying her with amusement.

"He's hot," she said again. "And he's looking for a wife."

"You're married. And pregnant." Kerri refused to

take the bait.

"That doesn't mean I'm blind. He looked interested, too."

"In what?"

"In you, of course. Wake up, Kerri. You've got the perfect opportunity to flirt with him later. Invite him in when he comes to deliver that tree. Better yet, ask him out. He's made it clear he's interested—and looking for something serious."

"I'm not asking him out." She could just imagine how that would go. Ryan probably saw her the same way she'd always seen him before today. Just a kid he used to know who'd grown up.

"Why not?"

"I'm not his type. Ryan Miller barely knew I existed when we were in school."

"He definitely knows now." Sunshine sighed. "You underestimate yourself, you know. You're hot, too."

"Right." She'd never been a beauty. She'd been a sturdy child with a plain face and spent most of her junior high years with a mouthful of braces. These days there never seemed time to do her hair or makeup. Her mom was right; she was letting life get away from her.

Sunshine was shaking her head. "You're still coming for Thanksgiving tomorrow, aren't you?"

"Of course," Kerri assured her. "Wouldn't miss it for the world."

"I wonder what Ryan is doing. He's all alone now his grandfather is gone."

Kerri had heard about John Miller's passing and

sympathised with how Ryan must miss him. "He'll be eating at the firehouse," she said. "What?" she added when Sunshine raised an eyebrow.

"For someone who's not interested in the man, you know an awful lot about him."

"The firemen always have a big Thanksgiving dinner, and they all go. The ones who aren't working do the cooking and keep the food warm for the ones who are, if they get called out. Everyone knows that."

"I didn't know that."

"City girl," Kerri teased her. Sunshine had lived in Chance Creek less than a decade, which made her basically a greenhorn.

"Whatever. It's too bad he's got a place to go. You could have brought him along as your plus one."

"Stop matchmaking." Ryan had never shown the slightest interest in her in all the years they'd known each other. He wasn't going to start now, despite what he'd said about being ready to get married. Besides, she had more important things to do than moon around after him. She had to find a way to save her home and business from her mother. Kerri thought about telling Sunshine about Sylvie's ultimatum and decided against it. She didn't want anyone to know how dysfunctional her family could be. She'd have to find a way to fix things on her own.

"I think I'd be good at it. Ryan is perfect for you." Sunshine snagged the last bite of Kerri's cornbread. Kerri shot her a look, but she didn't really mind. She'd eaten most of her soup and was full, anyway. "Isn't it time you settled down and found yourself a man?"

She'd be glad to find a man, Kerri thought, but first she had to sort out her future.

Sunshine sighed again when she didn't answer. "Do you want some help with those trains?"

Kerri quickly shook her head. The last thing she wanted was anyone to climb the stairs at Bess's house and see that the second floor was worse than the first.

"It won't take me long to pack it up," she lied, quailing inwardly at just how long it would take. After all, look what had happened when she tried to tackle the kitchen.

"Are you sure you won't miss them when they're gone?"

"Miss them?" Sunshine had to know she wasn't all that into trains.

"You told me once Bess collected things that had meaning to her. I thought maybe they meant something to you, too."

Kerri smiled despite herself. "Everything has a story," she admitted. "That does make it harder to let things go."

"You could do what I do with the avalanche of artwork Sienna produces. I can't keep it all, as special as it all is to me, so each year I choose the best pieces to keep in a portfolio, and I photograph the rest of them. As I go through, I note down anything special about them. I make little photo albums. One for each year."

"That's not a bad idea." In fact, it was kind of brilliant. Suddenly Kerri felt like she could tackle the project on her own. "I've got a speech-to-text app on my phone. I can record myself talking about the pieces as I sort them. Later, I can add to the descriptions. I could make photo albums, too."

"I bet George would love a copy if you made one about the trains," Sunshine said. "When you get around to it, of course. The trains themselves will be a big enough present on their own."

The more Kerri thought about it, the more she liked the idea.

"I also bet Ryan would go on a date if you asked him," Sunshine added.

"Give it up already," Kerri said.

"You know you love me," Sunshine teased her. "No matter what I do."

"You're right, I do," Kerri admitted. "You're the best friend ever."

"If I'm that good, buy some dessert, and I'll steal half of it, too."

CHAPTER 3

WHEN RYAN LUGGED the six-foot-tall white pine to the front door of Kerri's house the next morning, it was like stepping back into the past. He'd delivered a Christmas tree with his grandfather to this house every year until he left home at eighteen. Kerri's grandmother had placed her order each January for the following December until this year. Bess must already have been too sick to make the call.

Ryan wondered what Kerri would think if she knew he had a white pine growing on King's Mountain tagged with her name, just the same. His grandfather had always been keenly aware of his customers. When Bess hadn't placed her order at the usual time, Grandpa John made a notation in his notebook and tagged a tree for her anyway. After she passed, he'd crossed out Bess's name and substituted Kerri's, sure that come December, she would want one. He hadn't lived long enough to learn he was right.

Ryan took a deep breath and let his grief pass through him. Grandpa John's death had left a gap in the fabric of the town, and he was afraid he couldn't fill it. There were so many details to remember. So many people for whom his grandfather's deliveries had brought joy.

"Hi, Ryan." The front door swung open before he could knock, and warm air wafted out of Kerri's huge old house. Maple trotted inside happily. Ryan didn't blame her. Grandma Bess's house had always felt like a true home to him. She was the kind of woman who was a grandmother to everyone she met, boisterous and happy, with a laugh that warmed a room. When he was a child, Ryan had made a point to never miss accompanying his grandfather on this delivery. Bess baked the best pecan snowball cookies and never sent them away without a tin to take home.

During those deliveries, Kerri always hung in the background while her grandmother directed them to set the tree in the front hall, since there wasn't any room in the living room. He wouldn't call Bess a hoarder, exactly, but she came awfully close, seemingly unable to part with anything that caught her eye.

Ryan peeked into the living room. Still full to the brim. Kerri hadn't gotten rid of anything, as far as he could tell.

At least she didn't seem to be adding anything.

Despite the clutter, Ryan had always loved this house. He'd made it a game to discern the true dimensions of each room he'd been allowed in and to notice all the details he could. He'd counted the windows and deduced the layout of the second floor based on his knowledge of the first. One year he'd bragged that his grandfather's cabin had two bedrooms, knowing Kerri would counter that her house had more. She hadn't disappointed him.

"We've got six bedrooms upstairs." She'd lifted her chin smugly.

"Show me," he'd said.

Kerri had shaken her head decisively.

That day he'd gone home and drawn a set of floor plans for his dream house. It would be laid out like Bess's, and it would be as cheerful as she somehow made the yellow house, despite all the extra stuff.

His would be a lot less cluttered, he'd decided. He was too used to his grandfather's tidy cabin to accumulate so many things he would never use.

"Where do you want this?" he asked Kerri, lifting the tree he'd brought. Today she was wearing a soft white sweater that clung to her curves, and her pretty, heart-shaped face was flushed. Her dark curls were loose, and they fell just below her shoulders.

"Actually, I have a favor to ask you."

"Shoot." He liked the way she looked at him, sliding her gaze his way from under her lashes, as if she was a little afraid he might do something unexpected.

"Would you help me transport it to the hospital, set it up in the parking lot and then, when I've got it decorated, help me carry it into George Metcalf's room?"

A smile tugged at his mouth. "Of course." That was a nice thing to do for an old man who'd lost something important to him. Ryan had heard all about the flood from the guys at the fire station who'd been the first on the scene to help George with his injuries.

"I'll need to bring these boxes, too," she added, pointing to a large stack of them piled just inside the door. "Some of them hold the decorations I made for the tree. The rest are full of train sets. I figured George might want them to replace the ones that were ruined. Bess had quite a collection, and I figure George will get a lot more use out of them than I ever will."

"That sounds like a good plan." If the rest of the house looked like the living room, it would take a lot more than the contents of those boxes to make a dent in emptying it. "I'll put the tree back in my truck and load those."

"Thanks. I really appreciate it." Her answering smile tugged at something deep inside him, and he wondered once again when she'd made the transition from school-girl to the kind of woman who could make him look twice.

In elementary school she'd been a skinny kid with a long ponytail, curls escaping as the day went on. He remembered her getting hurt once in a dodgeball game and how she'd gotten right up to keep playing, all the while struggling to hide her tears. She'd dated Kenny Sutcliff for a while in high school but had broken up with him in junior year.

These days people talked about her the way they talked about Storm Hall over at Willows clothing store, Fila and Camilla at Fila's Familia, and the other merchants who made up the heart of Chance Creek's downtown. She was on her way to becoming a pillar of the community.

Unlike him. These days he felt like he was getting nowhere fast. Maybe that's why Kerri hadn't paid any attention to the way he and the others had joked about finding wives.

Not that he was joking.

"I'll get my coat and purse," Kerri said.

No pecan snowball cookies, then. Maybe she didn't know how to bake them. Or maybe the thought of offering some to him had never crossed her mind. After all, she had no idea Bess had known they were his favorite. "I'll take this back out."

By the time he'd wrestled the tree into his truck again, Kerri was ready. He hefted a couple of boxes and carried them out. Kerri picked one up and followed him.

"I didn't know Bess collected trains," he said over his shoulder as he went down the steps.

"They reminded her of her older brother, Gavin, who went through a serious train phase."

"Oh, yeah?"

"Once, when they were on vacation in Texas, he found a whole box of them being sold for three dollars at a garage sale. He bought them without their parents knowing. When it came time to go home, he hid all his clothes under the bed and filled his suitcase with them." Kerri grinned. "No one realized what he'd done until it was too late. Their mother was furious, but Gavin played with the set for years, so it was all worth it, or at least that's how Bess told the story. He died when he was in his last year of high school. I guess her parents left his old bedroom the way it was, and after they were gone, she added to it over the years."

Ryan nodded as he deposited the boxes in the back of the truck and reached for the one she'd brought. He'd forgotten Bess had lost a brother early. Her mother and father, too, if memory served him right. She'd inherited the house and store in her early twenties. Had married and lost her husband young, as well.

She must have had some lonely years in this big old place.

As he loaded the truck, Ryan wondered how Kerri was doing living here now that Bess was gone. Did the silent hours between dusk and dawn get to her the way they did him sometimes in the cabin? Throughout his childhood, his grandfather's snoring had commenced at ten-thirty every night and continued until six in the morning. Sometimes Ryan still listened for those snores, but of course they never came.

When they were done loading the boxes, Kerri locked up and joined him in the cab of his truck.

"Buckle up." He immediately wished he could take back the words. It was what his grandfather had always said to him when they rode together, as if he'd never grown up. It was a bit of a joke between them—but Kerri didn't know that.

She held up her seat belt, clicked it into the latch ostentatiously and sent him an amused look under her lashes that warmed his soul. Maybe Bess had said corny things like that, too. At the very least, it seemed like Kerri wasn't going to hold it against him.

What would it be like if she belonged in his passenger seat?

Ryan wasn't sure what he even meant by that. As his girlfriend?

His wife?

Somehow the idea didn't seem as out there as it would have just a month or two ago. They weren't kids anymore. They'd both grown up.

Was she as ready to get on with life as he was?

Little Kerri Olsen, Ryan mused as he drove. Who'd have guessed she could get under his skin?

Then reality set in. If he wanted a wife, he'd better find a job.

A little of the brightness went out of the morning.

IT FELT STRANGE to be riding in the cab of Ryan's truck and even stranger still to know the contents of the train room were all packed up in the back of it. When she'd stood in the doorway of the room after she got home from Orchards last night, trying to decide where to start, the task had seemed overwhelming, but Sunshine's idea had made all the difference.

Just like the downstairs hall, Bess had kept the upstairs hall clear, but the rule about putting anything in it hadn't carried as much weight because visitors never made it that far into the house. Kerri had squared her shoulders, lifted the nearest train set and put it out in the hall. Once she'd taken that first step, everything else became easier. She'd alternated between taking photos and using her voice-to-text app to record all the information she remembered about the pieces, then packed each train set in a box as she went. The landscape and building pieces didn't have as many stories attached to them, so they packed up quickly. When she'd filled a few boxes, she carried them downstairs and left them by the door.

The process took time but not as much as she'd feared when she started. Soon the room was emptying out and the boxes by the front door were piling up, but otherwise she wasn't creating any additional mess in her home. The more she'd done, the more she'd wanted to do. As she went through things, she set aside the smallest trains to make into ornaments, which she'd accomplished later while watching television. When she'd packed the last train away, an unfamiliar satisfaction filled her. There was space in the house, and she felt like she could breathe a little better.

Maybe the house could breathe better, too.

After an uncomfortable fifteen minutes in the parking lot during which Kerri decorated the tree as quickly as she could, she slipped into the hospital to talk to the administrator while Ryan stood guard over it.

It took some convincing to get the serious woman to let them bring it into George's room, but once they'd muscled the tree through the doors, everyone who caught sight of it was entranced by the train-car ornaments.

Buoyed by the reception her tree was getting, Kerri helped Ryan lug it to George's room. His family was gathered around his bed, and his daughter, Susan, came to meet them as soon as they opened the door.

"Kerri! Oh my goodness, what a surprise. Dad, look what Kerri Olsen brought you!"

The old man, who'd been resting back against his pillows, opened his eyes and peered at them. "A tree?"

"Not just any tree," Kerri announced. "A train tree." They moved it nearer to him so he could see, his family parting to let them through.

"A train tree," George repeated faintly. He sat up a little, and his son, Richard, hurried to plump his pillows to support him. "Why, that's a 1955 New Haven diesel." George pointed an unsteady finger at one of the train cars hanging from the boughs. "And a Southern Pacific tender. And that's a Golden Eagle caboose."

"There are a lot more where these came from." Satisfaction filled Kerri as interest animated him. "I've got a stack of boxes full of trains, tracks and scenery out in Ryan's truck. We'll run them over to Susan's house, if that's all right with her, and you can open them on Christmas morning." As strange as it had felt to pack up the trains, she was thrilled to know they were going to someone who would truly appreciate them. Her mother was right; it was time to let some of Bess's things go.

"No need to bring them all the way to my house," Susan said. "I've got my truck in the parking lot. You can pile them in there, and I'll take them home later." She turned to her father. "But you'll have to get better so you're not still here at Christmas," she warned him. "It's bad enough spending Thanksgiving in the hospital! We'll have your place all fixed by then, and after the holidays we'll help you set up your basement again."

"When you do, I'll come by and tell you all the stories that go along with these train cars," Kerri promised.

"You know their history?" George lit up.

"Of course." She bent closer. "I know those stories by heart."

"I'll have to learn them," George said faintly.

"I'll give you something that can help," she told him. "When I packed the trains, I took photographs of them. As soon as I can, I'll put the stories and photos together and turn the whole thing into a little book for you so you can look them up if you forget."

"That would do the trick." The old man was positively beaming now, and Kerri swore he looked healthier than he had when they'd walked in.

Ryan, standing close beside her, touched her arm, and she knew what he was trying to communicate; she'd done a good thing. Was she beaming, too? She had a feeling she might be.

They talked for a while longer, but it was clear George was tiring, so they said their goodbyes and returned to the waiting room, Susan promising to follow them and help them transfer the boxes to her truck.

"Kerri—can I ask you a favor?" A nurse hurried to meet them. Teresa Schultz had been a senior when Kerri was a freshman, a star on the soccer field. "We were wondering if you could make us a tree like the one you made for George? A group of us donate one to the women's shelter every year. We usually decorate it with a set of ornaments someone purchased in the nineties, but they're showing their age, and I love what you did with the trains."

"I gave all the ones I have to George," Kerri said. "I'm sorry." She would have loved to help them.

"Oh, it doesn't have to be trains. It could be anything cute and cozy. I just meant we'd love something unusual. I think our regular trees remind the women of the homes they've left, you know what I mean?"

Kerri nodded. "Something unexpected could give them a fresh way to see the holiday," she mused. "I might be able to do that. Let me think it over. I'll call you tomorrow." Her mind was already racing with possibilities.

"Thanks." Teresa returned to the reception area.

She turned to find Ryan watching her with a look in his eyes she couldn't quite place. Something almost possessive but proud at the same time, as if she was one of his people—

No. She couldn't let herself spin stories like that about a man who'd never noticed her before. She was lonely right now. The holidays were looming, and Bess was gone.

Ryan touched the small of her back, sending another shock of awareness through her. She liked the feel of his hand on her body. Wished he would touch her more.

Kerri closed her eyes a moment. She shouldn't think about Ryan's hands... period. Certainly not about them touching her. She had a crisis to solve.

Why would he now?

"Here comes Susan," Ryan said.

Kerri opened her eyes again as he stepped away from her. When George's daughter joined them, she let Ryan lead the way out of the hospital so they could move the boxes into her vehicle. It was just the season making her think she was attracted to him, she told herself. Christmas made everyone a little crazy. She couldn't afford to get tangled up with Ryan Miller. Not when she needed to focus all her energy on saving her home and business.

CHAPTER 4

RYAN SPENT THE rest of the day harvesting trees and bringing them to display in the sales area of the farm. When he opened to the public this weekend, the place would throng with people, some of them wanting to search through the cut trees and others who wanted to wander the fields to cut down their own.

At four thirty he cleaned up and drove to town for Thanksgiving supper at the firehouse. Just as he turned off the highway, however, his pager went off, alerting him that a fire was in progress several blocks away—at an address he knew. He turned on the revolving red emergency light affixed to his truck. Arriving minutes later, he found the crew already on scene, most of them milling around in front of a small gray house. Its windows were thrown open wide despite the chill of the day. Smoke was streaming out of them, but Ryan could tell from the relaxed attitudes of the men the fire had already been put out.

He parked, turned off the emergency light and got out. "Is Mrs. Fisher okay?" She was a long-term customer; he'd delivered a tree to her just a couple of days ago. She liked having her house decorated for Christmas when she came home from her daughter's house after Thanksgiving dinner.

"She's fine. So are her cats, despite their best efforts." Ed detached himself from the rest of the crowd and came to talk with him. He was nearing sixty and balding but still an active, energetic man.

"What do you mean?" Mrs. Fisher's penchant for cats was well known in town. He'd spotted at least eight of them when he'd set up the tree for her, all healthy, happy animals from the looks of things.

"Seems she bought a new ornament this year."

"Let me guess—of the feline persuasion?" Mrs. Fisher always had her ornaments laid out in their boxes when she expected him, ready to decorate her tree the moment he put it in its place by the front window. She'd collected hundreds of cat-themed decorations over the years.

"Actually, it was a fish—given to her by her great-niece."

Ryan chuckled. "That's a departure for her."

"Sure is. There's a twist, though." Ed raised his eyebrows for effect. "The fish wasn't an ornament at all. It was a cat toy. Stuffed with catnip."

"Oh no."

"Oh yes." Ed was enjoying this too much. "You can imagine what happened when she hung it on her tree."

"Total mayhem?" Ryan guessed. Eight cats, one catnip-filled toy? Sure sounded like trouble.

"Total mayhem," Ed confirmed. "Several of them jumped up to get it, knocked over the tree, which landed close enough to a plug for a metal ornament to touch the socket. There was a spark, and the tree caught on fire."

"Did it burn up?"

"The tree is done for. So are most of the ornaments—and the rug in her living room. You could call it a… *cat-astrophe*."

Ryan groaned. "A man your age should know better than to make a pun that bad."

Ed grinned. "Don't suppose you've got another tree you could give her? Mrs. Fisher is distraught."

"I bet she is." Ryan thought it over. "I've got the balsam fir in my truck I was bringing for the firehouse. I can give it to her and grab another one later. We weren't going to put it up until tomorrow anyway. I even brought a stand for it. She can have that, too, if hers was damaged."

"I'll help you carry everything in."

Mrs. Fisher was grateful when she caught sight of them lugging the fir into her house. Some of the men had already dragged her rug outside, and she was trying to remove a burn mark on the hardwood floor. "I could save only a handful of ornaments," she fussed as she watched them set it up by the window. "I'll have to go to the store tomorrow."

"I bet my missus has an extra string of lights you could have," Ed told her.

Ryan thought about the train tree Kerri made for

George. Was there any chance she could whip up some cat-themed ornaments?

Wouldn't hurt to ask. Especially since it would give him the perfect excuse to see her again.

TEAPOTS. AND TEACUPS. And spoons.

Kerri stirred sugar into the fresh cup of tea she'd just poured and nodded with satisfaction. Bess had collected them along with every other kind of kitchen implement. She had a number of regular-size teapots that would be far too large to turn into ornaments, but she also had a collection of the most darling single-serving teapots you'd ever seen. Tiny, decorative and pretty, they would be perfect.

She'd been racking her brain trying to come up with an idea for the tree she was making for the women's shelter. The most obvious choice was to hang small stuffed animals on it for the kids, but she was afraid that would remind the mothers of the gifts they couldn't give to their children.

She wanted to do something different. Something whimsical and fun with no associations to anything in particular. The brightly colored teapots were cute as buttons. Teatime was a comforting theme, and she could choose the ones decorated with shades of red, silver, green and gold.

While she was at it…

Kerri turned in a circle, taking in the disorganized clutter. She could give each woman at the shelter a practical gift, too. They'd all move on eventually, and when they got their own places, most of them would be starting from scratch. Wouldn't a collection of high-quality kitchen tools be a big help as they prepared to begin their new lives? She had enough to make gift baskets for each of the women living there now.

A new inspiration struck. Bess had one whole cupboard of miniature baking items. Kerri could package those as gifts for the kids. In the process she could clear enough things out of the kitchen that maybe she could actually use it for its intended purpose.

Energized by that thought, she got to work. Like the trains in the train room, the teapots had stories behind them, too, and Kerri wanted to be sure to document them. At least she didn't have to carry everything downstairs, she thought as she took a few into the hall, got out her phone and photographed them.

When she'd chosen the items to use on the tree, documented them and dictated notes about their provenance, then packed them carefully into a couple of boxes, she got out some old tablecloths and laid them on the floor in the hallway, creating a space to sort through everything else. By the time she got to the cupboards, the countertops and kitchen floor were bare, which gave her more places to sort things.

She was surprised to find it didn't bother her to use the hall as a sorting area today. After all, she'd stacked boxes here to bring to the hospital and moved them out within twenty-four hours without incident. She'd used the upstairs hall to sort the trains, and it was empty again, too—as was the train room. At no point during the process of cleaning that room had she felt any hoarding tendencies take hold of her. In fact, if anything, the reverse had happened. The more she'd packed, the more she'd wanted to do. She thought things would go the same way with the kitchen.

It took a long time to empty the room, especially when it came to taking down Bess's collection of vintage cooking implements that hung on the wall. By the time she was done, she was standing in a sea of items.

Quelling a momentary flutter of panic as she surveyed them, Kerri got to work and grouped them together, like with like, moving between the kitchen and hall. She counted the names on the list Teresa had emailed her. Nine women, fourteen children. Kerri pictured them making do in the shelter, the mothers trying to heal from their pasts and create a whole new future for their families.

She threw on a jacket and boots and hurried through the snow to her store, where she grabbed a bundle of large handled bags and brought them back to the house. Out of her winter things again, she went around filling one bag for each adult. When she had nine of them, she filled fourteen more with kids' versions of the kitchen wares. By the time she was done, she'd put a substantial dent in the collection. Fired up now, Kerri decided she'd keep going.

First she filled more bags, figuring she could donate them to the shelter to keep on hand for future clients and their children. She grouped the leftovers in boxes, some to take to her store and others to donate to charity. She saved a set of dishes for herself for normal use, a set of china for special occasions, and only those pots, pans and kitchen implements she knew for sure she'd use, plus a few vintage items that reminded her of her grandmother that she knew she'd like to display.

In the end she lined up all the bags and boxes in the front hall, telling herself again she'd make sure everything was gone within a day or two at most. Returning to the kitchen, Kerri stopped short. The room was even more enormous than she'd realized, now that everything was cleared from the walls, shelves and countertops.

In fact, it was a spectacular space.

Something between joy and heartache filled her. When was the last time Bess had seen the room like this?

She shook off the sad thoughts before they could paralyze her. The room was ready now for a new future.

Her future.

This kitchen was made to be the heart of a house that was filled by family, and she couldn't help imagining herself at the center of it, her husband and children spread around her. She could work magic here, she knew. She could fill stomachs and hearts with her cooking and love. She could supervise homework, dispense wisdom, dance with the man she loved…

But she was going to lose that future if her mother had her way. Kerri took a deep breath and stiffened her resolve not to let that happen. She took a snapshot and sent it to Sylvie with an accompanying text: *See? I've already tackled the kitchen! Doesn't it look great?*

Any hope she had that her mother would respond just as enthusiastically was dashed a moment later.

Show me the rest of the house.

Kerri knew the empty train room wouldn't impress her, so she didn't bother running upstairs to photograph it. Instead she remained where she was. This beautiful kitchen deserved to be used for its proper purpose, and she wasn't going to let her mother ruin the joy she felt after setting it free from all the clutter that filled it. She still had time before she was due at Sunshine's place. Why not bake pecan snowball cookies to bring along instead of the store-bought sugar cookies sitting in the cupboard?

Ryan popped into her mind, which was odd, until a memory surfaced from when she was a girl. She'd been standing awkwardly in the doorway between the kitchen and hall when he and his grandfather brought in their tree. Bess had sent her running for the cookie tins she'd prepared for them.

Ryan loved pecan snowball cookies. Bess had made them for him every year.

The corner of her mouth tugged upward at the memory.

Did he still love them?

She told herself not to be silly. It didn't matter what Ryan liked or disliked. She was going to a friend's house tonight, and it was only right for her to contribute something to the meal.

She gave the countertops a quick clean, determined

to do a more thorough job on the whole room tomorrow, then got to the fun part. Enjoying the sensation of having so much space, she fetched ingredients, almost tempted to dance as she made the cookie dough. When her phone rang, it startled her. She slapped a hand to her pocket and drew it out.

Her mother again. Kerri accepted the call. Maybe she'd come around.

"Hi, Mom."

"You sound cheerful."

"You saw my beautiful kitchen. I'm baking my first batch of Christmas cookies in it now." She ran her hand along the ingredients she'd set on the counter—flour, sugar, butter, pecans and vanilla flavoring.

"So, I was right; the rest of the house is still a mess."

"I cleaned out the train room, too. That's two rooms in two days. I thought you'd be impressed." Kerri set up her phone on the counter and kept working.

"Does that mean you'll be ready to show the place soon?"

"Show it?"

"When you put it up for sale."

Kerri couldn't believe what she was hearing. "I don't want to put it up for sale. I want to stay here. I'm cleaning it out to prove to you there's nothing wrong with me living in Bess's house." She pulled out Bess's favorite ceramic mixing bowl and a wooden spoon, determined not to let her mother rattle her.

"A couple of clean rooms doesn't get me my money, does it?"

"I'll go to the bank on Monday. It's a holiday week-end, Mom, in case you haven't noticed." She measured out her ingredients.

Her mother made an impatient noise. "In other words, my future isn't your priority."

"I never said that. I said the bank is closed. I'll get you the money!" Kerri was having a hard time holding on to the high spirits that had filled her just moments ago, but she kept going. Why was her mother so determined to ruin things for her?

"How?"

"A second loan. Or cash advances on my credit cards. Or something." She mixed the cookie dough with a little more force than was necessary.

Her mother's expression softened. "You're living in a dream world, honey. The same one Mom always lived in. There's no way you can round up thirty grand in less than a month. You've got to shake off the hold the past has on you and focus on your future. Our future. Sell that property. Come to California."

"Why would I come to California?" Kerri knew the question was rude, but so was throwing her out of her house. Did her mom really think they'd be best friends after something like that?

Her mother blinked on her screen. "I told you I was expanding my business. Think about it, Kerri. You and me. Working together. Finally living in the same town."

Was she serious? Kerri wasn't sure. "You're trying to get me to sell Bess's house so I'll come work for you?

I thought it was because you needed the money."

Her mother winced. "I told you I'm doing it for your own good. So you don't become just like her."

Kerri wasn't sure she bought that, and she was afraid of saying something she'd regret. "I've got to go. I'll be late to Sunshine's house."

"Think about coming to Sacramento. And then call a realtor."

"Happy Thanksgiving, Mom." Kerri hung up, feeling as wrung out as a washcloth. She pocketed her phone, defeat weighing down her shoulders. If anyone should understand what she'd accomplished today it was her mother, but Sylvie had acted like cleaning two rooms was the least she could do. Maybe she should forget about the cookies.

No, Kerri decided. She was going to finish what she started. She turned back to the cookie dough, scooped it onto a tray and got the first batch in the oven.

She should call Ryan. He'd cheer her up.

Kerri stopped in her tracks, one hand on her phone, unsure where that thought had come from. If anything, she should call Ryan to set up a time to bring that tree over, not to chat with him. It wasn't like he was a friend—or anything else, no matter what Sunshine thought.

But as she made the call, she found herself wishing he was.

CHAPTER 5

"HEARD YOU GAVE our tree to the cat lady," Jacob Monk said when he and Ryan were filling their plates at the buffet table that had been set up to hold the special holiday meal. The firehouse was packed with men—and a few women. Most of the department was male, but a couple of female firefighters had joined the team in recent years. So far, except for Mrs. Fisher's cat disaster, there hadn't been any other calls. Ryan knew that could change in an instant, and he hoped he'd get to finish his meal before it did.

"I'll bring another one tomorrow," Ryan assured him. When their plates were heaping, they took them to a nearby table and found places to sit. Maple curled up under the table, careful to stay out of the way of the men's feet and knees. Ryan side-eyed Jacob as the blond man fed her a morsel of turkey. Jacob had been a defenseman on the high school football team. He tackled every problem in life like it was an opponent on the field, with brute force and zero hesitation. Some-times that made him the best person to have backing you up. Sometimes it made being his friend a liability.

"You better not spoil her."

"With the way you let Maple follow you wherever you go, *I'm* not the one spoiling her, buddy." Jacob wiped his hands on a napkin before tucking into his food. "What are you going to do after the holidays? Have you found a job?"

"Not yet."

Jacob leaned closer. "Wish you were working here. I'd take you over Robert any day."

"He's doing fine." For the past nine months or so, Ryan had tried hard not to resent Robert Perry, the man who'd filled the position he couldn't take last winter.

"Exactly. *Fine.*" There was a world of meaning in the way Jacob pronounced the word. "His heart isn't in it."

"He's just adjusting to the place." Perry came from Idaho. The fire chief who'd recommended him was a friend of Ed's.

"He's taking his sweet time."

Ryan had a feeling the man was homesick. Robert vacillated between keeping to himself and trying too hard to fit in with the others. He'd managed to step on just about everyone's toes since he'd arrived. Sometimes it was bad luck. Other times he seemed to do it deliberately.

Ryan looked around the room, taking in all the faces he knew so well. He fit in easily here because he'd known most of them his whole life. There'd been an unusual amount of turnover at the station around the time he graduated, the old crew retiring and a new one getting started. He'd been in school with most of the people sitting at these tables. Only his volunteer status kept him from truly being one of them.

His phone buzzed in his pocket. "Hold on." He pulled it out and was surprised to see Kerri's name on his screen. She'd probably looked up the tree farm and found his number on the website he'd created after his grandfather got ill. He'd planned to call her tomorrow to ask about the cat ornaments, but he was happy to talk to her today. Jacob, looking over his shoulder, saw her name, too. Ryan elbowed him away and answered the call. "Hey, happy Thanksgiving. You getting any turkey?"

"I will soon. I'm going to Sunshine's place in a minute. But I wanted to let you know I'm ready for the tree to take to the women's shelter. I've got all the decorations together. Any chance you can bring me one when you've got a minute? And I need to pay you for the one we took to Charlie."

"I'm happy to donate both trees."

"You don't have to do that."

"I want to."

Jacob cut him off. "Hi, Kerri," he said loudly. "How's it going?"

Everyone at the table turned their way. Ryan elbowed Jacob again.

"Who's that?" Kerri asked.

"Jacob Monk. I'm at the firehouse." He decided not to ask about ornaments for Mrs. Fisher's tree right now.

Not with everyone listening in.

"I must be interrupting your dinner," Kerri said.

"You're not interrupting anything." Ryan vowed he'd get even with Jacob later. "How about I stop by later tonight? Do you know when you'll be home?"

"Around nine, I guess. We're all working tomorrow, and Sunshine's pregnant. She needs her sleep, so I'm sure we'll leave early. But you don't have to bring it tonight; any time will do."

"I'll see you at nine."

When he ended the call, Ryan faced the rest of the crew. "What?"

"Since when are you and Kerri Olsen a thing?" Jacob asked. "You've been holding out on us."

"Kerri from Kerri's Collectibles?" Daniel Wallace said. "I've thought about asking her out." Daniel was a few years older than Ryan, a tall man with a laid-back attitude.

"She's never at the Boot," Eli King complained. "I'd ask her to dance if she was." Eli was Nicholas King's cousin, but he wasn't part of the Mountain Man group; he lived on flat ground.

Ryan didn't like the turn this conversation had taken. "No one gets to ask her out or to dance or anything else. Hands off."

"Ooh," Jacob crooned. "Sounds serious."

"Sounds like you're going to get a face full of gravy if you don't shut up. All I'm doing is delivering a tree to her."

"You're *giving* her a tree, you mean. Admit it; you

like her." There were a few appreciative chuckles around the table.

"Kerri's decorating it for the women's shelter. You ever think of doing something good for someone else?"

"Jacob?" Brandon Strauss, who was sitting across the table, laughed. "He's never volunteered for anything in his life." Brandon had been a wide receiver on the football team. He could pull a ball out of the air no matter how far off course the quarterback threw it. He was known for finding a way through any fire to get to people trapped in burning buildings, too.

"I have so."

"When?"

"I volunteered to beat your ass at pool as soon as dinner's over, so let's get going."

Ryan was grateful for the new topic, knowing Jacob could have spent the next hour teasing him about Kerri.

There was nothing going on between the two of them, but he still didn't like the sound of her name in anyone else's mouth. Maybe he didn't have the right to tell Daniel not to ask her out or Eli not to dance with her, but he wasn't sorry he'd done so. Even if he never dated her, Kerri was still special. The guys he worked with here were a good bunch, but none of them was serious about settling down anytime soon. Kerri deserved a man who was ready to build a life with her.

He wished he was in a position to do so.

Ryan paused, a forkful of turkey halfway to his mouth.

Did Kerri Olsen have wife potential?

He hadn't been joking last night when he'd told the Mountain Men he was looking for one, but he'd never spent any time with Kerri. Thinking about settling down with her certainly qualified as putting the cart before the horse.

And he had no idea what she thought about him. When Nicholas had joked that Sunshine might have a wife for him, Kerri hadn't taken the bait. She'd remained cool and calm and answered all his questions in a measured tone. She'd betrayed no feelings for him during their ride to the hospital and back, either.

He was the one who'd struggled not to touch her—and failed, several times.

Maybe he should ask her out, whether or not he had his future sorted.

"You going to eat all that turkey?" Jacob asked.

"You wouldn't need mine if you hadn't fed half yours to my dog," Ryan groused, sliding his plate over anyway.

Around seven thirty he left the firehouse, the men's laughter echoing behind him, and drove home to pick up a tree worthy of a good cause. The night was clear, the stars shining as he made his way back to town. He knocked on Kerri's door at nine, anticipation curling low in his gut. Should he ask her out tonight? Knowing several other men at the station were interested in her sharpened his need to find out if she was someone he wanted to get to know better.

Like he needed to find out anything. His base instincts were ready to stake a claim on her. It was as if he'd never fully focused on Kerri before, and now that he had, he couldn't stop thinking about her.

"Come in. Are you as stuffed as I am?" Kerri asked when she opened the door a moment later. She had changed from this morning's outfit into a calf-length skirt and a soft blue sweater that made him ache to touch her. How had he ever thought Kerri was just another girl?

"I can barely move. We didn't get any calls this evening, so I had plenty of time to eat." And joke around with friends.

And think about her.

"I'm glad you had a calm day. I thought I heard sirens this afternoon."

"There was a small fire at Mrs. Fisher's house. Her cats tried to burn her house down." He filled her in on the details.

"I shouldn't laugh," Kerri said as she led him inside. "But I can just picture it."

"I gave her a new tree, but she doesn't have anything to decorate it with. I was wondering if you had anything cat-related that might fit the bill."

She smiled lopsidedly, and he felt it all the way to the core of him. "Actually, I do. I'd be happy to donate some ornaments."

"Good." He forced himself to stay with the conversation, when what he really wanted to do was tuck the loose curl that was tickling her cheek behind her ear. "I've got the tree for the women's shelter in the truck." He sniffed the air, suddenly alert to a new call on his senses. "Are those snowball cookies I'm smelling?" The scent took him straight back to being ten years old.

"Got it in one try. I baked them this afternoon. Come in and have one if you've got any room for it. Watch the bags." The hall was lined with them. "Those are for the women at the shelter," she added. "I've been decluttering."

"I've always got room for a snowball cookie." It had to be a good sign she wanted him in her house—and that she wanted to feed him, too. Buoyed by the thought, Ryan followed her into the living room.

"Have a seat. I'll be back in a minute."

It took him a minute to find an empty space on one of the overstuffed sofas, given the room was still filled to the brim with vintage sporting equipment. There were cross-country skis, lobster traps, fishing rods, snowshoes, woven baskets for berry picking and the like. Gear was stored in corners, piled on chairs and end tables, hung on the walls. He was surprised Kerri hadn't brought it all to her secondhand store to sell long before now.

He knew better than to ask about Bess's collections, though. He had, once, when he was thirteen, when he was too young and dumb to understand discretion.

He'd come, as usual, to deliver a tree and had been sitting right here in the living room with Kerri while Grandpa John and Bess talked in the hall. Ryan had been reaching for a cookie from a plate Kerri was offering when the question popped out of his mouth. "Why does your grandma have so much junk?"

"It's not junk!" Kerri had been furious. She'd snatched the plate from under his hand, jumped up and stormed into the kitchen, leaving him ashamed and wishing he'd gotten a cookie before he'd shot off his mouth.

"Gotta learn when to keep your trap shut," his grandfather had said afterward on their drive back to the mountain. "Especially around women."

Ryan had never questioned Bess's tendencies again.

Kerri came back with a plate of cookies and two mugs of tea.

"Thanks." He took the mug she offered him and a couple of cookies when she'd set them down.

"I've done a train tree, a kitchen tree, and pretty soon I'll do a cat tree," she said as she took a seat. Maple, who'd been nosing around, came to settle on the floor near them. "What's your Christmas tree's theme?"

"I've never had one." He braced himself for her reaction, figuring she'd have something to say about that.

"Your decorations are eclectic? I guess most people's are."

"I mean I've never had a Christmas tree. Not since I moved in with my grandfather, anyway."

Kerri stared up at him. "You've never had a tree? How is that possible? You live on a Christmas tree farm."

Ryan shrugged his shoulders. "I guess that's why in a nutshell. Working there, you end up thinking about Christmas trees all year long. By the time the holidays roll around, you've had enough." As she tilted her head, he wished he'd found a way to deflect her questions. Why was it any time he talked about himself, he wished he hadn't?

"Is that your grandfather's position, or do you feel that way yourself?" she probed. "Everyone needs a tree in the house to brighten it up at the darkest time of the year."

"I never thought about it." But he had. As a child he'd wished for a tree every time December rolled around, but he'd accepted his grandfather's pronouncement. Grandpa John never wanted to change anything about the cabin, no matter what time of year it was. "When I was little, my parents always decorated one." That was something he and Kerri had in common—the number of people they'd lost.

"It's never too late to start a new tradition," Kerri said, breaking into his thoughts. "Don't you want to have a bit of holiday spirit in your home?"

"I guess I'll have to. I'm in charge of the Mountain Man Christmas party. It's going to be on December twenty-second. You're definitely invited." He'd set the date but hadn't thought beyond that. Did he need decorations? Food? Drinks?

Party games?

He was out of his league.

"Thanks. That sounds like fun. If you need anything, let me know. I'll probably have something you can borrow."

"Great." He was grateful when she let the topic go. "It's pretty late to bring the tree to the shelter tonight," he pointed out.

Kerri nodded. "Just leave it here, and I'll take it over in the morning." She took a sip from her mug.

"By yourself?"

"If you help me put it in my truck tonight, I'm sure the ladies at the shelter will help me unload it."

"But you'll want to decorate the tree first before you take it in—so it's a surprise." He was grasping at straws, wanting to spend more time with her but not sure what she'd say if he asked her on a date. Kerri was a hard woman to read. On the one hand, she seemed open and friendly. On the other, Ryan had the feeling there was much more to her than met the eye.

Like the way she restored old furniture. He'd been to her store since he'd been home, and while the secondhand items hadn't surprised him, her restorations had. She didn't take a piece of furniture and make it exactly what it was before. She took broken-down items and transformed them into something else entirely. That took imagination as well as patience and skill and suggested a depth to her he hadn't suspected before. He'd done a lot of woodworking when he was younger, so he could respect the effort it took.

"Tell you what," he said. "I won't bother to unload it tonight. I'll come back at eight tomorrow morning. We'll take everything over to the shelter, park somewhere around the corner, and you can decorate the tree before we carry it inside. Just like we did at the hospital." He popped one last cookie in his mouth and washed it down with a gulp of tea.

"I can handle it on my own," Kerri said.

"I know you can. I want to help." He wasn't going to back down, even though he could tell Kerri wanted to protest. He stood up, figuring if he stuck around, she'd find some way to divert him from his purpose. "I'd better get home. I'll be back in the morning."

Kerri stood up and followed him into the hall to see him to the door, still looking like she wanted to argue with him. Maple got to her feet with a big doggy yawn and trotted after them.

"I'll call Teresa and let her know we're coming," she finally said, giving in. "Hold on," she added. "I'll send you home with more cookies." She ducked into the kitchen, and he followed her, stopping dead in the doorway.

"What happened?" he asked. The last time he'd seen this room it was stuffed to the gills. She wasn't kidding when she'd said she'd decluttered.

"Pretty amazing, isn't it?" Kerri asked. "There were so many things in here before, you could hardly turn around. That's where all those bags in the hall came from."

He nodded. That made sense. "This is some kitchen." He pointed to the empty space. "You need a table and chairs, though."

"I guess." She shrugged.

He figured she needed time to get used to the change before she thought about adding new furniture. He found himself relieved by the state of the room although it took him a moment to figure out why.

Kerri wasn't a hoarder.

Which was good, because he didn't think he could marry one. Which made no sense to be thinking about, since he still hadn't even asked her on a date.

But here he was, thinking about it.

What's more, his body was thinking about what it would feel like to get closer to her—a lot closer.

He needed to get out of here before he did something stupid like tell her everything that was going through his mind. Watching her sort cookies into different tins on layers of waxed paper, just like her grandmother used to do, was kicking his imagination into high gear, and that was all kinds of wrong. He wasn't fantasizing about her because she reminded him of her grandmother.

"Did you say something?"

Ryan swallowed hard. "No." He might have made a strangled noise, but he definitely hadn't put any of that into words. It was the domesticity of the scene that was getting to him, something his life had lacked for a long, long time. He wasn't looking for a substitute mother—or grandmother. He was looking for a wife. A woman who'd take the time and care to make his house a real home. A woman who'd plan for his happiness the way he wanted to plan for hers. Someone soft and warm and—

"Ryan?" Kerri was looking at him in concern. He'd made that noise again.

Ryan cleared his throat. "Sorry. Maybe I'm getting a cold."

She nodded. When she'd finished with the cookies, he followed her out into the hall.

"Enjoy," she said, handing them over.

"Thanks." To the surprise of them both, he dropped a kiss on her cheek. Her skin was soft and smooth, and the subtle scent of her shampoo made him want to lean in closer. He caught himself just in time. "Happy Thanksgiving," he said again gruffly, as if that explained what he'd just done. Ryan figured he'd better get out of here while the getting was good. "Maple, come."

Maple followed him out into the cold, and Ryan shut the door firmly behind them. He strode to his truck, taking a deep breath of the icy winter air.

What the hell had just happened?

He'd kissed Kerri Olsen.

And she hadn't stopped him.

HE'D KISSED HER.

Hadn't he?

Ryan had leaned down, and she'd felt a brief brush of his lips against her cheek. That had been a kiss. She was sure of it.

But why? Was he interested in her?

Did she want him to be?

Kerri lay in bed analyzing every minute of their time together for hours before sleep finally claimed her that night. In the morning, it was the first thought on her mind when she woke up.

Ryan had kissed her. A very light, friendly kiss.

But still. He'd watched her like a feral thing as she'd packed up his cookies, until she'd gotten jumpy as a hen around a fox. She hadn't been able to decipher his expression. Had that been interest or merely impatience?

The kiss seemed to suggest the former.

Kerri got out of bed, showered, dressed and had her breakfast. By the time eight o'clock rolled around, she was a bundle of nerves, but when Ryan showed up, he was all good cheer and hearty greetings, as if nothing out of the ordinary had happened the night before. Kerri decided to follow his lead. Maybe she'd been making a mountain out of a molehill. Maybe Ryan kissed all his female acquaintances goodbye.

He'd better not.

Kerri squashed the errant thought. She had no reason to feel possessive of Ryan Miller. He was just a guy she'd gone to school with. Someone who was helping her out. Nothing more, nothing less.

"Where's Maple?" Kerri asked, noticing the dog's absence.

"I've got something for you in the truck. She decided she needed to guard it," he said as she went to collect her coat.

"You've got something for me? What is it?" A curious thrill shot through her at the idea of Ryan going out of his way for her. Had he brought her coffee?

If so, why would he leave it in the truck?

"You'll have to come outside to see. Hope you like it, or I'll have to take it back up the mountain."

That didn't sound like coffee. Eager to find out what it was, she followed him outside, rounded his truck and gasped.

"Where did you get that?" And why had he brought her a dining table set? A beautiful dining table set, from what she could see.

That was a much bigger deal than a cup of coffee.

Suddenly uncertain, Kerri wasn't sure what she should do. She was all too aware of Ryan's gaze on her.

"I made it—about ten years ago." He opened the tailgate, revealing fully the table that was braced in the truck bed—and Maple, who was lying with her head on her paws underneath it. The chairs that made up the set were stacked to one side. "Come take a closer look." He climbed into the bed and put out his hand. Kerri took it, more unsettled by the moment. His hand swallowed hers, and he pulled her up easily. Suddenly face to face with him, Kerri held her breath.

He'd brought her a dining room set? One he'd made himself?

What did that mean?

He stepped back as much as he could in the tight confines of the truck bed. "Take a look."

He steadied her with a hand on the crook of her arm as she did so, and Kerri found it hard to focus on the table at all. "This is beautiful," she said when she could find words again. The table was farmhouse style but pared-down and elegant, with a wide plank top and a solid, wooden base. The matching chairs were well crafted. "Ryan, you're really good at this."

"If you want it, it's yours." He was still much too close to her, and her heart was pounding. This was a hell of a gift, and he was a hell of a man—

"I couldn't possibly take it. Why aren't you keeping it?" Was she babbling? She felt like she was.

"No room at my place. You'd be doing me a favor taking it off my hands."

"I can't imagine that." It would fit so nicely in her kitchen, Kerri thought. Every time she saw it, she'd think about him—

As if she wasn't thinking about him enough already.

"How about this," Ryan said, moving closer to run a hand over the tabletop. "Let's put it in your kitchen for now, and you can give it a test run. If you don't like it, you can sell it in your store and take a cut of the proceeds."

"Deal," Kerri said decidedly, already knowing she'd never want to give it up. She'd be able to eat her meals in her newly spacious kitchen at a table for once instead of perched on a sofa in her still-crowded living room. It was a perfect fit for the splendid room her kitchen had turned out to be.

And he'd made it himself.

A little shiver went through her at the way his hand ran over the tabletop possessively, as if he knew every inch of it, since he was its creator. How would those hands of his feel running over her skin?

She shook the impossible idea away.

Maybe it wasn't impossible, though, a part of her argued. He was giving her a dining room table and chairs, for heaven's sake. He had to be a little interested in her.

Buzzing with awareness, she helped him move everything into her house. She was grateful for the errand that awaited them afterward, because the sight of the beautiful dining room set positioned in front of the window in her beautiful, newly cleaned and organized kitchen nearly brought her to tears.

Blinking them away, she helped Ryan load all the bags in her front hall into the truck bed beside the tree he'd brought. Maple had begrudgingly hopped out of the back when they'd unloaded it. Now she padded over to the cab expectantly. When Kerri had shut and locked the house's front door, Ryan helped her into the passenger seat. The quick pressure of his hand in hers sent another little thrill through her body, but she was up in the cab before she could do more than register what he'd done. Maple jumped in and sat on her feet.

"Buckle up," he told Kerri.

"You said that last time. I've been in a truck before, you know." She pulled the seat belt over her shoulder and fastened it.

"Just thinking about your safety." He shot her a grin that melted her insides until she was amazed she could still keep upright.

"Maybe you'd better think about your own," she quipped.

"Don't I know it." He shut her door and rounded the truck to take his place in the driver's seat. Kerri ran those words through her mind over and over on the way to the shelter, wondering what he meant. Was he suggesting he was as affected by her as she was by him?

No, that couldn't be it.

Could it?

The ride was too short to give her time to come to any conclusions. Just as Ryan had suggested, he found a parking spot around the corner and helped her get the tree into its stand on the sidewalk. He stood guard while she quickly decorated it and helped her carefully carry it inside. Ryan ordered Maple to stay in the truck. Even a perfectly mannered dog might not be welcome in the shelter. She gave the two of them a morose look as they made their way to the back door.

Teresa met them there with Sarah Ripperson, who ran the place.

"Hello, you two! The tree looks amazing." Sarah directed them into a large room full of couches and easy chairs, a somewhat old-fashioned television, several baskets of children's toys and two large bulletin boards on the walls. "I've told everyone they're not allowed in until tonight, when we'll have a special tree-lighting ceremony. I love the teapots and teacups. What a great idea, Kerri."

"Thanks." She'd supplemented them with a string of Christmas lights and red-and-white-calico bows, and now she thought it was one of the most cheerful trees she'd ever seen. She supposed since Sarah was keeping everyone out, she could have decorated it inside the building, but it didn't matter now.

"It's so cute," Teresa said. "Where did you find all

this stuff?"

Kerri shrugged. "I run a secondhand store" was all she said. She didn't want anyone to think badly of Bess. Not that her collections were ever much of a secret.

"We're very grateful for your contribution," Sarah said.

"Ryan provided the tree," Kerri told her. "I can't take all the credit."

"She can take most of it," Ryan said.

"Well, thanks to both of you," Sarah said. "I know the women and children will be thrilled when they see it later."

"We brought some gifts, too," Kerri said. "We'll be back in a minute."

She and Ryan had to make several trips to get all the gift bags into the shelter. Teresa helped Sarah find a place to hide them away until the holidays.

"You really went above and beyond," she said when they were done.

"We were happy to do it," Kerri said. "Everyone needs some holiday cheer."

When they'd said their goodbyes, Kerri followed Ryan outside to his truck, nerves fluttering to life again. She had the feeling he would bring up that kiss now they'd accomplished their errand.

"I'll run you to your shop."

"Thanks. I need to open soon."

"Look," he said when they were in their seats. "About last night."

Kerri waited to hear what he had to say, wondering

if he'd try to brush off what happened as an accident or if he'd acknowledge what he'd done. The resonance of his deep voice had her on pins and needles. There was something so masculine about the way he sat so easily in his seat.

The way he watched her.

"What about it?"

"I don't have any excuse for kissing you. It just felt right, and I did it."

Kerri let out an unsteady breath. She knew what he meant. Every time he was close to her, she wanted to touch him.

"Oh." She didn't know what else to say.

"Want to help me make my tree deliveries tonight?" he asked. "I like to do them at the end of the day when people are home from work. I could pick you up when you close the store."

"Sure." Kerri bit her lip. Had she sounded too enthusiastic? The truth was she didn't have any other plans tonight, and she had no desire to rush home to an empty house. Evenings were the worst since Bess was gone. It used to be she'd come home to hear Bess singing as she dusted her collections, a simple dinner warm in the oven. Bess always managed to cook something despite the lack of space in the kitchen, even when she'd fallen ill.

Ever since she passed away, the house seemed too big for just one person. Friends had suggested getting a dog, but she couldn't imagine keeping a pet away from Bess's collections, even if she did love watching Maple navigate carefully around the stacks, sniffing each item with intense curiosity.

"I've got nine of them to drop off," Ryan said. "It'll take about an hour and a half."

"I've got nowhere to be tonight," Kerri assured him. Would this count as a date? It was a pretty unconventional one.

"Glad to hear it. Wouldn't hurt my feelings if you brought some more of those cookies along. If you have any left."

She laughed. "You already ate the ones I gave you?" When he nodded, she said, "Will do."

Ryan pulled to a stop in front of her store. "See you later." He looked like he wanted to add something more, or steal another kiss, but in the end he didn't.

She was disappointed.

"See you," Kerri said and got out.

She was afraid the day would crawl, but the store was so busy from the moment she opened, she barely had time to think about Ryan or the evening ahead of her. Chloe Weston, her sole, part-time employee, came in to help in the afternoon. She was a local girl who was taking classes at Montana State in Billings three days a week. Most Friday afternoons, she ran the store while Kerri ran errands and worked on upcycling furniture she found at auctions and garage sales. Kerri had always liked sourcing pieces other people thought were past repair, finding a way to fix or repurpose them and then painting them cheerful colors. You wouldn't furnish a whole house with her creations, but they packed a punch if you put one or two into a room. Some she did in a color palette that called to free spirits. Others, she painted in the faded red, white and blue that fit in any country-style home.

Sometimes Chloe came along to auctions to keep Kerri company and help carry heavy items. She was often willing to come in and help on a moment's notice if an emergency came up. Kerri didn't know what she'd do when Chloe graduated and went to work full time somewhere else.

Her upcycled items made up just a portion of her inventory, though. She stocked all kinds of things, from antiques and secondhand furniture to quilts, wall-hangings, artwork and more. Customers streamed through the shop, looking for just the right gifts for their loved ones. Kerri did her best to make suggestions, rearranging her stock every time someone bought a large enough item to leave a gap in her displays.

During a slow moment, she called the local bank, but as she suspected, they wouldn't schedule a loan appointment until the following week. Kerri made one for Monday and relayed the information to her mother, hoping that would get Sylvie off her back for a few days.

After they finally closed the shop late in the after-noon, she managed to run home, change and freshen up before Ryan arrived.

He showed up in a rugged work jacket and knitted hat.

"I brought hot chocolate from Orchards." He handed her a cup as she came outside, shutting the door behind her, and sipped from his own, letting his gaze travel over her as he took in her jeans, ankle boots, sky-blue parka and white hat and mittens. "Glad you could make it tonight."

"Me, too." The cold tickled her nostrils. "Look, it's snowing." She gestured to the large flakes floating lazily down. They'd already had an early storm that had left several inches on the ground, but that was more than a week ago, and the snow had gotten dingy. Now everything was blanketed with a fresh, fluffy covering of the stuff.

"It's getting Christmas-y." He wasn't looking at the snow, however. He was looking at her. Kerri's excitement turned to something more complex. She wished Ryan would reach for her and thought she saw answering desire in his eyes. Her heart pounded in anticipation. Would he take her in his arms? Kiss her for real?

In the end, however, he only nodded toward the truck. "Better get going. We've got a lot of stops to make."

"Okay."

She wondered why he'd hesitated. Was he still deciding whether he was interested in her that way, or was he simply a gentleman? Maybe he thought he had to wait until the end of the date to try for a kiss.

A few days ago, the idea of kissing him would have seemed as unlikely as getting invited to fly to the moon, but ever since his lips had brushed her cheek last night, she'd wanted him to do it again.

Didn't he want to?

She supposed he wouldn't be here if he didn't.

Kerri decided to settle down and let the night go how it might. Once she stopped agonizing over Ryan's next move, it turned out to be more fun delivering Christmas trees than she had supposed. Everyone was happy to see them pull up. Most people spilled out of their houses before Ryan even shut off the engine. Kids jumped up and down. Dogs barked at the excitement. In between stops, Ryan let the radio play, the local station already filling the airwaves with holiday tunes. He regaled her with stories about the guys he worked with at the fire station—young, testosterone-addled men who seemed to get up to as much trouble on their time off as they sorted out during work hours. Many of them were single, and they seemed to suffer through a lot of bad dates. Some of Ryan's stories had Kerri laughing until she nearly cried.

After they left their last stop, he was telling her about Brandon Strauss, another man they'd both gone to school with.

"About eight years ago, Brandon takes this girl mini golfing on a first date," he said. "You know Brandon. He's got a competitive streak a mile wide, and he's the sorest loser I've ever met."

Kerri nodded. She remembered that from high school. He had golden hands on the football field, catching a number of important passes over the years, but woe betide his teammates if they let him down.

Ryan continued his story. "What he doesn't know is his date is the star player on her university's golf team.

She was from Billings. He met her at a club there."

"Got it." She could already see where this was going. Brandon had lost his cool once at a high school dance when he'd lost at the foosball table in the games room. He'd kicked the thing and ended up having to go to the hospital. Sounded like he hadn't learned his lesson.

"At first he thinks she's getting a lot of lucky breaks," Ryan said, "but by halfway through the course, he realizes she knows what she's doing. They end up neck and neck the whole time, which is killing Brandon. He's doing everything he can to get ahead. On the last hole, they're still tied. He's praying she screws up."

"Did she?"

"Not a chance." Ryan grinned. "She gets a hole in one. Brandon loses it. Now he needs to get a hole in one, too. If not, she wins, and there's no way he can stand that. The whole point of taking her there is to show off his prowess, right?"

"Of course," Kerri said, shaking her head. *Men.*

"So Brandon gets in the zone and takes his shot."

"Well?" Kerri demanded when he didn't go on.

His smile widened. "Guess his date is as competitive as he is. She doesn't want to lose any more than he does, so just as he goes to putt the ball, she slaps him on the ass. Calls him a *cute buckaroo*. He's so shocked he whacks the daylight out of that ball. It ricochets off a miniature windmill and shatters the window of the front office. Glass everywhere. Kids screaming. Mothers going ballistic."

"What happened?" Kerri could imagine the scene.

"His date takes off at a run. Jumps the fence and skedaddles. Turns out she was a track star, too."

"That's awful!" But Kerri was laughing.

"The manager tackles Brandon before he can take off after her. Won't let him go until he calls his folks and they come to pay for the damage, since he doesn't have enough cash in his account to cover it himself."

"He must have been dying! Did he ever see her again?"

Ryan shook his head. "I think he stayed out of Billings for a couple of years after that."

Kerri laughed. "Poor Brandon."

"He's still single. Don't think he's gotten over it." He looked her way. "You're a good delivery partner, you know that?"

"I'm enjoying myself." She was.

"Glad to hear it." His smile warmed her. "Not sure why we haven't spent time together before. You know—when we were younger."

Kerri wasn't sure what to say. Why would they have spent time together? "Guess we ran in different crowds." As in he was a football star, and she was the mousy girl whose grandmother couldn't get rid of anything.

"We should change that."

A little thrill chased down Kerri's spine. They'd come to a stop sign. Before she could answer he leaned toward her. Kerri found herself leaning toward him, too. They met in the middle, and the kiss he gave her sent tendrils of desire all the way down to her toes.

Only when someone honked their horn behind them did they part again, and they exchanged a long look before another honk made Ryan straighten and press his foot down on the accelerator.

After that they kissed at every stop sign, and Kerri's body was buzzing with pent-up need by the time Ryan dropped her at her door. He walked with her up the path and waited while she fumbled with her keys, feeling suddenly like a teenager again.

Was she supposed to invite him in? Take him to bed?

She pictured opening the door, pulling him inside, making out in the hallway, stripping off their clothes as they climbed the stairs. Pushing him down on her bed—

In the… *cat room*?

Horror stopped her cold, and Kerri stared up at Ryan, keys clutched in her fingers.

"You can't come in," she blurted, then snapped her mouth shut. Why had she said it like that? How could she explain the problem?

How could she get him out of here before he guessed what it was?

Ryan's brows shot up. "Okay," he said slowly.

"I mean. It's just…" Kerri trailed off, unable to finish her sentence. He'd seen Bess's living room, after all. He knew what the place looked like, but…

Kerri felt like she always did when someone made it into the house, like she'd been stripped bare and found wanting. It made no difference to say they were Bess's collections, the hoarding Bess's disease. She lived here alone now. How could she possibly explain the bedroom she slept in?

The pathetic single bed jammed into a corner? Cat statues, vases, plush toys stacked halfway to the ceiling?

"You aren't ready," Ryan said when she didn't go on. "That's okay, Kerri. You're worth the wait."

Oh God, this was worse. At least if Ryan was upset, she could blame him for being an ass, but he was being... considerate.

Why on earth was she blinking back tears?

Kerri turned away, using the excuse of unlocking the door to cover her confusion.

"Good night," she squeaked before she slipped inside and shut the door quickly behind her.

Shame overwhelmed her as she turned the lock as quietly as possible so he wouldn't hear it click if he was still standing outside.

Somehow, she knew he was.

If you could die of an emotion, she'd be gone by now. Shame burned her from the inside out, carving slices of her self-esteem into ribbons of loathing.

She had to clean out the rest of the house—and her mother was right; she couldn't add a single thing to it. Not ever again. She couldn't become like Bess. She had to empty the house soon. *Now.* Before anyone suspected how bad it had gotten.

With her heart beating so hard she wondered if her rib cage could contain it, Kerri pushed off from the door, crossed to the stairs and climbed them. The distance to the second floor seemed endless and too short at the same time. Forcing herself to look at the cat room—her *bedroom*—with fresh eyes was even worse than she'd imagined. She clearly saw the jungle of figurines large and small. The cat pincushions, jewelry boxes, paintings and nightlight covers. The stuffed animals and pillows. Kerri made her way through it all to sink down on her sagging mattress.

Why had she accepted living like this for all these years? Why hadn't she asked Bess to move this collection somewhere else? To sort through it and give away the excess?

Why hadn't she ever taken Bess to a doctor to get treatment for a problem that had so obviously gotten out of control?

Why hadn't her mother done so?

Kerri took off her coat and gloves and set them aside, then hugged herself, trying to press away the pain and embarrassment that were threatening to overwhelm her. She could never bring Ryan to a room like this.

Could never allow anyone up those stairs.

Despite her best efforts, one tear fell and then another, but Kerri tried to hold the rest back. She'd sat on her bed like this so many times before, crying silently into one of the latch-hooked cat pillows. Screaming into it sometimes.

She had never let Bess see her pain, however, and she wouldn't let Ryan see it now.

Ryan.

He had asked her to make ornaments for Mrs. Fisher. He'd be back in the morning and expect her to have them ready. She needed to clean this room right now, put the past behind her and forget it.

But as she wiped away her tears and stood, Kerri wondered if the shame would ever go away, even if Bess's collections did. Wouldn't the memory of how she'd agreed to live—the lies and coverups and minimizing—stay with her? Didn't it tarnish her even now?

She wanted to sink back down on the bed and never get up.

Ryan would probably be the one to find her if she did allow herself to perish from shame, she told herself. Someone would call 9-1-1 when she didn't show up for work for a few days. The rest of the firefighters would be right behind him.

Taking pictures, probably.

Kerri sighed. There was nothing for it. She had to make those ornaments now. Had to clean out this room—and face Ryan in the morning.

Just the thought of it made her pull out her phone. She picked up her coat and walked downstairs to hang it in the hall closet. Sunshine answered on the third ring.

"Are you free for an hour?" Kerri asked as she retraced her steps upstairs. "Any chance you want to attach hooks to a bunch of little cat statues to make ornaments out of them?" As she began to sort through the room, setting aside any objects she found that were small enough, she couldn't seem to make her hands stop shaking.

"I can't think of anything I'd rather do than make ornaments out of little cat statues," Sunshine said. Kerri was so grateful for her answer, she would have hugged her if Sunshine was in the room.

"Even though it's nearly nine?" She hoped Sunshine didn't hear the wobble in her voice.

"Especially since it's nearly nine." Sunshine laughed. "Seriously, I've just put Sienna down for the night, and Cole's here to keep an eye on her. I wouldn't mind getting out of the house, even for a little while. It's been ages since we had a good chat—just the two of us."

"Come right over. I'll make some tea."

When Sunshine agreed, Kerri put away her phone and got busy moving the tiny figurines downstairs to the kitchen.

She could handle just about anything with a friend by her side.

CHAPTER 6

AFTER A LONG night thinking it over, Ryan was no closer to figuring out what had gone wrong with Kerri the previous evening. Fresh out of the shower, he stared at himself in the mirror, wondering why she'd sent him packing like that.

Every time he'd kissed her, she'd kissed him back without reluctance, and he'd been hard pressed to keep his hands off her by the time he drove her home. He wasn't some boy so driven by lust that he couldn't handle the rejection of not being asked inside. It was the way she'd done it that confused him. She'd been as eager as he was to keep the party going until they reached her front door.

Then it was like someone flipped a switch.

And he'd been the only one around.

What had he done?

He found himself going over and over that walk from the truck to the house. Something had happened. They'd reached the front door—and her expression had changed.

She'd been—

What?

Not afraid. That hadn't been fear in her eyes before she turned away from him. There'd been something in her gaze he couldn't decipher, however. Some black emotion that made her go from wanting him to wanting him gone.

Now he didn't know what he was supposed to do. Did he pursue her and hope she opened up to him?

Did he back off and wait for her to make the next move?

He finished getting ready for the day, exited the bathroom and found he had two messages when he picked up his phone.

He'd missed a call from Cole and another one from a number he didn't recognize. Both had left a voice mail. Cole simply asked him to call back when he could. The stranger's message was longer.

"Hi, Ryan, this is Nathan Briars from the California Forestry Department. Sorry to call you so early on a Saturday. Ed Brookings gave me your name. Explained how he hired you last year but had to let you go and hire someone else when your grandfather got ill. My condolences, by the way. Losing family is always hard."

Ryan jotted down the man's name, wondering why Ed would pass his number along to him.

"I'll get to the point," Nathan said. "I need to fill a position here in Sacramento, and from what Ed told me, you sound like the man for the job. He's already forwarded me your resume. Give me a call on Monday so we can arrange a time for you to fly out here and talk." He gave some more particulars about the job and pay scale, rattled off a number, and the message ended.

Ryan stared at the notepad where he'd written Nathan's name and number. Ed must have gone out on a limb to make this happen. The salary was far higher than anything he'd find around here.

Taking the job would mean leaving Chance Creek, though, and leaving was the last thing he wanted to do.

Still. How many times would he be offered the chance to move up in the world?

His mind spinning, he called Cole next. Maple trotted into the room from his bedroom, where she'd been sleeping, and flopped down happily beside him, tail thumping.

The phone rang twice before Cole picked up. "Hey, Ryan. How're things in those big old woods of yours?"

Confusing, Ryan thought but didn't say out loud. If he did, Cole would probably be so taken aback he'd hang up. Marriage to Sunshine had softened the man's rough edges over the years, but he was still a guy. "I'm doing all right. What's up?"

"I plan to bring Sienna out soon to cut down a tree for our place, but Sunshine and Emma are looking for one for Orchards. If you're coming into town today, would you mind dropping one off there? I think they're hoping to decorate tonight."

"No problem at all. I planned to head to town to run some errands before I open the tree lot later this morning. I'll throw one in the truck and stop by Orchards."

"Thanks. Any news on the job hunt?"

"I just got asked to come and interview for a job out west," he said. He could still hardly believe it, but saying it out loud made it more real. "With the California Forest Service. Sounds like a good position."

"California?" Cole said slowly. "Didn't know you were considering leaving town. I'd sure hate to see you go." He cleared his throat. "Besides, where would we get our Christmas trees?"

Ryan appreciated Cole's attempt to keep things light, even if he was as shocked as Ryan was at this turn of events.

"I probably won't take it." He couldn't imagine leaving Chance Creek again, especially now he was getting close to Kerri. "I'll be over with the tree as soon as I can."

"See you then."

After he made himself coffee and a couple of slices of toast, he took them to the sofa, where he did his usual juggling act with his plate and cup until a thought struck him.

He left the remains of his meal on the kitchen counter, shrugged into his coat, shoved his feet into his boots and went outside. He'd taken one set of furniture out of the stash he had in his workshop. He might as well take out another one. When he was alive, Grandpa John had been adamant that nothing changed in the cabin, but he'd always told Ryan he could do whatever he wanted once he was gone. Maple came, too, eager to join in the fun. She sniffed around the interior of the cold building as he turned on the lights and looked through the furniture stored there.

He finally found what he was looking for: a coffee table he'd built years ago, back when woodworking was one of his favorite hobbies. He wrestled it out from among the other pieces and carried it toward the door.

"Maple. Come on, girl."

Maple looked up at him reproachfully from the pile of old rags she'd just settled on, but she got up and followed him back to the house.

Ryan installed the coffee table in his living room in front of the sofa and made himself another piece of toast. This time he was able to set his plate down somewhere other than his lap.

Even though it was barely seven thirty in the morning, he chased down the toast with a snowball cookie, closing his eyes as he bit into it. An avalanche of memories washed over him, but before they could overwhelm him, his phone buzzed to life again, waking him from his reverie. It was Kerri. Ryan sat up straight and answered.

"Hello?"

"Hi, Ryan." Kerri paused. "Listen. About yesterday…"

He waited, but the silence on the line stretched out so long he was afraid she'd hung up.

"Like I said, I can wait," he assured her. He wanted a lot more with her than a quick tumble in the sheets. Last night his thoughts had been full of the future they could have together—if she didn't send him packing. "I just hope you'll keep helping me with deliveries. It'd be expensive if I had to hire someone for the job." He held his breath. Would she get the joke?

When Kerri chuckled ruefully, he let it out again.

"Yeah. I guess I can still be your delivery boy."

"Good. That's settled then. I'll be at your place in about an hour."

"I can get the cat ornaments to Mrs. Fisher by myself."

"I'd prefer to come with you," he said firmly. He knew if he didn't see her again soon, the awkwardness between them would grow no matter what they said now. "Can't wait to see the look in her eyes when you give them to her."

"Okay." She sounded a little hesitant, though.

"Great. I need to deliver a tree to Orchards, too. We can grab some coffee." He wasn't going to give in.

"I've got to open my store at ten."

"I need to be back on the mountain by eleven. We'll work fast." He waited. Would she find another excuse to beg off?

"Okay," she said quietly.

Relief whooshed through him. He stood up to carry his plate to the sink. "I promise I won't kiss you." He immediately wanted to kick himself. He'd been hoping to do just that.

"That's a shame."

"What?" Her answer brought him up short. He replayed the conversation in his mind. Did she mean...

"That's a shame," she repeated. "I kind of liked all that kissing."

Suddenly his day looked bright again. "Then scratch what I just said. I'll kiss you all you want. But that's it. I mean it, Kerri. There's no rush for us to do anything else." As much as he wanted to. It was killing him to play the good guy, but he knew how to be patient in the process of gaining a bigger goal in the end.

Somehow Kerri had become his goal.

Another pause. "Okay. I'll see you later."

He got the message. No more talking about what might—or might not—happen between them in the future.

Which suited him just fine, because he couldn't explain anything he was feeling right now.

He'd come home to Chance Creek wanting to get on with life, and he'd looked forward to settling down with a woman, but it had never crossed his mind Kerri Olsen would be the one. Even when he'd made his mental list of single women in Chance Creek and added her to it, he hadn't put her at the top. Only when he saw her walk into Orchards a few days ago did the truth of the matter punch him in the chest.

She was the one for him. She was kind and caring. Sweet and sexy. She liked his dog and baked his favorite kind of cookie. Was embedded in the community and added something to the life of the town. She was artistic—and a businesswoman, too. In short, she cared about a lot of the same things he did.

But it was none of that. It was a feeling. Like if he

couldn't get closer to her, he wouldn't find the happiness he craved. It made no sense and all the sense in the world.

"See you soon." He hung up, grabbed his things and got back into his winter gear. Maple lifted her head and gave him a look.

"I'm not rushing just because it's Kerri. I have to hurry, or I won't be back before eleven," he told the dog. "Don't want to keep my customers waiting."

Maple lifted a furry eyebrow at the word *customers*, as if she knew he kept giving trees away.

"Don't be judgmental," he told her. "Are you coming or not?"

Maple stood and was at his heels in a second, and not for the first time, Ryan was grateful no one had stepped forward to claim her.

When he climbed into the driver's seat of his truck, Maple hopped obediently into the passenger one. She lay down and stared up at him with her perpetually sad eyes. All that sorrow was a trick, and Ryan knew it, but he reached into the glove compartment and gave her a dog biscuit anyway.

In moments it was gone.

The drive to town settled him down somewhat, but when he pulled into Kerri's driveway and parked, he could feel his pulse dancing in his veins. This was like being a teenager again, he thought ruefully.

"Come on," he told Maple. She followed him out of the truck to the front door, where he knocked.

"Come in!" Kerri called from inside.

Ryan opened the door and was greeted by the smell of fresh snowball cookies and the sight of a half-dozen boxes lined up in the hallway with all kinds of cat ornaments poking their heads out and looking his way. Kerri emerged from the kitchen. Today her sweater was salmon pink, which somehow made her even more kissable, but she wasn't exactly meeting his eye, so he figured he'd better warm up to that.

"Do you think Mrs. Fisher will like them? I left them uncovered so you could take a look."

"I'm sure she will." When Maple slipped past him to investigate the cat ornaments, Ryan restrained her. "Careful. You break it, you buy it."

"Don't listen to him." Kerri came closer and bent down to hug Maple. "With a face like yours, you can break anything you want. No jury would convict you." She scratched behind the dog's ears. "Grab a cookie while you're waiting," she said to Ryan. "There's a plate in the living room. I'll close these up and get them ready to go." She rose to her feet again and got to work.

Ryan snagged a cookie from a plate she'd set on the edge of a cluttered end table and sat on the couch, Maple at his feet. He was sharing the cushion with an old-fashioned lobster trap. He traced a finger over the hole in the metal mesh and spared a moment to sympathize with the lobsters who'd met their end inside before it had become a decoration. Caught before they'd even realized it was too late. He understood how that felt.

Kerri pattered up and down the stairs in the hallway

and reappeared a few minutes later. "That's the last of them! I boxed a bunch of larger, decorative cat items I thought Mrs. Fisher might like to have. I've got a tin of cookies for her, too. I left my purse upstairs. Give me a minute, and I'll grab them."

Ryan carried all the boxes outside and carefully arranged them, wedging them in between Christmas trees and the side of the truck bed. "Leave those alone," he told Maple, who'd jumped up to nose them interestedly. "Down."

Maple jumped down again and made a beeline for the passenger side door. Kerri joined them there, and Ryan opened the door for her with a flourish. With a leap, Maple got in first.

"You're going to have to move over," Kerri told her. She ducked under Ryan's arm and climbed gingerly into the seat. The dog shifted over as Kerri sat down, then tried to climb on her lap. "No, sweetie, not right now. Oh, shoot. I forgot the cookies. Hold on."

She made to hop out of the truck again, but Maple, not wanting to be left out, lunged for the door, too. The dog landed on her feet on the driveway, but not before Kerri tripped over her, pitched sideways and would have cracked her head on the pavement if Ryan hadn't caught her.

"Whoa!" He held her tightly, his heart beating hard. "That could have ended with a trip to the hospital. You okay?" That had been close. A vision of Kerri splayed on the pavement, hurt, made his heart clench. He'd seen what accidents could do to people during his time with the Marines.

Suddenly reluctant to put her down, he carried her to her front stoop, sat down and settled her in his lap.

"I'm fine." But her eyes were wide and her breathing unsteady.

So was his, for that matter. "You sure?"

She nodded. "I can't believe you managed to catch me."

"I can't believe Maple tripped you." He breathed in the scent of her shampoo, trying to get his heart to slow down. You could lose people in an instant. It had happened to him when his parents died. It had happened during his time in the military, too. When things went wrong, you didn't see them coming. One minute everything was fine. The next it was all over.

"She didn't mean to. I'm just clumsy."

Maple pressed herself against Ryan's legs, whining worriedly. Kerri patted her, and Maple licked her hand in apology.

"I'd better keep an eye on you then." He kept his arms firmly around her. As his heart slowed, his awareness of her closeness grew. "I like you in my arms," he said. "I know you're safe here."

"I feel safe here," she admitted.

Warmth flooded Ryan's chest. He didn't think she could pay him a bigger compliment. He would do whatever it took to protect her, he decided then and there. Not just in a physical way, either. He'd do what he could to give her a good life.

He heard Nathan Briar's voice in his mind. *I've got a*

position to fill…

If he took that job, he could be a good provider for a wife and kids.

He was getting ahead of himself. Wasting an opportunity for a kiss right now by getting hung up on the future. Ryan tried to focus on the beautiful woman in his arms, but just as he bent closer to Kerri, she wriggled a little.

"We'd better get going. I don't want to be late getting back."

He hesitated, but then he understood. She needed firm ground beneath her feet. The fall had scared her, too.

He let her up.

"Cats," she said as he got to his feet. "Mrs. Fisher's house. I'll grab those cookies." A moment later she disappeared inside.

"Right." Time to get on with their deliveries.

But he would've done anything to keep her in his arms.

SHE SHOULD HAVE kept her mouth shut.

If she hadn't reminded him they needed to get to work, Ryan might have kissed her again. She had a feeling he'd been thinking about it.

Now they were parked in front of Mrs. Fisher's house. When Ryan came around to open the door for her, Kerri climbed out, tin of cookies in her hand. Maple followed, but a command from him sent her right back into the seat. Ryan gave her a treat from the glove compartment.

"You're going to have to sit this one out," he told Maple. "I'll grab some boxes," he added to Kerri.

"Thanks."

As usual, they made a good team. Ryan piled a stack of boxes on the front porch and went back for more while she knocked on the door. When Mrs. Fisher opened it, a multitude of cats twining around her ankles, Kerri got a whiff of molasses—and smoke.

"Kerri, hello! Oh, my goodness, I wasn't expecting a visit this morning," Mrs. Fisher said. "Come in out of the cold." She was a tall, thin woman with iron-gray hair dressed in black pants, a red turtleneck and a green holiday apron dusted with flour.

"I heard about the fire. Ryan Miller and I brought something to cheer you up." Kerri handed the tin of cookies to her and reached down to pick up a couple of boxes.

"Ryan already brought me a tree! What's all this?" Mrs. Fisher asked, ushering her inside. "Careful. My cats can't seem to understand it'll hurt them if we step on them."

Two were already winding around Kerri's feet. She took care not to tread on them as she made her way through the door. Mrs. Fisher helped her out of her jacket.

"Those are snowball cookies," Kerri said, nodding to the tin. "And these are ornaments for your tree. Come and look." She brought the boxes into the living room, set them on Mrs. Fisher's coffee table and opened them to display their contents.

Mrs. Fisher gasped. "Those are wonderful! Where did you find all those cat ornaments?"

"I made them."

Mrs. Fisher clasped her hands together like a little girl. "They're for me?"

"Of course! I hope you like them."

"They're perfect. I need to put them up right away. I've been feeling ridiculous having a tree with no decorations on it." Mrs. Fisher carefully picked one up and took it over to the balsam fir standing near her front window. She considered the tree a moment, then hung it on a branch about two-thirds of the way up before coming back for another one.

Ryan brought in some of the larger boxes and went back for more.

"What are those?" Mrs. Fisher asked Kerri.

"Grandma Bess collected all kinds of cat decorations. Did you know that?" Kerri asked, handing her another ornament.

"No, I didn't." Mrs. Fisher took it and found it a place on the tree.

"I don't have a good use for them, but I thought you might. They're special pieces. There's a story to many of them I can share with you if you like." Just like she'd done with the trains and kitchen items, she'd photographed the cats as she'd cleaned them out of her bedroom and recorded their stories. She had no idea how long it would take her to make the photo books, but she'd get them done when she could.

"I'd love that!"

Kerri bent to pet an orange tabby who'd jumped to lie on the back of the couch as two Siamese cats wound lazily around her ankles. A couple of gray cats cavorted under the Christmas tree. It would be a miracle if the thing lasted through the holiday, Kerri thought.

"The tabby is Leo," Mrs. Fisher said. "The Siamese are Castor and Pollux, and the grays are Abigail and Anne." She stopped, bent down and picked something off the hardwood floor. "I keep finding shards of glass and porcelain no matter how many times I vacuum."

Kerri knew it had to hurt to lose years of work collecting the perfect pieces. She hoped the ornaments and decorations she'd brought would go a little way to easing Mrs. Fisher's pain. She continued to hand the ornaments to her one by one, patiently waiting for the older woman to find the best places to hang them on her tree, grateful she and Ryan had gotten such an early start.

When Ryan finished unloading the truck, he shucked off his outerwear, too, and moved all the boxes into the living room, spreading them out so they'd be easy to access. When he opened one, a black cat hopped into it and curled up to nap.

"Schrodinger, behave yourself," Mrs. Fisher said. "I hope there's nothing breakable in there," she added to Kerri.

"I packed them carefully," Kerri assured her. "I hope you can use these things. Just let me know if you see something you don't want, and I'll take it away again."

"I've never met a cat I didn't like, real or porcelain," Mrs. Fisher assured her. "Oh, I could just hug you two! Look at this tree. It's a Christmas miracle."

She came to give them both a big squeeze and turned out to be surprisingly strong. Kerri found herself squashed against Ryan's chest. When she looked up, he was grinning boyishly. Her heart gave a little throb, and she couldn't help but grin back at him.

Mrs. Fisher gave them one last squeeze, let go and clapped her hands together. "Gingerbread time! Ryan, close the front door before all the cats get out. Kerri, why don't you open the rest of those boxes? We can decorate the whole house."

"Do you think we have enough time?" Kerri asked Ryan in a low voice when Mrs. Fisher went into the kitchen.

"I'll keep an eye on the clock." Ryan stepped around a couple of cats to close the front door, careful not to trip over them. Mrs. Fisher bustled back in and handed out gingerbread as Kerri opened the rest of the boxes. Schrodinger resettled on the floor when she tipped him out of the one he'd curled up in. When she was done, she delved into the nearest one and handed a plush cat to Ryan and a cat painting to Mrs. Fisher and kept a cat statue for herself.

"Where should we put these?"

"The plush cat goes there." Mrs. Fisher pointed to the sofa. "The painting can go on the mantelpiece and the statue on that table."

They settled into a rhythm, Kerri unpacking the cats and distributing them, then all three of them stepping around each other according to Mrs. Fisher's instructions.

"It's like we're dancing," Kerri announced as she threaded her way between Ryan and Mrs. Fisher, hopped over a gray cat who had moved to sit in the center of the room and narrowly avoided stepping on the tail of an elderly Siamese one. "Whoops!" She stuttered left and pivoted when the Siamese took a swipe at Schrodinger and sent him streaking across the room. The second gray cat got tangled in her feet, and Kerri fell backward. Ryan caught her, nearly dropping a cat-shaped stone doorstop he was hefting.

"That's the second time I've had to save you today," he murmured in her ear as he stood her back on her feet. "Doesn't that mean you owe me something?"

"Like what?"

"Like a kiss, of course," Mrs. Fisher said. She held a sprig of mistletoe over their heads. Kerri noticed a tiny cat figurine held the greenery in its paws.

"A kiss would do," Ryan agreed. He bent toward her, but Kerri pulled back.

"We're not alone," she murmured.

"Well, if you're not going to kiss him, I will," Mrs. Fisher exclaimed. She put the mistletoe in her apron pocket, caught Ryan's cheeks in her hands and gave him a loud smack on the mouth. "There. That's how it's done."

Kerri laughed at the expression on his face. "Mrs.

Fisher, you're going to land on Santa's naughty list." The woman was inspiring, though. What she wanted, she reached out and took.

"Doesn't matter. I've already got the best present I could want." Mrs. Fisher surveyed the room with satisfaction. "It certainly looks festive in here now, although I think I'd better knit some red and green hats and scarves for the statues that aren't already holiday-themed. I should have planned a Christmas party." Mrs. Fisher sighed. "It's been so long since I've been dancing. No one dances at parties anymore."

"You're right. It's a real shame." Ryan, who'd pulled himself together, approached Mrs. Fisher and held out a hand. "May I have the honor?"

She laughed. "There isn't even any music playing."

"I can fix that." Kerri tapped her phone and turned on a Christmas tune. Ryan led Mrs. Fisher in a waltz around the room. Kerri went back to the boxes and pulled out the last three items. Two were statues.

"Over there, dear." Mrs. Fisher pointed to the windowsill as she floated by in Ryan's arms. Kerri placed the statues carefully. The last item was a wreath of sorts, carved out of wood, depicting four cats chasing after each other, the paws of each one just barely reaching the tail of the cat ahead of it. They wore Santa hats and collars of mistletoe.

"Would you mind hanging that on the front door for me?" Mrs. Fisher said. "Ryan, enough. Go help her."

"You sure?"

"I'm sure. Thank you for the dance. While you two figure out how to hang that up, I'll get us something to drink." Mrs. Fisher bustled off to the kitchen again.

They found snow had begun to fall again when they got outside, muffling the sounds of traffic passing. Kerri zipped up her coat as Ryan looked at the nail in the door and then at the wreath.

"Which way is up?" A snowflake caught in one of his eyelashes, and Kerri had the urge to brush it away, but the gesture seemed much too intimate.

"I think we get to choose." She pointed at an orange tabby. "Put that one on the top. It looks just like Leo."

Ryan spun the wreath to the orange cat and nodded. "If Leo ever bothered to run."

She knew what he meant. Leo had spent the entire time they'd been here sleeping on the back of the couch. If it hadn't been for the slow rise and fall of the cat's stomach, Kerri might have thought he was a decoration himself.

Ryan hung the wreath and stepped back.

"Thanks for sticking around. I'm sure you didn't anticipate spending a whole morning this way," Kerri said.

"I've enjoyed myself. Honestly." He gestured at the wreath. "Is that straight?"

Kerri surveyed it. "I think so."

"You can't tell from there." He gently tugged her closer before wrapping an arm around her. "Now what do you think?"

But Kerri wasn't paying attention to the wreath anymore, and neither was Ryan. He leaned down to kiss her briefly.

"That's more like it," he said when he pulled away. "I was afraid I'd scared you away."

"I was afraid Mrs. Fisher might have won your heart in there," Kerri returned.

"Nope." He bent and kissed her again. Kerri braced her hands on his chest and melted into his embrace until a cat wound between their ankles and startled them apart.

"You're new. Do you want to go inside?" Kerri asked the cat, trying to hide her confusion. How could Ryan Miller—the boy she'd known all her life—make her feel like this? Like she only existed to be in his arms.

Like she was meant to be his.

"We'd better get going. We still need to deliver Sunshine's tree," Ryan said.

EVERY TIME HE kissed Kerri, it was harder to let her go. He would have liked to keep her by his side throughout his day, but they both needed to earn a living.

"The Christmas party," he said as they drove to Orchards.

"What?" Kerri asked.

"Mrs. Fisher said she needed to have a Christmas party. That reminded me I'm in charge of throwing one for the Mountain Men. Don't suppose you'd help me."

"I already said I'd lend you anything you need. What kind of party do you want to have?"

"Hell if I know. Got any more collections you need

to clear out of Bess's place? Maybe there's a good theme somewhere in there."

Kerri thought it over. "I haven't cleaned out the living room, music room, sewing room, plant room or library. And then there are the small collections."

"The small ones? Where are they?" He turned a corner.

Kerri was quiet a moment. "In the bathrooms."

"Oh." He tried hard to stifle a laugh but wasn't altogether successful. "Sorry."

"You should be. It isn't funny," Kerri said. A blush was creeping up her neck and mottling her cheeks.

"It kind of is, though." He liked teasing her, as long as she knew he didn't mean anything by it.

She groaned. "No, it isn't."

"Fine, it's not funny at all. Let's see… I don't think the sewing collection is going to cut it. Neither will your library, although I did see a post once on social media in which someone made a Christmas tree out of books, so maybe I'm wrong. Maple would have a field day with a bunch of houseplants. That leaves the music room. Can't play an instrument to save my life. What else is in there?"

"Records. A lot of them. I could look through them and see if she has some Christmas albums."

"Does she have a turntable? Because I sure don't."

"Not one that works," Kerri admitted.

"What about the small collections? I want to know all my options."

"Owls," Kerri said.

Ryan laughed. He couldn't hold it back this time. "Because nothing says Christmas like a bunch of owls, right? Can you imagine the look on my friends' faces when I usher them into the house and wave them into the living room, where I've arranged an ice chest of beer, some snacks—and a few dozen owls staring back at them?"

Kerri's lips twitched. "A few dozen? Don't you mean a hundred?"

That gave him pause. "Both bathrooms are full of owls? Hell, a man might struggle to let go, so to speak, when he's using the can if he's got an audience like that."

She shrugged but she was smiling. "The downstairs bathroom has a different theme."

"Well? Don't keep me in suspense, Kerri Olsen."

"Cacti."

"Like… succulents?" This got better and better. And her blushes were getting more pronounced.

"Sort of a desert theme," she said.

"You've got a mighty strange idea of what counts as Christmas decorations." He reached across and took her hand, giving it a squeeze to assure her he was only teasing.

"I think I've proven that anything can be a Christmas decoration," Kerri said tartly. "Besides, you forgot all about the living room. You've seen Bess's vintage outdoor sports collection."

"That's right. That's the most sensible option of the bunch. I guess the question is, should I throw a sensible, sporty Christmas party, or should I throw a cacti-themed one and keep the guys guessing about my sanity?"

"Only you can answer that."

"How about this?" he said in a burst of inspiration. "The party is on December twenty-second. How about you come over a day or two in advance and surprise me?"

"I get to decorate any way I want?" Kerri brightened.

"That's right."

"Can Sunshine and Emma help?"

"Every chef in town can help you if you want. It's up to you." He liked the way her eyes lit up at the thought of it.

He liked the thought of her in his house, too.

"Deal," Kerri said.

"Really?" Ryan pulled into a parking spot outside Orchards. He felt like he'd pulled one over on her somehow, getting her to do the hard work for his party. She could decorate with hedgehogs for all he cared, as long as he didn't have to come up with a theme himself.

"Really."

"I like you, Kerri Olsen, you know that?" he said as he cut the engine. "You're one of the good ones."

"I think you're one of the good ones, too," she said.

CHAPTER 7

O RCHARDS WAS BUZZING when they arrived. Mothers with young children and retired folks getting together for their morning coffee filled many of the tables. Emma came to meet them when she saw Ryan wrestling the tree through the door.

"Thank you for dropping one by! Let's put it in the back for now. We'll set it up tonight after we close."

Ryan followed her past the counter and into the back. Kerri waited until they returned.

"Do you want your usual, Kerri?" Emma asked.

"You know it."

"One raspberry turnover coming right up. What do you want, Ryan?"

"I'll take one of those cheesecake things you make."

"You got it."

"Ryan!" Cole came through the door. "Thought I might catch you here. I was going to help you get the tree in."

"It's already in back."

"Is that my husband?" Sunshine came out of the

kitchen and gave Cole a big kiss. "What are you doing here? Miss me already? I left home only a couple of hours ago."

"Came to town for a few things. Thought I'd stop by."

"To see me? Or because you needed a snack?" she teased him.

"Both. I wouldn't say no to a cup of coffee either."

"Coming right up."

"I'll bring everything in a minute," Emma said. "You go sit down, Sunshine."

Sunshine grumbled, but she followed them to a table where they all sat down, and soon she was smiling again.

"You seem happy," Kerri told her.

"I am. Getting to have my restaurant and a family is a dream come true." She rubbed her belly. "I wasn't sure I could have both, and now it's all going so well. Ryan knows what I mean, don't you, Ryan?"

He wasn't sure he did.

"Oh, come on, you said you were looking for a wife last time I saw you." Sunshine poked Kerri. "Speaking of which, when are you going to settle down?"

"What?" Kerri squeaked.

"I'm serious. You've got a house. You've got a business. You need a family. You two were made for each other."

"Sunshine!"

"You might have a point there." Ryan spoke over her. "But you also might be sticking your nose in where it doesn't have any business being. If and when I decide to marry Kerri, I'll be the one to arrange it. I don't need a matchmaker running roughshod over us."

"Kerri said I'd be good at it," Sunshine said, unperturbed.

"I did not!" Kerri sputtered. He was pretty sure she'd throttle Sunshine if they were alone. Probably throttle him, too, if she could.

"You definitely said you wanted a family."

Kerri looked like she might get up and walk away. "I'm not against settling down," she finally said. "But I've got some unfinished business to take care of first and—"

"What do you mean, unfinished business?" Sunshine asked.

"I mean Mom gave me an ultimatum a couple of days ago. She wants her money. All of it. By Christmas." Kerri sat back in her chair, looking like she wished it would swallow her whole, and Ryan had the feeling she'd said far more than she'd meant to.

"We just spent an evening together making ornaments." Sunshine leaned forward, all joking forgotten. Ryan knew how she felt. Kerri had just dropped a bombshell. "How come you didn't mention any of that?"

"I… don't know," Kerri said helplessly.

"You owe your mom money?" Ryan asked. If she did, it concerned him, too, at this point. He was trying to figure how to make her a part of his life.

Kerri gave him a wary look but nodded. "When

Bess left me the house and business, it was with the understanding I'd take out a loan for the amount of Mom's share of the inheritance. I got the best loan I could, and the money will be in Mom's account by the end of next week, but it's not enough to cover what I owe her."

"How much will you fall short?" Sunshine asked.

"About thirty grand."

Sunshine whistled. "She wants you to come up with that before Christmas?"

"That's right."

"I'm sorry to hear that." Ryan had no idea Kerri's living and work situation were precarious. Here he'd been running her around delivering trees when she had real problems to solve.

Kerri looked down at her hands. "I wasn't going to tell anyone about it," she said. "I shouldn't have said anything now."

"Why not?" Sunshine demanded. "We're your friends. That's why we're here. I don't understand why she's putting you through this, though. Why can't she wait for the thirty grand if she's getting the rest up-front? It's not like you're trying to stiff her."

Ryan nodded his agreement, but he knew money made people do all sorts of strange things. He was sure he'd met Kerri's mother once or twice when he was a kid, but he didn't remember her.

"I offered to set up a payment plan. I'm perfectly happy to sign a contract if that makes her feel better, but I don't think it's about the money. Mom wants me to move to California and work for her."

Move? Ryan bristled at the idea.

"Move?" Sunshine echoed. "You mean you'd sell Bess's place?" She looked as shocked as he felt. Kerri had never mentioned leaving Chance Creek. Every instinct in him wanted to take her hand and impress upon her the fact that she had to stay. He wanted her here with him. "You can't leave," Sunshine said, as if she'd heard him. "You love it here. You have a life here. Besides, you hate minimalism."

"Minimalism?" Cole asked. Ryan hadn't found his voice yet. All the plans he'd been building in his mind were coming crashing down. No wonder Kerri hadn't wanted to take their relationship to a deeper level. When had she intended to tell him she was going to leave town?

"Kerri's mother owns these terrible stores that don't sell anything," Sunshine told her husband.

"They sell things," Kerri protested. "Mom carefully curates her wares."

"Carefully curates, my ass," Sunshine said indignantly. "Her stuff is ridiculous. You've said so a hundred times. You can't work there."

"My mother designs housewares," Kerri explained to Cole and Ryan. "Sunshine is right; she keeps to a minimalist theme, which isn't my style, but they're high-quality items and she seems to do well."

"Minimalism isn't that bad," Cole said reasonably.

Sunshine turned on her husband. "Minimalism is awful!"

"Why are we talking about minimalism?" Emma asked, coming to join them. She'd brought a tray filled with their orders and passed out coffee and pastries.

"Kerri's moving to Sacramento to work at her mother's horrible, empty boutiques." Sunshine split her muffin in half but didn't take a bite of it.

"Sacramento?" Ryan repeated. That was where the job Ed had wrangled for him was located. "Are you really thinking about moving there?" He couldn't imagine Kerri in California any more than he could picture himself there.

"It's not my first choice." Kerri poked at her turnover with about as much enthusiasm as Sunshine had for her muffin. "But I guess it's a possibility."

"What about Kerri's Collectibles?" Emma asked.

"If I can't convince my mom to change her mind, I'll have to sell it with the house. It's all one property. Look, I don't want to move," she added. "I'm going back to the bank on Monday to see what I can do to get the rest of the money. I'm cleaning out Bess's collections to prove to my mom I'm not like her." She played with her fork for a moment, cutting her turnover into ever-smaller pieces. "That's what this is about at the heart of it," she said finally. "She's still angry at Bess for never cleaning out her house."

"Does your mom really think she can force you to sell?" Sunshine demanded. Cole must have nudged her. "What?" she asked him. "I have to know where we stand. It might be the difference between keeping my friend in town or not."

"Mom has every right to ask for her money. Bess should have left everything to her," Kerri said.

"What would your mother do with a small-town store and a six-bedroom house?" Sunshine was losing her temper.

"What am I doing with a six-bedroom house?" Kerri countered. "It's too big for one person, right?"

"Wait, I thought you wanted kids," Emma said, taking her seat. "We were talking about it last month, remember?" She'd brought herself a blueberry muffin and pinched off a bite.

"Of course she wants kids. Kerri's always wanted kids. A ton of them," Sunshine said. Her eyes were bright with unshed tears, and Ryan thought she was close to losing control.

"I do want a large family. I was an only child," Kerri explained. "I always wished I had brothers and sisters."

"Me, too," Ryan said. When everyone looked at him, he shrugged, happy to draw their attention and give Sunshine a chance to settle down. "Just for the record. Always thought I'd have a big family someday to even it out." He slid a glance Kerri's way, curious about her reaction to his pronouncement, but Kerri was studying her fork again. "I just got offered a job in Sacramento," he added.

That made Kerri look up. "You did?"

"With the California Forestry Service."

Sunshine pushed her plate away abruptly. "No. Don't you dare. The two of you can't join forces and take off like that."

Hadn't Cole told Sunshine about the offer? The man refused to meet his gaze. Ryan guessed he'd been saving that information, hoping Ryan would turn down the job and he'd never have to tell Sunshine about it. Ryan was more Cole's friend than Sunshine's, but she was possessive of the people around her and wouldn't want any of her acquaintances to leave.

"We haven't joined forces," Kerri said.

Not yet, Ryan thought, but if he had his way, they would. "I don't want to leave Chance Creek any more than Kerri does, but I can't get by selling Christmas trees," he said out loud. "There aren't any firefighter positions with the local department right now, but the California Forest Service is hiring—for a position with a lot more responsibility."

"So you're going to take off—just like that?" Sunshine folded her arms over her chest.

"Like I said, I want a family someday, and when I've got one, I want to be able to provide a good life for them."

Sunshine's gaze skipped from him to Kerri and back again. He could almost see her struggling to keep a sharp retort to herself.

She lost the battle.

"So both of you *want* to stay but neither of you are willing to do the work to make it happen."

Ryan didn't know how to answer that. Kerri didn't seem to, either.

When Sunshine opened her mouth to go on, Cole broke off a bite of her muffin and popped it in. "We've said our piece," he told her as she chewed and sput-tered. "It's up to them to figure it out now. We don't want you to go," he reiterated to Ryan and Kerri. "So put on your thinking caps and come up with a way to stay."

THE BELL JINGLED as an older woman entered Kerri's Collectibles later that morning. She walked through the displays, pausing a long moment at the Christmas ornaments.

"Looking to fill out your collection?" Kerri asked her. She was straightening a table of vintage Christmas cards nearby, going over and over in her mind every-thing that had happened since she'd asked Ryan to bring her that first tree.

She'd ridden shotgun on his deliveries.

Made three people very happy with custom-designed trees.

Had cleaned out a substantial portion of her house, a feat that seemed nearly impossible just a week ago.

Been kissed by Ryan—a number of times.

And now they were linked together, not just in her mind but in Sunshine's, Cole's and Emma's minds, too.

Her friends had acted like it made perfect sense for her and Ryan to make plans as if they were a couple. Ryan had gone along with it. He hadn't even blinked when Sunshine had gone on the offensive and talked about the two of them marrying.

Kerri couldn't keep up. Couldn't figure out what Ryan's game was. He'd been in the background of her entire life, then he'd disappeared for years while serving in the military. He'd come back last February, but their paths hadn't crossed until just a few days ago. What had she done to capture his attention now?

Had losing his grandfather made him focus on the future? Had living alone on King's Mountain made him realize he wanted a partner?

But why her?

There were any number of single women in town…

Her customer nodded. "None of this is quite what I had in mind, though. It's all a little bit too… wintery, I suppose."

Too wintery? Kerri tried to keep her lips from twitching. Her Christmas decorations were too wintery? That was a new one. "I'm sorry to hear that," she made herself say. "What did you have in mind?"

"You won't understand," the woman said. She was wearing a puffy gray jacket that threatened to overwhelm her slim figure.

"Try me." Kerri figured she was as understanding as anyone.

"I spent the best Christmas I ever had in Nevada about forty years ago." The woman paused as if to see if Kerri was following her.

"Really?"

Encouraged, she went on. "My husband was stationed there. It was our first Christmas as a married couple. We'd barely settled into our living arrangements and hadn't managed to find a tree yet. One evening I came into the living room, and my husband had arranged this—*display*, I suppose you'd call it—of cacti with string lights on them, some of them big, some of them small. He'd borrowed them from other people on the base. It cheered me up so much." She shook her head at the memory. "Every year after that we had normal decorations and a tree, but I've always looked back on that first year fondly." She sent Kerri a sheepish look. "I'm sorry, honey, didn't mean to dump all that on you out of nowhere."

"Don't be. I'm glad you did." The gears were turning in Kerri's brain. "And I might have the perfect thing for you. Can you wait right here for a few minutes? I just need to run across the lawn to my house. I'm Kerri, by the way."

"I guessed as much. I'm Connie. What if another customer comes while you're gone?"

"Tell them I'll be right back."

Kerri raced home to her first-floor bathroom. The windowsill was covered in live succulents of various heights and kinds, and she set to work carefully transferring them into a box. The cactus-patterned shower curtain could stay, but everything else could go. She packed the decorations according to size, small trinkets in one box and larger statues and art pieces in another. She could help the woman make ornaments out of the little ones and offer her the larger decor items should she wish to take them. Hefting the boxes, Kerri decided she would come back for the living plants.

When she burst back into the store, she was pleased to see Connie still waiting, looking through more

Christmas ornaments displayed by the cash register.

"Come take a look at these," Kerri called out, placing the boxes down on the counter. She pulled out one of the little cactus statues. "I could help you make these into ornaments. I have some larger items, too, you might be interested in. Why don't you go through these while I run back to the house for the last box."

Connie looked at the two boxes Kerri had just set down. "You have more?"

"I do." Kerri slipped out the door again. When she returned, the woman had most of the decorations spread out on the counter. "Did you find anything interesting?"

"I love them all!" Connie seemed much happier than when she'd walked into the store.

"Here are some live ones, if you like that kind of thing." She set the box nearby, and Connie peered into it, then looked up, eyes shining.

"It never occurred to me to start a collection of my own!"

"If you don't mind waiting a half hour or so, I could make all the little statues into ornaments you can hang on your tree. I've had a lot of practice doing that." Kerri gestured to the little succulent figurines Connie had lined up in a row.

"Really? You'd do that for me?"

"Of course. I love a project." Kerri fetched some metal hooks. "Why don't you come sit over here, and we can work on them together?"

Kerri showed Connie how to fasten on the hooks,

and they got to work. When the bell chimed a few minutes later, they both looked up to see an older couple making their way inside.

"Hi, Stuart. Hi, Lois," Connie called out to them. "Doing your Christmas shopping?"

"Trying to get it done today," Lois said. "What are you working on over there?"

"I'm making cactus ornaments. I'm going to have a Nevada-themed Christmas this year."

"Really? That's different!" Lois made a beeline for them, Stuart following. Kerri knew the couple vaguely from around town, and she gave them a welcoming smile. "I didn't know you did custom ornament making," Lois said to her.

Kerri quickly explained how she had sort of fallen into the business of making custom trees. The couple, delighted at the idea, ended up sitting down at the table, too.

"I can do a few of those," Lois said, already reaching for a cactus statuette.

"I can do a few, too," Stuart said.

"The more the merrier," Kerri told them.

When another group of customers walked in, two sisters and their daughters, they got sucked into the ornament making, as well. Each time the door opened, the new arrivals came to see what was happening, until Kerri felt like she was holding an impromptu class.

"You know what kind of tree I want?" Lois asked.

"Let me guess," Stuart said. "A wine tree."

The crowd around the table erupted in laughter.

"That's not a bad idea," a woman said.

"Not a wine tree," Lois said. "A butterfly tree. I love butterflies."

"I have some lovely stained-glass butterfly pieces at the back of the store." Kerri directed her toward them, and Lois ended up purchasing the lot.

"I'd like a star-themed one. My kids are into astronomy," another woman said.

"Mine are into dinosaurs."

Kerri helped her customers find what they were looking for, then helped them turn the objects into ornaments. For the rest of the afternoon, the store had a party atmosphere.

When her cactus ornaments were done, Connie paid for the whole collection, insisting on doubling the initial amount Kerri quoted for it.

"You're being too nice," she told Kerri. "You have to charge what things are worth, or you'll go out of business, and then what will we do? Stores like this one make up the life blood of a small town. We need you."

And she needed to stay right here, Kerri thought, as she watched her other customers happily at work making their ornaments.

Sunshine was right; there had to be a way to make it work.

CHAPTER 8

THE TREE SALES lot had been swarming with people ever since he opened at nine, so Ryan was grateful when Dane showed up around eleven and offered to stay to help.

"Don't you have work you need to do on your ranch?" Ryan asked him as they worked together to tie a tree on the roof rack of a midsize sedan.

"Taking a break," Dane said succinctly.

Ryan checked a knot, stood back and glanced at him. Something was troubling his friend, but Dane kept his attention on the rope he was tightening.

Ryan waited until the customer had driven off to take up the conversation again.

"Something happen?" he asked.

"Sometimes I wonder why I'm even bothering," Dane said. "Running a ranch. Keeping up my family's legacy."

"You need a reason more than that?"

Dane shrugged. "Guess I want one."

Ryan tried to guess what was bugging him. Why

would a man complain about having a spread as nice as the one Dane had inherited? His ranch was prosperous, as far as Ryan knew. He was well liked around town.

"I was thinking about decorating for the holidays," Dane said. "Then I wondered why I would take the trouble? Who's going to come around to see it? Not like I have a girlfriend or anything."

Ah. There was the problem, Ryan figured.

"Been getting out lately? Meeting new people?"

"Haven't had the time for it."

More like he hadn't had the inclination. Ryan knew vaguely Dane had gone through a bad breakup in his past.

"Make time for it. You need a woman to cheer you up." Ryan knew that wasn't particularly helpful, but he wasn't sure what else to say.

Dane made a face. He shoved his hands in the pockets of his jacket. "I had the right woman. Just let her get away."

"Then find someone else. There's plenty of fish in the sea."

"It's more like a pond around here. I feel like I've dated every woman in town. Besides, like I said, I had the right woman."

The way Ryan saw it, the right woman wouldn't have wanted to get away. He didn't say that to Dane, though.

"I know what you're thinking," Dane said, scanning the distant mountains.

"Doubt it."

"You're thinking I'm a fool for wanting back what I was dumb enough to lose in the first place."

"Wasn't thinking anything of the kind." Ryan took in the shadows under Dane's eyes and understood he was truly unhappy. Sometimes this season brought out people's private sorrows. Made them harder to stand.

"Eyes forward. Focus on the future, not the past. That's what everyone says."

"What do you say?" Ryan asked him.

"I say I lost the best thing I ever had, and there's no getting over a thing like that."

Ryan didn't contradict him, much as he wanted to. That was the way the man was feeling. No words were going to change it.

"Are you thinking it's time for you to settle down?"

Dane fixed him with a surprised look.

Ryan kept going. In for a penny, in for a pound. "We were all talking about it at Orchards the other day. I know I am."

Dane surveyed him, his gaze taking in more than Ryan wanted it to. "You and Kerri, huh?"

"Maybe." Ryan filled him in on what he'd learned, more to distract Dane than anything else. "Sounds like her mother is playing dirty pool, trying to force her to move to Sacramento. I can't figure out if she thinks she's saving Kerri or if she thinks Kerri owes her something." Once he started, he found it hard to stop. His thoughts had been full of the problem ever since he dropped her at her store.

"Not sure I understand."

They were interrupted by a family who'd found a tree they liked. After Ryan had rung them up and helped them load the tree in their truck, he answered Dane.

"You know Bess was a little… unusual."

"Heard her house was so full of junk you could barely move."

Ryan winced on Kerri's behalf. "It wasn't quite that bad, but close. Her mom says she's afraid Kerri will end up like her if she stays in Chance Creek. But she's also expanding her business in Sacramento and says she wants to employ Kerri. So which is it? You know what I mean?"

"You think she's trying to get a cheap employee?" Dane asked. He was more engaged now, and Ryan thought he'd succeeded in distracting him from his own problems.

"I don't know. I don't think Kerri would be happy there. And I think it would kill her to sell Bess's house."

"Not to mention her store," Dane put in. "But if you try to get in the middle of her and her mother, you'll end up with the two of them turned against you. Believe me, I know."

Ryan stopped short. He hadn't thought of that. He waited a moment to see if Dane would elaborate. "You're right," he admitted when Dane didn't go on.

"You're serious about her?"

It was more of a statement than a question, Ryan knew. He nodded anyway.

"Then you'd better fight for her. Don't let a good one get away, like I did."

"You'll find another good one," Ryan told him. He moved to straighten some of the cut trees, which were askew where they leaned against the wooden supports after people had looked through them. When Maple appeared from the direction of the tree fields, he leaned down to stroke her fur a time or two. She sat at his feet.

Dane thought about that, his mood souring again. "There isn't anyone as good. Guess I'd better get back to my own work. See you later."

Ryan started to ask Dane to stay, but he was already trudging toward the parking area, shoulders hunched against the cold.

KERRI HAD JUST left the bank Monday morning and climbed into her truck when her phone chimed. If it had been anyone other than Sunshine calling, she wouldn't have answered it—not even if it was Ryan.

For one thing, her mind was spinning out with worst-case scenarios based on the bad news the loan officer had just given her. For another, she was barely holding back tears.

"Well?" Sunshine asked when she took the call. "How'd it go?"

"It didn't go at all," Kerri said. "They won't lend me any more than they have already. They said the size of my home-finance loan makes a personal line of credit impossible. The loan officer made it very clear all the other banks would say the same thing. I tried my luck at a second bank just to be sure and found out she was right."

"Oh, Kerri, that's awful. What are you going to do now?"

"I don't know. I could try to get my credit card limit raised, but that will be a drop in the bucket, and my card is from the same bank. They might not even let me raise it. I guess… I guess I could apply for more credit cards, but if I'm turned down, that isn't great for my credit score."

She blinked back more tears that threatened to fall.

"You don't want to use cash advances to pay your mom, anyway. The interest rate would be outrageous." Sunshine's tone was brisk, as if she could bustle around and fix the problem through sheer efficiency. Kerri knew it had to be killing her not to be able to swoop in and make it all right. That was the kind of friend Sunshine was.

"I know, but I'm desperate. What else can I do?"

"What was Bess thinking when she set up your inheritance this way?" Her frustration was clear.

"She was hoping I'd get to keep the house and shop and she'd still be able to give Mom the money she needs. She was trying to be everything to everyone."

"Unlike your mother, who's nothing to no one." Sunshine stopped herself. "God, Kerri, I'm sorry. That was an awful thing to say. I just wish she'd stop trying to take away the things that are so important to you. I don't want you to leave."

"I know."

"Does she really need another store?"

"She thinks she does." Kerri didn't want to complain about her mother. "I'd better get home. If I'd known how things were going to go this morning, I wouldn't have scheduled Chloe for a full day, since I can barely afford her, but as it is, I'd better make use of the time and get a few things done."

"Okay, but call me if you need to talk, you hear me?"

"Will do."

Kerri hung up and started the truck. When her phone trilled out the sound for a video chat, she thought it was Sunshine again and accepted the call without looking at the screen.

"Had another bright idea?" she asked.

"I'm full of bright ideas," her mother said. "You know that."

Whoops. Her mother's face filled the tiny screen. Kerri quickly scrubbed an arm across her eyes and lifted the phone to face her. "Sorry, Mom. Thought you were someone else."

"How's the cleaning going?"

"Good. I emptied the cactus bathroom Saturday and the music room this morning." Mr. Owen from the high school had stopped by the store yesterday. They'd got to talking, and it turned out he was an avid audiophile. She'd had other customers, and Kerri wasn't enthusiastic about letting him upstairs in her house anyway, so she sent him on his way, then boxed up the whole collection last night after work, loaded it in her truck and drove it over to the school this morning before she opened her store for the day and turned it over to

Chloe. Mr. Owen martialled his first-period class to help him carry the boxes into the music room. He'd called her an hour ago and left a voice mail saying he and his students were having a blast sorting through the records, playing some of them on an old stereo setup stashed at the back of the music department's supply closet and looking over all the other music-related items.

"Impressive. Next thing you'll tell me is you haven't added anything new to the house."

Kerri opened her mouth to tell her she was right, then remembered the table and chairs Ryan had given her. Her mother noticed the change in her expression immediately.

"Kerri Jocelyn Olsen, do not tell me you brought something new into that house! What was it? Books? Records?" She shook her head. "Cats?"

"Not any of those," Kerri promised her. "Not anything to do with a collection."

"What, then?"

Kerri closed her eyes. This was going to sound so much worse than it was. "A dining set."

"Dining set. You mean dishes? For heaven's sake, do you not have enough of those already?"

"A table and chairs, Mom. You know I cleaned out the kitchen last week. I showed it to you."

Sylvie's eyes went wide. "You added an entire dining room table and chairs? For what? You've got no one to use it! And you're leaving soon! You can't bring that to California. Kerri—you're turning into a hoarder. You've got to get out of there, now!"

"It's not hoarding to have a dining room table!" But her mother was off and running on a lecture.

"You have to move. It's unhealthy to stay there. It's like you've been hijacked by my mother's ghost."

"Bess is not haunting me."

"You know what I mean." Her mother was tight-lipped. "She stole you from me once before. I'm not going to let her do it again. You clean out that house, and you put that property up for sale, or I swear to God…"

She cut the call, leaving Kerri shaken. She'd never seen her mother so angry.

She started the engine, drove home and hurried to heat up leftovers for a quick lunch. As she pulled food out of the refrigerator, she had to admit this had gone far past her mother wanting her rightful share of the inheritance from Bess. Her mother was determined to pry her out of Chance Creek. To move her to Sacramento.

And she was just as determined to stay put, Kerri decided. Which meant she needed to brainstorm every way she could possibly get her hands on thirty grand in the next few weeks.

Robbing a bank was out of the question, as was any kind of illicit enterprise.

Could she take a second job?

Kerri pulled out her phone as she heated up a bowl of soup and found a site that listed local jobs. Linda's Diner was looking for a server. Could she work a few shifts around her store's hours? Kerri thought it unlikely. The town's maintenance crew needed a receptionist. That looked like a nine-to-five job. She moved on. She wasn't qualified to be a carpenter or ranch hand. She didn't have an accounting degree or nursing skills.

She put the phone down as her soup began to steam. This was probably the wrong way to go about it. Most positions here in Chance Creek were filled by word of mouth.

I'm looking for work, she texted to Sunshine. *Will you put the word out for me? I'll do anything that pays.*

I can do that, Sunshine texted back. *Does this mean you're going to stay?*

I'm going to try, Kerri said.

Good. Come with Cole and me to the Dancing Boot on Friday. We miss you lately. We can hear all the latest gossip and tell people you need work.

I will, Kerri responded, despite usually begging off any plans involving dancing. She hadn't seen Sunshine enough lately with everything going on.

As she ate, Kerri thought about what her mother had said about losing her. She'd used language like that before, claiming Bess had taken her when she was the one who'd left town. It was true she'd asked Kerri to come with her, but Kerri had begged to stay. The last thing she'd wanted was to uproot herself, leave all her friends behind. Leave Bess—and the store.

She still felt the same way.

Was her mother angry with her for choosing Bess—and Chance Creek—over her?

Was that what this was all about?

"THE CHIEF WANTS to see you in his office," Brandon said when Ryan entered the firehouse on Thursday, Maple trotting happily by his side. Brandon was lying on a couch in the common area of the firehouse with his legs hooked over one arm rest.

Jacob looked up from his place at the table, mouth full of cereal. He raised an eyebrow as if to say, "What did you do?"

Ryan wasn't sure why Ed would want to see him. As far as he knew, he was caught up on all the new training protocols, and he hadn't had a big enough role in the last fire to need to make a statement.

As a volunteer Ryan had at least one full shift at the firehouse a week, usually from noon on Thursday to noon on Friday. Ed let him bring Maple to stay so she wouldn't be lonely at the cabin. The rest of the week he spent on call. When he was running deliveries in town, he could respond to emergencies quickly. When he was home on the mountain, it took a lot longer to make it into town, but Ed tried to make sure there were volunteers spread throughout the large community.

This week there'd been only a few calls to interrupt his days, but he'd been busy enough with tree sales. He'd spoken to Nathan Briars about the job in California on Monday. Nathan had emailed him a bunch of information to look through, and they'd scheduled an interview in Sacramento for December 19. Ever since, Ryan had turned over the possibilities in his mind. There was no reason not to go to the interview. Meanwhile, he'd keep looking for work in town.

"Thanks for the heads-up," he told Brandon. He set off for Ed's office in the back of the firehouse, tucked behind the kitchen and the sleeping quarters.

Should he take the job in Sacramento if it was offered to him? Would Kerri end up moving there, too? What if she didn't?

The questions kept reverberating around his mind. He'd ended up doing an extra shift at the firehouse from Monday to Tuesday, which meant he'd spent Tuesday afternoon and all of Wednesday catching up on deliveries and restocking the tree lot. He and Kerri had texted a few times, but that was the extent of it. He wanted to spend more time with her, but nothing seemed to be going right this week.

The door to Ed's office was open when he got there, but he knocked before he stuck his head in.

"Come on in," Ed said from behind his massive oak desk. Every time Ryan saw it he wondered if that desk had been put here when the firehouse was built a hundred years ago.

"Heard you wanted to talk to me."

"I heard you've got an interview coming up in Sacramento."

"Thanks to you."

Ed waved that off. "All I did was forward a resume."

"Seemed to do the trick."

"But…?" Ed steepled his fingers and raised his eyebrows.

"But nothing," Ryan bluffed. "It sounds like a good

job. Thanks for putting in a word for me."

"A little bird told me you might prefer to stay in Chance Creek." Ed watched him carefully.

A little bird? Did he mean Cole or Sunshine? Or was he simply guessing?

"Chance Creek is my hometown," Ryan acknowledged, "but sometimes you have to jump when opportunity comes knocking." Which was a hell of a thing to say when he didn't even know if he would jump if he was offered the job.

"That's what I think," Ed said. "When I hear about a good thing, I want to pass it on to the people I think deserve good things."

Ryan heard the compliment. "Thanks. I do appreciate it. It's just taking me a little time to wrap my head around the idea of leaving."

"You're the kind of man who's going to rise," Ed said. "You need a job with scope for growth."

Ryan nodded. He supposed that made sense. His gaze caught on a pair of old-fashioned snowshoes leaned against Ed's desk, and he grabbed at the chance to change the subject.

"New hobby?"

Ed made a face. "Something like that. The wife finally wore me down, and we bought a cabin near Silver Lake. She's driving all over trying to find vintage outdoor gear to decorate it. Skis and fishing poles, that kind of thing. I don't know if it's the season or what, but she's been having trouble finding what she wants. Friend of mine offered these to us. I knew I'd better snap them up."

Ryan thought about the lobster trap at Kerri's house. He knew where to find plenty of vintage outdoor gear. Maybe he could persuade her to sell him an item or two to give to Ed to show his appreciation for all the man had done. It would be a good excuse to see her again. "Might have a lead for you. I'll get back to you about it."

"Keep me posted on that interview, too," Ed said.

"Will do."

Back in the break room, he tried to join the usual banter among the other men but found his mind was elsewhere. A few of the men were playing pool. Others watched TV to pass the time. Ryan's shift passed slowly, with only two call-outs to break up the monotony. Once to help an elderly gentleman who had a stroke and once to a small grease fire that was already out by the time they arrived. In between the calls, he managed to catch a bit of sleep, Maple curled up nearby. When his shift was finally over Friday morning, Ryan stepped outside and called Kerri before heading home, grateful for the excuse Ed had given him to get in touch with her again.

"Hi, Ryan," she answered. She sounded tired, Ryan thought. Had she had a hard week?

"Can you help me with a gift for a friend this afternoon?" he asked. He explained about the new cabin Ed and his wife had bought. "Millie is decorating it with vintage outdoor gear, snowshoes and skis, that kind of thing. I wondered if you wanted to part with that lobster trap. Maybe a few other things."

"You can take it all, as far as I'm concerned."

She sounded discouraged. "I think Ed and Millie would be happy to pay for whatever you want to part with. And I'd like to make them a tree, if you've got anything that would work for it." Now that he'd thought of it, he knew that was the way to go. Ed was a proud man, and it might be hard to get him to accept the gift of some larger items, but how could he turn away a decorated tree? "Could you help me with that this afternoon?"

She thought about it. "Sure. Chloe is in this afternoon, so we can look through things at the house. I probably have enough small stuff that we could pull it off. But we were going to use it for your party, remember?"

"I think the Brookings would appreciate it more. Sounds like Millie will want to buy most of the bigger stuff you have, if you're selling it." After all, Kerri seemed to clean out a room each time she donated a themed tree.

She hesitated. "That's not a bad idea. Sounds like Ed and his wife would really like the vintage things Bess collected."

"You sure you won't miss them?"

"I won't be here to miss them."

Ryan's gut twisted, and he lowered his voice. "Did something happen?"

"No bank will loan me any more money. I'm looking for extra work, and I can't find that, either."

"I'm sorry to hear that." He made a mental note to

ask around for her. He wanted to ask her more questions, but he hesitated. Did he have the right to quiz her on her financial situation? Or was he supposed to sit back and wait and see what happened, even if her plans were important to him?

"What about you? How's life?" Kerri asked.

"Same old same old." He wished now he'd found a way to take her to dinner or something earlier in the week, despite how busy they'd both been. "Things get hectic this time of year. I've sold a lot of trees and delivered a lot more. Spent a few nights at the station." He searched for something else to say. "I've got an interview on December nineteenth. I'll be flying out to Sacramento for a night. You must have been there a bunch of times. What do you think about the place?"

"It's... okay," Kerri said. "Honestly, Mom usually comes to visit me here in Chance Creek. The few times I went there, we did a little sightseeing, visited museums, stuff like that. I always got the feeling Mom works so hard she hardly knows the place herself."

"Got it." He wasn't sure he did, though. If he had to move somewhere new, he would immerse himself in the place. Do his best to recreate the community he'd lost here.

"You'll have to tell me what you think when you go."

He could tell she was trying to sound cheerful, but he heard the pain underneath her breezy tone. She was losing heart, and he didn't want her to do that.

"You want to come with me?" he asked. Now that

he'd thought of it, it seemed like the perfect answer. He could spend some time with her. They could share their impressions of the place. Get a sense of how they interacted with each other away from their comfort zone.

A pause. "To your interview?"

"To Sacramento. We can stay overnight and check it out. Your mom would like to see you, right? It would give you two a chance to talk. And we could have some fun, too." He'd try to get the smile back on her face.

"I… sure. Why not?"

Ryan's heart lifted. "Let's hash out the details when I see you. Give me about an hour and a half." He had to drive all the way to the cabin and back again.

"See you then."

Energized, Ryan stowed his gear away and went to search for Maple. She was facing off with Brandon and Jacob, a wrench in her mouth.

"She thinks we're playing keep away," Jacob said.

"We've tried to persuade her she's wrong," Brandon said. "It's not getting through her thick skull."

More like Maple was having fun leading them on a merry chase, Ryan thought. "Maple, mine," he called.

Maple came bounding over and dropped the wrench into his waiting hand. He held it up. "This what you wanted?" he teased Jacob.

"Yep."

Ryan tossed the wrench to him. Maple barked and chased it, thinking the game was on again. Ryan whistled her back. "Playtime's over," he told the dog. "I'm off."

"Off to see *Kerri?*" Jacob asked innocently.

"None of your business."

"MEGAN? WHAT ARE you doing here?" Kerri asked when she opened her door to find the real estate agent on her front stoop. Ryan wouldn't arrive for another hour at least, and she'd wondered who was knocking at this time of day.

"Your mom said it was an emergency. I do whatever I can to keep my clients happy. Can I come in?"

"Of course." Thoroughly confused, Kerri stepped back and ushered Megan Lawrence into the front hall. She'd known her forever but couldn't imagine why she was here.

Megan handed her a brochure from Carmichael Realty, where she worked. Kerri had heard rumors that Megan's career in real estate had a rocky start as she'd tried to compete for listings against the older, established agents in town, but today she looked polished and confident.

"My mom called you?"

"She told me you're in a rush to sell. Personally, I think it's a shame you're leaving. I've always loved this house—and not many people get to commute across their lawn to work."

Understanding came all at once.

"Mom sent you here to list my property?" She tried to keep her rising anger out of her voice. It wasn't Megan's fault Sylvie had no concept of boundaries.

Megan nodded. "I'll miss your store when you move. Kerri's Collectibles is my favorite place to shop, you know," she added. "When I have money, which isn't too often these days."

"House sales not going well?" Kerri managed to ask. Did her mother really think these scare tactics would work? She hadn't talked to Sylvie since their disastrous last call except for a single text exchange. Her mother had let her know she'd received the funds in her account from the loan Kerri had taken out.

And then she'd asked where the rest of it was.

"They are for Lainie." Megan leaned closer and lowered her voice, although they were alone in the house. "She takes all the good listings and leaves me with the worst ones."

"I'm sorry to hear that."

"She can't take this one, though, can she? I'm the one who found it. Or rather, it found me, I guess you could say."

"I…" Kerri trailed off, finding it difficult to explain the mistake now that she noticed how happy Megan looked about getting the listing.

"I understand wanting to move closer to your mom," Megan added. "If I could have my parents back, I'd move wherever they did. But…" She bit her lip. "I was still surprised to hear you were leaving."

"I…" Kerri didn't know what to say. She wasn't leaving if she could help it. "I'm… thinking over my options." It was too embarrassing to admit her mother was trying to force her hand.

Megan's face fell. "You're not sure about moving? I brought the sign because your mom said it was a rush job. All the paperwork is in there." She nodded to the brochure where some loose pages were tucked inside. "I thought we could fill in the representation agreement today."

Kerri could tell Megan was trying hard not to let her disappointment show, and she felt a surge of anger toward her mother—and Lainie Carmichael, Megan's boss. Why had she hired Megan if she didn't mean to help her build a client base?

"We can fill out the agreement," she heard herself say.

"Awesome!" Megan lit up. Then she bit her lip. "I mean, I'll miss you a ton, Kerri. I wish you didn't have to go. Is there somewhere we can spread out the paperwork?" She looked toward the living room.

Kerri quickly maneuvered Megan into the kitchen and sat her down at the table Ryan had brought for her. It didn't take long to fill in the forms, but the whole time, Kerri felt a little sick. It didn't mean anything, she kept telling herself. She wasn't actually going to sell her house.

Not if she could help it.

"I'll need some photos," Megan said, standing up when they were done.

"I'll send some," Kerri hastened to say. No way would she let Megan walk through the house.

"Usually I do that."

"I've got better photos than you'll be able to take.

They're from when Bess was young. Before she…"

"Started collecting?" Megan said tentatively.

"Right."

Megan nodded, and Kerri ushered her into the front hall.

"I'll put up the sign on my way out," Megan said, lingering by the door. "Thanks for the business, Kerri. I appreciate it."

"Of course," Kerri said helplessly. Megan was putting the sign up now?

How had she gotten herself into this mess?

"I'll be in touch soon," Megan promised. "We'll have to set up an open house." She glanced into the living room, one hand on the doorknob. "Kerri, I hope you don't mind me saying so, but you'd better declutter a little bit before we do. People like a blank slate, so they can imagine what their possessions will look like in a house."

"Sure," Kerri said. "Talk soon."

"Don't worry," Megan said as she left. "We'll have the place sold in no time."

CHAPTER 9

MAPLE WAS CONFUSED when they headed back to town only twenty minutes after they arrived at the cabin, but like any dog, she was perfectly content to go for a bonus truck ride.

Ryan was humming along to the country song on the radio when he turned onto Kerri's street and noticed the sign on her lawn.

What was that?

For Sale.

Shock hit him like a fist to the solar plexus. Kerri wasn't just talking about leaving town.

She actually meant it. She was selling her house.

Which meant this trip they were taking to Sacramento wasn't some lark. When he decided whether to leave or stay, he'd be deciding his future with Kerri, too.

He gripped the steering wheel, his thoughts churning. He'd expected to have more time. You were supposed to think long and hard about choosing a woman to marry, weren't you?

He'd taken Kerri out—if you could call it that when

all they'd done was deliver trees—only a couple of times. Could he really make a major life decision based on such a small foundation?

Could he let her go if their choices didn't mesh? He wasn't sure he could. Kerri had been getting under his skin since the day he spotted her at Orchards. He thought about her constantly. Fantasized about her more than should be legal. Kept picturing the path their lives could take together—

Someday.

Ryan looked at the sign again.

Seemed like someday might be closer than he thought.

How on earth was Kerri going to survive selling Bess's place? He'd already spent eight years away during his time in the Marine Corps, so he knew what it was like to be somewhere else and ready to be home again. Kerri had lived here all her life. Would she be able to make a home somewhere else?

A surge of anger made his fingers tighten on the steering wheel. Why was Kerri's mother being so unreasonable? Why was the only decent job offer he'd gotten in another state?

Why were Grandpa John—and Bess—gone? None of this would be happening if they were still alive.

Ryan took a deep breath. He'd never lost control when it counted, and he wasn't going to lose it now. Kerri needed him to stay calm. To make a plan that worked.

Was Sunshine right—was there a way for them to

stay, if they only looked hard enough? Was there something he'd missed?

He thought of his daily check-ins on the job forums, finding the same low-paying, no-benefit entry-level positions day after day after day. What choice did he have but to move if he wanted to be a good provider? Kerri had told him she couldn't find extra work, either. Couldn't get another loan for a lousy thirty grand.

Had she come home from her store one night this week and given up? Is that why she'd decided to sell?

If he'd paid her more attention, would she have fought harder to stay?

Ryan turned off the truck's engine and got out, Maple leaping out after him. He remembered how he'd felt when Sunshine revealed Kerri wanted a big family. His reaction had been visceral, a strong tug inside to prove he was the one she should have that family with. Caveman stuff, but real nonetheless.

Sick of feeling thwarted, Ryan strode to her front door. You didn't always get what you wanted in life. Maybe he needed to move to Sacramento to take that job. Maybe Kerri needed to sell her home and business to get square with her mother. That didn't mean they couldn't be together—or build a new life with just as much meaning. Plenty of people left their hometowns to get ahead in the world.

The important thing was not to lose Kerri while they figured all this out.

WHEN KERRI OPENED her door, Ryan was frowning on

her doorstep. Maple, sitting calmly beside him, lifted a paw, licked it a few times and put it down again.

"Come in, I've got some snowball cookies if you want them. Sorry about the mess." She tried to sound more cheerful than she felt. At least she was getting to see Ryan. As his shoulders filled her doorway, she felt something shift inside her. Maybe the loan officer had let her down. Maybe she couldn't find extra work anywhere. Maybe she was angry at her mother—and at fate, too.

Ryan was here. Just being near him made things a little better.

He stepped inside and looked around as if he'd never seen the place before.

In the hour since Megan left, she'd spread out everything in the living room as best she could and moved a bunch of items into the hall. Large objects were stationed on the floor. Smaller ones were lined up on the furniture. Miniature versions of the real vintage sporting equipment sat on the coffee table. The tray of snowball cookies was perched on the very end.

"Thanks, but I'm not really hungry."

That surprised her. When was Ryan not hungry for a snowball cookie?

"Well, they're right here if you change your mind. How about some hot chocolate?"

"Not today."

His voice was rough, as if he hadn't slept well. He kept his hands in his pockets, his gaze averted from hers. What had happened since they'd spoken earlier?

Had something gone wrong at the firehouse?

Like always when Ryan was near, she itched to cross the room and bury herself in his arms. She wanted him to kiss her again. Wanted his hands to trace their way down to rest on her hips and tug her closer. Instead, she gestured to some of the larger objects. A pair of skis, the lobster trap, some baskets.

"I wasn't sure what your plan was. Did you want to start with ornaments first or bring a few of the bigger items to Ed and Millie so they can take a look?"

"Maybe I should just take it all. Chances are Millie's going to want it anyway. If there's anything left over, we can figure out what to do with it. I'll make a couple of trips."

"Sounds great, if you're sure you don't mind." Kerri watched him carefully. What was wrong? He was acting like they'd just been introduced, not like they'd been flirting for days. "I've set aside some small things to make into ornaments. I can work on them while you're doing the first delivery of the larger pieces and have them ready to go before you're all done."

"Sounds good." Ryan grabbed an armful of gear and carried it into the hall to stack by the door. Kerri got to work slowly boxing up the smaller things, thoroughly unsettled. They hadn't talked about prices, but Ed and Millie were good people. They would give her a fair price and buy only what they could afford. At least she'd end up with a little money to put toward what she owed her mother. Maybe she could find places at the store for whatever was left over.

"Long day?" she asked after Ryan worked in silence for a while.

"Something like that. Kerri…" He trailed off and shook his head, as if thinking better of whatever he meant to say.

"What?" she prompted him. She put down the box she'd been filling and faced him.

"Sunshine said…" He broke off and sighed.

Sunshine said a lot of things. Kerri waited to see which one had Ryan tied up in knots.

"You want kids?" He finally met her gaze, and Kerri's stomach swooped.

"Yes. Sure. Of course." Hell, now she sounded like she was hoping he was offering to provide them. "I mean, someday. When the time is right."

"Right."

"You want kids, too?" she blurted after an awkward moment. What was she saying? What were they even talking about? She sat down on the sofa and began to move the miniature items around on the coffee table, bunching them into meaningless groups.

"Yeah. I do." That look again.

"How… many?" she asked. Somehow she was on her feet again. She didn't know what was happening here. A minute ago she was afraid he was angry about something. Now he looked like he might toss her over his shoulder and take her to bed. He was watching her hungrily, a flare of desperation in his gaze she couldn't quite understand.

"A houseful. I want…" He paused again, and Kerri

leaned toward him. What did he want? "I want a home. A real home. I want a wife."

A shiver traveled through her. He'd said that before when they were all at Orchards that first day.

She craved a family, too. A place to belong. A person to belong to.

She craved Ryan.

"I want to be someone's wife," she said and felt a blush overtake her. She'd never said something so baldly true before. She should have said she wanted a husband, but that didn't encompass what she was after. That sense of being possessed—not in a carnal way, not in a passive way, but in a way that meant the man doing the possessing wanted you and only you. She wanted Ryan to want her like that.

He was watching her like he might devour her. Like he might cross the room—

In two steps he was there.

"Kerri." It was a guttural groan that told her everything she wanted to know. They crashed together, Ryan circling one arm around her waist, one hand tangling in her hair. This time when he kissed her it went on and on, his hands lifting her up to her tiptoes. Kerri couldn't get enough of him, couldn't get close enough to him. She tugged at the hem of his shirt, and he peeled it over his head. She fumbled with his belt while he unbuttoned her blouse.

All the while he kept on kissing her, his hands exploring her body wherever it was exposed. His hunger for her was evident, and she was sure he was in no doubt that she felt the same way.

When he lowered her to the floor, kicking aside a set of vintage boxing gloves and a croquet set Kerri had played with when she was young, she went with him willingly, shrugging out of her shirt and untangling herself from her bra.

Somehow he cleared a big enough space for her before setting her down and covering her with his body. They got his jeans off next—and then hers. At one point she felt Maple's cold nose bump against the arch of her bare foot, but Ryan sent the curious dog away with a single command, and they were alone.

Ryan's kisses heated her until Kerri thought she had to be glowing; every inch of her felt so good. He didn't make her ask about protection; he just took care of it. When he finally slid inside her, Kerri gave a low moan that echoed his deeper, more animal-like sound.

She let Ryan set the pace, moving with him naturally, letting go of all her swirling thoughts so she could feel every sensation without being distracted. The width of his shoulders and the bunch and release of his muscles called her to run her hands over his warm skin. He seemed to know her rhythm instinctively. Made her body hum with desire.

"Kerri?" A whispered question against her neck.

"Yes." She wanted everything this man had to offer.

"I don't know what's going to happen next. I don't know whether to take the job in Sacramento if I'm offered it or to stay and try to make things work out here."

"Okay." She didn't know what to do either. Sell and join her mother in Sacramento? Sell and stay? Refuse to sell and see if her mother called her bluff? None of it seemed important now. Not with Ryan bringing her such exquisite pleasure.

"I want to be with you, though. I know that for sure."

Kerri let out a long breath. He was coaxing her body to the point of no return.

"I want to be with you, too," she gasped.

"Here or in Sacramento?" His gaze held hers as they moved together. "I saw the sign out front."

The sign.

Kerri froze. He'd seen the sign and probably made all kinds of assumptions. No wonder he'd been so upset when he came in.

She should have told him what had happened with Megan right away. Suddenly Kerri wasn't in sync with him at all, and she wanted to be. She wanted nothing more than to get back into pace with the rhythm he'd set. "Yes. Here or in Sacramento. Anywhere. Mom was the one who called Megan and said I wanted to sell. And then Megan looked so disappointed when I hesitated," she explained. "Somehow I lost control of the situation."

Just like she was losing control over her body now. Everywhere he touched her sent sparks of pure sensation through her. "I don't want to leave," she told him. He was still moving slowly within her, tormenting her until she could barely hang on.

"If I take that job, will that change the way you feel about being with me?" He paused, bracing himself above her. Kerri moved her hips, not wanting him to stop.

"No." What she felt for him wouldn't change.

Something shifted in his eyes. Was that relief she saw there?

Kerri wasn't sure. When he stroked into her again, she shut hers, letting his movements take her right to the edge.

"We can build something together. I know we can. No matter where we end up." Ryan's voice was labored. He was getting close, too.

Kerri was past being able to think anything through logically. She clung to him and a moment later cried out as her release overtook her. Everything else forgotten, she rode the feeling, Ryan somehow spinned it out long past what she thought was possible. It was like he knew her through and through already.

When they finally lay spent together, Ryan still half on top of her, Kerri was almost dizzy. What exactly had they promised each other?

She wasn't sure.

Ryan lifted his head. Touched her cheek gently. "We're going to figure this out. It's going to be okay. I promise."

Reality rushed back in and with it the realization she was lying on the floor in a jumble of outdoor gear, looking up at stacks of equipment the way she'd looked up from her bed at stacks of cat-themed objects all her life.

Suddenly the mess in her living room pressed in on all sides, and despite her best efforts, tears pricked her eyes. They didn't know what the future held. Didn't know if they could stay or would have to leave.

What if this thing between her and Ryan—whatever it was—didn't work out?

"Hey," Ryan said, trailing a kiss along her jaw. "I mean it. It's going to be all right, Kerri. I'm going to make it all right. Understand?"

She nodded. What else could she do?

With Ryan by her side, she could handle almost anything, but could she handle leaving everything else she loved behind?

When he disengaged from her and sat up, reaching for his clothes, more doubts crept in. Kerri remembered what he'd said at Orchards. The tree farm didn't make enough money to support him. There weren't any positions for him at the fire house. He might have to take that job in California, even if she decided not to work for her mother.

The good feelings Ryan had stirred within her were gone, leaving Kerri far too aware of her nakedness. Someone could see in from the street—

She scrambled to pull her clothes to cover her.

"No one can see you down there on the floor," Ryan assured her, guessing where her thoughts had gone.

But he'd seen her. He'd seen this mess. Seen the way she and Bess had lived all these years. For the first time she realized Ryan had been in her house more than almost anyone else in Chance Creek had, given how often he'd accompanied his grandfather on his deliveries.

What did he think of her—really?

"Kerri?"

"What?" The word came out far more sharply than she'd intended it to.

"I asked, which way to your bathroom?"

Bathroom? Pure fear spiked through her before Kerri remembered she'd already cleaned the cacti out of it. "It's right down that hall. I'll use the one upstairs. See you in a minute." She struggled to her feet, bringing her clothing with her, trying to strategically cover herself.

"I could join you," he suggested and kissed her shoulder.

Kerri stiffened. His kiss felt so good. Being with him had felt so good, but—

Maple came trotting back in from wherever she'd gone while they were together. Ryan bent to ruffle her fur, freeing Kerri to move again.

"Not this time." She wasn't sure why she still didn't want Ryan upstairs. After all, they'd just made love in a pile of Bess's stuff. He'd seen the kitchen at its worst, too. Several of the bedrooms had been cleaned out already. Why was she holding back?

Was there anything left in the house that would scare him away after all that?

There was an upstairs bathroom full of owls.

A laugh escaped her that was almost a sob.

"I'll be back." In an attempt to divert him, she went up on tiptoe again, kissed his nose and darted away, racing up the stairs before she lost control completely. She'd been with Ryan—and it had been amazing. He'd practically told her he wanted to get married—at least someday.

But people didn't always follow through when it came to loving you. Sometimes they left if you weren't exactly what they wanted you to be.

Sometimes you weren't special enough to be loved in the first place.

Kerri stopped halfway up, clinging to the banister.

Where had that thought come from? With it came a wrenching feeling in her chest and tears that pricked her eyes. She remembered being seventeen. The email she'd written to her father.

Deleting it before she'd hit *send*.

Kerri shook her head, trying to settle herself down. That was the past. She was so far over thinking about a man who'd turned his back on her before she was born. And she was the one who'd refused to go to California with Sylvie. Her mother hadn't *left* her.

Except, she kind of had.

This was getting her nowhere, Kerri told herself fiercely as tears slid down her cheeks. That was history—it had nothing to do with now.

She had a wonderful man downstairs who'd made it clear he was interested. He was making plans for the both of them. He'd made love to her.

But did that mean she was lovable?

Kerri raced up the rest of the stairs before the sob caught in her throat could make it out, flung herself into the bathroom and shut the door. She turned on the shower to muffle the sounds she was making. As the water ran and steam filled the air, she tossed her clothes to the ground, got in and braced her hands against the tiled walls.

She was losing her mind. That was the only explanation for why she was crying in the shower—no, sobbing in the shower—moments after being with Ryan. She definitely wasn't crying because he'd made her feel wanted—really wanted—for the first time since Bess died. Or because his arms around her made her feel safer than she'd ever felt even when Bess was alive.

This was grief. Just a natural result of spending months alone after her grandmother died. Or maybe it was the result of shedding so many possessions that reminded her of Bess.

Is wasn't because Ryan had allowed her to see what life could feel like if you didn't have to go through it alone—

Kerri didn't know how long she stayed that way, racked with tears, the water running over her, but it was turning cold by the time she'd cried the last of them, rinsed herself and turned the shower off. Her eyes were puffy and her nose was red, but she found a new outfit, dried her hair and reapplied her makeup. She hoped Ryan had left to take the first load to the Brookings' house, but when she came downstairs, he was outside loading up his truck.

Kerri busied herself in the living room attaching hooks to the miniature items to make them into ornaments, keeping her head bowed over the task even when he came inside, Maple following him.

"There you are."

"Sorry that took a while," she murmured.

"That's okay." He watched her a moment. Maple flopped down near her feet. "Kerri?"

She nodded, not wanting him to see her face.

"Will you really move to Sacramento if it turns out you have to sell this place?" he asked. "If I were you, I'd be too angry at my mom to think about working with her."

"I am angry," Kerri said after a moment and was glad she'd already cried herself dry. She had no energy left for strong emotions. "But she sees our history differently." She put down the ornament she was working on. "She thinks Bess stole me from her back when I was a teenager." Her throat tightened as she remembered the arguments they'd had.

"Stole you? How?"

"You have to understand Mom hated Chance Creek by then. She hated how people looked at her because of Bess's hoarding. She hated the whispers. She moved to New York as soon as she turned eighteen, and she came back only because she was pregnant with me. She didn't intend to stay longer than necessary to save some money, but it took far longer than she'd thought it would to accumulate enough. I held her back." Kerri lifted her hands helplessly. "When I was fourteen, she was ready to make a break for it, and I refused to go with her. Mom decided that was all Bess's fault."

"Was it?"

"Of course not. I was a teenager. I wanted to stay with my friends, and besides, Mom was barely ever around. I mean, she was here, but she wasn't here, if you know what I mean. Everything she did was online. She made all her designs on her laptop. She was up in her bedroom from morning to night, working, working, working. She said the conditions in this house were her constant inspiration to get the... heck... out of here." Kerri swallowed again. "Bess was the one who had time for me, even if she did have a store to run. Mom was too busy building her empire, even then."

"You chose the place where you thought you'd thrive. No one can blame you for that."

"Mom blames me. I broke her heart." Kerri bent over the miniature set of skis she was turning into an ornament. Even now she couldn't believe she'd been so selfish, demanding her own way.

Ryan thought that over. "You were fourteen," he repeated slowly. "Your mom could have made you come to Sacramento."

"I would have kicked up a real fuss if she did." Back then she was quite capable of pitching a fit.

"So what?" When she looked up, startled, he went on. "Kids fuss all the time when their parents make them do things they don't want to do. Parents keep parenting. Your mom could have demanded that you come. You would have sulked for a while and then you would have gotten over it, right?"

"I… guess." She didn't know what he was getting at.

"Maybe it suited your mom for you to stay with Bess."

Kerri stared at him. "You think…"

"I think she's had her cake and eaten it, too. She got to run off to California and start her business without having to worry about taking care of you, knowing Bess would do a far better job than she could, and she got to make you and Bess both feel guilty about it."

"I don't believe…" Kerri trailed off. It was possible. Now that she thought about it, her mother had never made much of an effort to convince her that living in California would be fun. The few times she'd made it to Sacramento, it was almost as if her mother had tried to keep her separate from the life she'd built there.

"I'm not saying your mom doesn't love you or that she doesn't want you out there now that you're grown up."

"She definitely wants me there now," Kerri confirmed, looking down again. She was in no doubt of that. But was it because her mother missed her or because she thought Kerri might be useful to her? "What about you?" she asked Ryan, still bent over her task. "Would you really take a job in Sacramento and give up living here? Does it make a difference what I do?"

"Of course it makes a difference." He came to crouch down beside her. Maple thumped her tail but stayed where she was. "I want to be where you are."

Her breath hitched. He... wanted her. She wanted him, too—so badly. Still, the last hour had brought up all the old fears she thought she'd conquered. He was talking a good game, but would he really follow through?

"What if I didn't exist," she pressed him. "Without me in the picture, would you take that job if it was offered to you?"

"I don't know." He thought it over. "Like I said, I want to get somewhere in life, but leaving Chance Creek isn't my first choice."

"It's not mine, either," Kerri said. The ache in her throat was back, despite everything. Happiness was so fleeting in this world. Just when she'd been old enough to really be part of Chance Creek, her mother had left. Just when she'd come into her own running her store, Bess had died. Now that she'd found someone to love—someone who might love her—

Both of them were being cast adrift all over again.

"Kerri," Ryan said softly. "Look at me."

She did so reluctantly, knowing he'd see the traces of her tears on her face.

"I know this isn't ideal. Neither of us knows what the future holds. We can still face it together."

Tears pricked her eyes again, even though she didn't think she had any left. Could they face it together? Or would the decisions they needed to make tear them apart?

Ryan put his hand over hers. Immediately, Kerri felt

the promise there. He was going to do his best to find an answer they could both live with. "We'll go to Sacramento," he said. "We'll see how we feel when we're there together."

Kerri nodded. Took a deep breath.

She pointed to the boxes remaining in the hall, needing to move the conversation to more solid ground. "Those aren't going to fit, are they?"

Ryan watched her a moment, as if assessing whether he could press her to keep talking about the future. He must have decided she'd reached her limit.

"I'll take the first batch to Ed and Millie and see if they want the rest." He kissed the top of her head and stood up. Maple got to her feet, too. "I'd rather stay with you. Talk this over more," he added.

"I know, but duty calls." She was past her limit for thinking about the changes she might have to face. "After you drop those off, come back and I'll help you take the second load over. We can bring the tree then."

"Sounds good." He helped her up, still assessing her. "Can I take you out later tonight? We should do something fun. We've both been working hard."

"I'm supposed to go with Sunshine and Cole to the Dancing Boot. Want to join us?"

"I'll be there," Ryan said.

CHAPTER 10

RYAN FOUND ED and Millie at home. When he led them outside to show them the contents of his truck, Millie was thrilled.

"I'll take everything you've got," she said.

"You sure? There's another truckload back at Kerri's place." Ed was looking a little shell-shocked and too late Ryan wondered if he should have brought over a smaller load first.

"Are you kidding? Of course I'm sure; It's a big cabin, and the way things were going I thought it was going to take me years to find enough stuff to decorate the place. Besides, I've got friends who will take anything I can't use. Don't worry," she told her husband. "I'll leave some room for your fishing trophies."

"If there's anything you don't want, I'll take it back," Ryan said. "Where should I put it all?"

"In the shop, I guess," Ed said with a sigh.

Ryan caught him alone a few minutes later as Millie was happily picking through the gear, exclaiming over each new treasure. "Did I mess up?"

"No," Ed said. "I like to give Millie a hard time about her secondhand shopping, but the truth is, she's right. She'll be able to get the cottage looking exactly the way she wants it before we have friends over next summer, and I won't have to drive her all over the western half of the country to find things. It's a win–win situation, really."

"Glad to hear it."

Ryan emptied his truck, went back a second time, filled it again and brought Kerri with him to deliver the tree. Millie couldn't stop exclaiming over the miniature snowshoes and skis and picnic baskets that hung from its boughs. When she showed Ed the fishing rods and fish, he was tickled pink.

"That was a hit," Ryan said when they drove off, leaving the Brookings to get busy decorating their cabin.

"I think so, too."

It was nearly six, so they stopped for fast food on the way back to Kerri's place and he dropped her off there, promising to meet her later at the Boot. He wanted nothing more than to stay with her, given the afternoon they'd had, but something told him Kerri needed time to find her equilibrium again.

Making love to her had been everything he'd known it could be, despite the location and circumstances, but he had a feeling the location—all those stacks of Bess's things around them—had gotten to Kerri at the end.

He was aware she'd been overwhelmed when she escaped up the stairs to take a shower, and he'd considered pursuing her, but then he remembered how cautious she'd always been to keep him in certain parts of the house. He'd always noticed how she stiffened whenever he came through the front door—even back when they were kids. She'd hovered around when he and his grandfather delivered each tree, and every time Bess invited them to have a cup of hot chocolate, she'd winced.

She'd been furious that time he called her grandmother's collections junk.

Bess's hoarding was a sore spot, and she wasn't over it, given how long it had taken her to tackle the problem.

Still, he didn't like it that she'd been crying upstairs, and it killed him he didn't know for sure what had caused those tears. She'd been as hungry as he was to get close, and the words they'd spoken to each other during the act seemed to promise they had a future together, but the minute it was over, it was as if she felt—

Overexposed.

Was it really only fear of being seen from the street that had her covering herself the way she had? Was the upstairs bathroom really so awful she couldn't bear to bring him to it?

Was she afraid now that he'd seen her—all of her—he wouldn't want her anymore?

Nothing could be further from the truth.

He needed to make that clear to her.

Of course, she could have run up those stairs because she'd been revolted by him.

A smile tugged at the corners of his mouth. She hadn't seemed revolted when she was crying out his name.

No, they were compatible; that was for sure. They weren't the problem—everything else around them was.

He was going to solve those problems, he promised himself. He'd found the woman he wanted, and he was going to do whatever it took to keep her.

After a couple of hours of hard work on the mountain, cutting trees to sell the following day, Ryan showered, changed and was just leaving for town when his phone buzzed. Jacob was calling.

"Hey, stop by the firehouse, would you? Got something I need to talk over."

"Can't we talk now?" He wanted to get to the Boot and grab a table before the place filled up. He had things to say to Kerri that wouldn't wait.

"Get your ass over here." Jacob hung up. Ryan sighed but decided he could make the stop and still get to the Boot on the early side. Nothing really got going until at least ten, which was when Kerri said she'd get there.

"Sorry, girl. You'll have to stay here," he said to Maple. She followed him to the door and whined as he shut it. Ryan hated to leave her behind, but the Boot was no place for a dog.

The station was packed when he arrived, the guys who were on shift tonight joined by a number of off-duty men.

"What's going on?" he asked.

"There you are!" Jacob came to greet him. "Kept us waiting long enough."

"I was busy."

"With your girlfriend? You and Kerri Olsen are quite the couple now. Heard you spent the day with her."

"I spent the day with Ed and Millie." It wasn't a total lie, and he was not going to discuss what he'd done with Kerri today with Jacob or anyone else.

"Right. Fess up. You've got a thing for her," Jacob said.

"My fist is going to have a thing for your face in another minute."

"Oooh. See? What did I tell you?" Jacob said to Brandon. "He's got it bad."

"All right. I'm out of here." Ryan moved to go, but several of the men got in his way.

"No, you're not. We're taking you out to celebrate," Daniel Wallace said. He was a stocky man in his mid-thirties, always up for a good time.

"Celebrate what?"

"Your big advancement. Ed told us you're going to take a position out west. Be a big shot in the California Forestry Service."

Jacob took his arm and marched him toward the door. "We're going to the Dancing Boot to get shit-faced tonight in your honor!" More cheers erupted.

Ryan made to argue, then decided against it. There was no stopping the tide of humanity sweeping him out the door, and he was already going to the Dancing Boot anyway. His firehouse friends probably needed a reason to blow off some steam. If he spoke up now, he'd ruin everyone's Friday night.

"AREN'T YOU GLAD you came?" Sunshine asked when she slipped a beer into Kerri's hand. She'd gotten a cranberry juice and soda water for herself and settled with an audible sigh into a seat at the table Cole had found for them.

Kerri nodded and took a long drink. "Aren't you tired after working all week?" Sunshine's belly was getting bigger every time she saw her friend.

"Gotta have a date night now and then or you get old and grumpy," Sunshine told her. She held up her glass of soda. "Cheers."

"Cheers." Kerri saluted her. It was strange to be out in public after the day she'd had. She kept expecting Sunshine to read in her face that she'd been with Ryan this afternoon. Everything felt different.

She felt different.

Her body hummed with the memory of the way he'd moved inside her even as her mind was tormented with visions of the way she'd dashed up the stairs afterward. It was all so embarrassing.

With a few hours of separation from the experience, she couldn't remember anymore why she'd been so upset afterward. Ryan had been—amazing. So what if the living room was a mess? It wasn't anything he hadn't seen before.

Besides, he'd been looking at her, not at the stacks

of outdoor gear.

Why shouldn't a man want her? Maybe her mother had been a driven businesswoman and her father had been a cheating man. Maybe life didn't always go smoothly. That didn't mean she couldn't be happy now.

Wearing a cute, flirty dress and cowboy boots, her hair and makeup done, she felt like she could take on the world, especially because they were sitting in the Dancing Boot and not Bess's living room. Out here she was just like everyone else.

"I heard you've been delivering Christmas trees all over town." Cole took a swig of his beer and smiled. "That hits the spot."

"I've been decorating some of them with pieces from Grandma Bess's collections. It's been the kick in the butt I needed to start cleaning out my house. I like knowing some of Bess's collections are staying together and will be cherished by their new owners."

"Besides, Kerri's going to be living in a teeny, tiny minimalist apartment in Sacramento," Sunshine said. "She won't have room for any possessions."

"I'm doing everything I can to prevent that," Kerri protested.

"I hope so, but I'm still worried your mom won't quit until she wins," Sunshine said darkly. "Then she'll force you to be a minimalist, too. You'll have to live the brand, right?"

"If I chose to work for her, I guess I'd do my best to represent her brand, but it's not like she'd decorate my home."

"Really?" Sunshine raised an eyebrow. Kerri took another drink. She had to admit her mother had found ways to influence her aesthetic choices when she was younger. She was good at making comments that sounded harmless enough but packed a sting once you were alone thinking back on them. She was all grown up now, though. Even if she had to sell up to pay her debt to Sylvie, that didn't mean she'd give her mother control over her life.

"Kerri," Sunshine began in a new tone, one that put her on automatic alert. "Cole and I have been thinking. We can't offer you a lot, but we'd like to give you a loan for a thousand dollars. We can spare that right now, and I bet a lot of other people could lend you a little. Or we could do one of those fancy internet fundraising things where a lot of people each chip in a bit, and the money would be a gift, not a loan. You know how people like to help each other here."

Kerri was already shaking her head. "No. Absolutely not. I appreciate the offer more than you can ever imagine, but it's going to take me years to pay back the home equity loan I took out. I'm not going to owe money all over town—and I'm not going to take charity, either. I would if my situation was desperate," she went on, overriding Sunshine's protestations. "If I lost my house to a fire or flood or something like that. This is a dispute over an inheritance. I don't want anyone else involved."

"Sunshine," Cole warned when Sunshine opened her mouth to argue her point. "You asked, just like we agreed, and Kerri said no, just like we knew she would. Let it go. We'll figure out another way to help."

"Thank you," Kerri told him. "From the bottom of my heart. Both of you. You're the best friends I could ask for." She reached across the table and gave their hands a squeeze.

"I just keep imagining how amazing it would be if you raised a family in that wonderful house of yours," Sunshine said, a hand protectively on her belly and tears in her eyes. "Just think what it could be like without Bess's collections. A blank slate for however you want to decorate it. Over time, you could update it. Modernize the furniture, get new drapes and repaint the walls. The rooms are sized so generously. The windows are fabulous. The ceilings are so high. It could be amazing—and you know we'd all help."

"I know." Now that she'd seen how the first floor had shaped up, she could imagine what the rest of the place could look like. Free of Bess's clutter, the living room was almost cavernous. She could fit two conversational groupings of sofas and love seats in there and still have plenty of room to walk around. There were low, built-in, glass-fronted bookcases on one wall that she'd almost forgotten since they'd been hidden behind piles of vintage equipment all her life. She'd taken a minute to look through them before coming to the Boot, and she'd already chosen a few old-fashioned books to read when she had time.

The room was meant for family gatherings, holiday parties, book club meetings. She could picture a life in which she hosted all of those—

Kerri stopped herself right there. She could have a good future no matter where she lived. Bess's house wasn't the only place she could make a home.

"Thirsty?" Sunshine asked.

Kerri realized she'd drained her bottle. She set it on the table carefully.

"Let me get you another," Cole said. "It's Friday night. You're allowed a drink or two."

Normally Kerri would wave him off. For one thing, she could buy her own. For another, one or two beers were enough to get her tipsy. Cole was out of his seat before she could tell him any of that, though.

"Here comes trouble," Sunshine said. She pointed to the door, where Ryan had just walked in surrounded by a bunch of his fireman buddies, who steered him straight to a table across the room from her.

He was so damn handsome, and she wanted to be with him so damn badly.

Kerri decided a second beer sounded perfect. What if she had to leave Chance Creek and he decided to stay? What if she pulled off a miracle, kept her home and business, and he decided he had to take that job in Sacramento?

"To Ryan and his new job!" she heard one of his friends shout. A round of cheers filled the room.

Her stomach sank, and Kerri gripped the table, suddenly feeling like the earth had tilted beneath her feet. Had he decided he was going to take the job in the hours since they'd parted? He hadn't even been offered it yet, had he? His interview wasn't until the nineteenth.

Ryan spotted her and smiled. She raised her eyebrows in a question. He shook his head and shrugged helplessly.

Kerri let out a breath. Someone had jumped the gun. Probably Jacob Monk. He was always looking for an excuse to celebrate.

"They seem happy," Sunshine said. A local band was warming up and a moment later began to play. The noise level shot up immediately, and couples took to the floor.

"I think they found out about Ryan's job offer," Kerri told her.

Sunshine made a face. "They're celebrating the idea of him leaving? Maybe he's a pain in the ass around the station."

Kerri had to laugh. "I don't think so. I think they're just happy for him."

"I'm not happy for him."

"I know." Kerri hesitated. "I told Ryan he could join us tonight."

Sunshine cocked her head. "Interesting. You two are really getting along, huh?"

Kerri shrugged. That was one way of putting it.

Sunshine reached across the table and touched her hand. "I'm happy for you. I think you deserve someone wonderful."

"You think Ryan's wonderful?" Kerri asked.

"I think he could be—as long as he stays here in Chance Creek where he belongs."

"Got it." She couldn't fault Sunshine for feeling that way, but she decided she'd done enough worrying about what the future would hold for one day. Right now she didn't want to think about anything.

Another burst of laughter and shouting came from Ryan's table as a waitress brought them more pitchers of beer. As she watched they raised their glasses in a toast and drained them. It looked like they were racing each other to see who could finish first. They slammed their empties on the tabletop.

"Fill them up again," Jacob crowed.

"It's going to be a rowdy night," Sunshine said.

"It's always a rowdy night at the Boot," Cole said, coming back with more drinks. He handed a beer to Kerri, who immediate took a long sip. "Ryan's here," he added.

"We saw," Sunshine said. "Are you going to ask me to dance or what?" she demanded.

"Do you mind?" Cole asked Kerri.

"Not at all." She glanced across the room at Ryan. He lifted his glass and nodded back, mouthing something. Was it an apology for being detained?

She nodded back, tapping her foot to the beat. If he didn't get over here soon and ask her to dance, she might just have to ask him.

"DRINK, DRINK, DRINK," Brandon chanted when the waitress brought a third round of drinks for everyone at the table. Ryan accepted his gladly and downed half of it in one go. He hoped Kerri understood he'd rather be with her, but he appreciated the fact that his friends wanted to celebrate what they saw as his good fortune, even if he wasn't sure how he felt about the job in California—or if he would even be offered it.

"I'm going to find me a partner and get on that dance floor," Jacob announced. He nudged Kyle off the end of the bench seat and got out of the booth, heading off without looking back.

"Me, too. Lots of women here tonight," Kyle said.

"Kerri's all by herself," Brandon told Ryan. "Better grab her up before someone else does."

"Sounds like a good idea." But as he moved to stand, he noticed Russell Taylor heading in her direction with a purposeful look on his face. Russell had been a pain in the ass on the football team in high school who always showed up late for practice but always wanted to be first on the field on game day.

Ryan found himself on his feet and across the floor before he knew what he was doing.

"Let's dance," he said, taking Kerri's hand and tugging her toward the dance floor.

"Hey," Russell said, cutting them off. "I was just about to ask Kerri to dance."

"You're late. As usual," Ryan said, keeping going.

"What the hell is that supposed to mean?"

Ryan didn't give him another look. He led Kerri in between the other couples, leaving Russell sputtering behind them, took her in his arms and began to sway to the music. When he caught her raised eyebrow, he knew she wanted an explanation.

"Old enemy," he said. "Hope you don't mind dancing with me instead of Russell."

"I thought you'd never ask."

He tugged her closer, and she threaded her hands around his neck. As they swayed together, Ryan fought an urge to bury his face in her hair. Holding her reminded him of being with her this afternoon. He'd memorized every expression that had crossed her face when he'd moved inside her.

Couldn't wait to do it again.

"See? What did I tell you? You and Kerri are a thing," Jacob shouted, passing by them with Kelly Scheer in his arms. Kelly waved at them over Jacob's shoulder.

Ryan stiffened, but Kerri laughed. "The whole town is going to know about us now."

"Do you mind?"

"No. It's inevitable when you date in Chance Creek." She swayed with him a moment. "Sunshine and Cole tried to lend me money to pay my mom."

He could guess how that had gone. "They care about you."

"Looks like your friends care about you, too. Do they think you're taking the Sacramento job?" She nodded toward the booth where some of the firemen were still hanging out.

"I told them I haven't even gone for the interview yet. Jacob insisted on celebrating anyway. Any excuse to spend the night at the Boot." He realized Kerri was one of the few people in his life who took the time to listen to him. Cole did. Sunshine was a pretty good friend, too, but sometimes she was too busy trying to boss people around to hear everything they had to say. He drew Kerri closer until she rested her head against his chest. "I'm glad I found you."

She laughed. "I've been right here the whole time."

"I should have gotten with you sooner."

"Gotten with me?" She laughed again. "Why is it so hard for people to use the word *dating* anymore?"

"I don't mind using that word. Would you date me, Kerri Olsen?"

"Considering what we got up to this afternoon, I hope so."

He tightened his arms around her. "Good. And I don't care who knows it. In fact, I hope everyone does." He saw the surprise in her eyes and wondered at it. "Why shouldn't I want the world to know about the two of us?"

"Because you used to play football and I'm just… Kerri Olsen."

"Just Kerri Olsen? Don't sell yourself short, woman." She was heaven in his arms, and his body was letting him know it wanted to get her alone again. Soon.

"Whatever you say."

He stopped. Pulled back and made her meet his gaze. "You're amazing. You got that? There's no one I'd rather be dancing with tonight." He lowered his voice. "No one I want to be with more when we're through here." He wished he could say more. Wanted to tell her all the plans he was making for the life they could spend together, but he didn't want to scare her off. Instead, he tightened his arms around her again, and after that they simply danced until the song ended.

"Want to join me and my friends?" Ryan asked when it did.

"I'm here with Sunshine and Cole," Kerri told him.

"Ryan!" Brandon and Jacob grabbed his arms. "Time for another drink!"

Ryan smiled at Kerri apologetically. "I'll come get you for another dance in a little bit."

Knowing he had a long drive home ahead of him later, he managed to nurse a mug of beer through the next few rounds, toasting with his friends but not drinking deeply. Each time he saw Russell—or anyone else, for that matter—make a move toward Kerri, he crossed the bar, headed him off, gathered her in his arms and swayed with her on the dance floor.

Kerri didn't seem to be holding back on her alcohol consumption. Each time they danced, she was a little tipsier. Ryan had the feeling she was drinking to forget that for-sale sign on her yard. Or maybe to forget the way she'd felt after letting him get so close earlier in the day.

He reminded himself she'd been dancing with him all night. If she had any regrets about this afternoon, she would have blown him off the first time he asked. Being with him had stirred up something, though. When he decided he could get away with it, he shifted places and joined Kerri, Cole and Sunshine at their table, leaving his firefighter friends to entertain themselves.

Toward midnight, Cole stood up and helped Sunshine to her feet. "You'll see Kerri home, won't you? I've got to get Sunshine in bed before she falls asleep right here."

"Of course. Night."

"You behave yourself," Sunshine warned him. "Or don't, if Kerri doesn't want you to."

Kerri swatted her. "Get out of here." She slurred her words a little.

"Told you I was good at matchmaking."

When they were gone, Ryan meant to suggest one last dance before heading out themselves, but his friends swooped down on them and ushered them back to their booth on the other side of the room. Kerri joked good-humoredly with his crew and did her best to keep up with them as they continued to toast Ryan. By their last dance, he was having to steady her on her feet. Ryan could see the bartender was getting ready for last call. Time to get out of here.

"Let's go," he said, although he could dance with her all night. She was so soft and warm in his arms. Sexy, too. At some point she had begun pressing tiny kisses to the side and base of his neck whenever he had her in his arms. His body was happy to respond, which made it hard to keep his wits about him.

"Where're we going?" she asked.

"I'm taking you home." He took her arm and led her toward the door, stopping to grab her jacket and help her get it on.

"Let's stay," she slurred.

"Bar's closing. Come on. Is your truck here?"

She shook her head. "I walked over. Sunshine's giving me a ride home."

"I'm giving you that ride. Let's go." He led the way to his truck, got her tucked into the passenger seat and closed the door. When he got in on his side, she shook her head.

"I don't wanna be alone. It's too damn… lonely."

She was three sheets to the wind, Ryan thought, but her honesty struck a chord with him. He didn't want to be alone, either. Especially not after the afternoon they'd spent together.

"I'd be happy to stay with you if you like." He'd assumed that's what they were going to do anyway.

"Not at my place. No can do. No one allowed upstairs," she pronounced.

Ryan stilled. Was she quoting someone? Quoting Bess? Had that been a rule she had to follow growing up?

He'd certainly never been upstairs at the house. Had anyone outside of Kerri's family?

Suddenly her reaction that afternoon made more sense. Bess had always seemed so cheerful and friendly when he was a kid, so he'd never had the feeling she was ashamed of her collections, but Kerri's body language had always been different. Stiff and wary, ready to attack the moment he made a negative comment. Was that because Bess was different behind closed doors?

Ashamed of herself? Ashamed of her house?

He'd been making inroads into that house as he'd

grown closer to Kerri, and today she'd let down her guard while he made love to her. In the aftermath, she'd panicked—

Panic. That was the emotion he'd seen in her eyes the first time they kissed on her front doorstep. That night she'd been as hungry for him as he was for her until she'd gone to open the door and remembered what was on the other side.

No wonder she'd drunk herself silly tonight. She'd broken all the rules today, hadn't she? All the ones she could stand to break. Letting him upstairs had been a bridge too far.

Wanting to spare her any more pain, he said, "I'd be happy to have you spend the night at my place."

"Your place?" she repeated drunkenly. "That's a good idea. You always come to my house, but I've never been to yours."

"You've been to the tree farm." He started the engine, relieved he'd found a solution.

"Never seen where you live," she repeated. "Probably in a cave," she added sleepily. "Underground. Like a bat."

He chuckled. "I'd be happy to show you where I live." He had nothing to hide, after all. Maybe the cabin was spartan and old-fashioned, but no one expected a bachelor like him to be an interior decorator.

Kerri fell asleep almost instantly as soon as they got moving. Ryan turned on the radio to keep himself company for the drive home, negotiating the roads carefully, although he'd switched to water more than an hour before they left the bar. When he finally pulled in and parked at the cabin, she woke up.

"Where are we?" she asked groggily.

"My place. Remember? You wanted to see it?"

She turned a sleepy, accusing gaze on him. "Trying to get me in bed," she murmured.

"You know it." If they did sleep together tonight, that's all they'd be doing, though—sleeping. No matter what they'd done earlier, he wasn't going to take advantage of Kerri when she was like this.

It took some doing to get her out of the car to the front door, then hold her upright while he opened it. Maple streaked out and disappeared into the gloom. Ryan let her, knowing she'd be back soon.

Inside, he settled Kerri on the couch, making sure she was comfortable. He went back to whistle Maple inside and shut the door before helping Kerri out of her high heels.

"Do you really like me?" she murmured when he tucked her under a blanket.

"Yes, I do." He smoothed her hair and brushed a kiss over her mouth, wishing he could do a hell of a lot more, but she'd drunk too much and he was a little worried that the cold night air hadn't sobered her up any.

Someone had to be sensible.

Even if it killed him.

KERRI WOKE UP in an unfamiliar bed, her head pounding and her mouth as dry as cotton. Squinting against the early morning light that illuminated the room she found herself in, she decided she had to be in Ryan's cabin, given the vague memory she had of asking him about it. Its knotty pine walls shone golden in the bright sunshine streaming through large windows, but a very plain nightstand and a large chest were the only other pieces of furniture. The bed had been made up with white sheets, a plaid blanket and a hand-stitched quilt. The effect was spartan but lovely in its own way.

Sliding out from underneath the covers, she spotted the dress she'd worn last night lying in a crumpled ball nearby. She couldn't see her parka anywhere. Dragging the covers with her as she went, she crossed the room and pulled open the closet door. Inside were tough canvas pants, plain work shirts and jackets that could withstand the wear of carrying trees around all day.

There were a couple of hoodies hung up on one side, and she selected a thick black one, relishing its warmth when she pulled it on. She fished out a pair of sweatpants that were far too large for her and put them on as well, rolling up the legs as best she could. When she felt along the shelf above the clothing rod, her fingers closed around a pair of socks. Kerri pulled them on gratefully. It was December in Chance Creek, and the cabin floor was freezing under her bare feet.

There was no mirror to be found, so she smoothed her hair as best she could before she opened the door and found Maple sitting right outside. The dog thumped her tail in a hello. Kerri gave her an affectionate pat before moving past her into the living room. Ryan was asleep on the couch, his feet hanging off the edge a little, fully dressed under a blanket. The living room was sparsely furnished, too. Just the couch and an easy chair on a wide plank floor. A lamp or two. There were some old books on the bookshelf and a single, pretty vase. A handmade rag rug covered the floor in front of the sink in the tiny kitchenette.

She ducked into the bathroom and freshened up as much as she could. Back in the main room, she tiptoed past Ryan's sleeping form and opened a cupboard, Maple following gamely along.

Inside were four mugs, four plates and four bowls. The silverware drawer held four each of knives, forks and spoons. All were a little old-fashioned, as if someone had bought a starter set in the fifties or sixties and never added to or replaced it.

At least Maple had dishes for water and food, plain metal bowls that were each partially filled.

Needing caffeine desperately, Kerri searched for coffee, but all she found was a can of instant stuff. Her mind raced as she made two cups. Was Ryan oblivious to creature comforts? What about his grandfather? Surely he could have afforded a luxury or two.

Kerri sighed and set the kettle to boil, spooning some of coffee powder into the plain gray mugs, which reminded her of the bowls her mother had crowed about.

Was Ryan a minimalist?

The kettle clicked off. Ryan stirred as Kerri poured the boiling water into the mugs.

He groaned, and Maple trotted over to investigate, sitting down beside the couch and licking his hand. Kerri leaned back against the counter.

"Good morning," she said. "You know this is an abomination, don't you?" She held up the instant coffee.

He rubbed the sleep from his eyes, peered at what she was holding and chuckled. "That's just for emergencies. I have coffee at the firehouse most days. Or I go to Orchards or Linda's Diner. I've been meaning to get a coffee maker. Just haven't gotten around to it."

Kerri relaxed a little—but not too much. You didn't live with so few possessions because it slipped your mind to buy them. Still, the sight of Ryan waking up, hair and clothes rumpled, made her smile. She wanted to slide under that blanket of his and see if a second encounter with him would be as nice as the first.

He pushed the blanket aside, stood up, made his way to the kitchen, rested his forearms on the counter and his forehead against the cupboards, closing his eyes like he was trying to sleep a little more standing up.

"This for me?" he asked when he spotted the second cup.

"That's for you."

"Thanks." He reached for it, took a sip, gave an appreciative groan and straightened. "That's what I needed." He rubbed a hand through his hair until it stood nearly on end.

Not a morning person, obviously. Kerri thought mornings were the best part of the day. As long as she got her coffee.

He took another sip. Made a face. "How about I drive you into town and we grab something better than this at Orchards?" He set the cup of coffee down again.

Kerri looked down at the clothes she was wearing. "Only if we can swing by my house so I can change."

That woke him up. He let his gaze slowly run down her body.

"I like your outfit." He grinned. "That stuff looks better on you than it does on me."

She doubted that. "I wasn't wearing much when I woke up." She couldn't remember if they'd gotten up to anything last night.

He frowned. "You were wearing a dress when I carried you into the bedroom."

"Carried me?"

"Had you sleeping on the couch until I made sure you were all right. I transferred you in there around two in the morning."

"Sorry to keep you up so late." He'd watched her sleep? That was embarrassing. And sweet, too.

"Glad to do it." His voice was warm and deep and wrapped around her like a soft blanket. "Soon as I got you settled in bed, I took over the couch and was out like a light. During my time with the Marines, I learned to sleep when I could."

"I bet." So she'd squirmed out of her dress on her own sometime during the night. Now she thought about it, she had a shadowy memory of doing just that. "Sounds like I wasn't a very fun date."

"You were fun." He tousled her hair affectionately,

and she thought she had to be positively glowing. She was fun? Good. "Glad you remember the dating part."

"Hm?" She'd just taken another sip of the awful coffee.

"We established last night that we're together—officially," he said as seriously as a schoolgirl.

Kerri had to smile. "I like that. Being official," she told him. She liked it a lot, especially after everything that had happened. Her weird reaction after they'd been together yesterday hadn't frightened him off.

"Good. Give me a minute and we'll go," Ryan said, heading for the bedroom. "We'll stop by your house to change on the way."

Ten minutes later she sat in the truck with Maple draped over her lap while Ryan started the engine. He seemed more alert now that he'd taken a lightning-quick shower and gotten dressed. She was still wearing his clothes under her jacket, glad not to have to shiver all the way home in her dress. She played mindlessly with Maple's fur.

"What do you do if you have company?" she asked.

"Company?" Ryan repeated as if it was a foreign concept. His gaze flickered over to her in the passenger seat, then quickly back to the road.

"You only have enough dishes for four and you don't even have a table. Didn't your grandfather live with you before he passed away?"

"Grandpa John wasn't much for entertaining. Not exactly a people person."

Kerri remembered the older Mr. Miller as being taciturn but not unfriendly.

"He never had anyone over?"

"No. He liked to grab a meal at Linda's Diner on Wednesday nights. He'd chat with a few of the other old-timers then. Saw plenty of people when he delivered their trees."

"He had an auto shop in town. He must have known lots of people."

"Sure. Knew them and liked them. Just didn't feel the need to feed them."

Ryan seemed uncomfortable with her line of questioning. Kerri knew what that was like. While Bess was alive, she'd hated it when people asked personal questions about their living arrangements. It was only slightly better now that Bess was gone. Still, Kerri was compelled to ask, "What about you? You have friends. The firefighters and the Mountain Men."

Ryan shrugged. "I see the Mountain Men in town. Same with the guys at the station. We hang out at the Boot or grab some food at one of the restaurants. I haven't hosted any dinner parties—yet. Guess that's going to change. I don't know how I'll fit everyone at the Christmas party I'm supposed to have. There won't just be the Mountain Men there; I'm supposed to invite other people, too. Make it a real party. My cabin isn't all that big."

"You never thought about updating it? I mean, don't get me wrong, it's really cute. It's just like stepping back into the sixties inside."

"Grandpa John liked it that way."

Now he sounded defensive.

"Was he a minimalist?" Kerri asked.

"Definitely not, and neither am I," Ryan said. "Grandpa John just liked to have things exactly the way Lily left them. Lily was my grandmother," he explained. "She died in childbirth, having my dad. Grandpa John raised my dad alone."

"And he kept the house exactly the way it was when Lily died?"

"That's right." Ryan pulled into her driveway and turned off the truck. "Go change. I'm starving."

CHAPTER 11

I F Ryan hoped that would be the end of the questions, he was wrong. Kerri stayed where she was. "Do you plan to keep it that way?" She looked for all the world like she was ready to take up residence in his front seat if that's what it took to get him to answer.

"Guess I still feel like it's my grandfather's house," Ryan admitted.

"Don't you think it was strange for him not to add anything to it for half a century?"

"Grandpa John never stopped missing his wife. You ought to understand that if anyone can. Look at Bess."

"We're not talking about Bess."

Maple whined, turning in a circle in the small space between the passenger seat and the dashboard, stepping all over Kerri's feet, the rising tension between them making her anxious.

"Sure we are. Bess collected things that reminded her of the people she'd lost. Trains because of her brother. Kitchen stuff because of her mother." He took in Kerri's surprised look. "She told me her mother was a wonderful cook and that her happiest times were spent in the kitchen learning at her knee."

"I didn't know you knew that."

"Bess was a little like the grandmother I never had," he told her. "That's why I loved delivering your tree every year."

Kerri took that in.

"Who did the outdoor gear remind her of?" Ryan asked.

"Her grandfather," Kerri said automatically. "I think he was a hero in her eyes. So strong and tough and afraid of nothing." She thought a moment. "The music is for her aunt Irene, who had an extraordinary singing voice. The cats were for all the cats she was never able to have since she was allergic to them. I guess she really wished she could have one."

"I think my grandfather was afraid he'd forget Lily if he moved on." Ryan let his gaze travel over Bess's house. "Thing was, he kind of forgot about everyone else. I imagine my dad was pretty lonely growing up. He and my mom married young. Had me right away. They died in an accident when I was seven." He thought a moment. "I guess in a way, I understand my grandfather. I have memories of Mom and Dad, but the older I get the more I second-guess if those memories are real or not."

"Your grandfather raised you after they were gone, right?" Kerri asked.

He could feel her sympathetic gaze on him. "That's right. Did a fine job. It was just… kind of quiet at the cabin. I liked it when Christmas came around and there were people everywhere in town. Parties to go to at my friends' houses. Trees to deliver to happy customers."

"Like Bess."

"Like Bess. She always made us come in and have some cookies, even though my grandfather tried to get out of it. He had nothing against Bess. Just preferred to be in his own head with his memories."

Ryan swallowed against the pain that welled up inside him when he thought about the silences that characterized his childhood. He'd always known he was safe and loved, and he'd always appreciated the order and simplicity of life with his grandfather. When he got up in the morning, he knew there'd be oatmeal on the table. His clothes would be clean. His backpack by the door. Any forms to be signed for school would be signed. There were no surprises. Nothing left undone.

There'd never been much talking, though.

Bess must have known that. Whenever their paths crossed, she'd enveloped Ryan in a hug and chatted his ears off, asking him questions and then more questions about his answers. She'd drawn him out in a way his grandfather never did.

"I think Bess knew Grandpa John had little to say, so she pumped me for every bit of information she could get. I liked it. All my friends complained about their relatives grilling them when they visited. When Bess did it to me, it made me feel... normal." He was beginning to understand why Kerri had run up the stairs yesterday after they'd been together. Talking about his past left him feeling exposed.

He didn't like that feeling.

"Bess had a good heart. She really cared about people. I remember the way she always hugged you. I sometimes wondered if she wished she had more grandkids. She probably did."

"You were always there when we delivered the trees, but usually you kept to yourself." Except that one time she'd got angry with him.

"We never talked at school," Kerri reminded him. "I figured you wouldn't want to talk at my house, either. You were always so popular."

He'd made up for the quiet at home by being as involved as possible out in the world. Kerri had kept more to herself. "Were you lonely?" he asked, feeling like he'd stepped out on a tightwire strung between two cliffs. He wasn't one to quiz people about their feelings.

"I guess I was—for different reasons than you. I had Bess and my group of friends. I didn't have a father, though. That made me feel like an outsider. When my mom took off when I was fourteen, I felt like I had even more to hide. Then there were Bess's collections, which have always been a kind of open secret. I know everyone knows about them, and I know they wonder about them. Bess did her best to keep the front hall clear so we weren't embarrassed to open the door, but any time someone stepped into the house growing up, I felt... shame, I guess. I did my best to avoid that happening. The only problem is, no matter what the reason, when you never invite people to your house, they assume you don't really like them. At least, that's what girls think."

His heart squeezed for her. Now that she'd put the feeling into words, Ryan realized he'd experienced a mild form of that shame. He spent plenty of time at friends' houses growing up and never invited anyone home, either. What would he have done with them in the cabin where there was no place to sit and watch TV, no video game consoles, no rec room—or even snacks to serve? Thankfully the tree farm was so far out of town he'd hardly ever been questioned about his lack of invitations, but the sense that there was something to hide at home—he knew that well.

"Grandpa John hasn't been gone long enough for me to put much time into thinking about updating the cabin," he admitted. "I know I should, but I don't know where to start. It feels... wrong, somehow." Even if he had brought in the coffee table.

"It took my mom threatening me before I tackled Bess's stuff. I'm not sure why I got paralyzed. I guess..." She thought it through. "I guess I felt like your grandfather did about Lily. Like if I changed things, I'd have to admit I've really lost her." She explained how she'd taken photographs of each item before letting it go. "I guess I hope it's a healthier way to preserve Bess's memory."

"Sounds like a really good idea," Ryan said. Maybe he could do something similar. Document everything in the cabin as it stood now. Write down memories of his life with his grandfather and the stories Grandpa John had passed down to him.

Kerri checked the time. "It's getting late. I'll be as fast as I can getting changed."

An hour later, after a quick stop at Orchards, where a decorated Christmas tree now stood in the front window, Ryan dropped Kerri off at her shop and drove back home. He didn't have to open the tree lot until eleven, which meant he had time. Inside the cabin, he looked around with fresh eyes, trying to see it the way Kerri had. It was a homey space; nothing wrong with it, really. It was simply a little... faded.

She'd mentioned there was no table, and Ryan realized that if Kerri stayed overnight again, it would be nice to have a place to serve her breakfast. He had just the thing stored in his workshop.

He stopped himself halfway to the door, pulled out his phone and walked through the house, documenting every room exactly as it was now, the way his grandfather had left it, taking his time to do a thorough job.

When he was satisfied, he went out to the shop, moved things around and found the table he was looking for. It was smaller than the one he'd given to Kerri, made for a breakfast nook or some similarly constrained space. Inside the house, it fit near the kitchenette, forming a natural second counter, which would make it easier to prepare meals.

Now that he'd started, he remembered more pieces of furniture that could spruce up the place. It took several trips out to the workshop to bring in everything he wanted. He replaced his grandfather's lamps with ones he had made, with wood bases carved with forest animals. He put a dresser in the bedroom. An entertainment cabinet in the living room. He put up a series of drawings he'd made in high school art, a required class he had secretly enjoyed despite complaining alongside his friends about having to attend it. He'd done them in the style of a botanist's sketchbook, drawing one of each type of tree they sold on the farm and labelling each of them carefully in black ink.

He had also made things for the kitchen. A spice organizer, a framed magnetic strip to hang his knives on, a couple of cutting boards big enough to make a pizza on. He kept telling himself he wasn't being foolish for bringing it all out, even if he ended up taking the job in Sacramento and having to move in a few months.

When he was done, he decided the cabin's transformation made it all worth it. It looked like a home.

Almost.

He turned around in the living room slowly. Something was still missing, but he couldn't figure out what it was. There was a gap near the window that needed something. What?

When it finally came to him, the answer made him laugh.

A Christmas tree.

WHEN ROSE JOHNSON came through the door of Kerri's Collectibles, Kerri was rearranging a clothing display, pulling all her vintage holiday party clothing to the front where the pieces would be easy to see. It had been a busy day, and she'd made a number of sales, which had put her in a good mood. Her hangover had dissipated, and she'd been humming along with the holiday music playing when the bells over the door rang, indicating she had a customer.

"Hi, Rose. How's business?" she asked. Rose was a petite woman with dark hair and blue eyes who was married to the county sheriff. She ran the jewelry store in town, sharing a space with Mia Matheson, a wedding planner. The two women always seemed to be having such a good time whenever she stopped by. Just like Sunshine and Emma. Sometimes she wished she had a partner like that.

"Pretty good! Your store looks fabulous, as always. I love your decorations."

"I have Bess to thank for them." Her grandmother had accumulated decorations over the years, but her collections had made it difficult to decorate much more than the exterior and front hall of the house. Kerri had absconded with the leftovers when she took over the store and loved to put them up each year. It had been easy enough to do so during working hours these past few days, but she'd done nothing with the house, even though the first-floor rooms were accessible now. She'd have to change that.

She noticed Rose scanning the showroom.

"Can I help you find something in particular?"

"I thought you'd have trees."

"I have a few back here." Kerri showed her a set of bottlebrush trees meant to go on a tabletop display.

"I mean real trees like the one you gave to George Metcalf and Mrs. Fisher."

Kerri smiled at how word had gotten around. Everyone knew everyone's business in Chance Creek. "Those were one-offs I made because someone asked me to. I don't have them for sale."

"Really? That's too bad. They're so original. I was sure you'd be making and selling more of them at your store."

"It never even occurred to me," Kerri said honestly. "The other day I helped a bunch of customers make ornaments out of things they bought here, though."

Rose joined her at the counter. "I don't have time for a do-it-yourself project. Could you make a jewelry-themed one for my store? You wouldn't believe how many people get engaged this time of year. I'm hosting an open house next weekend. Could you deliver a tree to me by Friday?"

"What a fun idea. I'd love to create a jewelry-themed tree for you." Kerri had a whole room of jewelry she could choose from. She wouldn't give away anything of value, of course, but just about everything Bess had collected was costume jewelry, and there was probably enough for a dozen trees.

In fact, maybe this time she wouldn't give the whole collection away at once. Maybe she'd split up the costume jewelry and create as many trees as possible. She could do a large one for Rose and several small ones to sell here in the store. She didn't think Bess would mind that at all. In fact, it would have made her smile to see the women of Chance Creek decorating their trees with her treasures.

"Really?" Rose beamed.

"Of course. I'll deliver it Friday morning, just like you asked," she promised. "You wouldn't mind if I made more than one and sold the others, would you?"

"Of course not," Rose said. "I assumed you'd be doing that already. I think they'd go like hotcakes."

Kerri was already thinking about the other rooms in Bess's house she hadn't cleaned out yet. "I really enjoy making the trees," she confessed. "I like seeing people's reactions to them."

"I bet. Make sure you charge me what it's worth." Rose waved Kerri's protests away. "I know you gave the ones to Charlie and Mrs. Fisher as gifts, but you can't keep doing that. You're a businesswoman, Kerri, and you've got bills to pay. Chance Creek is special because of its one-of-a-kind boutiques like yours."

Connie had said something similar. Kerri hadn't ever thought about her business making Chance Creek special. "I guess you're right. I'll see you Friday," she added.

"See you then. I can't wait!"

As soon as Rose left, Kerri called Ryan about ordering more trees. She could hear people laughing and calling to each other in the distance. It sounded like he was having a busy day on the tree lot.

"Hey, Kerri."

"I need another tree. Several of them, actually." She told him about Rose's visit.

"Sounds like a great idea to sell some of your creations. People are talking about them all over town."

"Are they?"

"Definitely. Tell you what," he continued. "Why don't I come get you when you close the store for the day? I'll run you up the mountain so you can pick out the trees you want and then I'll bring you back into town and we can grab some dinner."

"That's a lot of driving for you. Besides, Rose doesn't want her tree delivered until next Friday."

"But you'll want to get started on the ones for your store right away, won't you? People are buying Christmas trees now."

"I guess."

"I do that drive all the time. I don't mind it one bit. Let's get those trees, then let me take you to DelMonaco's. We're dating, remember? We need to go on dates."

"Okay. DelMonaco's sounds perfect."

"Great. See you in a few hours," Ryan said.

RYAN SHUT DOWN the lot promptly at five and shrugged into the button-up shirt he normally reserved for wearing to events at the firehouse. If Jacob saw him, he'd probably never let him hear the end of it, especially if he knew Ryan was dressing up for Kerri, but he didn't care. She was worth it.

When he stepped into Kerri's Collectables and she was nowhere to be seen, he assumed she was in the back room. He wandered the store until he found a shelf unit stacked high with dishes. The dish sets weren't very interesting, but he found a handmade mug with a mountain design etched into it that he liked. He wondered who had made it and what their story was.

Kerri would know.

"Hi, Ryan." Kerri emerged from the back room. She was wearing an oversize sweater over jeans. Her hair was tucked up into a messy bun, tendrils coming free. He had a strong urge to release that hair and watch it tumble around her shoulders, but he restrained himself.

Barely.

"Hi, yourself." He lifted the mug and gestured to the others on the shelf. "I'm thinking about buying this."

Kerri's smile broadened. "Hang on." She hurried off into the back room and emerged a moment later with another mug, almost identical in style to the one he was holding. Hers was decorated with a tree, with two red cardinals flying above it.

"I saw this today and it reminded me of you, so I set it aside. It's made by the same woman who made the one you're holding."

"I'll take both. They can be our lucky coffee mugs when you're at my place."

"I hope they're lucky enough to contain some decent coffee next time I'm there." She softened the quip with a smile.

"They will be," he promised, then leaned in and brushed a kiss across her cheek. "Can't wait to get you at my place again."

"I can't wait either." She ducked away when he went

for another kiss, though, wrapped the mugs in tissue paper and put them in a bag.

"You're not ringing them up," he pointed out.

"They're a gift. I owe you for three Christmas trees."

He considered that. "Fine. I'll let you get away with that this time. But don't think I'm taking any more handouts."

"It would be too bad if you didn't, because I have something else for you." She reached under the counter and pulled out a tin. Snowball cookies. She slid them across to him, then walked over to grab her jacket and keys.

Ryan cracked the tin open and took a deep breath. "Oh, that smells good. You know what I like, don't you?"

They shared a look as she returned. "Do I?" she said sweetly.

"You know you do," he growled. He leaned over the counter and stole a kiss.

When he pulled back again, she came out from behind it, and they made their way to the door.

"I packed a lot of cookies in there," Kerri told him. "Make sure to share them with your friends."

"Hell, no. Let them get their own damn cookies," Ryan said. If he brought them to the station, they'd be gone in a matter of minutes. Same if he shared them with the Mountain Men.

In his truck, they took their usual positions, Ryan in the driver's seat, Kerri in the passenger side, Maple laid out on top of her like she was a lap dog and not an oversized furry beast.

Kerri nudged her toe against a tiny red cooler at her feet. "What's this?" she asked.

"It's a secret," Ryan said.

She grinned. "Is that right?"

"Yep."

She scratched the scruff of fur on Maple's neck. "You'll tell me what it is, won't you, girl?"

"Don't you try to turn my dog against me," Ryan objected. He turned on the radio, and they were quiet the rest of the way out to King's Mountain. When they got to the tree farm, he drove the truck right out to the lot and turned on the tiny Christmas lights he'd strung around the sales area and through the tree lots.

"It's beautiful up here at night." Kerri turned in a circle to take it all in. "I can't believe you've been keeping this all to yourself."

"You could have come here any time over the years."

"Bess always ordered a tree and trusted you'd pick a good one for her. If I'd known it was so pretty up here, I'd have made her let me come and pick them out myself."

"Go ahead and look around a little. I'll be back in a minute," Ryan directed and then took the tiny cooler into the shed, where there was running water and a two-burner electric stovetop. In earlier years, his grandfather had run a concession stand out of the building, serving hot chocolate and treats he bought in town. Ryan rinsed out the two matching mugs he'd just acquired and made hot chocolate with real milk and whipped cream he pulled from the cooler. Coming back out into the cold, he stopped short when he saw that Kerri was lying down in the snow, making an angel.

When she stood up and brushed herself off, Ryan handed over her mug of hot chocolate. "How many trees do you need?"

"I'm thinking four little ones. If they sell, I can get more."

"All right. Drink up, then we'll get to work."

They savored their hot chocolate but didn't linger over it, since the evening was cold. When they were done, he ducked back into the shed, set the mugs on the counter and returned with two bow saws. "Here's the deal. Each of us finds two trees. Whoever makes it back with them first wins."

"You're on."

He handed her a saw, and she tucked it under her arm, put two fingers in her mouth and whistled like a referee to start the contest, then dashed off into the woods. Maple leaped after her.

Ryan didn't mind she'd stolen his dog. He knew where the perfect little trees stood, and he set off toward them at a determined pace, leaving the glow of the string lights behind. When he found a nicely shaped three-foot spruce, he sawed through the trunk and set it aside, looking for another one.

It took him longer than he'd expected to settle on the next one, but he finally located a sweet little white fir. He had just bent down to set the saw against its trunk when something hit him hard between the shoulder blades.

A snowball.

Ryan whirled around, but Kerri was nowhere to be seen.

He quickly scooped up enough of the white stuff to make a snowball of his own and went to look for her. He heard the crunch of shoes in snow and saw a flash of icy-blue jacket out of the corner of his eye. Ryan ducked. This time her missile sailed past him.

"Missed!" Quick as a wink, he straightened and hurled a snowball back at her. He heard a distant thud. Maple barked, confirming a hit. He jogged in the direction of the sound. Another snowball whistled past his ear.

"Missed again!" He scooped up more snow. The forest was perfectly silent as he ducked behind a row of trees, crept along in the shadows and peered into the dark. A snowball hit the top of his head.

"Got you!" Kerri cried from behind him.

Ryan whirled around to see her smirking, two small trees leaned up against a larger one, the bow saw he'd given her resting against them.

"How did you cut those down so fast?"

"I've got skills." She shrugged.

He moved closer. "Where are your gloves?"

"Didn't want to get sap all over them."

"Your fingers are going to freeze. Come here."

When she did so, he drew off his gloves and took

her hands in his, chafing them to warm them. She looked so beautiful in the soft glow of the Christmas lights, her face tipped toward him. He drew her closer and lifted one hand to cup her cheek. Slowly, he leaned in to kiss her.

KERRI WAS BREATHLESS when they finally broke apart. The night was magical. The lights strung between the trees, the bird houses dotted around—it was all so beautiful it made her heart hurt. How could they possibly recreate this in Sacramento? There wouldn't even be snow for Christmas there.

She couldn't shake the feeling that whatever she was building here with Ryan possessed an expiration date that would come due as soon as they left Chance Creek County. She knew that was silly. Love should transcend any hardship.

But she knew that wasn't always the case.

They chose the last small tree together and carried all four of them to the truck. Whenever he got the chance, Ryan slid one of her hands in his pocket, lacing his fingers through hers, and her fears about the future calmed a little. After Ryan fetched the mugs and hot chocolate supplies, they loaded up the truck. When Kerri went to get into the cab, Ryan stopped her.

"I just need to give Maple some food at the cabin before we go. It's not far. Let's walk." Maple's ears perked up and she barked once.

The path through the woods was full of shadows, but it was easy to follow. Just a minute or two later, they arrived at the little house. All the way there, Maple darted forward and circled back to urge them on. Now she whined to be let in.

Ryan opened the door, turned on the lights and gestured Kerri inside. If she'd been surprised by the tree lot, she was blown away by the transformation that had taken place since the last time she was here.

Gone was the sparse cabin. In its place was a perfectly decorated woodland cottage. More furniture had been brought in, similar in design to the dining table. Had Ryan made all of it?

There was a shoe rack by the door now. Kerri slipped off her boots and put them away, then walked around the cabin in awe, reaching out to run her fingers along the bookshelves. She examined the art on the wall.

She turned around to look at Ryan. "What inspired all this?" She swept out a hand to include everything.

He shrugged. "You did." He led her over to the couch, and they sat down. "I remembered what you said about documenting Bess's things before letting them go. I photographed the cabin as it was, and that made it all right to try something new."

"You made all this furniture?"

He nodded. "When I was a teenager. I didn't have the cabin in mind when I made most of it, so there's a lot more where this comes from in my shed."

"Where did you design it to go?"

"In the house I wanted to own when I grew up. I made plans and everything."

"I'd love to see those."

Ryan stiffened, only for a moment, but Kerri spent so much time watching him these days she caught it instantly.

He seemed to be thinking over her request. In the end he nodded and held out his hand. When she took it, he led her into his bedroom and gestured for her to take a seat on his bed. He moved to the trunk at the end of it, opened it up and fished around inside.

"Grandpa gave me this trunk when I first moved in, so I had a place to put my stuff. It was hard enough to let me take over this room, but he was adamant that the main part of the cabin couldn't change at all."

Kerri ached for the little boy he'd been, trying to keep himself hidden away so as not to disturb his grandfather's memories. Surely his refusal to change anything was just as bad as Bess's tendency to keep everything?

Ryan brought a sketchbook with him when he joined her on the bed. Kerri was curious to see what was in it, but as he took his seat, he ran his fingers over the quilt.

"Mom made this just a few months before she and my dad were hit by a drunk driver. This is the biggest change Grandpa John allowed me to make to the decor in here when I came to live with him. He didn't have much choice," Ryan added. "I refused to sleep unless it was on my bed."

"Did he save any of their things for you? What about photo albums and things like that?"

Ryan looked thoughtful. "I bet there are a few of those somewhere around here. I haven't gotten around to looking for them. Haven't sorted through my grandfather's clothes or personal items in his bedroom, either."

"I can help with that, when you're ready, if you like." For a woman who collected so many things, Bess hadn't possessed much when it came to items that were truly personal. Kerri had gone through her closet, donated her clothing and sorted through the things in the medicine cabinet soon after her death. It had been a very emotional day, and she would have loved to have company through it. She was sure Sunshine would have been glad to help, but that would have meant letting her upstairs.

"Thanks."

She touched the quilt. "Your mother must have put a lot of work into this." At least he had one memento of her. She didn't have much to remind her of her own mother.

Who was still alive, she told herself sternly. She could pick up the phone and call Sylvie any time. Ryan didn't have that luxury with his folks.

"I've been thinking about how I'll feel taking it to California," Ryan said. "It feels like it belongs here in Chance Creek, you know?"

"It belongs with *you*," Kerri said firmly. She couldn't do much, but at least she could tell him what she was pretty sure his mother would say if she was here. "Show me your house plans."

He opened the sketchbook and paged through it, passing drawing after drawing of furniture. He must have sketched his designs before creating them in real life. Interspersed among them were landscapes she recognized from outside town and a few animal sketches.

When he opened the book to a set of house plans, it took her only a moment to realize why the layout was so familiar.

"That's… my house," she said, tracing a finger over the lines of the drawing.

"Your house seemed like the best place in the world when I was a kid."

Kerri's breath caught in her throat. She'd never realized how important his visits were to him, but now she imagined them from his point of view. Being the object of Bess's attention must have felt like being wrapped in a warm quilt to a boy without a mother or grandmother of his own. Those visits had been so fleeting, but so important—

"I'm not after you for your house, though," he said roughly. "That's not what this is about—you and me."

"I know," Kerri assured him. She did know, although she wondered if subconsciously that's what had attracted him to her in the first place. Still, the way he made love to her left her sure she was the main attraction now.

"I don't want you to mother me like Bess did."

"I know." She understood his attachment to the place, though. And why he'd been so eager to give her his table and chairs. They'd been designed for her house.

"I've got a lot of furniture in my shed," he said, and she knew he was trying to keep the conversation on even ground. "When I finished making enough for my dream house, I kept going."

"I'm glad. The things you make are beautiful. Your parents would be proud."

He nodded, then shifted, as if the moment had become too much. "Don't know what to do with it all. I can't fit it in the cabin. No way I can bring it all to Sacramento, either. I'll have to give it away to the guys at the firehouse or something if I leave."

"Or you could sell it. It's beautiful, Ryan. You could make some real money off the pieces you don't want to keep."

"You think?"

"I do. I could sell it at my shop if you want." She was sure it would pull in customers, which would help her business, too.

Suddenly the need to find thirty grand pressed down on her so hard she found it difficult to breathe. Not only did she love her house, but also Ryan loved it, too. She couldn't lose something so important to both of them.

"That would be great," Ryan said.

Kerri pushed down the panic threatening to overwhelm her. She still had time. "We could load up a few pieces now. Give it a try."

"That sounds like a good plan."

CHAPTER 12

B Y THE TIME he'd brought the truck around and they'd loaded three or four pieces of furniture into it, Ryan's stomach was rumbling, but he was reluctant to leave the quiet mountainside where he got Kerri to himself. She was beautiful, and very kissable, but she was more than that. She understood him in a way no one else ever had.

Except Bess, maybe.

He could be himself in a way he wasn't around other people. He couldn't imagine showing those house plans to Cole, for example. Or Jacob.

Especially not Jacob.

"That's all for now," he said as he snapped the tailgate into place.

Kerri looked around one last time. "It really is beautiful here. It's almost a shame to head back to town."

"We don't have to," Ryan said. "I can rustle us up some food, and we can have a quiet night right here." Up on the mountain, he felt like they were far away from their problems.

"I'd like that," Kerri said softly.

He came to stand beside her and slid an arm around her waist, tucking her against him. They stood that way in silence for a few moments, drinking it all in until it became too much for Ryan. He leaned down and kissed her, lingering this time, enjoying the taste of her and the softness of her mouth beneath his. Back in school, Kerri had always seemed timid, but she met his kisses boldly, as if wondering what had taken him so long to get around to them.

Her eyes were shining in the soft starlight filtering down between the trees when he pulled away.

"Come inside. I'll get dinner on."

In the cabin, Maple getting underfoot, Ryan told Kerri to sit down while he cooked, since there wasn't much room in the tiny kitchen. He took some pasta and sauce out of the cupboard and some ground beef out of the fridge and set to work.

"Did you know your father?" he asked as he shaped some meatballs. It was a question that had been nagging at him. How could anyone abandon someone as wonderful as Kerri?

She didn't answer right away.

"You can tell me to mind my own business," he assured her over his shoulder.

"It's a fair question," she said. "It's just a little embarrassing to admit that my mom was spending time with someone completely inappropriate. My dad was married," she explained. "Mom gave him the option of being involved, but he didn't want to break up his family over something that was just supposed to be a little fun on the side." Kerri sighed. "I think the two of them were simply careless. She didn't mean to get pregnant, and neither did he. Once she was, she wanted to see it through, and he didn't. It's that simple."

"Nothing is that simple. Did you ever try to get in touch with him?" He couldn't imagine having a father in the world he didn't know.

"I thought about it a lot when I was a teenager, especially when Mom moved to California. A lot," she repeated, smiling a little. "I had all the fantasies about my dad turning out to be this wonderful guy who'd dote on me. Mom meant well, but like I said, she was too busy working to spend much time with me. And then she left."

"Was that when you thought about tracking him down?"

Kerri nodded. "A few years later. I finally talked to Bess about it. She wanted me to make up my own mind, but she said something I've never forgotten. She said, 'Family is made from the people who share their stories with you. The people who show up again and again.' I thought that over for the whole summer I was seventeen, and I watched who showed up. And who didn't." She looked down at the ground. "It's funny. There were several people in my life I almost hadn't noticed before. People who weren't flashy or forward but who were always there when I needed them. Then there were the ones who always had some exciting drama happening. I realized I spent a lot more time thinking about those exciting people than they did thinking about me."

She cut off, and Ryan wondered where her thoughts had gone.

"My dad never showed up," she finally said. "Not once. He never even sent a birthday card or a Christmas present. Why would I want someone like that in my life? In the end it wasn't hard at all to let go of the idea of contacting him."

Ryan nodded. He guessed he could understand that.

"What was a lot more difficult was trying to figure out where my mom fit in. Like I said, she did her best. When I was little, we drew together. She'd design the kind of wares she wanted to sell in her store, simple things with clean lines. I'd draw the most vibrant things I could think of. Fields of sunflowers. Rainbows and bluebirds and tulips." Kerri laughed. "Poor Mom. I wanted to swim in Chance Creek, hunt for bugs, play with puppies, find old furniture to strip down and repaint in crazy colors. She wanted cool, modern interiors, bare walls, muted desert tones." She sobered. "She was so lost in thought about all the things she didn't have, she couldn't see the things she did."

"I hope the people around you appreciate how much you let them off the hook," Ryan said.

"What's the use of blaming someone for being themselves?" Kerri asked. "Why would I want to try to force a man to be a father when he already had a family he'd chosen? Why would I want to make my mother stay in Chance Creek when her dream was calling?"

"You ended up having to care for your grandmother

alone," he pointed out.

"I don't regret a minute of it. But... I do feel guilty."

"Guilty? Why?"

"Think about how my mother felt growing up in that house, Bess's collections taking up more and more space, leaving less and less for her. To Mom, those collections were her rivals for her mother's attention and love. I knew that, even as a child. That's what made it hard to say no to moving to California with my mom when I was fourteen. I knew when Mom announced she was leaving, she was making a last-ditch effort to get her mother to choose her over those collections."

"But the collections won," Ryan said.

"That's right. They did. Mom couldn't see the broken part of Bess that relied on them. And Bess couldn't stop herself from hurting Mom. When I chose to stay, my mom must have felt like the past was happening all over again. I chose Bess over her. Not only that, I chose Bess's house and store—the places that had stifled my mother. In a way I chose those collections, too. I chose everything they stood for to me: family, continuity, history. All the things my mom couldn't stand. It was never quite the same between us after that."

There were so many things he wanted to say, but Ryan knew he couldn't. Kerri would take any criticism of her mother as criticism of herself, and he didn't want to push her away.

"I think that's why I can't find the money to pay off my mom," Kerri said. "I think I'm supposed to choose her this time. I've been keeping my head in the sand, hoping there was another way, but it's the only way, isn't it?"

Ryan wasn't sure that was true, but if it was, he wasn't planning to lose her over it. "If you go, I'll go, too," he promised her, and this time he felt like he could live with that decision. He didn't want to leave Chance Creek. Didn't want to leave the legacy his grandfather had left him.

But he'd go if he had to.

He was choosing Kerri and the possible future she represented to him. One in which he got companionship, love—and the family he'd always wanted.

She searched his face. "Do you think we'd work in Sacramento? What if this relationship is just a Chance Creek thing?"

He understood her fear. They were both so rooted here, it seemed possible they could wither when they moved. "We can make it work there," he said. "Trust me."

"I do," she said softly. "Trust you, that is."

Something shifted in his chest. She trusted him? It was as if she had handed him a fragile bird he could crush in his fingers with one wrong movement. He swore to himself right then and there he'd be worthy of her.

He set down the spoon he'd been stirring the sauce with, turned off all the burners in use, crossed the room, sat on the couch and gathered her onto his lap. This time his kiss was raw and hungry, and soon they were on their feet, lurching toward the door to his bedroom.

He helped her tug her sweater over her head, reached one hand over his shoulder to pull his Henley off, as well. He was bare chested, but she still had a tank top on. Its spaghetti straps seemed impossibly thin to hold up such full breasts. Ryan bent to drop kisses along her skin, angling her toward his bed.

He tossed the quilt aside, picked her up and snuggled her under the covers, quickly joining her.

They made fast work of helping each other out of the rest of their clothes.

"I want you," he told her huskily as he took care of protection and pulled her on top of him. He groaned as she fitted herself against him, struggling to hold his desire in check. He wanted to spend the rest of the night making Kerri feel good.

"I want you, too." She lifted her hips and lowered back down, taking him inside her. She was so hot and ready for him, he was nearly undone right then.

All thought of going slow left his mind, and instinct took over. His fingers dug into her hips as he moved inside her, keeping the pace Kerri set. She must have been as hungry for him as he was for her, because she rode him hard, her body tensing and flexing as they met.

Her breasts were a feast for his mouth, her nipples taut under his tongue. He explored her body until he couldn't hold back.

"Ryan," she said, arching back with her release. He lost any remaining control he had, crashing his hips into hers until he followed her over the edge, bucking and calling out his own pleasure.

Kerri was laughing when she collapsed on top of him afterward, her forehead pressing against his chest. "What are we going to do for the rest of the night?" she asked.

"Eat the dinner I was making for you, then do this again."

"If we're that fast next time, we can do it about a thousand times tonight." She was still giggling, and the girlish sound made him smile. He rolled over, flipping her onto her back, and braced himself above her.

"I'm down for that."

"Up for it, you mean. Oh," she breathed as he fitted himself inside her again. She was just as ready for him this time as she was before, but this time he had a lot more control. She was right; their first round had been lightning quick. He set out to show her he could take all the time in the world to make her feel good. "Ryan," she breathed when he'd coaxed them both into a state of feverish need a long time later.

He finally took pity on her, stroking long and purposefully, moving inside her just the way he knew she liked it best. She shut her eyes, tilted her head back, her fingers clutching the bedclothes. When she finally gave a cry, he was ready, too.

They finished together, their bodies clenching and releasing, the sounds of their pleasure mingling until both were drained. This time as they panted together, Kerri wasn't laughing.

"Dinner or another round?"

"Both," she said.

"GOOD, YOU BROUGHT your grandmother's famous snowball cookies, Kerri," Emma said a few days later. "I've been craving them." She popped one into her mouth and sighed with pleasure.

"You're supposed to wait to eat any until we've all filled our tins," Sunshine admonished her.

It was Tuesday, and they were at the annual cookie exchange party Sunshine and Emma hosted at Orchards. They'd begun the tradition a couple of years ago, and it had become one of Kerri's favorite parts of the holiday.

After Saturday night, she and Ryan had been together every moment they could, spending their nights together in his cabin, but the cookie exchange was women only. They'd parted with a promise to get together later. She couldn't wait. She couldn't seem to get enough of Ryan, nor he of her. This was what falling in love felt like, she thought more than once, wonder overtaking her. She was so lucky.

Or she would have been without the constant worry of what her mother might pull next.

"I'm sorry. Hope you brought extras," Emma said with a smile.

"I did. I know how they tend to disappear," Kerri told her.

Sunshine and Emma had pushed several tables together at the front of the restaurant, and all the women in attendance set their plates of cookies on it. They'd each brought enough so that everyone could take several of each kind to take home to their families, with extras to consume at the party, too.

Kerri knew the guest list could easily have gotten out of hand, but Sunshine and Emma did their best to keep it reasonable. Autumn Cruz was there, as was her sister-in-law, Claire Lassiter, who had an interior design business. Claire sometimes came to Kerri's store looking for a particular item, but Kerri knew she found most of the furnishings for her clients in Billings or even bigger cities. The Matheson women were there, too, including Morgan, whose vineyard was beginning to get a reputation outside Chance Creek; Hannah, who was using her veterinary degree to work with rangeland animals, like the bison herd she and her husband had founded on the Matheson land; Mia, whose wedding planning business was booming; and Fila Matheson and Camila Whitfield, whose restaurant, Fila's Familia, was a favorite in town. Rose Johnson was there. So was Bella Mortimer, a local veterinarian.

As the wine and conversation flowed, Kerri tried to relax, but the more she enjoyed the other women's company, the more she realized how much she was going to miss it if she was forced to sell her house. She'd gotten nowhere as far as raising more money was concerned, except for some additional sales at the store. She'd lowered prices and put big sale signs in her windows and seen a bump in her profits. Still, it wasn't nearly enough.

She did her best to join in the conversation, taking a

turn around the table and filling her cookie tin with the delicious offerings, but she felt like her smile was forced. She'd looked at the calendar before coming here and found Christmas uncomfortably close at hand. The holidays were going to be awful if her mother sued her.

"We won't announce it for a few more months, but yes—the festival is on," Claire was saying when Kerri put the lid on her brimming tin of cookies. Unlike many of the other women, she didn't have a family to share them with, so she'd put most of them out in the store this week, along with little cups of juice, for customers to enjoy, saving just enough for herself—and Ryan—to get her through the season.

"What festival?" she asked.

"The Matheson Winery Music Festival. We've got twenty acts booked to play over a weekend next June. We had to make some changes to the property in order to score a permit, but we worked with the county to figure it all out. The chamber of commerce is excited because we'll be bringing in tourists from all over Montana—probably. Maybe the Dakotas, Idaho and Wyoming, too. It should be a blast."

"You'll have to let us know when we can buy tickets," Hannah said. "We can all go and hang out together."

"Will it be family friendly?" Mia asked.

"Of course. We expect people to bring their kids. There will be all the usual things to keep them occupied. Face painting and so on."

As the women talked it over excitedly, Kerri's happiness slipped away again. What would her life look like in June?

Would she even be here?

Would she even be allowed to make that choice, or would fate force her hand?

Neither she nor Ryan were fully masters of their futures right now. If she lost her business and they were both struggling to get work, wouldn't it make sense for them to move to Sacramento? He could work for the forestry department. She could work for her mother. They'd be financially secure.

The idea left her cold, however.

She forced herself back to the present.

No matter where she ended up, she could always come back for Claire's music festival, she told herself sternly. Besides, there must be all kinds of festivals in Sacramento. She could probably watch live music every day of the week, if she wanted.

She'd make new friends.

Wouldn't she?

When her phone vibrated in her pocket, she was almost relieved, and she excused herself to take the call.

It was her mother.

"Where are you at?" Sylvie asked when they'd said hello. "Sounds busy."

"Sunshine's cookie party. I've told you about it."

"Right. Any excuse to eat sugar and drink wine, I guess," her mother said.

"Mom." She made her way into another room.

"What? I'm right, aren't I? You don't get that kind

of hubbub if there isn't a little alcohol in the mix."

"Aren't you going to any holiday parties?" Did her mother have to disapprove of everything?

"No. You know how I feel about that kind of thing."

Kerri wasn't sure she did, but now that she thought about it, she couldn't really remember her mother talking about many social engagements lately. When she first moved to Sacramento, she'd dated a man for a few years, but she'd never introduced Kerri to him, and Kerri had the feeling he might have been unsuitable in the way her father was.

Sylvie talked about her employees, usually to vent about their mistakes, but she didn't mention friends very often. She was always so busy with work, which was her passion, as she reminded Kerri often.

"Are you hosting one at the store?" Kerri asked her.

"Why would I host a party at the store?"

Kerri could picture the frown on her mother's face. Sometimes she wondered why her mother was even in retail. When she was starting out, she made many of her own products. She loved design and was a whiz at pottery. She'd emphasized the uniqueness of her wares in her marketing and lived on a shoestring as she tried to get her business off the ground. When she'd discovered she was pregnant with Kerri, however, and moved home, she lost a lot of momentum. It had taken her years to get her business off the ground again. Instead of creating her own pottery, she began working with manufacturers and extended her line into textiles and other home goods.

It was designing products that her mother loved. She'd always had mixed feelings about her customers.

"To raise your brand awareness. You could have a cookie party," Kerri teased her mother, knowing that would get a rise out of her.

Sylvie didn't disappoint. "A cookie party? How on earth does that fit the ambiance I'm trying to convey?"

"A cookie party is cozy and comfortable. People like to linger over their treats and glasses of wine. You could invite people from the neighborhood so they get to know you and your wares. They'd start to feel at home in the Outpost."

"Anyone who needs cookies and wine to be interested in my store isn't my target audience."

"Don't you want to know your neighbors? Become part of the fabric of your community?" Kerri thought of all the people who came through her door. The way she knew their stories and their likes and dislikes. That allowed her to identify the kind of products they might be drawn to.

"That's your problem. You're always getting so attached to things. Your community. Your friends. Your house. Your store. You have no sense of the freedom you get when you don't have ties like that," her mother said.

"You have three stores." She hoped her mom had some friends and a sense of community, as well.

"But I'm not attached to their location. I could leave California tomorrow. Move my business to Greece if I really wanted."

Kerri stopped pacing. "How would that work?" She certainly couldn't move her store anywhere else and expect to thrive. Not right away, anyhow. Her business was tied to Chance Creek. People came to her store because they knew her. Trusted her. Liked her way of doing things.

"I thought you were at a party," her mother reminded her. "I'm sorry I can't transmit an entire MBA in a five-minute conversation."

"I didn't ask you to."

"Look, I called to find out if you've gotten any offers on the house."

"No," Kerri said shortly.

"Well, call me when you do. We can start planning. I think you should stay with me awhile rather than getting your own place right away. I'll be down in San Francisco most of the time. When I come back, it'll be handy to have you nearby so we can brainstorm together."

"Even if I sell my property, that doesn't mean I'm moving to Sacramento." Kerri had always taken care to refer to the house and store as Bess's, even after she'd inherited it, out of respect for her mother's feelings, but she was done with that. Her mother wasn't respecting any of her boundaries.

"What are you talking about? What else would you do?"

She thought she'd shocked her mother. Good. Sylvie needed to know she wasn't in charge of everything.

"Whatever I want. If I sell, I'll be fancy free, right?

With cash in my pocket. *I* could go to Greece."

"That's ridiculous. You're going to come right here and help me. I need you."

You never came to Montana when I needed you. Kerri didn't say the words out loud, but they were true. Sylvie hadn't come when her first boyfriend broke her heart. She hadn't come when Kerri took over the store and revamped it from top to bottom.

She hadn't come when Bess got sick.

"Let's talk again soon, okay?" was all she said. "I'd better get back to the party."

"Kerri!"

Kerri ended the call, slipped her phone in her pocket and returned to the others. She couldn't feel triumphant, though. Her mother held all the cards, and she'd have to face her when she traveled to Sacramento with Ryan. If he got the job he'd been offered there, she'd have to make a decision no matter what her mother did. Everything seemed to be conspiring to force her hand, but in the end she'd have to make the choice that was best for her.

Even if it wasn't right for Sylvie.

"Everything okay?" Sunshine asked.

"Just my mom. She's expanding her business, and I think it's making her a little crazy."

"That could make anyone crazy," Sunshine said.

But Kerri thought it was more than that. For a woman who was achieving all her dreams, she didn't sound very happy.

CHAPTER 13

"**R**OUGH DAY?" KERRI asked when Ryan arrived at the store after his shift at the firehouse ended Friday morning.

"Rough twenty-four hours. We had a bunch of calls last night. Didn't get much sleep. You ready to deliver Rose's tree?" He was looking forward to spending some time with Kerri and focusing on happier things.

"I am. I got a little carried away," she confessed. "I found an old stand, set the tree up and decorated it in advance, because I wanted to make sure it would turn out all right. Once it was up, it seemed a shame to take everything off and have to do it all over again at Rose's place, so I wrapped it in burlap. It might be tricky getting it over there in the back of your truck."

"I've done tricky things in the back of my truck before." Hell, that hadn't come out right. "I mean…"

"Don't even try to make that sound better," Kerri advised, trying hard not to smile but failing.

"I could show *you* a few tricks." Ryan tugged her close and rested his hands on her hips.

"That would give the town something to talk about." She wriggled away. "Come on. I told Rose we'd be over there soon. Chloe, I'll see you later, okay?"

Chloe waved from the counter, where she was checking out a customer.

"How'd the tree turn out?" Ryan asked.

"Terrific. I can't wait for you to see it."

Together they wrestled the carefully wrapped tree into the back of Ryan's truck, but when Ryan went to lay it down, Kerri stopped him.

"I don't think that's a good idea. It needs to stay upright." She made a face. "I really should have waited to put the ornaments on." She thought about it. "How about I ride in back with it? It's only a block or two to Rose's place."

"I don't know if that's a good idea."

"I'll stay sitting down, and you'll drive slowly. It's the only way."

Ryan rubbed a hand over his chin. "I'm going to regret this."

"No, you won't."

In the end he gave in, but they'd only just pulled away from the store when the sound of a siren came from behind them and Cab Johnson pulled alongside.

"Tell me I'm not seeing a grown woman ride in the back of a truck with no seat belt on," he called out of his rolled-down window.

"That's definitely not what you're seeing," Kerri called back.

Ryan stuck his head out his window. "We're going

to Rose's store. It's just a block or so."

"Just a block or so is a block or so too many," Cab said. "See you there," he added, pulled in front of them and kept going.

"You all right back there?" Ryan asked her when he was gone.

"I'm fine. Hope I don't end up in jail."

"Somehow I don't think you will."

Cab was waiting for them at Thayers, however. "No more riding around like that," he warned them as he came to help Ryan unload the tree.

"Definitely not. It was a one-time thing," Ryan said.

Rose came bounding out of the store, pulling on her parka. "Is that my tree? I'm so excited! I know it's going to be beautiful."

"Couple of felons brought it over," Cab told her. "I don't think you should be associating with people like this."

"You say that about everyone," Rose said, laughing. "According to my husband, this town is full of miscreants."

"It is," Cab said. But he was grinning.

"I hope you like it," Kerri said to Rose. "I think it's my best so far. It was worth risking arrest to get it to you."

The men carried it inside, Rose and Kerri trailing along after them. They stood the tree upright where Rose directed them, then Kerri made Rose turn around while she unwrapped it carefully and set a few things to rights.

"Now you can look!"

Rose turned, put her hands to her mouth and exclaimed, "It's gorgeous! It's just what I hoped it would be, Kerri! It's going to be perfect for my holiday open house tomorrow. I'm putting everything on sale and serving snacks. I hope I'll be mobbed."

"I'm sure you will be."

"What's going on in here? Are you folks having a party without me?" Carl Whitfield came into the store, unwrapping his scarf from his throat. He was Camila Whitfield's husband, a wealthy rancher with a property outside town that belonged in the movies. A tall man with close-cropped hair, Carl was older than most of the people in Ryan's circle of friends and mostly ran in a different crowd, but Ryan had been to his spread a few times. When the Whitfields threw a party, it was a big deal, but they also liked to invite friends over to watch football games. They had the biggest sectional sofa in their den he'd ever seen. They had their own movie theater setup in their basement, too. Ryan preferred the game days, everyone sprawled around on the comfy couch passing snacks and cheering for their team.

"Hi, Carl," Rose said. "The real party isn't until tomorrow, but come see my tree. Kerri decorated it for me."

Carl shrugged out of his coat as he came to join them. "I swear, I've been in and out of this jacket all day. I'm trying to finish up my Christmas shopping. I don't know why every store is blasting its heat when they know we're all dressed for cold weather. Wow," he added and stopped when he got a look at the tree. "Is that… jewelry?"

"Jewelry ornaments for a jewelry store," Rose confirmed. "Isn't it amazing? Kerri did a cat-themed tree for Mrs. Fisher, a train one for George Metcalf and a kitchen-themed one for the women's shelter."

Carl considered the tree for a long moment. "I don't suppose you could whip up a few ranch-themed ones in the next week?"

"How many is a few?" Kerri asked, perking up. Ryan guessed why. Here was an opportunity to make a little money.

"An even dozen, if that's possible. I've already got an order in with Ryan, here, for the trees themselves." Ryan nodded. "We've got the usual decorations, red and silver round things. You know what I mean. Ranch-themed trees would be much better. I've got some people coming in from out of town next Saturday, and I want to wow them. If you could deliver them a week from today, that would be perfect."

"I could do that."

"You don't have a ranch room," Ryan said to her. "Where would you get the decorations from?"

Kerri laughed ruefully. "You're right, I don't have a ranch room, but I do have a ranch *shed*. A big one. I haven't been in it since Bess passed. Honestly, it's so big, I've been refusing to even think about it." In the back of her mind, she'd thought she'd have a tag sale someday—just open the shed doors and let people go to town with its contents. None of it had any sentimental value for her.

"That's a tight deadline," Ryan pointed out.

"I think I can make it work."

"Just bill me for the cost of them—and add an extra fee to expedite them. Deliver them to the house next Friday," Carl said again. "Or will you need help with that?"

"I'll help her," Ryan said.

"Great." Carl pulled out his phone and read a text. "I've got an appointment in a half hour I completely forgot about. Rose, I'm sorry. I'm pressed for time. Can you show me a few things Camila might like?"

"I know just the thing," Rose said. "Come this way. Kerri, thank you so much for the tree. Stop by tomorrow for my big sale if you can. And don't forget to bill me."

"You know what? Let me pay you right now," Carl said. "One less thing for me to worry about later. What are you charging per tree?"

Kerri named her price, but Rose butted in.

"Kerri gave me a big discount because I'm one of her first customers. Her regular price is double that, at least."

"Let's call it five hundred per tree, delivery included?" Carl asked.

"That's still a bargain," Rose said. "If we were in Billings, it would be way more."

"Five hundred is great," Kerri hurried to say. It was far more than she ever dreamed of charging.

Ryan did the math in his head. She'd just earned six

thousand dollars. That went a fair way toward the thirty grand she owed her mother.

Carl tapped away on his phone. "Send me your info, would you? I'll transfer the money right now."

"So much for sneaking a few minutes with my wife," Cab said to Ryan a moment later as Kerri and Carl conferred, then Rose led the rancher toward a jewelry case. "Guess I'd better get back to work."

"Thanks for overlooking our crimes," Kerri said to him, rejoining them.

"Crimes?" Cab asked. "Did you commit more than one?"

Kerri leaned closer to him and whispered, "I feel like I just got away with highway robbery." She looked over her shoulder to where Carl was talking with Rose. "And your wife was an accessory to the theft."

"I have a feeling the real crime is how many trees you've given away already," Cab said kindly. "Carl's a smart businessman and knows what things cost. See you later. Behave yourselves," he added on his way out the door.

When he was gone, Ryan moved closer to Kerri. "You sure you can do twelve trees in less than a week?"

"I'm going to have to. I already got paid, and I'm not giving any of that money back. It might be enough to convince my mother to give me more time." She didn't look at all sure of that, though.

"Maybe you can sell more of them to someone else."

Kerri's phone buzzed. She put up a finger to tell

Ryan to wait and answered it. "Hi, Megan." She listened a few moments. "Next Saturday? I'll be at work, like usual, I guess. Oh," she added a moment later. "I... don't think I'm ready for an open house yet." She met Ryan's gaze helplessly.

"Tell her you're not selling your house," he urged her.

Kerri waved him off. "The living room? It's all cleaned out." She frowned. "Well, I would be ready if..." She broke off again. "You haven't had an open house in a month? Is the market really that bad?" She listened some more. "I'm sure it'll get better soon." Another pause. "Wow. That is bad." Kerri sighed. "Fine. Let's do an open house. But under no circumstances do I want people touring the shop. Not while I have customers." Another pause. "Ten to twelve next Saturday? I guess..." Megan must have been talking. "I know. My mom can be very persuasive. Fine. I'll be ready." In another moment she hung up.

"Why didn't you tell her you're not going to sell?" Ryan demanded when she ended the call.

"Because Megan's so desperate to grow her business."

"You can't sell your house just so Megan can keep her job." Ryan jostled her a little, as if to shake some sense into her.

"I know." Kerri shook her head. "But maybe she can drum up some customers or another listing. People like walking through open houses. She can hand out her business card to everyone."

"What if she actually manages to persuade someone to make an offer?"

"I'll cross that bridge when I get to it. I mean—I don't have that thirty grand yet. I might still have to sell my house. As soon as I have a minute, I'm going to forward all that money Carl gave me to my Mom, but it's not nearly enough."

Ryan hated to admit it, but she was right. She might have to sell her house.

And if he couldn't find a decent paying job in town soon, he might have to sell his as well.

AS SHE STRODE through her house the following Wednesday morning, Kerri was satisfied at how the place had shaped up. After work on Friday, she'd gone through all the stacks of books in the library room, plus the ones on the shelves in the living room, saved the ones she liked—just enough to fill her bookcases—and carted the rest to her store for a special book sale on Saturday. She'd gotten the local radio station to mention it several times and was happy with the stream of customers that visited her shop. At her highly discounted prices, she hadn't earned a lot from selling them, but she'd added a few dollars to her savings and sold two of her little jewelry trees, too. She'd driven the leftover books to a donation station at the end of the day.

That evening, before heading to Ryan's place, she'd distributed a number of plants from the plant room around the house. The next morning, Ryan helped to carry the rest of them to the store before driving back to

King's Mountain, and she'd held another special sale, clearing her sales table by midafternoon, much to the chagrin of some customers who didn't hear about it in time. She asked Ryan to bring her a few more trees that evening, and she decorated one with baby items and another with vintage Christmas cards after helping him make his deliveries. She priced these higher than she had the previous ones she'd made. She spent that night at her house while Ryan went back to the cabin. They'd been reluctant to part, but she had so much to do.

On Monday she got up early and brought everything from the sewing room into the store, which set off an avalanche of customers the minute the radio announcers did their thing. Kerri knew she probably needed to do more with social media, but everyone in town still listened to the local station. She had to intervene a couple of times when the squabbling over her vintage fabrics got too heated, but in the end, the sale was even more successful than the previous ones. The baby item tree and the third jewelry tree sold, too. She called Ryan again, who was happy to bring a few more trees and take her out to dinner, as well, when his deliveries were done. They spent a couple of hours in the shed that night going through the ranch gear and managed to sort a lot of it into different categories, but she hadn't been that successful in locating items she could use to decorate Carl's trees.

She held back wide velvet ribbon from the fabric room to make garlands for the trees and gingham cloth to drape around their bases for tree skirts, but she had only two days to go before her deadline and still didn't have enough ornaments to do the trees justice.

She was just about to leave for work when her phone buzzed.

"Well? How's it all going?" Sunshine asked when she took the call.

"Fantastic." Kerri had been updating her about her sales. "I never thought I'd say this, but it's too bad Bess didn't have more collections. A few more months of sales like these, and I'd be able to pay off Mom."

"You've still got the wall of Chance Creek photographs, right?"

"And whatever's in the shed I don't use for Carl's trees."

"How are those coming?" Sunshine asked.

"Not great," Kerri admitted. "Most of the stuff in that shed is real ranch equipment, old useless stuff no one's going to want, not little things that I can turn into ornaments."

"I'm sure you'll figure it out."

"I hope so."

"Are you going to sell those Chance Creek photos next?" Sunshine asked.

"I think I'll wait until next week. It's going to take every minute I have between now and Friday to gather enough ornaments." Then she needed to clean her house from top to bottom if a bunch of people were going to traipse through it on Saturday. She wondered if she could make an owl tree.

"You'll get it done. Come by later if you can."

"I'll try."

Kerri flipped the open sign at ten o'clock and was grateful when customers began trickling into her store not soon after. When she sold her last jewelry tree and the vintage card tree before noon, she knew she should be thrilled, but she was too nervous about her impending deadline to savor the small victories. She created a few more trees out of odds and ends she had around the store and displayed them prominently.

Halfway through the morning, a couple in their early forties spent a long time walking around the place, their heads close together as they murmured to each other about what they saw. She noticed them staring for quite some time at a crack in the wall near the ceiling in the back corner of the store and became convinced they weren't shoppers—they were interested in the property itself.

Had Megan sent them over?

If they asked, Kerri could tell them that crack had been there all her life and didn't indicate any serious problems with the building. She'd had the foundation inspected earlier this year, and it was perfectly sound. They didn't ask her anything, though. Just left some time later without buying anything, leaving Kerri thoroughly out of sorts.

Just before noon a group of women came in, all in their early twenties, one with a distinct baby bump. They wandered through the store, oohing and ahhing about everything remotely baby related, especially a second baby-themed tree she'd created. One of the women came to a stop in front of a rocking chair Ryan had built.

"Ann, come look at this," she called to her friend.

The woman with the baby bump came over to the chair. "Oh, it's beautiful. Do you mind if I try it out?" she asked Kerri.

"Not at all! Let me know if you have any questions." Ryan's furniture had been getting a lot of attention lately, and several pieces had sold. The woman sat down in the rocking chair and let out a grateful sigh.

"It's a shame there isn't a matching one," she said to her friend. "It would be nice to have one for Kevin to sit in, as well."

The friend turned to Kerri. "Is the builder local? Does he take commissions at all?"

Ryan hadn't done commissions in the past as far as Kerri knew, but it couldn't hurt to ask. "The builder is local. If you give me your contact information, I can put you in touch with him. Would you like me to put a hold on that chair for a couple of days while you get it figured out?"

"That would be wonderful, thank you so much."

"When are you due?" Kerri asked.

The woman smiled, stroking her stomach, "Mid-January."

Bells twinkling alerted Kerri to more customers walking through the door. She wrote the customer's name—Ann Whittler—on a sticker and slapped it on the back of the rocking chair before checking on them. A man and his young daughter were wandering around the shop. The little girl stopped short when she saw the last jewelry tree Kerri had made.

The girl tugged on her dad's pant leg. "Daddy! look, it's a tree for a princess," she squealed.

He looked at the tree and laughed. "It sure is, sweetie."

"Can we buy it, please?" she begged, drawing out the last word for a good few seconds.

The father walked over to inspect it.

"I don't see why not. We'll take it," he told Kerri.

When everyone had left, Kerri was alone again. She knew she should be happy. Everything had gone well today. She'd made some sales, and people were showing interest in Ryan's furniture. Still, she turned off the radio when "Jingle Bells" came on for the third time that afternoon. She wasn't in the mood for Christmas music today. She wasn't really in the mood for Christmas at all.

CHAPTER 14

THIS CLOSE TO Christmas, Ryan opened the tree lot to customers during the week when he could. Today it felt like half of Chance Creek was wandering through the rows of trees, debating the merits of a Douglas fir over a blue spruce. Maple was having a blast, going from family to family to soak up all the praise and pets she could get. Ryan wished Kerri could be here, but she had her own business to run.

"Excuse me."

Ryan looked down to see a little boy who had run ahead of the rest of his family. He crouched down beside him. "Is that your tree? Do you need it wrapped up?"

The little boy stared at him for a moment, then nodded and ran back to hide behind his mother's legs.

Ryan followed him, greeted the family, rung up their purchase and was inundated by another wave of customers, who all seemed to have found their dream tree at the same time.

An hour or so later, when things quieted down, he

noticed a man in an expensive-looking suit who had just arrived at the lot. The stranger scanned the crowd, spotted him and approached. Ryan was curious to see what his business here was. He wasn't dressed for picking out a tree, and he didn't look like he'd arrived here on a lark, following the signs from the highway.

"Ryan Miller?" the man asked.

"That's me. How can I help you?"

"Grant Wallace." The man held out a hand for him to shake. Ryan obliged. "I was hoping we could talk in private for a moment."

Ryan surveyed the crowd. No one seemed to require him currently. He nodded toward his workshop. "We can talk in there."

Grant's smile didn't reach his eyes. "Perfect." He followed Ryan into the small building. "Lanie Carmichael mentioned that this plot of land may be coming up for sale soon. When I heard that, I felt like I had won the lottery—again." He paused, as if waiting for a question he knew Ryan would ask.

"You've won the lottery?" Ryan recognized the kind of man this was. If he hadn't asked him, Grant would have found another way to boast about his good fortune.

He wondered how Lanie knew he was considering selling the place. Had Kerri told Megan something and Megan passed it on to her boss? Or had someone at the firehouse been running his mouth around town about Ryan's job offer?

He supposed it didn't matter.

"I did. Biggest jackpot in Montana's history."

"Lucky man."

"I am a lucky man," Grant said smugly. "Been investing ever since, and I've done very well for myself. I'm also a man who knows what he wants, and I want this land. I'm ready to settle down."

Aren't we all, Ryan thought, but he didn't say it out loud. "You're interested in Christmas trees?" He was already getting impatient with this conversation. He'd been enjoying the day and the bustle of his customers, the clean, fresh air and the sense of anticipation that permeated the tree lot this close to the holidays.

"I'd like to find out more about the property," Grant said.

He hadn't answered the question. Ryan looked at his watch. "I have to finish up here. It'll be an hour still. How about you come back then? Or we could schedule another time." He wanted to see Kerri. He figured he'd bring her a few more trees tonight, seeing how fast she was selling them. She'd told him to bring another piece of furniture or two, as well.

"I'll wait," Grant said. He wandered off, but fifteen minutes later, when Ryan was busy with customers again, he saw Grant take a seat in one of the Adirondack chairs outside the shed as if he owned the place already.

The presumptuous action rubbed Ryan wrong, but he figured he might as well let the man stick around. If he did end up taking that job in Sacramento, he'd have to sell to someone.

True to his word, Grant waited. Ryan sold ten more

trees, then started closing up. It wasn't a long process. He cleaned and stored the saws and other tools in the shed. Gathered up the tablet and credit card reader he used for his sales transactions. Made sure the precut trees were upright against their supports. When he was done, he found Grant still sitting in his chair.

"Ready for the tour?"

"Perfect!" Grant slapped his hands on his knees as he got up. He might have money now, but he hadn't grown up with it, Ryan reckoned. He was a little rough around the edges—and much too eager to talk about his good luck. People who'd grown up with their wealth didn't need to do that.

"Let's start with the cabin."

"The cabin?" Grant shook his head. "No need to bother with that. It's the property I'm after."

All right, Ryan thought. "The property it is, then. I own three hundred acres. About two of those are cleared for the cabin and its surroundings. The tree farm takes up about ten acres, with another half-acre cleared for the staging area."

"I'll have to clear a lot more of it." Grant hummed a little, pondering that.

Ryan's stomach sank. "I have a good faith agreement with the other property owners on the mountain not to cut down any more trees than I need to. The Christmas tree lots are set up to be sustaining. Each year we plant as many as we cut down."

"Maybe you've got an agreement, but that doesn't mean I have to honor it."

His cockiness set Ryan's teeth on edge. On the one hand, Grant was right; he couldn't control what anyone did with the property after he'd sold it. On the other hand, he cared about this land—and the other people who lived nearby.

"What exactly do you plan to do with the place?" he asked.

"You know Carl Whitfield's spread?" Ryan nodded. "I want something even better. I worked on his first house here in town, you know."

"You're a builder?"

"Plumber by trade, before my big win. But now I don't have to work. I'll put my house over there, and I'll dig out that spot." He pointed to a place where the land naturally dipped into a round hollow. "That's where the lake will go."

The lake?

"I'll build the helipad over there," Grant continued, pointing to a higher, flat region. "My house will be a lot bigger than that old cabin of yours. Maybe twelve thousand square feet. I'll add a rooftop patio so I can look out over my lake."

Ryan did some quick mental math. Twelve thousand square feet was more than ten times as big as the cabin, which his great-grandfather had built by hand. Maybe it was a little snug, but that wasn't a good enough reason to knock it down for some soulless mansion. He couldn't imagine what the other Mountain Men would think about a helicopter flying around.

Grant was still going on about all his plans, like

stocking the lake with fish and buying zebras to run around in the woods.

"I've always been partial to zebras. It'll mean an end to all this Christmas tree business, of course. No one gets to come on my land without an invitation. Unless I decide to get a couple of lions and tigers, too, and start charging admission."

When Ryan found his fingers clenching into fists, he forced himself to shake them out and stuff them in his pockets.

"Not sure zebras will take to a Montana winter" was all he said.

"Where there's a will, there's a way."

Ryan stifled the urge to march the man right off his property.

"Do you need to see anything else?" He did his best to keep his tone friendly. No need to make enemies, even if he'd be damned if he was ever going to be this man's friend.

"Nope. I've seen enough. Got a few more proper-ties to look at, but I've got a hunch this will be the place. You'll be hearing from me."

"Sure thing." The man could talk all he wanted. Didn't mean Ryan was going to listen. Or sell to him.

Maple whined as the man walked away.

"I know, girl, I don't like him either."

AFTER A QUICK dinner that evening, Kerri faced Bess's ranch collection again. Bess's grandparents had owned a small spread not far from town, and Bess had grown up visiting there often. When they passed, her parents had kept it, but when they were gone, Bess sold it.

Had she already lost control of her collections by then? Kerri wasn't sure, but she knew she had at least started them by then. Alone in that big house, before her short-lived marriage, she'd begun to fill the empty spaces with things.

Kerri always thought that when Bess went through her family's possessions prior to selling the ranch, she must have started out with the intention of keeping a few keepsakes and giving away the rest.

How had she slipped into saving almost all of it? And how had she moved so much of it into town? She must have had help. Some of the furniture in the house originated on the ranch, and the shed contained broken down tools and equipment of all descriptions—even an old tractor. Bess must have loved her grandparents very much to want to keep so many of their things.

In contrast, she'd kept nothing to remind her of her husband, as far as Kerri could tell. Bess had wed a man from western Montana, and he'd moved into the house, but the only thing he'd left behind when he died was a baby. Kerri's mother had no recollection of her father. Bess never talked about him much. There was no collection that represented him, either, which Kerri supposed said a lot about the relationship.

She'd heard rumors over the years that her grandfather had a penchant for fishing, hunting and driving fast. The year after Sylvie was born, he went hunting in northern Montana with a bunch of his buddies and flipped his truck taking a turn too quickly on a logging road on his way home. Kerri might have guessed Bess collected the outdoor gear piled in the living room in her husband's honor, except Bess told her once point blank she hadn't.

Kerri had heard rumors about her grandfather's roving eye, too, which did a lot to explain Bess's feelings on the topic.

Bess had deserved much better.

Have you found enough ornaments yet? Sunshine texted. Kerri straightened and stretched her back, glad for the excuse to take a break.

Not even close, she texted back.

The longer she spent combing through the piles, the more discouraged she got. There was no way to use any of this stuff on a Christmas tree.

Sunshine didn't answer. Kerri kept sorting. She wasn't thinking straight when she took on this job for Carl. She'd been so desperate for the money, she hadn't asked for time to look through this old junk first to verify she could produce the trees he wanted.

"Knock, knock," someone called from the doorway.

Kerri whirled around, her heart beating hard. All she could see through the open shed door was darkness. "Who's there?" she called.

"It's us. We came to help," Sunshine called back, stepping inside into the light. Emma and Autumn Cruz followed her.

"But…" Hadn't Sunshine just texted her from Orchards?

She spotted the phone in Sunshine's hand and understood. Her friends had already been walking across the lawn when Sunshine texted. They must have parked at the house.

"Sunshine said you were struggling to find decorations for Carl's trees, so we brought some," Emma said.

"I struck gold," Autumn announced. "Claire had a client in Bozeman last year who hired her to do up his place with a rustic ranch Christmas theme, then changed his mind after she'd sourced all the decorations. She gave them to me, thinking I could use them at my bed-and-breakfast, but I use only a fraction of them when I decorate."

"And I have a ton of child-sized ranch items that were supposed to be toys but aren't up to code anymore," Emma said. "They belonged to a relative of mine, but she gave them to me, thinking maybe I'd have kids soon." Emma shrugged wryly. "Not sure what that says about her intentions toward my unborn children, but I think the toys will make perfect ornaments." She dug into one of the bags she was carrying and pulled out a small, rustic metal pail and garden rake.

"Lisa Matheson gave me these," Sunshine said triumphantly, pulling out a kitschy metal cow. "She's got dozens of them. She said they were decorations used at the county fair for years. When she joined the committee, they were in the process of upgrading. Lisa ended up taking them home. She forgot all about them until she was cleaning her attic last month."

Kerri was overwhelmed by their generosity—and

their good timing. "Those are all perfect!"

"Where should we work?" Emma asked, looking around the dim interior of the shed.

"Not here, that's for sure," Kerri said. "I've decided this shed is where dreams go to die." She thought about bringing them to the house. After all, she'd cleared out almost all of it. The furniture and curtains were dated, and she hadn't had time to do a thorough scrubbing, but she'd swept and dusted. It was good enough.

Unless more than one of her friends wanted to freshen up at the same time. Everyone would know there had to be a second bathroom upstairs.

A bathroom full of owls.

A familiar tightness constricted her chest. Her stomach twisted at the thought of the way her friends would whisper about her after they left.

She couldn't risk it.

She brought them to the store instead, shaking off the familiar burn of shame as best she could.

Her friends accepted her decision without question and spread everything out on the floor in the open area in front of the checkout counter, where they could separate the loot into twelve different piles. They talked and laughed happily as they sorted through the items they'd brought. Kerri did her best to join in, wanting to be… normal.

She'd always wanted to be like everyone else.

When she found herself blinking back tears, she excused herself for a moment, retreating to the back room to pull herself together. How had Bess done this for so many years? Kept her head up high no matter what people thought?

Kerri had witnessed her pain. The quick swipe of a wrist across her eyes when she was making dinner after overhearing people gossiping about her at the store. The nights she'd stayed home instead of joining friends at their houses, knowing she'd never reciprocate the invitations.

In Kerri's experience everyone was exquisitely aware of all the ways they fell short of society's expectations and wondered why people spent so much time talking about everyone else's failures instead of finding reasons to praise them. That would do a lot more good in the world.

When she pulled herself together, she discovered her friends had decided to group the ornaments by theme.

"We can have more than one ranch animal tree," Sunshine said.

"We can have several ranch-implement ones," Emma said.

"Look at these tiny frames," Autumn said, showing off a set she'd found in the store. They were rustic wooden squares about three inches wide Kerri had sourced from a going-out-of-business sale at a craft store in Wyoming. "We can put something country-themed in them."

Kerri nodded. "I know just the thing." She pulled on her coat and boots, raced to the house and retrieved it, glad for something active to do so she could shake off the old fear of being the object of gossip. "Look," she said when she returned. She'd found a checked calico cloth with ducks, geese, cows, chickens and goats on it.

"That's perfect," Autumn said. "Each frame will contain a single animal and a border of the check pattern." She got to work making them.

"I'll get snacks and hot chocolate going," Kerri said. She went in the back again where she had a break room set up for herself.

Several times over the next few hours she urged her friends to go home and let her finish, but each time they refused, and it was past midnight by the time they were done. The ornaments for each tree were neatly packed into bags. Emma had made garlands and bows to add to the trees, and Kerri knew she'd have access to the Whitfields' old ornaments, too. Those common elements would make the twelve distinct trees seem more of a piece when they were all decorated.

"Let us know if you need any more help," Sunshine said as they were leaving.

"You've done so much already," Kerri said. "I won't have any problem finishing them. Ryan is coming with me to deliver the trees on Friday morning, and he'll stay to help me decorate them."

"Call me when you're done. Don't forget to take photos," Sunshine said.

"Will do. Thanks!" She waved to them from the doorway as they made their way to their vehicles.

As she locked up for the night and returned to the

house, she was tired but jubilant.

Until she remembered she still owed her mother a lot of money she didn't have.

"MAPLE, NO!" RYAN said, but it was too late. Maple stuck her snout into one of the open boxes in Kerri's front hallway and carefully closed her mouth around a tiny trowel ornament.

"No! Bad Maple!" Kerri raced from the living room, where she'd been sorting through Christmas lights, dropped to her knees, took hold of Maple's jaw and extracted the trowel from her mouth.

Ryan reached them a moment later, a little surprised by her overreaction. He'd noticed how anxious Kerri was as soon as he arrived with Carl's twelve trees that morning. Was she afraid Carl wouldn't like what she'd done?

Maple laid her head on her paws and let out a baleful woof. Kerri softened at the sad eyes the dog cast her way. She bent down to scratch Maple's ears. "I'm sorry, I didn't mean to yell."

Ryan crouched down next to her and put a hand on her shoulder. "Want to tell me what you're upset about instead of taking it out on my dog?" He meant it as a joke, but he could tell from Kerri's expression it hadn't landed right.

Standing again, he took her hand and pulled her up into a hug.

"C'mon, what's bothering you?"

Kerri rested her head against his chest. "I think I

screwed up. Carl's going to hate these decorations. They're way too rustic for a guy like him. Camila is going to think they're ridiculous, and everyone's going to laugh at me. They'll ask for their money back, and I'll have to get it back from my mom."

"Hey. Hey, settle down. We'll figure it out—and I'm sure Carl will love his trees."

She just shook her head. "Let's just get this over with."

"Kerri." He lifted her chin. "The trees are going to be perfect." He wished he could fight her worries the way he fought fires, extinguishing them thoroughly. Someday he'd figure out how to do just that.

"I hope so." She pulled away and bent down to close the box Maple had purloined the ornament from. He could tell she was far from convinced.

Ryan followed her lead and set to work loading the boxes. When they were done, he helped Kerri into her seat and whistled for Maple, who jumped in with her. Ryan took his place and started the truck.

"This guy came by the other day out of the blue," he said to distract her. "Wanted to buy my land. Told me he was going to knock down my cabin, build a mansion, dig a lake and stock the forest with zebras."

He hoped she'd find it funny, but a glance her way told him she was horrified.

"You're selling your land?"

"Not if I can help it. You know I love it here. I'm still looking for local work, and I'm definitely not going to make any decisions until we check out Sacramento."

Kerri nodded slowly. "I guess it feels like so much is out of my control. Even if I somehow found all the money I owe my mother, you could decide you want that job in Sacramento and leave Chance Creek."

"It would be hard for me to go anywhere if you weren't coming with me." He slid another glance her way. "But it would be hard to ask you to leave your home if you found a way to stay. The tree farm business isn't enough to pay my bills, though."

"I wish I had the kind of money it takes to think you can transform a Montana mountainside into the Serengeti."

He laughed. "I hear that, but you know what I hate more than the idea of someone knocking down Grandpa John's cabin and tearing up my tree farm?"

"What?"

"The idea of not being with you. Wherever you go."

KERRI KNELT BY one of the trees Ryan had helped her set up in the Whitfields' great room, sorting out ornaments before she began to decorate it. Her hands were shaking and her mouth was dry. She'd been in awe as Carl ushered them in, just as she'd been the few times she'd been over before. She always forgot just how wealthy the Whitfields were. The house wasn't exactly ostentatious, but every inch of it exuded class, and Kerri was positive she'd made a huge mistake. Carl was going to hate those gingham animal prints in their tiny rustic frames. He'd hate the metal cows and barnyard animals. He'd hate the miniature ranch implements, too.

Had she been out of her mind?

She thought she was going to be sick as she hung one last tiny frame on the tree she was decorating, then adjusted the round red and silver Christmas balls and gingham ribbons and bows that unified the theme throughout the trees. He'd ask for his money back and then what would she do?

"You okay?" Ryan asked. She'd set him to work on one of the ranch animal–themed trees, and he was doing better at it than she'd thought, given that he hadn't had a tree since he was a child.

"Not really," she admitted. "What if Carl despises them?" Carl had left them to the work, disappearing into the recesses of his large home soon after they arrived.

Ryan shrugged. "He asked for ranch-themed trees, and that's what you're giving him. If he decides he doesn't like them after all, that's his problem, not yours." He stepped back and looked at the ones they'd finished. "I like them. He'd be a fool not to."

"Shh!" Kerri looked around to make sure Carl hadn't reappeared, but they were still alone. She was grateful for Ryan's support, but she couldn't afford to offend the man who'd paid her so much for these trees.

She got back to work. Forty-five minutes later, when they'd moved each of them into the places Carl had shown them when they'd first arrived at his ranch, Kerri decided they weren't that bad after all. They were whimsical and Christmassy and made the Whitfields' large first floor feel homey. The butterflies in her stomach settled a little, but when she glanced at Ryan and caught him watching her back, they fluttered to life again.

He'd made it very clear how important she was to him earlier this morning. She had a feeling she was coming to a crossroads in her life, and she had no idea how it would all turn out.

"Are you ready for us? We're coming in!" Carl called from the hallway.

"Ready!" she hastened to say, nervously wiping the palms of her hands against her jeans.

Carl was covering Camila's eyes with his hands when they appeared, directing her steps so she didn't bump into anything.

Ryan moved to Kerri's side, took her hand and squeezed it.

"Carl," Camila complained with a laugh when she nearly stumbled. "Are we there yet? Show me the big surprise."

"Just a second." He maneuvered her to where she could see almost all the trees at once and lifted his hands from her eyes. "Ta-da! What do you think?"

Camila lit up. "Oh, my goodness. They're perfect! Where did you get all those ornaments? These are so much better than our old ones! They're so unique."

"Exactly," Carl said with satisfaction. "Our old trees looked just like everyone else's."

Camila turned to Kerri. "I've heard about the trees you've been selling in your store, but I haven't had time to come see them for myself."

"I made the first one as a gift for someone who needed cheering up, and it kind of snowballed from there," Kerri explained.

"I hope you have a business card," Carl said.

"A business card? Why?" Kerri asked him.

"Because I know exactly what's going to happen next. We're going to hold our party, and by the end of it I'm going to have ten people asking who provided my decorations so they can hire you."

Kerri scoffed at the idea. "You're just being nice."

Camila laughed. "Carl is never nice when it comes to business."

Carl elbowed her. "That's a fine thing to say about the man you love."

"It's true." She turned to Kerri. "If Carl says people are going to want your product, you'd better believe they'll be knocking down your door. He's great at predicting what's going to sell."

"Lots of businesses need seasonal decorations for parties, for their corporate offices, that kind of thing," Carl said. "I'd be happy to put you in touch with a few people."

"O-okay," Kerri said. She told herself not to get too excited. It was too late in the season for anyone to hire her now. Maybe next year.

If she was still in Chance Creek.

"You'll need a separate name for your tree business," Carl added. "Kerri's Collectibles doesn't get it done, if you know what I mean."

"Carl!" Camila said. She held her hands up in exasperation. "See what I mean?" she asked Kerri, then poked a finger in her husband's chest. "That's exactly what I was talking about. When it comes to business, you aren't nice."

Carl shrugged. "Being nice doesn't make the sale. Get a better name," he told Kerri. "Get some business cards. Take photos of all the trees you've done so far to show people what you can do. Put together new ones, some fancy, some suited for smaller mom and pop businesses. Photograph them all and make a website—and a brochure."

Kerri swallowed. "Sure. I'll do that," she said. She had a feeling Carl saw right through her, though. She didn't know where to start to get all that done.

"Here's the thing," he said. "I've got a lot of contacts. I can help you—but you've got to do your part. Name, website, business card, brochures. When you've got those, come see me. Meanwhile, I'll send you anyone who asks about these." He waved to the trees again, then pulled his phone out of his pocket when it buzzed, glanced at the screen and frowned. "Sorry. I need to take this."

Camila saw Kerri and Ryan to the door. "Carl is serious, you know," she said. "He loves to help people start businesses or make them better. If you do what he says, he can send a lot of customers your way."

"Thanks," Kerri said, but she wasn't sure she could match Carl's energy.

"Thank *you*. I love the trees," Camila said. She waited for them to get their coats on. "Now all I need to do is furnish an entire house in the next three days."

"An entire house?" Ryan asked, leaning against the doorjamb as Kerri zipped up her coat. "You guys bought another one?"

Camila laughed and shook her head. "We built a guesthouse. It was supposed to be done at the end of October, but it's been one delay after another. The building passed its final inspection last week, but I just found out this morning our decorator dropped the ball. The furniture we ordered isn't arriving until January— and half my family is coming for Christmas. I've got to hit up the stores in town this afternoon."

Kerri exchanged a look with Ryan. "Make sure you stop at my place. I've got some fabulous handmade wooden furniture by a local artisan."

"Kerri," Ryan protested.

"A local artisan?" Camila perked up. "I'd love to see that. I'll give you two a head start to drive into town and follow you there as soon as I can."

"What?" Kerri asked Ryan a few minutes later when they were driving toward town. She had felt his gaze on her since they walked away from Camila and Carl's place.

"A local artisan?" he repeated.

"That's exactly what you are. I'm just doing what Carl said. Improving my branding."

CHAPTER 15

"YOU WANT IT all?" Ryan asked Camila an hour later. They were standing in the corner of Kerri's Collectibles near the store's front windows, where Kerri had positioned all his pieces. Kerri was at the counter, ringing up another customer. Camila had looked over the items he'd made and finally asked to buy almost every one. He'd never felt quite so exposed as he did while she was looking over them. There was nothing fearsome about Camila Whitfield, but it was a hell of a thing to wait for anyone to pass judgment on something you'd made by hand.

"Everything except that café table set."

She was buying a larger dining room table and chair set, so he couldn't blame her for leaving the small one out.

"I told you I have to furnish an entire guest house," Camila went on. "This will give me a good start. You've got a certain style that flows through all your pieces. It will make the house seem cohesive, no matter what other furniture I add. I'll still need to find a number of dressers, end tables and things like that, but this is a good start."

"Glad you like it. I hope you don't feel like you need to buy any of it just because you know me. I won't take it personally if you walk out that door empty-handed."

Camila shook her head. "This isn't a pity purchase, Ryan. Carl has rubbed off on me. I call it like I see it. What I see is some fabulous, one-of-a-kind furniture. I wish you had more." She looked around the store one last time, as if she was afraid she'd missed something.

"Can you fit any more?" Ryan joked. She'd bought a lot already.

"I'm sure I could, but I've got enough for now. You know what I really need, though?" she asked. "Promise not to laugh. Everyone else I've told has."

"Laugh about what?" Kerri asked, coming to join them.

"I need a ruin." Camila smiled at their expressions. Kerri looked blank, and Ryan was sure he looked just as confused. "Our place is so new," Camila said. "Too new. It needs some ambiance. Have you ever heard of a folly?"

"I have," Kerri said. "Rich people used to put them in their gardens. They'd build a fake Roman temple or something like that and make it look like it was falling apart. Like it had always been there."

"They were made to be focal points," Camila said. "Conversation starters. Something to give the place a little whimsy or gravitas. That's what I need. Something that belongs on a ranch that gives it a sense of history."

Kerri laughed. "Like a broken down eighty-year-old tractor? Every ranch needs one of those, don't they?"

Camila's whole face lit up. "You have one of those?"

Kerri laughed again. "I do, as a matter of fact, but I was joking, Camila. You don't want an old tractor."

"That's exactly what I want. An old tractor would be perfect."

"If you can find a way to tow it to your place, you can have it. I've been dreading having to get someone to remove it. It's sitting in my shed out back."

"What's the make and model?" Camila asked.

Kerri shrugged. "I haven't the foggiest idea."

"I'll run and look," Ryan said. "It will just take me a minute." He pulled out his phone. "Want some photos?"

"That would be great," Camila said. "I'll need to show them to Carl before I commit."

A few minutes later he was back, forwarding the photos to her.

"Thanks. That really is perfect," she said, looking through them. "I'll get back to you as soon as our company has gone home. I might have to sweet-talk Carl a little. Don't let anyone else have it before then, though."

"I won't," Kerri promised. "Who else would want it?" she asked Ryan in an undertone when Camila wandered away, drawn by something else in the shop.

A few minutes later, when Camila was satisfied there was nothing else to buy, Kerri rang her up. Ryan loaded what he could in his truck and delivered it to the Whitfield place. When he came back for a second load, Kerri was hunched over a check book on the counter.

"What are you doing?" he asked. He hadn't seen one of those things in ages.

"Writing you a check. Do me a favor and don't cash it until Tuesday. I never have much extra in my account, so Camila's payment needs to go through first."

"I'll hold on to it a couple of days," he assured her. "I hope you took your cut." She bent her head, and he sighed. "Kerri, tell me you took your cut. No one would have seen my furniture if you hadn't displayed it in your store."

She squirmed a little. "It doesn't feel right," she said. "You're my boyfriend."

He liked the sound of that, but still. "It is right. Look, if you're going to be a businesswoman, you can't go around doing special favors for everyone you know, because you know everyone in town!" He took her hand. "Besides, it'll help you pay off your mom. You know," he added, lowering his voice, "I don't need any of this money right now. I could put it toward what you owe her. I want us to build a future together."

She was already shaking her head. "That's not how I want to start our relationship, and it wouldn't be enough anyway. I need to do this on my own."

"What affects you, affects me," he argued, but she wouldn't hear of it.

"We have to do this right."

"We are doing this right." He took her into his

arms. "Look at us. You're getting rich on Christmas trees. I'm getting rich on furniture sales."

"I don't think either of us qualifies as rich." But she let him hold her. He bent to kiss her a moment later, and she met him happily halfway. Afterward, Ryan tore the check out of her book and ripped it up when he confirmed she'd given him the full amount. He did some calculations in his head and named a number. "The rest is yours. That's the usual commission a store takes."

She shook her head but wrote a new check out for the amount he'd dictated.

"I will put my share toward what I owe Mom," she told him.

"Should we go out and celebrate tonight?" he asked as the bell over the door rang, announcing another customer.

"It had better be a short celebration," Kerri said. "I've got to finish getting ready for the open house tomorrow, start gathering the decorations for your party next week and pack my bags, because Monday we're on a plane."

He'd almost forgotten they were flying out to California.

Almost.

"A short celebration then."

"Okay. Are you ready for your interview?"

"I'm ready," he assured Kerri. He needed to be, for her. For their future.

"It will be an adventure," she said, as if trying to

reassure herself as much as him.

"It will be something."

"THANKS FOR THE ride," Kerri said on Monday morning when Ryan dropped her off at the flagship Outpost store in Sacramento in his rental car. Their first flight had left at an ungodly hour of the morning. The second flight had been delayed by a half hour, but they'd still landed before lunch. They agreed he would pick her up at dinnertime, and they planned to go out for dinner before checking into their hotel room for the night.

She'd spent Saturday night at Ryan's cabin, talking late into the night about what they might find on this trip. Sunday they'd split up again, so both of them could get a little sleep before their early-morning departure. She knew Ryan had expected her to invite him to stay at Bess's house to simplify driving together to the airport this morning, but she still wasn't ready to invite him upstairs.

She hadn't probed the feeling last night while she was packing and didn't want to think about it now, either. The house wasn't hers yet. It was mostly emptied and clean, but she hadn't had a chance to furnish it.

Hadn't replaced her single bed.

She wanted the space to feel like it represented her before she invited him into it. She hoped he understood.

To her surprise, he killed the engine and got out, too. "Can I meet your mom?"

"Don't you have to get to your interview?"

"I've got time."

She took a deep breath, pushing down on a rising tide of panic at the idea of Sylvie and Ryan in the same place. Why shouldn't he meet her mother? She had high hopes for this relationship, after all.

"Okay."

They entered the store together, where Kerri breathed in the calming scent being subtly wafted through the showroom by diffusers. Her mother thought of all the details.

"Kerri!" Sylvie crossed from behind a counter to meet them. "There you are."

"Here I am," Kerri agreed and submitted to her mother's idea of a hug. It was more like a squeeze of her biceps—a test of her strength, Kerri always thought when her mother's fingers closed around them. "Mom, I want you to meet Ryan Miller. He flew out here with me for a job interview. He's my… friend."

"Boyfriend," Ryan clarified, leaning in to shake Sylvie's hand. "You have a wonderful daughter. I hope you know that."

"Boyfriend?" Sylvie's brows rose delicately. "Kerri has never mentioned you."

Kerri saw the blow land. "You've been too busy trying to force me out of my house to talk about my dating life. How is everything going?" She took Ryan's hand and held it proprietarily.

Her mother ignored the jab—and their clasped hands. "It's going well" was all she said. She kept her gaze on Ryan, sussing him out, Kerri thought. "What company are you interviewing with?" she asked him.

"The California Forestry Department. Fire suppression division."

"You're a firefighter?" Her disbelieving tone made it clear what she thought of that.

"Basically."

This wasn't going well at all.

"It's incredibly important work," Kerri rushed to say. "Living here in California, you should know that, Mom. Ryan makes beautiful furniture, too," she added.

"But firefighting is my main gig." He wasn't going to back down, was he? Kerri knew her mother had offended him. She was good at that. Kerri had a memory of her saying something slighting to Sunshine a few years back on one of her infrequent visits when Kerri had taken her to Orchards. Now that she thought about it, Kerri remembered she'd avoided bringing friends home when her mother still lived in Chance Creek, as much to avoid this kind of confrontation as to hide Bess's hoarding.

After an awkward pause, Ryan looked around the store. "Nice place you have here. Kerri, I'll be back around six. Hope you have a good day." It was clear he thought that unlikely. "Sylvie, nice to meet you. See you again soon."

It almost sounded like a threat. Kerri walked with him outside.

"I'm sorry for that," she said. "Mom is… well… Mom."

"She wants you to herself," Ryan said. "I think she's

mad you brought me along today."

"She was pretty touchy when I said I have a hotel room for the night," Kerri affirmed. "Don't hold it against her, okay? She's probably nervous, too. She's trying to prove to me that I should come here to live, and she knows I don't want to. She knows I'm angry at her for forcing my hand."

"Do you think you two will argue? You can call me any time if you need me to rescue you."

"I appreciate that." She leaned into him, and he put his arms around her, creating a safe space for her inside them. She loved his quiet strength and the knowledge that he cared about her. She could depend on him.

"See you later." He gave her a kiss and got into his rental car. When he was gone, she returned inside.

"Finally. Now we can get down to it," her mother said. "Let me show you around and then we'll visit the other stores. I haven't told them we're coming today. I like to keep everyone on their toes."

"You could have been nicer to Ryan," Kerri told her.

Sylvie waved that off. "I was nice."

"If that's nice, I'd hate to see you angry." Kerri faced off with her mother. "Ryan is very important to me. I expect to have him in my life for a long time. If you want to spend time with me, you'd better change your attitude toward him."

"Don't count your chickens before they hatch" was all her mother said. "That's what I've learned when it comes to men. Now come and see this."

Kerri gave up, knowing if she argued any more, she'd say something it was difficult to take back. Maybe if her mother didn't choose men who were already in committed relationships, she wouldn't be so disappointed by them.

It didn't take long to go through the store. Kerri had seen most of the products on her mother's website. In person, she got a better sense of the quality of the pieces and the care with which her mother had chosen them.

The retail space was beautiful, though spare, and the employees, in their uniform of green linen pants and cream-colored shirts, were impeccable.

The only thing missing was customers.

Kerri surreptitiously checked the store hours etched on the front window. The shop was definitely open. Had been for over an hour. Not one person walked through the door the entire time she was there, however.

"Just wait until you get out here for good," her mother said as they drove to the next location. "There's so much we can do together."

"There must be some great live music in this city," Kerri said conversationally. She had no idea if Sacramento had a music scene or not, but she enjoyed listening to bands and going dancing.

"I meant going on buying trips, doing inventory. Increasing our social media presence—in a tasteful way, of course."

"Of course." That all sounded like work. "But we

could do fun things, too, if I lived here. I know there's shopping and restaurants, but there must be some good hiking around here, too, isn't there?"

Her mother sent her a strange look. "Sounds like someone thinks she's going to have spare time when she moves here."

"Evenings? Weekends?" Kerri prompted. "There's always spare time."

Her mother laughed, but the sound was brittle. "Now we know why you have one store and I'm about to have four!"

They arrived at Outpost's second location, and soon Kerri was too busy getting a tour and oohing and aahing over the same inventory she'd seen at the first store to push the issue. Once again, the retail space was impeccable, as were the employees.

And the store was empty almost the entire time she was there.

They stopped for salads at a restaurant on their way to the third store.

"Am I going to meet any of your friends while I'm in town?" Kerri asked as she poked through her lettuce looking for some of the yummy bits.

She saw a flash of something on her mother's face before Sylvie got her emotions under control and shrugged.

Didn't she have friends?

"You're here only until dinnertime," her mother trilled. "You don't have time to meet my friends. We barely have time to see my stores."

Kerri didn't point out there was only one more to go and an entire afternoon stretching before them.

Sylvie must have felt the afternoon pressing on her, too, because she spun out the tour of the third store until they were practically crawling from object to object. When her mother got a phone call, Kerri breathed a sigh of relief. She took the opportunity to visit the ladies' room in the back of the store and joined the two employees at the sales counter when she returned.

"Seems awfully quiet. Is it some kind of holiday in town?"

The two young women looked at each other.

"It's always like this," the one named Audrey said. She was a slim brunette with a wide-eyed look that made her seem perpetually surprised.

"We get hardly any foot traffic in this location," the one named Heather said.

"The other locations aren't any better," Audrey said. "I've filled in at all of them."

"The showroom is beautiful," Kerri said, trying to contain her surprise. How was her mother getting by with so few customers?

"It's precise, you mean," Heather said. Audrey elbowed her.

"Precise?" Kerri repeated.

Heather pulled a tape measure out of her pocket and walked to the nearest shelf. "Six inches," she said, measuring the space between two items. "Six inches, six inches, six inches." She went down the row. "It has to be perfect, or your mom gets quite upset."

"Heather," Audrey warned.

"You know what? I'm sick of not speaking up," Heather said to her, returning to the counter. "Your mom makes a ton of sales—online," she said to Kerri. "I have no idea why she even has a storefront, let alone three."

"Four," Audrey put in.

"But I figure, whatever," Heather said. "She wants storefronts, she can have them. I'm grateful for the job, even though I'm bored out of my mind."

"Heather," Audrey warned again.

"The thing is, your mother isn't well," Heather said, an edge creeping into her voice. "Someone's got to do something about it."

"What do you mean?" Kerri felt like the conversation was going off the rails. Like they were three people talking, but the words weren't coming out quite right.

Her mother wasn't well?

"She's obsessed with measuring everything. She does it over and over again." Heather leaned closer. "She comes in at night and does it, too, as if she thinks we're not doing it right during the day. I saw her. My boyfriend and I were out driving the other night. When we passed by, there was someone in the store. I thought there was a break-in happening until I recognized your mother. She was walking around with a tape measure, going around and around the showroom."

"I don't think she has an apartment. I think she's sleeping at the flagship store," Audrey said, then bit her lip as if she'd surprised herself by speaking up.

"That's not true. She stopped that a long time ago," Kerri protested.

"Are you sure?" Heather asked.

Audrey elbowed her again, harder this time. Heather shut up. Both of them stiffened.

Kerri knew without turning that her mother had re-entered the room.

"What's going on?" Sylvie asked.

"These two are telling me all about your products," Kerri rushed to say. "You've done a fantastic job training them, Mom. You should be proud."

Just for a second, her mother softened. "Thank you." Then she lifted her chin. "All right, back to work, you two. Come on, Kerri. I've got a list of apartments for rent. I know you're not ready to make decisions like that yet, but you can at least get a sense of the city and what's available."

"I'd love to see *your* place," Kerri told her.

Her mother waved that idea away. "We won't have time."

"Oh." When Sylvie turned toward the door, Kerri turned back to Heather.

See? Heather mouthed.

Kerri nodded and followed her mother. She didn't know what else to do.

CHAPTER 16

R YAN WALKED UP a carpeted stairwell to the office where he was meeting Nathan Briars for the job interview. The CAL FIRE offices were located in a neighborhood of low-rise office buildings not far from the Sacramento River. Along the wall were canvases printed with fire-related images: a man escaping a fire, streaked with ash; a plane dropping water; a group of firefighters posed at the base of a massive old-growth redwood, saved by their efforts.

Ryan understood that the job he was interviewing for was important and that the business of firefighting didn't happen if someone wasn't in an office some-where organizing everything, but the photo of the firefighters stopped him in his tracks. They looked exhausted, their faces grimed with ash and dust, their eyes red from smoke and lack of sleep, but they looked triumphant, too. He knew how it felt when the tide of a fire finally turned your way. The terror and glory of facing a wall of flames and beating it back.

He tore himself away from the photo and made his

way up the stairs to a wide room with a receptionist desk positioned near the door and chairs ringing the rest of it. Several young men and women, all talking over each other and laughing, had collected in the seats on one side of the room. The other side was empty.

As Ryan walked up to the desk, the receptionist looked up at him and asked, "Are you here for training?"

He shook his head. "I'm here to interview for the Resource Assessment Officer position."

"Take a seat over there, please. Someone will be with you shortly." She motioned to the empty chairs nearest her desk.

Ryan sat and picked up a magazine, but he couldn't help looking over at the men on the other side of the room waiting for their training. They had to be firefighters already, here to upgrade some specific skill. It reminded him of his days with the Marines, which seemed like a long time ago now. He missed the undercurrent of competition that existed when people knew they were going to test their skills. He thrived on that kind of challenge, and he hadn't been pushed like that lately.

He missed Maple already. It was strange not to have her nosing around the place, coming back now and then to get a reassuring pat. If she was here, she'd be across the room making new friends. He'd left her with Adam, knowing she'd enjoy her time on his ranch while he was away. He'd closed the tree lot today and tomorrow, as well, and hoped no one made the trek all the way up the mountain only to find he was gone.

A balding man in a suit came into the room, consulted with the receptionist and came to meet him. He extended a hand when Ryan stood up. "I'm Nathan Briars. You're Ryan Miller?"

"Yes, sir." Ryan replied. Some military habits died hard.

"We don't stand much on ceremony here, son. Just call me Nathan."

They walked down a short hallway and entered Nathan's office. The room was decorated in grays and blues. Nathan sat down at a utilitarian desk, his back to a wide window.

"Let's get started." He consulted his computer screen. "Tell me about the work you did for the Marines."

Ryan talked about his time there. How he had taken on more responsibility as he went. As he explained the work he'd done, he took in Nathan's office and tried to picture himself in a similar one, working at a similar computer. He definitely wouldn't sit with his back to the only window in the place, he told himself.

If he got a window.

"You'd have quite a bit of responsibility if you came to work for us," Nathan told him. As he laid out the expected outcomes for the position, Ryan tried to look interested. Nathan was right; it was a job that required experience and clear thinking, but it also required a heck of a lot of sitting.

Restlessness filled him just thinking about it.

As the interview progressed, Ryan knew it was going well, but the sick feeling in his stomach got worse.

If he ever worked a desk job, he wanted it to be one like Ed's, where he still went out on calls even if he wasn't the one leading the way into burning buildings.

He wanted to connect with the men and women battling the fires, and he wanted to know the constituency who would depend on him. He couldn't imagine sitting in a room like this, in a building like this, at a desk like the one Nathan was sitting in, his back to the window. He couldn't imagine spending hours at a time pouring over statistics and financial charts. Maybe if there were wraparound windows overlooking forested hills, or maybe if Maple could spend her days at his feet. Maybe if he got to do site visits every week or so.

Maybe.

After they'd talked for the better part of an hour, Nathan sat back in his chair.

"I have to admit, this interview was pretty much for appearance's sake," he said. "The job is yours if you want it. You're qualified, and Ed Brookings has a lot of good things to say about you. That's all I need to know."

Ryan's fingers dug into his thighs. Could he stand this kind of life, year in, year out, if it gave him the security to provide for his family?

Could he stand it for Kerri's sake?

He wanted to believe he was made of stern enough stuff to handle anything if he put his mind to it.

But being willing to do so and pulling the trigger

were two different things.

"Thank you," he finally said. "I need to take a day or two to think it over. My family has lived in Chance Creek a long time."

"Understood," Nathan said. "I'd appreciate it if you can get back to me soon, though."

"Will do."

THEIR NIGHT IN Sacramento wasn't a success. Ryan was thoughtful when he came back from his interview. Even though he said the meeting went well, it was clear to Kerri he wasn't excited to take the job. She could sympathize. She was far from sold on the idea of moving to Sacramento and working with her mother. They went out to eat at a highly recommended restaurant, but both of them picked at their food. They drove around to see holiday light displays and try to get a feel for the city, each of them doing their best to seem cheerful, but they struggled to pull it off. Back at the hotel, they made love, and for a short time, Kerri was able to lose herself in Ryan's arms. As soon as they were done, however, it all came back. She struggled to sleep in the unaccustomed surroundings despite his reassuring presence.

Kerri wasn't sure why she didn't tell him what Heather and Audrey confessed—that her mother needed help. She was still processing what had happened. Still trying to figure out if what they said could be true—and if it was her place to do anything about it.

One thing seemed crystal clear, though. No life they

might build together in Sacramento would resemble the one they might have in Chance Creek.

Their flights home were uneventful, and they made it back to Kerri's house a little before noon. Ryan pulled into her driveway, killed the engine, turned to her and took her hand.

"Are you okay?"

She nodded, although she wasn't sure she was.

"Look, change is always hard. We can make it work anywhere we chose to go. We could be happy there."

But we could be happier here. She didn't say the words out loud. He knew that already.

"We're both tired," Ryan went on. "How about I come by after work? We'll get takeout and talk about the future."

"We'd better talk about your party the day after to-morrow," she said. "You can help me take down the Chance Creek photos in the front hall while we do that. I want to hold a sale for them tomorrow," she ex-plained. "I haven't had time to come up with a theme for your party yet. I was supposed to come and decorate a day or two early. I've entirely dropped the ball."

"Right. The party." He'd dropped the ball on it, too, as far as preparations went. He'd invited everyone he knew and let it be known people could invite their friends, as well. Other than that, he hadn't done a thing. He checked the time on his phone. "I'd better stock up on snacks now before I pick up Maple. I can get booze later."

"I'll gather up all the extra decorations I have. Let

me know if there's anything else I can do to help." Kerri leaned over to kiss him before getting out of the truck and heading into her house. She'd told Chloe she'd be back by noon, and she was grateful to have a few minutes before it would be time to cross the yard to the store.

She put her bags down in the foyer, toed off her shoes and walked the first floor of the house, empty of the collections that had been wall to wall for as long as she could remember. It really was a beautiful home. Original floors, one-of-a-kind built-in cupboards, craftsman-style woodworking and leaded windows. It seemed even more special now that she'd been away from it for a night.

Her mother had driven her around Sacramento and pointed to various buildings that had rental vacancies. None of them looked as inviting as this house was.

Kerri stood in the middle of the living room and allowed herself to imagine what it could look like full of Ryan's furniture—and a few of her own whimsical, one-of-a-kind pieces.

The shrill tone of her phone broke her out of her reverie. Kerri pulled it out of her pocket.

"Hello?"

"Hi, Kerri, it's Megan. Great news! Someone has made an offer for your place. They're really motivated. You won't have to worry about them backing out."

"Oh." Kerri gripped the phone, knowing she need-ed to stop this right now but not knowing if she should at the same time. Ryan could still decide to take the job in Sacramento, and she hadn't made enough money to pay her mother off. Not even close. "That's... uh... great."

"There's just one thing," Megan rattled on, unaware of her confusion. "They want a really short escrow period."

"How short?"

"As short as possible. They'd like to take possession by mid-January at the latest." Megan hesitated. "Kerri, I know how hard this has to be for you, but you'd better take this offer seriously. There won't be many more at this time of year."

"I'll... think about it," Kerri said.

"Don't think too long," Megan said.

As Kerri ended the call, she looked around the living room again. What if she'd been wrong all this time? What if this house was never meant to be hers?

Overwhelmed, she went to the kitchen to make a cup of tea. As the water heated in the kettle, she ran a hand over the wooden table Ryan had given her. She loved having something he'd made in her house. Loved having him in her life. He was putting himself out there for her, considering the job in Sacramento because he wanted to give his future wife and kids financial security. If he hadn't met her, he probably would be waiting to find the perfect job here in town.

As for her, if she moved to Sacramento, wouldn't she be enabling Sylvie by helping her open yet another store? Heather's accusations had scared her. If they were true, Sylvie's behavior had gone way past hardworking and into out-of-control territory.

Moving to California couldn't be the right choice if it meant enabling her mother's problems—and making Ryan miserable.

After all, there was no reason she had to move to California even if she accepted an offer on the house and store. She'd have to split the profits with her mother, but if she moved in with Ryan on King's Mountain, there'd be plenty of money left over to start something new. She could rent a storefront in town for now and move her inventory over. She could get a professional website to advertise her Christmas tree decorating business. Ryan could take the time he needed to find a job here in Chance Creek that suited him—or to expand his furniture-making business. The cabin was small, but in time, if things worked out, they could start their family there and expand as they went.

Ryan might not have proposed yet, but he'd made it clear he had marriage on his mind.

Maybe…

Kerri bit her lip at the audacity of the idea bubbling up inside her.

Maybe she should buy a ring and beat him to the punch.

She loved Ryan. Loved him. Could be just as happy on King's Mountain with him as she could be in town.

It would be cramped in his cabin. It would be hard to start her business over in a new location. They might struggle before they got their finances clear and their work lives on track, but they'd be together, and that's what really counted at the end of the day.

Trying to hold on to Bess's house and store was keeping her at the mercy of her mother's fears, and that wasn't doing either of them any good. As hard as it was to part with the property, it was beginning to look like the right thing to do.

Kerri thought about that, her heart beating hard. Why not stop being a victim and start taking charge of her life?

She could call Megan right now. Accept that offer.

No, she thought.

She needed to take this a step at a time.

Bess hadn't gotten help for her hoarding. Her mother hadn't gotten help for her perfectionism.

Too many times she herself hadn't reached out when she'd needed a hand.

That changed right now.

Kerri searched through her junk drawer for a slip of paper that Sunshine had discreetly given her after Bess's funeral. On it was the number of a counselor she'd never called.

"There's nothing wrong with talking to a professional when times get tough," Sunshine had said that day before pulling her into a comforting hug. Kerri had never told Sunshine how much her support meant in the hard months after Bess passed away. She had a feeling she didn't need to, that Sunshine knew anyway, but she promised herself one day soon she would. Kerri typed in the number on her screen, took a breath, and tapped Call.

"Marsha Overton's office, how can I help you?"

"Hello, my name is Kerri. I'm looking to book an appointment. It's urgent."

"You're in luck; I have a cancellation. Can you come in tomorrow morning at nine?"

"I'll be there."

RYAN HAD JUST lowered himself into one of the Adirondack chairs by the tree lot shed with a mug of hot chocolate when he heard a car door slam in the parking area. He sighed. So much for taking a break. The lot wasn't officially open for sales today, but when someone made the journey all the way out here, he wasn't in the habit of turning them away.

When he stood up and spotted Grant Wallace coming his way, however, he wished he'd stayed out among the trees. The man ambled up to him, cocked his hat back on his head and surveyed the territory around them.

"Sure is pretty up here. I came to see if you're ready to field an offer."

"Depends on the offer, I guess." It depended on more than that, but Ryan figured he'd let the man have his say. If Grant gave him a low-ball number, he could send him packing and make all this simple.

Grant named a figure that made Ryan blink. He could do a lot with that kind of money.

The man wasn't messing around.

"I want this place as soon as you can move yourself off it," Grant said. "I'm hoping to break ground the minute the snow is gone."

"I'll have to think it over," Ryan told him.

"What's there to think about? I offered more than the place is worth. This is your chance to get ahead. There's no way you're getting rich selling a few trees every December. Am I right?"

He was right, although Ryan refused to tell him that. "It's still a big decision" was all he said.

"I'll give you forty-eight hours," Grant said. "And don't even think about coming back with a counteroffer. That's my final number."

Ryan nodded. "Duly noted."

Grant hesitated. Muttered a little. Kicked the snow with one boot. "I want an answer right now," he complained.

"I understand that," Ryan said. "I'm not playing games. I'm just making sure I do what's right."

Somewhat reassured, Grant left soon after. Maple came out from where she'd been hiding nearby around the corner of the shed.

"What do you think?" Ryan asked her. If he sold the property to Grant, he might be able to persuade the man to give him enough up front to pay off Kerri's mother before Christmas. Kerri would be able to keep her home and her business. She might even let him move in.

Except she'd finally have to show him the second floor, and he was beginning to think she'd never do that. What exactly had Bess stuffed those upstairs rooms with—a collection of mummies?

Kerri would probably refuse to take the money from him, anyway. She was so damn proud.

He paced the length of the shed and back again.

If they were married, she'd feel differently, wouldn't she?

Maybe it was time he proposed, even if they hadn't been together that long. He'd known right from the first time she asked for a tree how he wanted all this to turn out.

His thoughts raced ahead, creating a possible future. He could pay off Kerri's mother. Move in with Kerri and use the rest of the money he got from Grant to start a business of his own. He could purchase more equipment. Use the shed on her property as a workshop to build his furniture.

Ryan stopped himself. Building furniture wasn't a steady business.

There had to be some investment he could make with the cash that would set them on their feet. Kerri deserved that much.

She deserved a proposal fit for a queen, too.

She had to pay her mother before Christmas, which meant he needed to propose to her tomorrow. Which meant he needed tonight to make his plans.

Ryan pulled out his phone and called her. He left a message when he got her voice mail.

"Hey, I'm going to be tied up tonight, but I'll stop by at lunchtime tomorrow. Do you think Chloe could watch the store for an hour or so, and we can go somewhere to talk?"

"I DON'T UNDERSTAND," Kerri said to Marsha Overton the following morning. "I was hoping you'd tell me how to fix my mom." She'd asked Chloe to run the store all day and was relieved when the younger woman jumped at the chance to make a little more money ahead of the holidays.

It was less money to give her mother, but that didn't matter if she was going to sell the place anyway. Kerri needed time to think over her plans—and prepare for Ryan's party. Ryan hadn't come over last night after all, and she hadn't taken down the photo collection. Instead she'd sat up poring over her bank accounts, loan statements and the offer sheet Megan had sent. If she sold the property and gave half the proceeds to her mother, she'd have a tidy nest egg to start over with. As much as it broke her heart to think of turning her back on her home, she'd decided in the early hours of the morning it was her only viable option.

Now she was sitting in a small office on the out-skirts of Chance Creek. She crossed her legs and shifted in the comfortable chair Marsha had directed her to at the start of their session.

The counselor smiled at Kerri from her seat. "I'm sure you were. The thing is, we can't change anyone except ourselves, no matter how much we wish we could. The sooner you own that, the sooner your life will change for the better."

That didn't make any sense, as far as Kerri was concerned. She'd explained that her mother was the one who was forcing her to sell her home and business. Her mother was the one opening stores all over California when her business was online.

Her mother was the one measuring the placement of her inventory with a ruler in the wee hours.

"I'm trying to clean up the mess my mom is making," Kerri said.

"Right. You're reacting to your mother's attempts to control you, and by doing so you're letting her do just that."

"But what else can I do?"

"You can learn to make your own decisions based on *your* wants and needs."

"But if my mom has OCD and needs my help…"

"If your mother needs your help, you'll have to decide whether to give it to her, based on your own plans for your life. As far as I can understand, she's making a living. Paying her bills. Following her passions. Right?"

"I… guess. But she's scaring her employees."

"If they're really afraid, they can quit, can't they?"

"Well, sure, but… what if Mom gets worse? What if she can't handle work in the future?"

"I suppose under those circumstances, she might have to sell her business and live on the proceeds. Or move in with you, if you offered her a place. Maybe *she'd* have to see a counselor," Marsha said gently. "That's not a future that's happened yet, is it? Why don't we focus on what's happening now. Tell me about you." She waited, her expression encouraging.

"I'm…" Kerri trailed off. How could she explain anything about her own situation without getting right back to what her mother was putting her through?

Marsha waited patiently.

"I'm the owner of a secondhand furniture store who creates unique pieces by upcycling some of my items. I'm also getting into making custom Christmas trees."

"That sounds great. Are you in a relationship?"

Kerri felt her cheeks warming. "Very much so." That was the one place in her life where things were going right. "I've been dating a guy for a few weeks, and we're getting pretty serious."

"After a few weeks?" Marsha made a face and wrote something down. "That seems to happen a lot in Chance Creek. My colleagues and I joke there must be something in the water." She looked up. "Are you sure you know this person well enough to be serious already?"

It was a fair question. "I've actually known him most of my life," Kerri explained. "He was just one of the people in the background of my existence… and then he stepped into the foreground."

"Got it." Marsha nodded. "What does he think about your mom?"

"They didn't hit it off. He thinks she's trying to control me. But he's willing to move to Sacramento if that's what I want to do. He just interviewed for a job out there." She told Marsha more about their trip.

"Sounds like he cares about you. Do you want to move to Sacramento, Kerri?"

"No," Kerri said firmly. "I don't. Not at all. Even though my mom wants me to come and even if Ryan can make more money there. I don't care if we're living paycheck to paycheck. I don't even care if I do have to sell my place if I can move in with Ryan and stay in the area. That's what I decided yesterday. I think…" She couldn't believe she was going to say this out loud. "I think I'm going to accept the offer on my place, and I'm going to propose to him."

"Wow," Marsha said. "For someone who thought she didn't know what to do, it sounds like you've made some major decisions. But, Kerri, don't you think if you're going to marry Ryan, you should ask him *his* vision for the future before you sell your house?"

Kerri thought about that. "I'm afraid if I don't take the offer now, I'll lose my nerve and won't be able to make myself take it later," she explained.

"Let me give you some advice," Marsha said. "When you feel rushed to choose something because you're afraid you'll change your mind, that's the sign of a bad decision. The right decision makes you feel calm, not chaotic."

Kerri let out a frustrated sigh. "But it seems so exciting to show up at his place with a lot of money in my bank account, a ring and a solution for everything."

"You can still do all that," Marsha assured her. "Just talk to the man first."

Back at home, Kerri mulled over their conversation as she began to take down Bess's enormous collection of Chance Creek photographs. She still had time before Ryan was coming for lunch. If she was going to sell the house, she needed to finish emptying it. The first few rows were easy enough. She could stand on the ground and reach them. She set each one on the floor and leaned it against the wall. When she couldn't reach any more, she fetched a chair from the kitchen and climbed up on it.

It was slow going, hopping on and off the chair as she took the artwork down, having to move the chair over every few minutes.

Kerri had decided she'd talk over her plan to sell the property with Ryan at lunch, laying out all the information and testing the waters to see if he was open to her moving into the cabin with him.

If that conversation went well, she could plan her proposal. Maybe she'd do it on Christmas morning. She still loved the idea of surprising him with their future all tied up nicely in a bow. They could live at the cabin. She could help with the trees after work. He could build more furniture and sell it in her new storefront when she found one. They could decorate Christmas trees and deliver them together.

The next photo was a little out of reach. Kerri considered moving the chair but instead went up on tiptoe and stretched as far as she could.

Should she propose to him over Christmas morning brunch? Or take him on a moonlit walk in the snow on Christmas Eve?

Should she propose in bed after making love to him?

"Oh!" Kerri shrieked as the chair she was standing on tipped over and she had to leap clear of it just as she'd closed her fingers around the framed photo she'd been reaching for. It smashed to the ground as she landed hard and tumbled over, glass flying in all directions. Kerri lay on her back on the floor, staring at the ceiling, trying to catch her breath.

When she was sure the fall hadn't killed her, she sat up slowly and rotated each of her ankles, testing them to see if she was hurt. She was probably going to be sore tomorrow, she concluded as she got to her feet carefully, but jumping free of the chair when it went over had probably saved her from a broken ankle.

She hobbled into the kitchen, fetched a broom and dustpan and came back to deal with the glass. When she'd managed to dispose of it, she picked up the mangled frame and the photo.

To her surprise, a piece of paper that had been wedged between the photo and its mat fluttered down to the floor. She stooped, picked it up and unfolded it.

A smile tugged at the corners of her mouth as she read the note at the top in Bess's neat handwriting.

Bowl and serving platter. Sylvie Olsen, age 5.

The drawing was childish but contained a wealth of detail. Kerri immediately recognized the platter she'd donated to the women's shelter just a few weeks ago. Even as a kid, her mother had a good eye.

Why was the drawing hidden behind a photograph, though?

Kerri eyed the other pieces of art she'd taken off the wall, went over to them, and pulled another framed photograph from one of the stacks. She turned it over and undid the frame. In between the photo and the backing board was another drawing. This one was labeled, *Woven blanket. Sylvie Olsen, age 11.*

Kerri recognized the blanket from the linen closet. Sylvie had caught its folds and patterns in the main part of the drawing, but in the bottom right-hand corner, she'd drawn another blanket Kerri didn't recognize. The pattern on this one was more sophisticated. More pleasing to the eye.

Had Sylvie been improving on what she saw around her? At eleven?

For the next hour, Kerri unframed all the photos she'd taken off the wall and got back on the chair to take more down. Behind each one was a piece of art her mother had made, from as early as three to as old as eighteen, when Kerri knew her mother had left home. Bess had saved dozens of them, hidden in plain sight.

Hearing a knock on the door, she called, "Come in." Ryan could help her figure out what to make of all this—and help her reach the photos that were too high for her.

"I knew it," her mother said as she walked in the door. "You're just like Bess. Look at this place!"

CHAPTER 17

"**W**HO'S THAT?" RYAN asked Maple as they pulled up to Kerri's house. A taxi was just pulling away, and someone in a long, black wool coat was entering the front door. By the time he'd parked, the door was shut again, leaving him to wonder who was visiting Kerri—

And if he should come back later.

He hadn't counted on company when he'd packed the picnic basket for their lunch. Ryan supposed there was nothing for it except to proceed, even though another person's presence was going to put a damper on his romantic plans.

"Come on," he said to Maple as he let her out of the car a moment later. "Behave, okay? We've got to put our best foot forward."

Maple gave a quiet "woof" and trotted toward the door as if she'd never done anything but behave.

On his way to the front door, Ryan rehearsed in his mind all the things he wanted to say to Kerri when he had her alone. He had a romantic spot picked out and a ring in his pocket. Thermoses of hot chocolate and a cold bottle of Champagne to celebrate with afterward.

First he'd tell her he planned to take Grant's offer and sell the tree farm. Then he'd say they could use the money to pay off her mother and furnish Bess's house. After that, he'd tell her he wanted to spend his life—

The door was open a crack when he reached it. Maple nosed it the rest of the way open and bounded into the front hall before Ryan could stop her. "Knock, knock," he called quickly and followed her. "Kerri?"

Ryan stopped short when he spotted Sylvie in the front hall, towering over Kerri, who was kneeling on the ground, Maple trying to lick her ear.

"…just disgraceful," Sylvie was saying. "Stuff everywhere! At least my mother kept her collections tidy! What has gotten into you, Kerri?"

"Mom, I swear—"

Ryan knew instinctively it wasn't the first time Kerri had tried to have her say, but Sylvie didn't slow down for a minute.

"I knew when I heard about the offer, you would screw things up. I knew you wouldn't take it. I got on a plane first thing, because I knew you'd be just like my mother. Incapable of thinking about anyone other than yourself!"

"I…"

"You were always selfish. Always taking Bess's side. Always holding me back."

"Then leave!" Kerri suddenly cried, surging to her feet. "If you hate me so much, get out of here! That's what you do best, isn't it? Disappear when people need you?"

Sylvie stared at her.

Kerri was just getting started. "Look around you, Mom. You think Bess was selfish? Then tell me why she saved every bit of your artwork she could lay her hands on! Tell me why she hid it away so you couldn't take it from her, the way you took yourself out of her life—and mine! You're the one who's selfish! I bet you don't have anything of mine—do you? Not one little scribble or drawing. Because that would just weigh you down. I'm sorry you ever had me! I know I've been ruining your life ever since I was born."

His desire to protect Kerri propelled Ryan to step between the women. "You happy now?" he demanded of Sylvie. "Or are you incapable of being happy until you force Kerri out of her home and ruin her business? Does it make you feel good to see her cry? Well, too bad. She's not going to." He turned to Kerri and took her hand. "I got an offer on the tree farm and I'm going to sell. We'll have plenty of money to pay your mom. Plenty left over to do whatever we want, right here in this house. If you'll have me, that is." He fished out the little velvet-covered box he'd recovered from his grandfather's room that morning, knowing Grandpa John would want him to use it for exactly this purpose. This wasn't the way he'd pictured his proposal happening, but he didn't care. He wasn't going to stand here and listen to Sylvie Olsen hurt the woman he loved for a moment longer. He got down on one knee, opened the box and held up his grandmother's wedding ring. "Kerri Olsen, will you marry me?"

To his surprise, Kerri laughed, a kind of half-hysterical hiccup that made him stand up in a hurry.

"Kerri?" Had he misread her feelings for him entirely, or was her unfortunate response to his proposal merely a reaction to its timing, which he had to admit wasn't nearly as romantic as he would have liked?

She put a hand in her pocket and pulled out a little velvet box of her own. "I was planning to propose to *you*, but my counselor told me I should talk to you about our future first." She opened the box to show him a wide, masculine wedding band. "It was my grandfather's. Bess saved it, of course." She took a shaky breath. "Ryan Miller, will you marry *me*?"

Hell, he hadn't expected that. Ryan took in the wedding band. Searched Kerri's face. Saw love staring back at him—and delight, too.

"You… want to marry me?" He'd hoped so, but now he realized he hadn't been sure she'd actually say yes.

"Of course I want to marry you! I want to live with you and work with you and fix our house and have children. I want all of it. I've wanted nothing else since I asked you for that tree that night at Orchards."

"You want all that—with me?" He wasn't sure why he needed her to repeat her answer, but he did. There was no room for mistakes right now.

"With you," Kerri agreed. "I want *you*, Ryan Miller."

"What on earth is going on?" Sylvie cried. "The two

of you have lost your minds! Look around you. This place is a shambles."

Ryan ignored her and bent down to kiss Kerri. "I want you, too, Kerri Olsen, and I will definitely marry you."

"Kerri, get away from him. He's not good for you. Anyone can see that!"

"I disagree," Kerri said. "I think Ryan is the best thing that's ever happened to me."

As they came together, Sylvie gave a cry that sounded like a needle scratching a record. "I don't understand what's happening!"

Ryan took his time kissing Kerri, but when they finally parted, he faced her mother. "What's happening is we are in love, and I'm selling my property so Kerri can pay you the rest of what she owes you. Kerri loves this house. She loves her store. And I'm going to make damned sure she gets to keep both."

Kerri was shaking her head. "Mom's right. I got an offer on this place. I can sell it and we can keep the tree farm. You love that place. It means so much to you."

"This house means as much or more to you," he countered. "Happy wife, happy life, right?"

"You two are insufferable!" Kerri's mother stormed past them into the living room, where her footsteps came to an abrupt halt. She was back a moment later. "What happened to everything in there?" She didn't wait for an answer. She darted into the kitchen next and came back shaking her head.

"I showed you the kitchen when we talked on the

phone," Kerri reminded her, but her mother just ran past her up the stairs. They could hear her go one way down the hall and then the other.

When she appeared again, she descended the staircase slowly. "You emptied the whole house," she said.

"All except the owls and the Chance Creek photographs," Kerri said. "That was today's job, which is why it's so messy in here. I dropped a photo and found one of your drawings behind it. Then I had to check the rest of them to make sure I recovered them all before I gave the photos away. I was thinking, maybe I should donate the photos to the historical society." She picked up the stack of her mother's drawings she'd accumulated. "It won't take more than fifteen minutes to clean this mess up, Mom. But look what Bess saved."

She passed the stack of artwork to her mother. This time her mother looked through it, her lips parting in wonder as she took in how many there were.

"I had no idea she kept all these."

"Why did she hide them behind the photos?" Ryan asked. He placed a hand on Kerri's waist, wanting to kiss her again. To celebrate their dual proposals.

"Yeah, Mom. Why were they behind the photos?" Kerri goaded her. Ryan thought she knew the reason perfectly well, but he wasn't sure he could understand it.

"I don't know." All the fight was gone out of Sylvie.

"Yes, you do."

Her mother let out a ragged breath. "Fine. I guess the older I got, the more ashamed I was of Mom's collections. Her hoarding. She'd promise me at breakfast to get rid of some stuff, and by the time I got home from school there was more. We started fighting all the time. I began to try to clean out her collections for her." She lowered the stack of drawings. "She got so frantic when I did that. I'd sneak around, bag things up and take them to dumpsters around town in the middle of the night. When she confronted me about it, I pretended I didn't know what she was talking about. By the time I left home at eighteen, she could barely sleep at night, and I could barely stand to be in the house." She looked around the hall at the photos and paintings, half still on the walls, half strewn around the floor. "This front hall was the one thing we agreed on. She promised me she'd keep the floor and hall table neat, and she always kept that promise. I always kind of liked the Chance Creek gallery." Sylvie shrugged.

"I remember you saying that," Kerri said softly. "Bess knew you felt that way, too. I bet she hid the drawings behind the photos because she knew you wouldn't take them away in the middle of the night. You realize your drawings were her most precious collection of all."

Her mother pulled back. "What makes you think that?"

"She didn't hide any of her other collections from you, even after she knew you were pilfering from them. I don't think she could have handled losing your artwork. She loved you so much."

Sylvie wavered where she stood, her chin wobbling with the effort she was making to hold in her feelings.

When her face crumpled and she sank to her knees, Kerri was beside her in a moment.

"Mom?"

"I loved *her* so much," Sylvie sobbed. "I didn't want people to make fun of her—of us. I wanted to be proud of my mother. Of my home. But she wouldn't stop!" Her sobs made it hard to understand her words. "Now she's gone." She waved a hand as if to encompass the house. "It's… all… gone."

Kerri lifted a horrified gaze to Ryan, and he knew what she was asking him. Did Sylvie mean Bess's collections? Did she regret telling Kerri to clear out the house?

Ryan came to crouch next to them. "We can get them back. At least some of Bess's things, if that's what you need, Sylvie."

Kerri's mother sobbed harder. Kerri wrapped her arms around her, cradling her head against her shoulder.

"I'm sorry," she said. "I would have kept everything if I'd known you wanted it."

Ryan knew saying that had to cost her. Kerri had struggled to let things go; it was Sylvie who'd finally forced her hand. Now Sylvie wanted to torment her for doing just that?

Sylvie's grief was real, though, and he had a feeling she'd held it in for far too long. Who was he to judge people for the way they dealt with losing the people they loved. It had to be one of life's cruelest tricks, providing people to cherish and then taking them away.

He didn't know how to put any of his thoughts into

words, so he simply stayed where he was, offering his presence since he couldn't give them anything else. When Kerri began to cry, too, he figured it was long past time for both to let it all out.

He didn't know how long they stayed like that, but eventually the storm passed and the women dried their eyes. He fetched tissues from the bathroom at the end of the hall, wishing he'd seen it just once with the cacti still in residence.

"Are you okay?" he asked Kerri, handing a few tissues to her.

She nodded. "Mom? Are you going to be all right?"

"I don't know," Sylvie said. "I don't know about anything at all. I thought I hated all that crap Mom kept, but now that it's gone, it feels like I've lost her all over again. And my stores... they're not doing so well," she admitted, her voice cracking. "I don't know why I'm opening another one when the first three barely break even. I just... feel like I have to."

"Do you even like managing those stores?" Kerri asked her. "I thought designing products was your true love." She picked up one of Sylvie's drawings. "If you closed your storefronts, you'd have so much more time for the creative side of your business."

"Maybe you're right." Her mother smoothed the fabric of the coat she still wore, then shrugged out of it as if just becoming aware of how stifling it was. "But Mom was so proud of me when I opened the first one. She sent roses." Sylvie smiled crookedly at the memory. "She told me she cleaned out one of her shelves so she'd be able to buy some of my pieces."

"I remember that," Kerri said. "Bess got rid of three boxes of stuff. I was shocked."

"I sent her a set of my bowls," Sylvie said. "I thought she was coming around. I thought maybe if I did really well and opened another one, she'd clean out even more things. If I was successful enough I could... cure her." She lifted her hands. "I know how crazy that sounds."

"Her hoarding was never about you, you know," Kerri said. "It was about her own losses. It was a way to stave off her grief."

"I should have stayed and forced her to get help," Sylvie said.

Kerri shook her head. "If you start second-guessing the past, you'll end up like she did, stuck there, unable to move forward. My counselor told me something."

"You have a counselor?" Sylvie asked.

Kerri nodded. "She told me we can't change anyone except ourselves. Bess knew she was hoarding, and she could have found a counselor of her own. She didn't choose to do so. That's not your fault. It's not mine, either. The thing is, though, we have to face our own problems." Kerri took a breath. "You're struggling with perfectionism, aren't you?" she asked softly.

Ryan could read the tension in her. He kept quiet, letting the women have it out.

Sylvie nodded. "I think it's more than perfectionism. I can't seem to stop myself sometimes—just like Bess. I think... I think I need help."

"I know I do," Kerri said. She hugged her mother again. "We'll get help together, okay?"

"Okay." Her mother cleared her throat and began to gather up the drawings she'd let fall to the floor. "Where's your collection?" she asked after a moment, as if ready to move to a new topic.

"My collection?" Kerri climbed to her feet unsteadily. Ryan moved to support her.

"What did Bess save to remind her of you?"

Kerri looked around her slowly, as if cataloging the house in her mind, thinking through all the things Bess had kept. "Nothing. Not that I've found, anyway." Her lips pinched together, and she looked younger, suddenly. Close to tears again.

Ryan realized she was reading the situation all wrong.

"She didn't need a collection to remember you by," he told her. "Don't you see? You were the one person she never lost."

KERRI'S MOTHER WAS still subdued when they sat down to dinner at DelMonaco's that night.

"I feel like I've been hit by a bus," she said as she perused the menu. "And like I've woken up after being asleep for a long time. I owe you an apology, Kerri. I should have never tried to force you to sell."

"You were right about one thing," Kerri said. "I was getting stuck in my grief, like Bess did. I was afraid to sort through her things. Afraid to admit she was really gone."

"I should have been here to help," her mother said.

"You're here now." Kerri hesitated. "Do you want us to track down Bess's things and get them back?"

Her mother shook her head. "No, it's not the stuff I miss. It's Mom. But I know she loved me, and I hope she knew I loved her."

"I'm sure she did," Kerri told her.

When the waiter came, Sylvie spoke up again. "We need Champagne. We're celebrating tonight."

"Right away." The waiter took their orders and left.

"What?" Sylvie asked Ryan. Kerri looked up. Ryan was trying—and failing—to suppress a smile.

"What is it?" Kerri asked him.

"I've got Champagne in my truck," he admitted. "And a picnic."

"You have a picnic?" Sylvie straightened. "Why are you two here with me at DelMonaco's? I ruined your romantic proposal! Both of them!"

"The picnic will keep," he assured her. "Having it in the back of my truck in this weather is better than putting it in a freezer. I'll take your daughter out and wow her another time."

"I think our proposal was pretty romantic, anyway," Kerri said. She still couldn't believe her ring was on Ryan's finger, and his was on hers. Who cared if men didn't usually get engagement rings, or that he'd have to take it off so she could put it back on at the wedding?

The waiter returned with a bottle.

"To the both of you," Sylvie said when their drinks were poured. "And to whatever choices you make about your future. Kerri, you don't need to pay me by Christmas." She made a face. "In fact, I don't care if you ever pay me the rest of that money. I have plenty."

"Thanks, Mom, but I want to follow Bess's wishes. I'm still willing to sell so you can keep your property," Kerri told Ryan.

"No way. We'll sell the tree farm so you can keep Bess's house and store."

"Ryan."

"Kerri! Just the person I wanted to see!" Camila Whitfield made her way to their table, Carl following close behind. "I was going to call you as soon as we were home."

"What's going on? Do you want to join us?"

Camila waved that off. "I'm desperate for that tractor of yours. I told Carl all about it. He agreed it'll be the perfect backdrop to the cottage garden. It'll make the place look like it's got some history to it."

Kerri shuddered to think what Carl actually thought about that plan. "You're sure you want that old wreck on your beautiful ranch?" she asked him. If he did, he was a better husband than most.

"Absolutely. I couldn't have picked out a better one myself."

Kerri thought he had to be joking, but Carl looked dead serious.

"I was going to drop this off at your house, but you've saved me a trip." Camila handed Kerri an envelope. "We'll have some of our workers come and fetch the tractor after Christmas. I'll call ahead to let you know when. I want to get it positioned now so in the spring we can plant around it. Make it look as if it's always been there."

"That sounds like a terrific plan," Kerri said. "But you don't have to give me anything for that piece of junk. It won't run; you know that, right?" She could see the outline of a check inside the envelope, and she tried to hand it back.

Camila laughed and refused to take it. "We know it won't run."

"Really, it's free for the taking." Kerri tried again.

"Kerri, you'd better come talk to me sometime about running a business," Carl said, shaking his head at her. "But first do me a favor and look up that tractor of yours online, just so you know we've paid you the market value. Hope you all have a merry Christmas. We'll see you again soon."

"Merry Christmas," Camila said. Then they were gone.

Sylvie waited until they'd left the restaurant. "What was that all about?"

"We sold them the old tractor that was in the shed," Kerri said, chagrined that she hadn't been able to convince Camila to simply take the thing. "I guess I'm a little closer to being able to pay you off," she added, holding up the envelope.

Ryan pulled out his phone and tapped on it.

"What are you doing?" Kerri asked him.

"Looking up the tractor, like Carl said we should. What did they pay you?" He kept tapping on the phone.

Kerri humored him and opened the envelope, but when she pulled out the check, all she could do was gape at it.

Her mother took it from her. "Forty-five thousand, one hundred dollars?" she read. "Is this some kind of joke?"

"Nope," Ryan said, a smile spreading across his features. "I found a similar one on an auction site online. Looks like they paid you one hundred dollars above the winning bid on that one." He showed his phone to Kerri. "Vintage tractors are apparently a hot item."

"It's worth forty-five thousand dollars? Who would pay that for a piece of junk?" Kerri couldn't believe what she was seeing.

"The Whitfields," Ryan said. He took Kerri's hand. "The rich are different from you and me," he added.

"They're out of their minds," Sylvie said.

"Guess I can pay you what I owe you right now," Kerri said to her.

CHAPTER 18

"**W**HERE TO NEXT?" Ryan asked when they walked out of DelMonaco's. It was a crisp, clear night, but something about the feel of the air hinted more snow was on its way.

"We'd better drop Mom off at home and stop at my store to see what we can use to decorate your house for your party tomorrow night. I'm almost out of collections."

The drive to Kerri's place took only a few minutes. When they got there, Ryan expected Sylvie to head to the house, but she followed them to the store instead.

"I haven't seen this place in a long time," she said when Kerri had unlocked the door, turned on the lights and ushered them in. "I like what you've done with it." She wandered inside and gazed around her, touching a whimsical dollhouse Kerri had painted in confectionary pinks and pastels, a wooden croquet set Ryan bet was over fifty years old and a mailbox done up to look like a shark before she made a beeline toward the café table set Camila hadn't bought. "Since when are you selling quality furniture?" she asked, circling it and running a hand over the wood.

"It's a recent addition." Kerri met Ryan's gaze over her mother's head.

"This is fantastic work. I like the clean, simple lines," her mother said. "Wish I had someone to design things like this for me. I'm all about the home goods, but furniture isn't my forte, and so much of it is over-done." She turned to Kerri. "Could I get the card from your supplier? Or is this secondhand?"

"The supplier is right there." Kerri pointed to Ryan.

Sylvie turned and surveyed him with new respect. "Really? This is your work?"

Ryan nodded carefully.

"I suppose you followed someone else's design?" she said with a sigh.

"At first I did, but when I learned the basics, I start-ed designing my own furniture. That's half the fun of it," Ryan told her.

"Isn't it?" she agreed, perking up again. "That's what I've always said. I don't know why everyone isn't into design. It's a good thing they're not," she added, "or I wouldn't have a job." Her face took on a calculat-ing look. "You make these pieces one at a time?"

He nodded.

"That doesn't work for retail. I could put you in touch with a manufacturer, though. I've been wanting to expand into furniture for quite some time. We could start with a small number of pieces and see how we do."

"I'm not sure what you're asking," Ryan said. Did

she want to work with him?

"I'm asking if I can carry your line of furniture in my retail stores and online business. We'd have to figure out manufacturing, shipping… all of that. I have the connections, and I've got the storefronts. If I was selling quality furniture, I might get more people in the door. Doesn't matter, though," she added. "Online is where it's at."

"Do you think there's money to be made?"

"I do. Not a lot at first. Maybe not anything for a few years," she cautioned him. "But after that the sky is the limit as far as I'm concerned."

Ryan looked at Kerri. "I could move in with you and rent out my cabin…"

"But keep the tree farm," Kerri hastened to say. "You could keep making furniture to sell in my store."

"I'd still want to look for a full-time job. Like your mom said, it could take years to see a return on the furniture line."

"But we can make it work," Kerri said. "Together."

"Together," he echoed.

Her mother had wandered off again, darting here and there, sifting through the contents of the store as if she was on a treasure hunt.

"Kerri," she called, pulling a box off a bottom shelf near the back of the store.

Kerri made her way toward her, and Ryan followed.

"Why do you have junk like this in among all the cute things you're selling?" She reached into the box and pulled out an old-fashioned string of lights. "Do these even work?"

"They do," Kerri said. "I tried them out last month." She turned to Ryan as her mother continued to poke through the box, counting. "We could use these for your party tomorrow."

He rolled his eyes. "I still don't know how I'm going to fit all those people in my cabin. You've seen how small it is."

Kerri thought a minute. "Why not hold your party outside—at the tree lot? You can decorate a bunch of trees, build a bonfire and serve hot chocolate. You've got everything you need there already."

"You're right," Ryan said, warming to the idea. "People can use the concession shed to come in out of the cold if they need to. We can set out snacks in there."

"There are thirteen sets of lights in here." Sylvie set the box down and wandered off again. Kerri bent down to look at them.

"We can decorate thirteen trees. I've got all kinds of odds and ends as far as ornaments are concerned. They'll look great."

"Why aren't these up at the front of the store?" Sylvie demanded, pointing at a large box full of sleds, toboggans and saucers. "These are seasonal items. If you don't sell them now, you won't sell them at all."

"I don't have room up front," Kerri said.

"I'll take them all," Ryan said before the two of them could get into an argument.

"You'll take them? Why?" Kerri asked.

"For the party. I've got the best snow hill around. If

we're going to be outside, we might as well go sledding." He laughed at her expression. "No one's going to come in a dress. Besides, it's going to be mostly guys, and they'll need something to do or they'll drink too much."

"You're going to take them sledding?" Kerri still didn't seem to think it was a good idea.

"Trust me. And I want those owls, too. All of them." He picked up the box.

"Owls?" Sylvie asked.

"The ones from the upstairs bathroom," Kerri said.

"Do you struggle with hoarding?" Sylvie asked him.

"No, Mom, he doesn't," Kerri assured her.

After he'd loaded the box in his truck, Ryan found Kerri making a circuit of the store, collecting ornaments with an outdoor or dog-related theme, enough mugs and glassware to supply all his guests, several Christmas-themed trays and serving platters and a reindeer outfit for Maple to wear.

"Don't forget those owls."

"I won't." She found a few boxes.

"Are you going to let me see them in their natural habitat?" he asked.

Kerri made a face. "I'd rather not."

"Please?" He knew he was pushing it, but it seemed important for Kerri to trust him enough to allow him upstairs. After all, he was going to live there soon.

"Fine, but you can't make fun of them."

"I promise." He put his hand over his heart.

"I'm going to regret this." But she allowed him to

take her hand and walk with her to the front of the shop.

They made their way to the house together, leaving Sylvie to continue her exploration of the store. Kerri's shoulders were tight as she led him upstairs, and Ryan resolved to behave himself—as much as possible.

The second floor seemed tidy—what he could see of it. Several rooms were completely empty, and several more had their doors closed. Kerri didn't explain why, and he didn't push her to. He had no doubt when she was ready, she'd let him into every room of her house.

"Here it is." She gestured to the bathroom with a flourish.

The room itself wasn't unusual, nor were the fixtures, although they were dated.

The owls were rather alarming, he had to admit, but they had a certain pizazz to them. Several hundred statues of various sizes and designs were lined up on a series of shelves that marched up one wall. They stared down at him in rows.

"Go ahead. Laugh," Kerri said, leaning against the doorframe.

"Did you name them?" he asked, moving past her into the room to get a better look. "That's a snowy owl. That's a barred one." He pointed to them. "That's a great horned owl. Kind of had a thing for them when I was a kid," he admitted.

"I did name some. Spent a lot of time sitting on the can and staring at them."

Ryan smiled at that.

"That's Ernest." She pointed to a tall, especially serious-looking owl. "That's Thomasina." A tiny, delicate one. "That's Beauregard." She pointed to an owl that looked like it knew a lot more than Ryan did.

"Aren't you going to miss them?" he asked. "I can bring them back after the party is over."

"Let's cross that bridge when we come to it." She got busy snapping photos, then Ryan helped her pack them carefully. With the owls gone, the little room seemed bigger. And not nearly as interesting.

Sylvie came out to find them when they were loading the owls into his truck. Kerri locked up the store and together they walked her mother to the house.

"Are you going to be all right on your own tonight?" Kerri asked her. "By the time I finish helping Ryan decorate, it's going to be too late to drive back to town."

"You don't have to come up with an excuse to stay the night with your fiancé," Sylvie said. "I'll be fine. Don't rush back, either. I can open the store for you in the morning."

"Thanks." Kerri tried to hide her surprise, but when her mother pulled her into a big hug, she couldn't.

"I'm sorry," Sylvie said again. "Sorry I pushed you so hard. Sorry I didn't see what you were building here and how important it is to you."

"I'm sorry you felt I chose Bess over you," Kerri said.

"I'm looking forward to getting to know you better," Sylvie said to Ryan, "and to welcoming you into our family."

"I'm looking forward to that, too."

"WHY DO MEN have to turn everything into a competition?" Sunshine asked the next evening. Kerri was standing with her at the top of Ryan's sledding hill, which was only a stone's throw from the tree lot and shed. Several strings of fairy lights lined the trail that led here. Kerri and Ryan had decorated trees and positioned them around the tree lot. They looked lovely in the dark.

It helped that the night was clear and the moon was out. The sun had been down for hours, but she could see the sledders clearly ranging up and down the track.

Her mother was hanging back with a number of women from town whom she'd known when she was younger. Kerri had worried she'd be out of her element, but so far she seemed to be enjoying herself.

"Firefighters are a competitive bunch," Cole said.

"It's not just firefighters," Kerri said. "The Mountain Men have joined in, too."

"What are the rules?" Emma asked.

"Whoever makes it farthest on his sled wins," Cole said. Brightly colored hats and gloves were spread down the track, marking the farthest descents of each person.

"Kerri!" Ryan came jogging up, Brandon behind him, both of them carrying sleds. "C'mon, I need you on my team."

Kerri glanced skeptically at the plastic sled he carried with him. She was pretty sure there was a photo somewhere of her playing with it as a toddler. She'd brought it along with a few others she'd found stashed at Bess's house to add to the ones they'd brought from the store.

"On that death trap?"

"I won't let us crash, I promise."

"We all just re-upped our medical training, if things do go badly!" Brandon said eagerly, waving his "flying carpet." All the firefighters were as happy as puppies with the sledding game.

"That's not helpful," Ryan told him.

"Sorry." Brandon gave a whoop, broke into a run and threw himself onto his sled belly first. He slid down the snowy hill and launched into a snowbank. When he emerged from it, he dusted the snow off himself and raised his hands in a victory stance. "I'm the champion," he roared.

"You're barely in the running," Jacob Wright shouted from halfway up the hill.

"Our turn," Ryan announced loudly as he led Kerri to the makeshift starting line. He held the sled in place as she gamely positioned herself in front, then slid in behind her, wrapping his arms around her to hold the rope handle.

"Ready?" he whispered. His breath was hot against her ear, and she fought a shiver. Her heart always thumped a little harder when Ryan was near.

"Ready."

And then they were off.

Kerri shrieked as they went careening down the hill, bouncing off bumps in the snow, narrowly missing a yearling tree, racing past the markers the others had left behind. They beat the farthest ride by a good three yards. Kerri jumped up like Brandon had, put her arms in the air and crowed, "Victory is ours!"

"You had two people on your sled. That's grounds for disqualification!" Jacob objected.

"Sore loser," Ryan ribbed back good-naturedly.

Everyone looked at Ed, who was chief even outside the firehouse. He considered the two of them thoughtfully. "I'll allow it."

Ryan lifted Kerri into the air in celebration and swung her around.

"Looks like we make a good team," she said when he set her down again.

"Sure do," Ryan replied, leaning close to kiss her.

When they had tramped back up the hill through the snow, Sunshine was waiting for them. "I wish I could take a turn. You looked like you were having so much fun."

"Next year," Kerri promised. She accepted a mug of hot chocolate from Emma.

"Thought you'd like one," Emma said. "It's got some Baileys in it."

"Thanks."

"The owls are a nice touch," she added.

"They were Ryan's idea," Kerri said cryptically. He'd commandeered the boxes they'd packed. It was only when she'd come to check on his progress setting up snacks and drinks for the party a few hours ago that she'd seen how he'd set them up in the shed, the whole army of them lined up ready to judge any partygoer who wandered in looking for refreshments.

Ryan had run fairy lights among them, and tonight he'd kept the overhead lights off. Now the shed had a decidedly otherworldly air.

"So there's going to be a next year?" Sunshine prompted. "You and Ryan are here to stay?"

"Definitely. We're going to have to be careful with our money until we see if his venture with Mom has any legs. That will only be part-time work, however, so he's going to keep looking for something else after Christmas."

"When's the wedding?"

"First weekend in February," Ryan supplied, joining them. He had just put another log on the enormous bonfire he'd built in the center of the tree lot. They'd moved all the wooden supports to the side of the clearing and scattered folding chairs around. The partiers were beginning to drift that way toward the snacks, drinks, chairs and bonfire.

"Hey, Miller," Jacob Wright called out, heading for them with a pack of his fellow firefighters following. "The chief needs a word with you!"

Ed pushed his way through the group as they circled Ryan and Kerri. Maple came trotting up to see what was happening. She sat at Ryan's feet, tail thumping. "Heard you turned down that job I rustled up for you in Sacramento."

"That's right," Ryan said. He'd called Nathan this morning. "You know I'm grateful—"

"Grateful, my ass. That was just a test to make sure you have your head on straight. You'd have to be off your rocker to leave Chance Creek and move out there."

Kerri was pretty sure he was joking, but you never could tell with Ed.

"I'm glad to be staying," Ryan said, putting an arm around her waist and giving her a squeeze. "This is where I belong."

"Which is why I'm happy to offer you a job right here in Chance Creek. The department has an opening, after all. Can you believe it?"

"No. When did that happen?" Ryan looked around, as if counting heads of the firefighters who were at the party. Kerri knew he was wondering who'd quit, since that was the only way there could be a position open.

"Robert Perry cleared out last night. Left the state," Jacob said.

"Guess he was homesick," Ed said. "He moved back to Idaho. The job's yours if you want it. It was always supposed to be yours, after all."

"Absolutely. Of course I want it." He turned to Kerri. "I can still design things on my own time for your mom."

"Of course. You love fighting fires," Kerri assured him. She knew he could do both.

The rest of the firefighters mobbed him. When new drinks had been distributed all around, Jacob lifted his glass in a toast.

"To Ryan and Kerri—and to sticking around!"

"To sticking around," Sunshine sang out, lifting her

hot chocolate and clinking it with Kerri's mug.

"To sticking around," Kerri cheered along with the rest.

It sounded like heaven to her.

Late that night, when everyone else had gone home, including Sylvie, who had already managed to upgrade all the beds at Kerri's house to queen-size ones, Kerri sat with Ryan in front of the tree he'd put up in his cabin. She'd insisted he use the one he'd saved for her, loving the idea that his grandfather had picked it out last January for Bess. It brought a little of his spirit—and Bess's—into the cozy room.

"That went well," she said, snuggling against him. She was exhausted—and happy. It was a wonderful combination. To her surprise, her mother had stayed late at the party. She'd introduced herself all around, chatted with Kerri's friends and acquaintances, laughed and joked with the firefighters and even flirted a little with one of the physicians who worked at the hospital.

"It did. Are you sure you want to celebrate Christmas here this year?" They'd talked it over and she'd insisted.

"I'm sure. I think it's important to celebrate it here at least once. The cabin deserves that much, and you deserve the memory."

He kissed her long and slow. "What about next year?"

"Next year we'll celebrate in Bess's house. Our house," she corrected herself. "We'll have an enormous tree—and we'll put it in the living room."

"Already got one tagged for us," Ryan put in.

"And we'll invite everyone who doesn't have family to spend the holiday with."

"Sounds good."

"And maybe we'll have a new addition to our own family, so we can start a whole bunch of new traditions."

"That sounds like the best idea yet." He slid an arm around her and maneuvered her down, covering her with his body.

"We agreed to wait until after the wedding," she said against his shoulder. "Ryan."

"Sure thing. Just practicing." He kept kissing her.

"Good idea," she admitted, closing her eyes and thoroughly enjoying the sensation. "We'd better practice a lot."

CHAPTER 19

R YAN STOOD IN front of the mirror in his bedroom and tugged at the knot in his tie. Fiddled with it a little more. Then sighed and pulled it undone. Each time he redid it the thing looked more disheveled.

"Nervous?" Cole asked. He, Jacob and Adam were putting the finishing touches on their own outfits. He took the tie from Ryan and tied it around his own neck—perfectly on the first try, like the show-off he was, then loosened it and passed it back to Ryan so he could loop it around his neck, tighten it and flip down the collar of his shirt.

Ryan had asked Cole to be his best man after the dual proposal with Kerri. As far as he was concerned, Cole was the best possible man for the job: serious enough to keep things on track, friendly enough to get a party going. Cole had deputized Adam to be his backup, since Sunshine had given birth to baby Kate only two weeks ago, and he wanted to be able to help her if she needed him.

"I didn't think I was."

"At least you don't have to worry about her being a no-show."

"Why's that?"

"You said she was ready to propose to you when you proposed to her. Had a ring and everything."

"That's right." He grinned to remember it.

"That's some fairy-tale nonsense if I ever heard it."

"I'm not worried about her running away," Ryan said. He was absolutely sure Kerri would be here to walk down the aisle. He was even more sure he wanted to marry her. "Except for my time deployed, I've never lived anywhere else than right here in this cabin. It's just weird knowing that I've already spent my last night here."

"Are you getting cold feet about moving in with Kerri?" Adam asked.

"No. Bess's place is the right place for us. It has room for us to grow. This cabin gets tight with any more than two people in it. I just hope I'm able to find someone to rent this place who really loves it, like I do."

"Wish I could rent it," Jacob said. "I'm sick of living at home. What?" he added, taking in the glance the other men exchanged.

"That's the first time I've ever heard you admit you live in your parents' basement," Adam said. "I'm renting a suite," he parroted, copying the way Jacob usually spoke about his living situation.

"It is a suite," Jacob protested. "It's got its own door. It's not like I'm eating dinner with Mom and Dad. Much."

The rest of them laughed.

"If you want to rent the cabin for a while, I'd be happy to have you," Ryan said. "As long as you don't trash it." He met Jacob's gaze and held it. "Place has a lot of history for me."

Jacob sobered. "I'd treat it right. You know I've always been jealous of this property. I could help you with the tree farm, too, if you ever needed it."

"It would be good to have someone's eye on the place." He clapped a hand on Jacob's shoulder and named a figure for the rent.

"I can do that," Jacob said.

"Well, we'll need to sign a contract when I'm back, but as far as I'm concerned, I'm happy to give you the keys today."

"Awesome!" Jacob's expression turned serious. "There's just one more matter to negotiate."

"What?" Ryan couldn't imagine what it could be.

"Who gets custody of Maple." He gave the dog a scratch behind her ears. "You come with the cabin, don't you?"

Ryan shoved him good-naturedly. "Stop trying to steal my dog!"

Maple barked.

"All right, all right. Probably time for you to head out there, big guy."

Right. He had a wedding to get to. Ryan pulled on his jacket, while Jacob adjusted the forest-green ribbon that had replaced Maple's usual collar so she would match the wedding party, and Cole and Adam checked themselves in the mirror.

"You'd like to stay here with me, wouldn't you, girl?" Jacob whispered to Maple as he worked.

"What did I just say?"

"Doesn't hurt to try."

Ryan pointed a finger toward the door. "Go."

Jacob held up his hands in surrender. "Fine, I'm going."

They made their way out of the cabin and down the lane to the tree lot. Maple trotted along happily beside them, fully prepared for her role as ring bearer. Ryan, Adam and the rest of the Mountain Men, as well as many of the off-duty firefighters as could make it, had spent yesterday getting the tree lot ready for the wedding. Rental chairs were lined up in rows. The trees on either side were strung with fairy lights, and an archway was festooned with roses in place of an altar.

Ryan walked up the aisle to his place next to Reverend Halpern, who presided over the church Ryan grew up attending. Cole, Adam and Jacob took their places by his side. Jameson held Maple back at the head of the aisle until it was time for her cue.

As Ryan looked out at the faces of his friends in the crowd, he felt totally at peace. Finally secure in the knowledge he was about to get everything he wanted. His cabin, his town, his wife.

KERRI'S LIVING ROOM had been turned into a makeup studio and hair salon for the occasion of her wedding. Even months after clearing out all the collections, she still marvelled at how spacious and bright her house felt.

She shrugged off the robe she was wearing and stepped into her dress. Back in early January, Emma and Sunshine had closed Orchards for the day to go shopping with her, an honor Kerri felt deeply, but in the end, they hadn't needed nearly that long. The moment she tried on the first dress Kerri knew it was the one. Caitlyn Warren, the proprietor, convinced her to try on a few more just in case, but none of the others even came close.

Kerri felt the same way putting it on now. It was perfect.

Her mother helped her with the fastenings.

"It is so unfair you get to look that hot while I still haven't lost my pregnancy weight," Sunshine said. She posed in front of the mirrors they'd set up in one corner of the room.

"It's my wedding. I'm supposed to be the hottest one there. Besides, you had Kate two weeks ago, and you look fabulous!" Kerri fussed with her updo. Baby Kate was asleep in a nearby car seat. Claire Lassiter and Morgan Matheson had volunteered to watch her during the ceremony so Sunshine could be the maid of honor.

"What about Ryan?"

"Ryan gets to be the hottest person every other day of the year."

"Awww." Emma cooed. "That's so sweet."

Sylvie approached with her veil. "Hold still." She attached it to Kerri's updo, then stepped back to eye her handiwork. "Perfect!" She turned to Kerri's friends.

"Ladies, could my daughter and I have the room for a minute?"

"Of course." Emma, Autumn and Sunshine went into the kitchen, taking Kate with them.

Sylvie moved to stand directly in front of Kerri. She sighed happily. "Look at my beautiful daughter—in her beautiful house. You've done such a good job with the place."

"Thank you." Kerri was proud of the transformation she'd wrought so far. Ryan had brought the furniture he'd made to fit it, she'd added a few funky pieces of her own and together they'd bought throw rugs, mirrors and new drapes. It would take time to fill the house with their own possessions, but Kerri wasn't in any hurry. She knew it was going to be lovely.

She'd finished the last of the photo albums she'd made to document Bess's collections and had them printed into hardcover books. She'd kept one of each for her family and distributed the rest to the appropriate people. Afterward, she'd felt lighter, as if she'd set down a burden she hadn't realized she'd been carrying, and she got the sense that somewhere Bess felt the release of that burden, too.

Kerri smoothed out the satin of her dress. "What did you want to talk about?"

Sylvie twisted her hands together. "Would you let me walk you down the aisle? I know we haven't always had the best relationship, and I understand if you don't want to or if you've already asked somebody else..."

Kerri cut her off. "I'd love that, Mom."

"Really?" Her mother seemed surprised.

"Really," Kerri said.

"One more thing." Her mother pulled out a black velvet rectangular box and handed it to Kerri. "Bess passed these down to me when I turned thirty. I think she was waiting for me to get married, but…" She trailed off with a shrug. "Maybe it could be your something borrowed?"

Kerri opened the box. Inside was a pearl necklace and matching earrings.

"They're beautiful."

"The second I saw your dress, all I could think of is how perfectly they would match it."

Kerri pulled her mother into a hug. "Thank you." She carefully replaced the earrings she was wearing with the pearl ones and held up the necklace. "Would you help me put this on?"

"Of course." Her mother turned her around, fastened the necklace and rested her hands on Kerri's shoulders, looking at both their reflections in the nearest mirror. "You are a beautiful bride."

"Thanks."

"We'd better get going. It's almost showtime."

Kerri, Sunshine and Autumn were right outside the door when Emma opened it, clearly trying to eavesdrop.

"Is everything okay?" Sunshine whispered.

"Everything is fantastic. Are you ready?"

"We were born ready," Emma said.

In a flurry of activity, the women moved toward the front door.

Carl had offered to lend her and the rest of the wedding party an old, restored jalopy to drive from her place to the tree farm, but Kerri wasn't interested in taking her chances with anything less than four-wheel drive on the treacherous road up King's Mountain. Ed Brookings had offered his services instead. He was waiting to usher them into his twenty-year-old F-350 when they came outside.

"She might not be pretty, but she's dependable," he told Kerri, patting the truck's hood.

"I think she's fine." At least she wouldn't end up in a snowbank on the way to the ceremony.

When they arrived at Ryan's tree farm, they found the cabin deserted, as planned, which meant Ryan and his groomsmen were already in place in the sales lot for the ceremony.

The women ducked inside to make last-minute preparations. Sunshine texted Cole to let him know they were coming.

As Kerri stepped outside again to walk to the tree lot, she was pleasantly surprised to note that woodchips had been laid down the whole way so she wouldn't have to walk on the snow.

Ryan had thought of everything.

"WHERE IS SHE?" Ryan murmured to Cole. He kept his gaze trained on the break in the woods where the path led from his cabin to the tree farm's sales lot.

"She'll be here. Sunshine's moving slow these days," Cole joked. "Still exhausted from having the baby."

"As long as she gets here sooner or later."

"Here they come," Adam said.

There was a flurry of movement, and Claire Lassiter and Morgan Matheson appeared, carrying a baby in a car seat carrier. The crowd oohed as they took their seats.

Next, Jameson released Maple, who trotted happily down the aisle, tongue out, rings glinting on the ribbon around her neck. Cole bent to ruffle her fur and detach the ribbon long enough to get the rings into his safe-keeping. "Sit," he commanded. To Ryan's surprise, Maple sat.

But his attention—and everyone else's—was caught by a new bustle of motion at the head of the aisle.

Sunshine was the first to appear, elegant in a floor-length forest-green gown and matching little jacket. Like Cole said, she was walking slowly, but he was pretty sure that was due to the solemnity of the occasion, not to any after-effects of Kate's birth. Emma and Autumn followed her, wearing matching outfits.

And then Kerri appeared on her mother's arm.

Ryan was unprepared for the emotions that ran through him at the sight of his bride. Her snow-white gown accentuated her dark hair and brows. Her hair had been pulled up in an elaborate style, crowned by a long veil. Her gown was fitted to the waist and then fell in waterfall folds to the ground. She looked like the snow queen herself had stepped out from some frozen fairy tale and come to join him in the human realm.

How had he ever been unaware of the beauty of this

woman? How could he have stood to go through his life without her by his side?

Ryan had no answers for those questions. All he knew was that she was necessary to his existence from now on.

Sunshine, Emma and Autumn took their places near the archway, and finally Sylvie placed Kerri's hand in his own.

"Be good to her," she whispered. There were tears in her eyes, but they were happy ones, and Ryan was grateful that in the process of winning Kerri he'd somehow helped bring these two women together again.

"I will," he whispered back. He met Kerri's gaze. Saw the happiness there and knew his own was shining back. He would be better than good to her, he promised himself. He would make her his whole world. He leaned in toward Kerri. "Buckle up," he whispered.

She smiled. "Click," she said, pretending to strap herself in for the ride.

KERRI WAS TREMBLING as she stood with Ryan, Reverend Halpern's words flowing over them. She knew that binding her life to this handsome, kind-hearted man was going to bring her more happiness than she'd ever known before.

Last night they'd stood in Bess's house—their house now—and talked of the life they meant to build there. They'd been discussing waiting a few months to try for a baby, but the truth was neither of them wanted to wait that long.

Her mother was in the process of closing two of her storefronts, consolidating her business into the remaining one and her online store and finding manufacturers who could help her expand into selling furniture as well as home goods. Kerri knew they'd be seeing Sylvie far more frequently than in the past, especially with Ryan collaborating with her on a furniture line. She wondered how her mother would take to grandparenting and looked forward to finding out.

Kerri repeated her vows, let Ryan slip a wedding ring onto her finger and put one on his, loving each step of the ceremony.

"You may now kiss the bride," Reverend Halpern said.

She let Ryan take her into his arms, the way he had dozens of times before, but this was different. Now they'd told the whole world they loved each other—and that they meant to stay together forever.

"I love you," Ryan said in a tone only she could hear as he bent to take possession of her mouth. She melted against him, wanting to be in his arms—in this moment—forever.

"I love you, too," she whispered against his mouth as they broke apart.

"Ladies and gentlemen," Reverend Halpern said. "May I present Mr. and Mrs. Miller."

Cheers rang through the clearing. Sunshine, Emma and Autumn kissed her. There were congratulations from all sides as they walked back down the aisle and along the trail to the cabin.

As soon as they were inside, Ryan shut the door, leaned her against it and kissed her again. Thoroughly this time.

"Kerri Miller," he said. "I can't wait to get you alone tonight when all those people are gone."

Kerri laughed. "You get to have me alone every night from now on," she reminded him as he swept her into another ravishing kiss. "Let's go enjoy all the people who love us enough to come to a wedding outside in the snow."

He groaned against her neck. "I suppose I can wait a couple of hours. But that's it," he warned her.

"A couple of hours," she agreed. "And then I'm all yours."

She was looking forward to it—and to the rest of their lives.

Be the first to know about Cora Seton's new releases! Sign up for her newsletter here!

www.coraseton.com/sign-up-for-my-newsletter

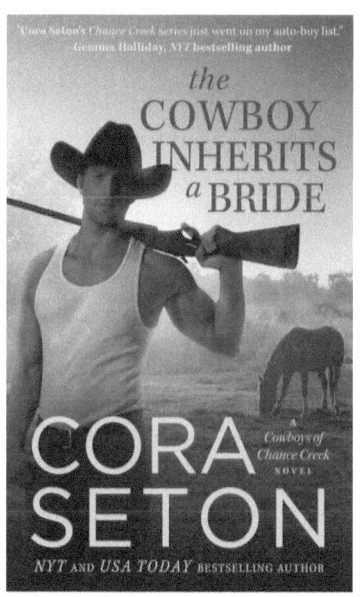

Read on for an excerpt of
The Cowboy Inherits a Bride.

S UNSHINE PATTERSON STRODE down a cracked and pitted sidewalk on the wrong side of a very small town. In fact, she wasn't sure Chance Creek, Montana, even deserved that designation. It was the kind of place you passed on the freeway from one city to the next—a grid of streets surrounded by miles and miles of pastures, rivers and far off mountains. If she was honest, its rural location made her downright nervous, but there was no turning back now.

Her beaded kitten heels rubbed a blister on her little

toe, her shoulder ached from lugging her overstuffed jute handbag, and her wheeled suitcase bumped and jerked over every crack in the cement as she dragged it behind her. The bus ride from Chicago had been a nightmare of men with body odor, screaming small children and pimply faced teenagers dressed all in black, and the cabbie who brought her most of the way from the bus station had dropped her off unceremoniously four blocks from her destination when she informed him that smoking in a taxi was against the law.

But those were minor irritants compared to the events of the last month. She had already brushed them off.

This was the first day of her new life—a life without Greg Albright—and nothing could stop her from showing him she didn't need him or his award-winning organic restaurant. No longer was she the kind of naïve young woman who invested all her savings into her boyfriend's bistro, only to find out he was sleeping with one of the waitresses. From now on she was the kind of woman who went her own way and owned her own business, thank you very much.

Thank God Aunt Cecily had left her a property in downtown Chance Creek as an inheritance or she would be sleeping on the streets of Chicago right now. Her parents would always take her in, of course, but there was no way she was returning to Lake Forest to face a chorus of *I told you so's* from them.

Chance Creek was a steep step down from Chicago, but she refused to dwell on that. She wouldn't be here long, anyway. She had a plan. She would start with a small vegan cafe in the building Cecily had left her. Within the year, she would sell the business and graduate to a larger restaurant—perhaps in Billings. Five years from now, when she had taken Montana by storm with her cutting-edge vegan creations, she would make the leap back to Chicago and show Greg just what a phony wanna-be he was compared to her own brilliance as a chef and restaurateur.

Not that she was looking for payback. Bad karma and all that. Sunshine sighed and picked up her pace. What she really wanted was smoking hot sex with a man who could make her forget Greg ever existed. Unfortunately, she doubted she'd find such a man within a hundred miles of sleepy little Chance Creek.

She navigated her way around a particularly nasty crack in the sidewalk. Four blocks ago, when she'd exited the cab, she'd been pleased to find herself in a well-kept-up neighborhood of small homes and shops. She'd even passed a bookstore and a cute little diner she immediately took note of as a potential rival for her customers. After two blocks of walking, the shops were gone but the neighborhood seemed solid enough. Two more brought a distinct drop in quality of both the curb appeal of the homes and their inhabitants. Sunshine had pointedly ignored the stares and comments from a group of men loitering around a truck up on blocks in front of one of the more run-down houses. The few shops here showed a serious level of decay. She bit her lip and noted how a little elbow grease and some money... well, a lot of money... could really spiff things up. The wheels of her suitcase got stuck in another crack and she stopped and fished her cell phone out of her bag. Balancing the slim phone on one shoulder against her cheek, she took hold of her things and teetered onward. "Hi Kate, it's me," she said when her friend picked up. "I'm almost there. Just another block."

"Why are you panting?" Kate's cultured voice made Sunshine long for her company. She could use a friend by her side right now.

"I asked the cabbie to stop smoking and he, in turn, asked me to get out of his car a few blocks early."

Kate chuckled. "When are you going to learn to let sleeping dogs lie?"

Sunshine could picture her friend at her desk at the law firm of Simons and Schiller back in Chicago, where she'd already worked her way into a junior partnership. Kate was always cool and collected, always knew exactly what she wanted and got it. Her fiancé, if she ever decided she wanted one, wouldn't steal her money and kick her to the curb. And despite what she'd just said, when Kate told cab drivers to put out their cigarettes, they did.

"Probably not in this lifetime."

There was a pause, in which Kate evidently decided her point had been sufficiently made. "So—what's the neighborhood like? Overrun with cowboys?"

"Not exactly. It's got lots of potential, though. Lots of character." She tried to believe her own words. If one more thing went wrong she might sit down on the sidewalk and cry.

"Right." There came the clicking of fingernails on a keyboard. Kate was multi-tasking, as usual. "Can you see your café yet?"

That brought a smile to Sunshine's face. *Her* café. She liked the sound of that. This time she wouldn't have a partner. She planned to do everything herself. She couldn't get screwed if no one was there to do the screwing.

"Not yet. Any minute." She crossed a street and found herself on a block that seemed almost abandoned. Several older automobiles sat parked at the curb. A barbershop edged the opposite corner, next to a pawn shop and a corner store. All three storefronts sported iron bars over their windows. On her side of the street, she confronted an empty lot sprouting weeds and cast-off tires. It grew a healthy crop of broken glass and liquor bottles, too. She tottered past it uncertainly.

"Well?" Kate asked. "I'm breathless from the suspense. What does it look like?" From the tapping sounds carrying across the phone line, Sunshine deduced her friend wasn't too breathless to work.

Sunshine approached the building whose street address matched the one on the letter she'd received from Aunt Cecily's solicitor. It was large, square, and sided with blue metal. A wide shop window framed what looked to be an expansive waiting room of some sort. Sunshine shaded her eyes to see inside better. A shoddy wooden counter separated the seating area—done in cracked brown tile and plastic chairs—from whatever went on in the rest of the building. A gap to the right of the counter led to a door to the back.

"Well?"

"It's…" Sunshine's gaze slid upward to take in the large painted sign over the entrance to this monstrosity. "It's… a rifle range."

"What?" The incessant clicking of her friend's fingers on the keyboard stopped and Sunshine knew she had Kate's full attention now. "Your aunt left you a rifle range?"

"That's what the sign says. An indoor rifle range. Is that even possible?"

"Send me a picture. Now."

Sunshine did as she was told and snapped a picture that would show Kate everything. No sense trying to hide this latest disaster. Not from her best friend. When she got back on the line, Kate whistled.

"I think I've heard of indoor rifle ranges, but there must be some mistake. I thought your aunt left you a restaurant."

"She did. I think. There's some sort of space up front, and…" Sunshine craned her neck and made out the unmistakable shape of a refrigerator behind the counter, along with a stove. A sinking feeling in her stomach told her that maybe she was the one who had made the mistake. Had Aunt Cecily left her part of a building? Or a building already rented to someone else? Would she be able to evict the tenant anytime soon? Where was the apartment Cecily had promised her?

"Is the rifle range occupied? Can you hear shots?"

Kate's voice brought her back to the present.

"No… wait." Now that she was paying attention, she heard muffled thumps that could be shots fired inside the building. Her blood pressure ratcheted up another notch. "Yes—someone's shooting in there. In my building! What do I do?" Her voice squeaked on her last sentence and she willed herself to calm down.

"Is the solicitor there?"

Trust Kate to be practical. "No. Wait… maybe." A man in a suit stood up from one of the plastic chairs in the waiting room and made his way to the door. He pushed it open and stuck his head out. "Miss Patterson?"

"Yes," she called and then spoke into the phone. "He's here. I've got to go."

"Call me the minute you find out what's going on."

"I will." Her throat was dry and her hands slippery with perspiration as she slipped her phone into her purse and waited for the man in the suit. She noticed through the dirty plate glass window that the other occupants of the waiting room were taking a distinct interest in this meeting. All in their late twenties or early thirties, except for an older gentleman who could have been one of their fathers, to a man they wore jeans, work shirts, and cowboy hats. She couldn't see their feet, but she'd bet they'd all have boots on. At least they weren't as bad as the men down the block. She didn't peg them as troublemakers—just not the kind of men who favored vegetarian restaurants. One of them turned toward the back of the building and gave a shout. Was he calling the rifle range's owner?

She turned her attention to the man who had come outside to meet her. He was balding, in his fifties, she estimated, exuding an air of distraction which didn't inspire confidence. How she wished for someone like Kate beside her. Someone who would cut through all the baloney and lay things on the line.

"Miss Patterson, I'm Abe Moffat. We spoke on the phone."

"Hi, Abe. Call me Sunshine, please."

"Sunshine. Lovely name." He seemed at a loss for what to say next. They surveyed the building in front of them uncertainly. "So. Here it is."

"Yes. I... uh... didn't realize there was a tenant in it."

"Well, yes. I believe I mentioned that there was an irregularity in your inheritance, Miss... Sunshine."

"No, I don't think you did, actually." She tried to channel Kate. Kate wouldn't put up with any of this.

"Well, it is a little peculiar." Abe reached into a pocket, brought out a cloth handkerchief, and mopped his face with it. Sunshine wasn't sure she'd ever seen anyone actually use a cloth handkerchief. "I decided to check into it a bit with one of my colleagues from Billings before bringing it to your attention. Maybe we should go somewhere else to talk," he said, glancing at the audience in the rifle range's waiting room.

She followed his gaze and nearly stopped breathing as a man walked out of the back to stand at the counter. He was tall, broad-shouldered and suntanned, with hawk-like features and a stare that pinned her in place from thirty feet away. As much as she wanted to escape his eagle-eyed gaze, she had an equal and opposite urge to preen under it. Now that was a man, and Greg… Greg could have his sordid waitress fling, because Greg wasn't fit to tie this guy's shoelaces.

"No, Mr. Moffat. I'd like to stay right here while you explain what the irregularity with my inheritance is." She found it hard not to stare right back at the man at the inside counter. How tall was he? Six foot one? What would it feel like to rest her cheek on one of those broad shoulders?

Abe swallowed hard. "All right. I'll try to explain. Your aunt found herself in a bit of a predicament when she wrote her will. Perhaps you should read her own words on the subject."

Sunshine tore her gaze away from the window and waited for the lawyer to fish a faded envelope from the folder in his hands and give it to her. Drawing out a sheet of paper filled with Aunt Cecilia's looping scrawl, she held it up and squinted to make out her aunt's words. The letter was dated some three months ago, two months before Aunt Cecily passed away.

Dear Sunshine,

I'm afraid I've done it again. I know I promised you a restaurant when you graduated from the culinary institute, but then you and Greg joined forces and were doing so well for yourselves with Chez Rosetta, that when a friend hit a rough patch I thought you'd never miss the old thing. However, from what you've let slip during your recent visit, I predict tough times ahead for you, honey. And now I'm in a real pickle. I've promised my building twice over, to two young people I really care for. All I can do is give you both a fair shake at it. After all, it is large and should contain enough room for each of you to pursue your dreams.

Abe will explain everything and I know it will all turn out for the best. It always does, doesn't it?

Love,
Aunt Cecily

Her aunt's words splashed over her like a bucket of ice water. "I have to share the building?"

"It's kind of a contest."

She blinked. "A contest? What does that mean?" She had banked everything on having a place to live and a café to run. This couldn't be happening.

The lawyer was clearly uncomfortable. "Cecily has stipulated that each of you must occupy the building continually for four months. You must run a business—a restaurant in your case, the rifle range in his—and live on the premises. If you abandon the premises, and she defines abandonment as spending more than one single night away from the building, Cole Linden immediately has the right to purchase it outright from you for a sum set by Cecily."

Sunshine couldn't believe her ears. This was ludicrous. "How much?"

"How much…?" he echoed.

"What's the *sum set by Cecily*?" Maybe it would be

enough for her to start over somewhere else. Somewhere more appropriate.

Abe licked his lips. "Sixty."

"Sixty thousand dollars?" That was outrageous for a building this large—it must be worth five times as much.

"Sixty dollars, actually."

Sunshine's mouth dropped open. Sixty dollars wouldn't cover a bus ticket back to Chicago. Why would Aunt Cecily do this to her? She glanced through the plate glass window at the man who leaned against the counter, his hands braced against it as he took her measure. "Is that Cole Linden?"

Abe nodded.

She met the man's gaze, pressing her lips together in a thin line. Who cared how hot he was? The bastard had weaseled his way into Cecily's good graces and stolen her inheritance out from under her.

"Is this his business? His… rifle range?"

"Yes." Abe took a step back, as if afraid she might lash out. Well, he should be afraid. They all should. This was her building. Her restaurant. And that man—Cole—was using it to promote violence and murder. Those cowboys in the waiting room were nothing more than thugs.

Cole Linden stared right back at her. He probably sensed she was a card-carrying member of PETA from where he stood. "What if he spends more than one night away?" She could arrange for that—just break both his legs and dump him near the Canadian border.

Unless he shot her first.

"Then you immediately inherit the building free and clear. But…" He held up a finger. "In either case, the absence may not be caused by the person who stands to inherit from it."

Damn.

"What happens at the end of four months?"

"If neither of you abandon the building, then it comes down to earnings. The person with the more successful business wins."

Well. At least that was something. Crazy Aunt Cecily must have known she'd take the challenge and succeed without a problem. Cole Linden and his stupid rifle range would be out of here in no time.

"Fine. But where exactly am I supposed to run my restaurant?"

"There." Abe gestured to the waiting room and counter. Sunshine squinted against the glare on the plate glass window. The stove behind the counter did have six burners. She thought she saw a sink, as well. The waiting room, while large, was no restaurant, however. She stifled an urge to shake the man. She'd have to bust her ass to transform the place into anything a respectable person would want to visit. "Where's my apartment?"

Abe seemed to have something caught in his throat. "There's an entrance at the side of the building. It's… cozy. And… it's not exactly *your* apartment." The lawyer's face went somewhat pink. His paisley tie seemed about to choke him.

She shut her eyes and counted to ten. "Spill it."

Abe shuffled the papers he clutched in his hands. "You'll have to share it with Mr. Linden."

"COLE, COME HERE—you've got to see this!"

Cole Linden carefully locked up the ammunition cabinet, exited the storeroom his father had converted to a safe room, and made his way to the front of the building where five men watched Abe Moffat confront a young woman who was decidedly angry. Cole didn't recognize the woman. The men in the waiting room he'd known all his life.

Ethan Cruz headed up one of the oldest ranches around now that his father had just passed away. He was engaged to the pretty but petulant Lacey Taylor, a girl Cole had known since she wore her hair in pigtails. Jamie Lassiter was a hired hand on Ethan's ranch, and his best friend. He had a way with horses that would keep him in demand no matter where he went, but he was loyal to Ethan. Cab Johnson, a large but quiet man, was the local sheriff. He'd ended up with the post when his father could no longer do the job. Cab was young to be an elected official, but he was well respected around town. Rob Matheson was a jokester, but a hard worker. One of four sons, he lived on the Double-Bar-K, the spread next to the Cruz ranch, which his father, Holt Matheson—currently occupying the seat beside him—ruled with an iron fist.

Cole had known every one of them for most of his life and appreciated their patronage—especially when they could have ridden out on their own spreads and tested any weapon they wanted without bothering anyone.

The only man to enter the range today that he didn't know well was the lawyer who'd brought him the news a week ago of Cecily Silverton's arrangement. News that left him shell-shocked in a way he hadn't thought possible. Sure, he'd known there was a chance that Cecily's death meant an end to the sweet deal that allowed him to keep the rifle range his father had opened twenty years ago, but she had always hinted she meant to leave the building to him, and she hadn't seemed like the type to lie to a man.

But Cecily hadn't left the building to him, at least not outright. She'd left it jointly to him and some silver-spoon niece of hers who probably spent all her time shopping and talking on the phone. He still had a chance to get the building—for the bizarre price of sixty dollars—if the interloper bailed within four months. But if she didn't, said niece would be his new landlord. If she allowed him to stay. Meanwhile, he had to share not only the building with whatever cockamamie business the debutante came up with, he'd have to share his apartment, too. His one bedroom, one bath, eight-hundred-square-foot apartment.

And what about the rest of his business? He'd still been in the Army, fighting in Iraq, when his father sent him the paperwork that made him a joint owner of Linden Holdings. It had never occurred to him not to sign, but now he knew that instead of a thriving business, he'd become partners in an enterprise drowning in debt. At the time, Linden Holdings had consisted of this building, two apartment buildings and the accoutrements of his father's deep-sea diving operation. Diving for treasure was Bailey Linden's passion. Thousands of miles away in a foreign desert, Cole hadn't realized his father had mortgaged everything else to the hilt to fund his trips until a new batch of paperwork had arrived in the mail for him to sign—paperwork that spelled out the deal his dad had struck with Cecily.

His father had told him they had no choice but to sell the range building to her, but had assured him it was only a temporary setback. Cole cursed himself for not asking the tough questions. He'd been too young to push his father for answers back then, and too ignorant to even know what to ask.

Now he knew all too well. His father had passed away less than a year after Cole left the Army and came home. When he took over the day-to-day operations, the amount of debt Linden Holdings was carrying staggered him. His accountant had sat him down and outlined the process of bankruptcy, but Cole refused to go that route. That would mean certain eviction for the tenants in his apartments—some of whom he'd known since he was a child.

But without the range, how was he supposed to keep paying down the mortgage on the two apartment buildings that stood on the back end of the property it fronted? Heaven knew the buildings should be paying their own way, but they weren't. Not with all the renovations they'd required in the last five years. He'd had to replace the roofs, rebuild the stairs, buy a brand-new hot water tank along with new appliances for most of the units. And don't even get him started on all the new flooring he'd put in to replace the decades-old carpets.

What the hell was Cecily thinking? He'd always liked the old woman, had been genuinely sorry when she passed away. Cecily was sweet to purchase the broken-down building and allow them to pay token rent to keep the range running. From time to time she'd stopped by, drunk a cup of the coffee he kept brewing all day for his customers, and seemed to take genuine pleasure in watching the men fire their various firearms at the paper targets in the shooting lanes. Cecily was great. But this... Sunshine... would be something altogether different. He was doomed and so was his range—and all the people who lived in his apartments, too.

He shoved aside a pile of paperwork as he watched the blonde question Abe. Maybe he deserved to lose it all. A better businessman than him would have raised the rents to twice as much as they were now, but over the years his father had accumulated Chance Creek's misfits and downtrodden. Cole couldn't bear to kick out any of them, or to watch their faces when he delivered the news that their apartments would no longer be affordable. He knew most of them were keeping afloat by the skin of their teeth, just like he was. Liliana Warner was a single mother who worked as a house-keeper at the Big Sky Hotel. William Lake was eighty-two and living on a fixed income. Scott Preston, a veteran who'd fought in Iraq, was supporting two sets of grandparents on his disability payments. How could he turn any of them out, let alone the others?

The worst part was he didn't have a dime saved to start over somewhere new even if he walked away from the company's debts. After five years of living on ramen noodles, Cole could see his way clear to putting his balance sheets back into the black soon, but if he lost the range, he'd lose the apartments, too, and then he'd have nothing. No business, no savings. He'd be starting over at twenty-nine. Some developer would come in and buy the apartments for pennies on the dollar, kick out the current tenants, do a nominal renovation, jack the prices up as high as the market would bear and make a killing.

He hated to think ill of Cecily, not after all she'd done for his family over the years, but if she wasn't going to leave the building to him, he wished she'd never even hinted at it. Losing it felt too much like a well-aimed kick to his nuts.

He took a deep breath as he focused on the woman outside the building. Holy cow, she was a knock-out. He leaned against the counter for a better look.

Holt cackled in his corner. "Thought you'd be interested."

"That's your new roommate? Lucky break." Jamie was staring at her too.

"Not bad," Ethan agreed.

"Wouldn't mind seeing that at the breakfast table,"

Rob threw in for good measure.

Cab held his peace and so did Cole. Pretty is as pretty does. She was definitely good looking, curved in all the right places with long, free-flowing shiny blonde hair that made her name not quite as ridiculous as it would otherwise be. She wore black leggings, and a nut-brown tunic that showed her curves to perfection. Her shoes were silly—tiny heeled things with thin beaded straps to hold them precariously on her feet. She had the determinedly healthy look he associated with yoga instructors. How old could she be—twenty-four, twenty-five, maybe?

This was his new landlord?

And roommate.

Lucky him.

"I'll bet that lawyer's explaining the details of Cecily's will," Holt said, and proceeded with a running commentary which nicely complemented the range of expressions flitting across the young woman's face. Shock, surprise, anger, horror—it would have been humorous if he hadn't known exactly how she felt. Then she looked in the window, met his gaze, and Cole felt like he'd been shot through the heart. She was more than pretty; she was drop-dead beautiful, with wide, expressive eyes and full lips that promised she could get up to all kinds of passionate shenanigans with the right partner.

He was not the right partner.

Although he would be a partner of sorts if she took her aunt's challenge and moved in with him for four months.

He straightened up and cleared his throat when he noticed the grins on his audience's faces. "She might bail. A girl like that isn't going to want to move into a rifle range, right?"

"Looks like a spitfire to me," Holt said.

"Cole can handle her," Jamie said. "He'll make her life so miserable she'll turn tail and run within the week. Within the day, even. Right, Cole?"

That's certainly the way he'd intended to play it, but now he wasn't so sure. Cecily wasn't a stupid woman and she didn't have a speck of malice in her. She wasn't one to lead a guy on for several years and then pull the rug out from under his feet. What if he was reading the situation all wrong? What if she'd had a plan of her own when she set up her will this way?

He watched the slender blonde gesticulate angrily at the lawyer outside. Abe looked pained and he had no doubt the man wished he hadn't been given this particular job to carry out. Even angry, Sunshine was beautiful. She looked smart, passionate, perhaps kindhearted.

Cole's next thought made his fingers press harder into the counter. Had Cecily left him *Sunshine* in her will?

And did he want to accept this bequest?

A smile curved his mouth as he considered this possibility. One look at Sunshine squaring her shoulders and approaching the front door told him she'd girded her loins for a knock-down, drag-out battle of the sexes, but suddenly he was sure he could win the prize without throwing even one punch.

Ethan glanced up and met his gaze. The rancher chuckled. "I've seen that look before. You've got a plan, don't you?"

"Yep."

They all jumped when the door banged open and the woman in question strode across the tile floor. "Cole Linden?" she said, stopping on the opposite side of the counter. She ignored Jamie's frank perusal and the muffled laughter coming from the rest of the crew.

"That's me." He forced himself to meet her gaze without blinking, found himself holding his breath to find out what she was going to do next.

"My name's Sunshine Patterson and I'm moving in. You have an hour to clear your things out of my apartment."

He raised an eyebrow. "You mean *my* apartment, don't you?"

Her jaw tightened. "*Our* apartment, Mr. Linden. I'll need the bedroom and half of the space in all the other rooms. I suggest you get to it right away."

Cole rocked back on his heels, surprised at how much it pleased him she was going through with this. After all, she could turn out to be a real pain in the ass.

Somehow he didn't think so. Somehow he thought she was going to be the most fun he'd had in a long time.

"There's only one bedroom and I'm already using it. I suggest you find some nice swanky hotel for the night."

That seemed to catch her off balance. She glanced away, squared her shoulders again and looked him right in the eye. "You wish. You and I both know I'm not spending a single night of the next hundred and twenty away from that apartment. This is my building and come fall I'll be waving bye-bye to you as you drive away with all your stupid guns."

"Firearms," five voices automatically corrected her. Cole squashed the smile that threatened to quirk his lips. Miss Sunshine had a lot to learn, and he'd be happy to teach her.

Jesus, he needed to get his mind out of his pants. At least for the moment. Plenty of time to go down that road later. Four whole months to be exact.

"I'm a woman. I need my own bedroom," Sunshine said. "You can take the couch."

Cole knew everyone was waiting to hear his next words. Knew also that if he blinked, he might as well walk away from the rifle range right now.

"Make me."

She flushed, and her eyes sparked with rage and something else. Tears? Heaven help him. Before he could react to them, though, she'd blinked them away and whirled around to stretch a hand out to Abe the lawyer.

"Give me the keys. If Mr. Linden can't be bothered to move his things, I'll have to do it for him."

She snatched the key the lawyer produced from his pocket and was out the door before any of them could move. She shooed away the transient man who had sidled out from an alley to check out the luggage she'd left on the street and began to haul it over to the side of the building where the entryway to the apartment was located.

"You gonna go after her?" Ethan asked.

"I guess so."

Right after he caught his breath.

End of Excerpt

The Cowboys of Chance Creek Series:

The Cowboy Inherits a Bride (Volume 0)
The Cowboy's E-Mail Order Bride (Volume 1)
The Cowboy Wins a Bride (Volume 2)
The Cowboy Imports a Bride (Volume 3)
The Cowgirl Ropes a Billionaire (Volume 4)
The Sheriff Catches a Bride (Volume 5)
The Cowboy Lassos a Bride (Volume 6)
The Cowboy Rescues a Bride (Volume 7)
The Cowboy Earns a Bride (Volume 8)
The Cowboy's Christmas Bride (Volume 9)

The Elliotts of Chance Creek Series:

House for Sale Navy SEAL Included
House for Sale Soldier Included
House for Sale Airman Included
House for Sale Marine Included

House for Sale Ranger Included

The Heroes of Chance Creek Series:

The Navy SEAL's E-Mail Order Bride (Volume 1)
The Soldier's E-Mail Order Bride (Volume 2)
The Marine's E-Mail Order Bride (Volume 3)
The Navy SEAL's Christmas Bride (Volume 4)
The Airman's E-Mail Order Bride (Volume 5)
The Navy SEAL's Second Chance Bride
(Volume 6)

The SEALs of Chance Creek Series:

A SEAL's Oath

A SEAL's Vow

A SEAL's Pledge

A SEAL's Consent

A SEAL's Purpose

A SEAL's Resolve

A SEAL's Devotion

A SEAL's Desire

A SEAL's Struggle

A SEAL's Triumph

The Brides of Chance Creek Series:

Issued to the Bride One Navy SEAL
Issued to the Bride One Airman
Issued to the Bride One Sniper

Issued to the Bride One Marine
Issued to the Bride One Soldier
Issued to the Bride One Sergeant for Christmas

The Turners v. Coopers Series:

The Cowboy's Secret Bride (Volume 1)
The Cowboy's Outlaw Bride (Volume 2)
The Cowboy's Hidden Bride (Volume 3)
The Cowboy's Stolen Bride (Volume 4)
The Cowboy's Forbidden Bride (Volume 5)

About the Author

With over one-and-a-half million books sold, NYT and USA Today bestselling author Cora Seton has created a world readers love in Chance Creek, Montana. She has thirty-five novels and novellas currently set in her fictional town, with many more in the works. Like her characters, Cora loves cowboys, military heroes, country life, gardening, jogging, binge-watching Jane Austen movies, keeping up with the latest technology and indulging in old-fashioned pursuits. She lives on beautiful Vancouver Island with her husband, children and two cats. Visit **www.coraseton.com** to read about new releases, contests and other cool events!

Blog:

www.coraseton.com

Facebook:

facebook.com/coraseton

Twitter:

twitter.com/coraseton

Newsletter:

www.coraseton.com/sign-up-for-my-newsletter